# THE AMSTERDAM FILE

A JACOB HUNTER THRILLER

DAVID ARCHER

DAMIEN WILD

The characters and events portrayed in this ebook are fictitious. Any similarity to real persons, living or dead, is coincidental and not intended by the author.



ISBN-13: 978-1-63696-470-6

ISBN-10: 1-63696-470-2

Printed in the United States of America

www.righthouse.com

www.instagram.com/righthousebooks

www.facebook.com/righthousebooks

twitter.com/righthousebooks

**JACOB HUNTER THRILLER**

The Kyiv File (Book 1)
The Bogotá File (Book 2)
The Havana File (Book 3)
The Amsterdam File (Book 4)
The Saint Petersburg File (Book 5)

# PROLOGUE

THE MOURNERS CLUSTERED TOGETHER, HEADS BOWED as a cold drizzle fell like icy needles from a sky of tarnished metal. They gathered in a desolate corner of a forgotten Queens cemetery—a fittingly bleak resting place for the woman in the plain pine box. Sturdy spruce trees battled the rising wind, their branches lashing yet unbroken. The scene was grim, a day that gnawed at your bones.

Jacob Hunter tightened his grip on Irina's hand as she stood silently beside him. He rolled his shoulders, battling the tension creeping up his neck as his breath clouded in the cold air. He wanted it over—longing to return to his apartment, bury himself in blankets with Irina, and forget this godforsaken winter day. But for now, he remained impassive, eyes fixed on the casket, willing himself to endure.

Inside lay Zerina Mills, once a brilliant field agent, now just another casualty. Not taken down by a bullet or a knife in a dangerous operation but stolen by a far crueler enemy: motor neurone disease. Twenty-six and gone with only a few mourners marking her passing. No family, no friends—just Jacob, Irina, and a handful of Skia operatives. She deserved better.

Grant Fletcher, the director of Skia, a clandestine security organization named after the Greek word for shadow, stood at the edge of the grave. His voice carried over the wind, low and measured, as he began the eulogy. "Zerina came to us like a gift from heaven, one we cherished and will miss greatly." His gaze flicked to Jacob and Irina, their eyes darkening with sadness as Fletcher continued. "She was rescued from an orphanage in Tirana, Albania, minutes before she and other girls were about to be sold into a sex-slave ring destined for the Middle East."

Fletcher's words cut through the rain-soaked gloom. He spent five minutes outlining the highlights of her short, brutal life—a girl who bounced through European foster homes until an American family took her in. She never really fit in—too fierce, too rebellious. Intelligence agencies eyed her even before she graduated high school; her physical and mental talents were impossible to ignore. Skia recruited her immediately after graduation, offering a new identity, a fresh start—but at the devastating cost of severing all ties with her adoptive family. It broke her heart, yet she accepted the sacrifice, her hatred for the criminals who tormented her burning fiercely. She returned to Albania, determined to crush the kidnapping rings that had once tried to steal her life.

And she had. Last year, with assistance from Jacob, Zerina had led an operation dismantling the region's largest trafficking ring. Gang leaders now rotted in Burrel Prison—the worst hellhole on the planet. Zerina had done it—she'd won. But fate had other plans.

"Two weeks after that mission, it was clear something was wrong," Fletcher said, his voice tightening. "Several months later, she was dead."

The silence that followed was suffocating as the drizzle turned into a steady downpour. Jacob closed his eyes, the weight of the moment pressing down on him. Zerina had been a warrior—she deserved to go out fighting. Instead, something that no bulletproof vest or combat training could stop took her.

When his number came up, how would he go? Ultimately, did it matter? Dead was dead.

The service ended, and the mourners bade their good-byes and got into a line of waiting vehicles. Jacob clicked his seatbelt, melted into the leather seat, and felt himself drifting off to sleep.

A nudge in the ribs and a soft Russian voice woke him. "*Zaichik. Ty spish? Priekhali.* Darling. Are you awake? We're home already."

He turned and smiled at Irina, her angelic smile banishing his morbid thoughts.

"Nightcap before bed?"

She nodded. "*Da*. But only one drink—we've got a red-eye flight to Amsterdam, remember?"

A smile creased Jacob's lips. "My first real vacation in years. I'll be so glad to visit a foreign country and actually get to enjoy it!"

"Did you not enjoy your visit to Moscow when you met me?"

He roared with laughter. "Apart from nearly getting killed a couple of times, that was the only part I enjoyed."

"Worth it, though, wasn't it?"

He leaned over and kissed her on the cheek. "And then some."

Despite the day's sorrow, tomorrow promised the gift of a new dawn.

"But why Europe in the winter, Yakov? We could go anywhere in the world, somewhere warm? Australia, for example."

He sighed. "I suffered enough in the heat and humidity of South and Central America to last a lifetime." He pulled her closer, whispering in her ear. "Cozy nights by a fire in the Dutch countryside, eating Edam cheese and drinking Heineken beer. Doesn't that sound romantic?"

She twisted her lips and shook her head. "You are a cunning devil. Yes, that does sound romantic. I can't wait to get there."

# ONE

A LIGHT DRIZZLE FELL UPON THE PAVERS, TURNING them slick and slippery. Laughter bounced off the walls of tightly packed slanting buildings, pressed close together in the narrow street. Tourists ogled a seemingly unending row of casement windows. Behind the glass, scantily clad women of all colors and ethnicities—but predominantly young and white—their faces covered in garish makeup gyrated, twisted, and twirled their bodies, running their tongues around their lips alluringly.

The majority of people strolling the red light district tonight—and every night—were merely curious, eager to see how the reality of Amsterdam's nightlife tallied with its famous reputation for unfettered freedom. To them, the women behind the glass were little different from the art hanging in the Rijksmuseum. The tourists grinned at them, shook their heads as they laughed at the prostitutes on display. Occasionally a man, or even couples of various gender combinations, might negotiate with the woman, hand signals and gestures on either side of the glass. A price agreed, they'd enter the inner sanctum to engage in sexual acts with strangers as other strangers ambled past only a few feet away.

"This is disgusting, Yakov. Can we go somewhere else?"

"I thought you'd be interested to see the red light district. It's a tourist mecca." His surprise was genuine; she was no prude, in fact the opposite in their intimate life. Irina did things no other woman he'd been with had been interested in.

She stopped, tugged on his hand, and looked up into his eyes. "Zerina's barely cold in her grave, and you..."

A mental head slap. How could he have been so stupid? The Albanian woman they'd mourned only days before had fought human sex trafficking with every fiber of her being. Still, he found himself justifying his choice to come to the district. "These girls are here of their own free will. The industry is properly regulated in the Netherlands."

"Yeah, right," she scoffed, shaking her head. "And you believe that, do you?"

Jacob fell silent for a moment as an alcohol-fueled female voice shrieked with laughter. He turned to see a couple in their early twenties making faces at a leggy blonde in red suspenders inside one of the booths. "Yes," he said finally but without a lot of conviction. "Of course, some might fall through the cracks. But on the whole—"

"On the whole!" she barked. "Even if one of them is being held captive by some pimp, a gang of criminals? If the government knows nothing about her? What then, huh? Does that justify"—her hand made a sweeping gesture, encompassing a half dozen booths—"letting this filth trade flourish?"

He squeezed her hand, encased in a woolen glove. "Sure, babe. You've got a good point." He hadn't suspected his own feelings would also tend toward disgust, but it was also tempered by pity, even for the women who were renting out their bodies voluntarily. "Let's get some of that apple pie I was telling you about."

"Anything to get out of this place." They picked up the pace, navigating the rabbit warren that was known as De Wallen, one of three red light districts in Amsterdam. Irina kept her eyes down as they squeezed between the throngs of people. "You know some of those women are in the cabins against their will, don't you?"

"Could be," he conceded. Jacob could have argued that the

Dutch authorities were all over the flesh-trade, keeping an eye on things. The women had regular health checks, their welfare was a priority, and everything was hunky-dory. But that would be a lie. Wherever there were drugs and prostitution—even in a legalized and regulated form—crime flourished. As much as Irina might want to liberate them all, set them on the straight and narrow, there was nothing either of them could do. "Let's get moving."

They traversed the relatively uncrowded Oudekennissteeg, a narrow alleyway bisecting densely packed brown-brick buildings. Jacob's eyes subconsciously scanned his surroundings. He wasn't expecting trouble—he'd been to the Netherlands before but never on assignment. In theory, he hadn't had the opportunity to piss off any local bad guys. In practice, he may have. Which was unfortunate, since the gangsters here were renowned for their brutality.

The underworld in the Netherlands, known as the *penoze*, had a reputation for ruthlessness the equal of any of the better-known mafias from Italy, Russia, or Albania. In recent years, a new brand of criminal gangs had emerged in the Netherlands—the Mocro mafia. Ostensibly headed up by Dutchmen of Moroccan heritage, it also included West Indian, South American, and Balkan criminals. Thanks to these dark and violent organizations, the Netherlands, together with Belgium, had become the European hub for the importation and distribution of cocaine and other illicit drugs through the giant ports of Rotterdam and Antwerp. On the surface, Amsterdam portrayed itself as a peaceful, happy city, where everyone had the freedom to do as they pleased. And to visitors like Jacob and Irina, there was no reason to be worried. The Mocro mafia wasn't interested in the average man and woman on the street.

The red-lit windows behind them faded into the shadows as they quickened their pace, shoes echoing off the damp cobblestones. Ahead, the narrow street opened onto the Oudezijds Achterburgwal canal, the water below an inky-black mirror reflecting the lights cast from street lamps, souvenir shops, and noisy bars. They crossed a small bridge, heads bent low as a frigid breeze picked up from the north, its bite amplified as it whipped off the surface of the canal.

"Is it far to this place?" Irina asked. "I'm gonna freeze to death if we don't get there soon."

He could sense her body shivering under her winter coat. Was it just the temperature making her body react, or had the sight of the hookers in their glass cages contributed to her agitation? "You're a Muscovite," Jacob chided, one eyebrow raised. "You can't be feeling cold. It's at least 50 degrees."

"That tells me nothing," she groaned. "What is it in normal units, meaning Celsius?"

Jacob grinned. It would take her a while to get used to Fahrenheit, the system he'd grown up with. As far as he remembered, it was just the United States and a handful of small nations sticking to the antiquated imperial scale. He did a quick mental conversion. "Ten Celsius."

"This is a different kind of cold, *zaichik*. It doesn't have to be subzero to be uncomfortable."

He nodded. The humidity and the wind certainly added to the level of chill. Besides, they weren't wearing the multiple layers you'd have on in the middle of a bitter Moscow or New York winter. He was about to respond when two large males in hooded sweaters rounded a corner and ascended the short bridge behind them. He tracked them in his peripherals as they got closer. There was no one else around. It was getting on for 9:30 p.m. on a Sunday. Understandably, the crowds had thinned out with the weather not helping the tourist trade tonight.

Jacob wrapped an arm around Irina. It seemed as if the men were standing farther apart than you would expect a couple of friends to be. His senses were going off like a fire alarm. Were they shepherding him and Irina, planning a mugging on two flanks? He turned, squared his shoulders, and glared at them. Only ten feet away now, and they were moving faster.

His fingers flexed, fists balling as a reflex action. A wispy fog descended over the shoulders of the approaching pair.

The two men had barrel chests and were almost as tall as Jacob, who stood at 6'2". Now their faces were visible. Both had dark brown eyes and sported trim beards, their complexion hinting at Middle Eastern or North African extraction.

The taller of the two stepped forward, his gait unhurried yet purposeful. He stopped a few paces from the couple, his hands tucked loosely in his pockets. A packet of Marlboros appeared in his meaty hand; he plucked out a cigarette and waved it like an orchestra conductor. "Hey, friend. You got a light for me?" He spoke in accented English, his tone not exactly friendly yet lacking the menace you might expect judging by his threatening appearance. Jacob's acute ear picked the man's first language as Dutch but with the influence of his own culture, the phonetic patterns of Arabic, affecting the accent.

Jacob's eyes narrowed as he assessed the situation, sensing Irina's growing disquiet as she gripped his hand tightly. The muscles in his neck tensed and bunched, his breathing quickening. Of course, this could be a perfectly normal interaction, the men genuinely lacking a lighter or matches. His gut told him otherwise, but there was nothing to base it on except raw suspicion. The man's companion, a couple inches shorter but still a big guy, sniffed as he nodded, eyes fixed on Jacob for a moment before flicking to Irina. The lustful glint in his eye sent a message to Jacob's brain: Toss the creep into the canal. He bit down on the impulse.

There was a brief pause, an eternity compressed into seconds. The chill of the night seemed to deepen, the quiet murmur of people in adjacent streets fading into the background. Jacob's eyes looked from one man to the other, watching for a knife or a gun. If they chose to attack, there were no witnesses, no one to come to their aid. He would have to call on every ounce of his training to deal with the two brutes. Irina had improved her martial arts skills, but the odds were still stacked against them. Finally he spoke.

"I'm sorry." Jacob felt the flaring of his nostrils. "I don't have one." It was a lie. A non-smoker with a cigar excuse, he carried a Zippo in his pocket most of the time. But the real reason for keeping a lighter was utility. It was a damned handy piece of kit. You could use one in all kinds of applications: to ignite flammable items as a distraction, as a signaling device if your phone flashlight failed, or hold it in your fist to magnify the power of a punch.

"What about the nice lady?" said the second man, a slight lisp affecting his speech. "You got a light, baby?"

It took every bit of willpower Jacob could muster not to lash out at the man with his fists. He set his jaw and said, "Disrespect her one more time, asshole, and you and your friend will both be taking a late-night swim in the canal."

The man raised his hands in a surrender gesture. "OK. Don't lose your shit, man."

"I don't have one either, I'm afraid." Irina shrugged apologetically, the 'baby' slur apparently making no impact on her. "But if you head back the other way, there's a couple of coffee shops full of people smoking their heads off. You'll find a hundred lighters there, I'm sure. It's less than a minute away." She pointed a finger toward the other side of the bridge.

Jacob, blood still boiling as the second man ogled his woman, nevertheless grinned. Irina's reply was beyond perfect.

The two men exchanged a couple of gruff words in guttural Dutch, then, without a backward glance, turned and melted back into the night, their departure as sudden and quiet as their arrival.

Irina's hand tightened around Jacob's. "That felt weird," she whispered, her voice trembling slightly. "Did it feel weird to you?"

Jacob rubbed his chin thoughtfully as their footsteps faded into silence. "Sometimes low-lifes like them get a buzz out of intimidating people. Nothing to stress over."

She chuckled in the back of her throat. "*Da.* You get assholes like them everywhere. There was no shortage of that kind of thug in the Moscow neighborhood I grew up in. Probably worse than those two."

He took both her hands in his. "Statistically, we are safer in Amsterdam than we are at home in New York."

She swept a loose lock of hair from her face. "I guess so." A bright smile stretched her cheeks, rosy from the cold. "He sure backed down when you told him you'd throw them off the bridge!"

"Like all bullies do when you stand up to them. The main thing to worry about here are professional pickpockets, not muggers." A broad smile from Jacob was enough; the furrows on her brow smoothed as her stress melted away. "Still," he added, "no need to tempt fate. Let's keep moving."

They resumed their walk, conversation put on hold for now. Despite his words of reassurance, there was something in the eyes of the two men that sat uneasy in his mind. He hadn't told Irina what he'd heard one of them say before they scrammed. *That's enough for now, Hassan.* Hassan was a common enough name these days, even in the Netherlands, and alone, that fact should mean nothing. Yet his thoughts drifted back to a mission he'd carried out seven years ago. One of his first operations as a Skia operative, in neighboring Belgium. One of the key figures they'd arrested back then had tried to dump the blame on a man called Khasan—a variant of Hassan—Kadyrov. Logic told him this could not be the same Hassan. The guy on the bridge would be thirty years old, maximum. Kadyrov would be pushing sixty by now. Still, it set off a train of thought he couldn't switch off.

His brain went into hyperdrive as he recalled the details of the case. It had been a long and sensitive mission. Foiling the multi-million euro drugs shipment had required detailed planning, lots of waiting around and observing from a distance, and meetings with shadowy and dangerous types. They had failed to pin the leader, a Belgian national called Valentijn de Vries, who was slipperier than a bucket of eels. His legal representative had somehow managed to get all charges against the man dropped. There were whispers of bribes and corruption in the Belgian legal sphere.

Something Jacob and his collaborators couldn't influence. Last time he checked, de Vries was still at liberty.

Jacob's nerves had been on edge a month before the Belgian sting, the biggest to date of his burgeoning career with Skia. Working under the alias David Reeve, he'd chewed his fingernails in the lead-up, lost twenty pounds in the heat of the case, and by the end of it, he thought his hair was starting to fall out. Sleep deprivation due to extended surveillance shifts had contributed to him crashing a vehicle in a high-speed chase. The accident had left a man—a local facilitator for the crime syndicate and close friend of de Vries—paralyzed from the waist down. With the Belgian police covering his tracks, Jacob had managed to dodge the blame for the accident. Rumors soon reached Jacob's ears that de Vries, the man at the top of the syndicate whom the authorities were unable to lay a finger on, was incensed about what happened to his loyal soldier and was hell-bent on revenge.

Jacob took a deep breath as they neared the bistro. Was he wise in choosing Amsterdam as a destination, so close to Belgium? He wanted to explain all of this to Irina, but she'd panic, for sure. The men on the bridge probably were just a pair of innocents. But why push your luck? Tomorrow they would cram in a day of sightseeing, then he'd book the next available flight to Tahiti. Irina was right—they should have gone somewhere warm for their vacation.

The route to the bistro was short—a direct path through another quiet side street that led into a small, well-lit square. The square was dotted with a few late-night cafés and a bench where a teenager in a bright-red quilted parka, arms ablur, thrashed drumsticks against a row of upturned plastic buckets. His skill and charm were such that the hat on the ground bulged with coins, even a few notes poking out here and there.

Jacob, never able to completely switch off from work mode, kept his eyes alert, scanning the crowd. Irina, as if reading his mind, reached out and squeezed his hand. "You're not still thinking about those two men, are you, Yakov?"

"No," he said curtly. "Well, maybe just a little."

"You've had a rough couple of months. Nearly getting killed in Havana, then Zerina dying so suddenly. It's just paranoia affecting you, *zaichik*." She wrapped an arm around his waist and snuggled into his chest. "You said before we were safe here. Have you had a change of heart?"

Jacob managed a small, reassuring smile. "We're fine, Irina. But it never hurts to be cautious." He shared his idea of cramming in the sights tomorrow and then jetting off to Tahiti.

She let go of him and stood back a pace. A radiant smile stretched across her face. "This is a beautiful city, you were right about that. But let's come back in the spring, shall we? I need sunshine."

He nodded. "I should have listened to you. We'll return when the tulips and crocuses are in bloom and we can sit at an outdoor café drinking pints of lager and gorging on cheese."

"Sounds perfect."

Finally, the red brick monolith—the Beurs van Berlage—loomed ahead. Once the beating heart of commerce as a stock exchange, it stood transformed, hosting conferences and exhibitions like a modern-day agora. At its far end, they entered the attached bistro, a quiet haven of rustic charm shielding them from the noise of the outside world. The wooden floors creaked softly underfoot, and the gentle murmur of conversation mixed with the clink of cutlery and the occasional burst of laughter. The aroma of cinnamon and baked apples filled the air. They found a free table near a window where they could watch pedestrians, cyclists, and trams rattling along the Damrak thoroughfare.

Jacob ordered two slices of apple pie, each generously dusted in a light mantle of powdered sugar, alongside steaming cups of strong brewed coffee. As they waited for the waitress to bring their order, Jacob steered the conversation to domestic matters.

Irina's parents had finally settled in a gated community in Florida, new identities arranged by Fletcher and a peaceful life stretching out in front of them. After running from the Russian

SVR, hiding out in Latvia for months on end in fear for their lives, it was a dream come true for the old couple. The house they'd scored was big enough for Irina's son, Vova, to stay with them until she returned from Europe.

"Are you sure he was happy to go to Orlando?" said Jacob, smiling at the waitress as she placed plates and cups on the table.

Irina shook out a napkin and placed it beside her slice of pie. "Are you kidding? He hated the idea. But it will teach him a lesson in not being selfish."

"Cut him some slack." Jacob rested his fork on the plate. "The kid is still adjusting to life in a strange country. He's been bullied for being different, wearing eye makeup and dressing like an emo."

"Goth," Irina corrected. She smiled wanly. "I think that's it."

"Whatever," Jacob said with a shrug. "And on top of all that, he's got teenage hormones raging inside him; his body's changing by the month. The last thing he wants to do is spend his winter break with a couple of oldies."

Irina shook her head. "They adore him, despite Vova being 'non-traditional,' as it's popular to call non-conformers in Russia these days. He actually sent me a text. Wanna read it?"

Before Jacob could answer, she was already scrolling through her phone to find the message. She flipped the device around; Jacob read the Russian text. Handing it back, he said, "He sure went from hating the idea to loving being there in a hurry."

"It's amazing how a trip to Disney World can change someone's mind." She laughed infectiously, eyes shining in the softly lit café.

Jacob joined in the laughter, holding her hand across the table. They must have looked like a couple of love-struck teenagers.

As they finished their dessert and prepared to leave the bistro, Jacob took a final, lingering look at the cityscape outside the window. The night was still relatively young, and Amsterdam's secrets were labyrinthine and mysterious. But they wouldn't be discovering them tonight. Irina had a twinkle in her eye, and he knew very well what that meant.

They stepped back into the cold night, their path illuminated by the soft glow of streetlights and headlights of cars, trams and bicycles.

"Sorry for the tour through the sleazy part of town," said Jacob. "I should have known better."

She tugged on his hand. "It's not your fault. I might have overreacted, to be honest."

"No, I—"

She shushed him with a finger placed to his lips. "It's a legitimate tourist attraction in this city. Everyone knows that. It's just... you know...Zerina's story kind of impacted my thinking."

"Quite natural," Jacob agreed. Zerina had hated the sex industry in all its forms, and to wander the streets of de Wallen so soon after her funeral was the height of bad taste.

"However," she whispered, making Jacob jump as she squeezed his crotch, "you know I'm no prude, don't you?"

His smile was so wide his facial muscles hurt. "I know it only too well."

# TWO

THEY WERE THE ONLY TOURISTS ON BOARD, SO THEY sat right up front behind the captain. The sky was china-blue perfect after days of drizzle, but the temperatures had plummeted. The man at the wheel, a smooth-talking native of Amsterdam not far off retirement age, had assured them the canals would freeze over in the next week. "You timed it right," he said with a lopsided smile. "Soon the waterways will be full of ice skaters. There hasn't been a total freeze of the canals since I was a boy, back in 1963."

Ten minutes into the tour, the long, narrow boat seemed to be on a collision course with the looming stone bridge. Irina gripped Jacob's hand tightly. He grinned as she clamped her teeth. A few seconds later, the vessel slipped through the gap in the centuries-old tunnel, the underside a patchwork of moss and lichen. Mere inches separated the boat's sides and glass roof from the stones.

"*Gospodi!* My God, that was close," Irina whispered when the boat emerged on the other side into bright sunshine and a cloud of squawking seagulls.

Jacob laughed as he pulled her close to his side. "They'd never even attempt it if there was a risk of not getting through safely."

"I know that." She slapped his wrist playfully. "Still, it's a close-run thing, and you can't blame me for flinching."

"You're very safe in my hands." The captain, wearing a badge that said *Dirk*, turned around, rubbing his neatly trimmed white beard. "I've only had one accident on the canals."

Jacob took the bait. "What happened? Anyone get hurt?"

"No injuries." His large belly wobbled as he chuckled. "Only my pride was wounded. A little kid escaped from her parents, came running up the aisle, and crashed into my legs. I lost balance, yanked down on the wheel, and steered the boat into the canal wall before I could make a correction. Minimal damage, but luckily the parents signed a letter to prove I wasn't at fault." He swung around and adjusted course as another tourist boat came at them from the opposite direction. "So I got to keep my job, which I've had for...lemme see...thirty-four years."

"Congratulations," said Jacob, musing that he had thirteen years left of his unbreakable contract. The end of his spy career seemed as far away as New York. He had a love-hate relationship with his job. He loved sticking it to the bad guys; he hated putting his life in danger every time Fletcher handed him a damned file.

They cruised the famous Prinsengracht, admiring the colorful canal houses with their crow-stepped and neck gables. Most had hooks attached at the top for hoisting loads directly from the water. The boat slowed for yet another bridge tunnel. Popping out the other side, they were confronted with a long yellow vessel, this one full of tourists who could care less about the weather.

"Oh, no!" cried Irina. The hulls of the two passing boats crunched together at their widest points. The sound was like giant fingernails raking down a chalkboard. Jacob and Irina exchanged a glance of disbelief. Dirk, hardly fazed, gripped the wheel firmly and wiggled his hips. He must have heard the loud noise and felt the contact, but he made no mention of it, keeping his eyes firmly toward the front.

At the end of the tour, they shook hands with the skipper, wondering if his assertion that he'd only had one accident might not be the gospel truth. On the other hand, maybe the other skipper had been at fault. “I’m glad we did that,” said Irina as they jumped on a tram for the next stop of the tour. “But I wouldn’t be in a hurry to go out with old Dirk again.”

“Me either,” said Jacob. “His retirement might be closer than he thinks.”

---

THE LINE at Anne Frank’s house was mercifully short. The winter season had its benefits after all. As they shuffled along, waiting to be admitted, Jacob felt a sense of pride that Irina had agreed to come. She had needed some serious convincing when it came to this one. She feared she would break down in tears, embarrassing herself. Jacob had encouraged her to read the girl’s famous diary before arriving in the Netherlands, and her emotions were already dialed in. The museum, dedicated to the heroic girl who’d hidden with her family from the Nazis in a secret annex behind a bookcase, was a must-see attraction. Jacob said she’d regret it later if she bailed on this opportunity. And so she’d relented.

Inside, Irina’s worry that she would lose her shit came true. Her eyes were brimming with tears minutes after ascending the steep stairs to the secret rooms. Only she wasn’t embarrassed at all. She was in good company. Among the handful of others in their small tour group, all of the women and one old man could not control the flood of tears. Although also moved by what he heard through his earpiece and what he saw in the cramped space, Jacob held his emotions in check. He knew Anne Frank’s story backwards, having read the famous diary a couple of times, plus a lot of other material on the Holocaust. Under the protection of patriarch Otto, the Franks and four other refugees had hidden in a tiny space, surviving off rotten potatoes and scraps. Most important, they had to keep absolutely quiet when outsiders came to the premises. Virtual house arrest for two long years. As the wooden floors creaked under his boots, Jacob could only imagine the terror they felt on the other side of the partition every time they heard strange noises and voices. Jacob had seen the horrors of Auschwitz in Poland, walked the vast empty fields, seen the suitcases and shoes of the dead, their bunks, the crematoria, the gas chambers. And yet, somehow the intimacy of the tiny house on the canal made the plight of these victims even more profound.

Outside on the street an hour later, Irina's eyes were red and spider-veined from constant crying. "I'm sorry, Yakov. I..."

He wrapped his arms around her as she buried her damp cheeks in his overcoat. "Nothing to apologize for. A couple of years ago, before I got inured to man's capacity for cruelty, I would have reacted exactly the same way."

She pushed herself away half a pace, staring up at him with incredulous eyes. "Bullshit. I have *never* seen you cry. Even when you speak about Sally-Anne Vincent, you only have determination on your face. Never grief."

He pursed his lips hard. She was right. "That happened over twenty years ago. The pain fades over time. Now it's just a dullness in my heart."

"*Nyet*, Yakov. That's also not true. In case you'd forgotten, I've spent dozens of hours—I wouldn't be surprised if it was over a hundred—trawling through databases for you, digging into archives, looking for that clue that will find whoever killed her." She jabbed a finger at his chest. "So I know exactly how obsessed you are with her."

He swallowed hard, then cleared his throat. "Come on. That's not fair. I simply want justice for Sally-Anne."

"Yes. And you vowed to never stop looking for the killer." She smiled warmly. "I'm not jealous of a dead girl from your past. But you know, I'm now as determined as you are to find the answer; then at least I know you'll be focused a hundred percent on me."

Every fiber of his being ached for Irina, but he wouldn't ever shed tears in her presence. Was he physically incapable? he wondered. Her ability to push jealousy aside, to understand his need to see this through to the end, melted his heart. "For the rest of this trip—and after we leave for Tahiti tomorrow—you will be my total focus. I love you, and that's all there is to it." He looked around to get his bearings. He'd memorized the map of greater Amsterdam, brought to mind the grid of the streets and walkways they needed to take to get to their next destination. "One more sight for the day, and then we're done, OK? Like I said, we'll come back another time. In my humble opinion, Amsterdam is the most beautiful capital in Europe, and you deserve to see it in its full glory."

Irina fished out a flyer from her jacket pocket and rested her finger on an attraction that she'd circled with black ink. "I want to go here."

He took the pamphlet, folded it up and handed it back. "The Heineken brewery?"

She nodded enthusiastically. "Why not? You get a free beer as part of the tour."

He frowned. "I was hoping to take you to the Rijksmuseum. Aren't you interested in seeing famous paintings by the Dutch masters? Rembrandt, Vermeer?"

She shook her head. "I know you value honesty, *zaichik*." She sighed and exhaled, sending out a cone of steam in the cold air. "After that harrowing experience at the Anne Frank house, I'd like a pint or two of lager followed by a sauna back at the hotel. Then you can rub my back, get me nice and relaxed. Then I'll take off your—"

"Heineken it is!" Jacob exclaimed, already recalibrating the route.

---

THE IMPOSING Rijksmuseum with its red brick and white stone façade stood before them like an ancient sentinel as they crossed the short Museumbrug bridge. Turrets climbed skyward, gables crowning its steep roof lines. The early sunshine was long gone, replaced by cement-gray clouds. Fluffy snowflakes began to fall obliquely in a gently rising breeze, lending the scene a fairytale quality. Despite the afternoon freeze, the line to the front door extended almost all the way back to the bridge.

"I thought we weren't coming here?" said Irina with a note of impetuousness. The timeless beauty of the Dutch neoclassical building with a hint of Gothic did nothing to entice her inside its walls.

"Don't stress," Jacob reassured. "It just happens to be on the way." He gave her a sideways look. "But since we're here, maybe you'd like to take a peek...?"

She stamped her foot in an exaggerated fashion. "You promised beer! I'm too tired to be traipsing around a building as big as that. We've got some massive museums in Russia, in case you've forgotten. The Hermitage, for example. Buildings like that can be like rabbit warrens; you're looking for the nearest exit five minutes after you enter."

He tugged her along as they made a left turn onto Stadhouderskade, leaving the lovers of culture to enjoy the museum's treasures without them. Jacob noted that, even in the miserable cold, Amsterdammers on bicycles were out in force. The clanging of the bike bells was as constant as the honking of car horns in Manhattan. You almost had to have eyes in the back of your head to avoid getting hit. Their journey took them through a linear park that hugged the southern bank of the Singelgracht canal. Naked tree branches waved eerily in the breeze, ruffled wavelets appearing on the surface of the canal. They hurried the one-third mile, eyes closed tight against the stinging snow, now more like icy pellets of sleet.

As they stood before the red-brick behemoth that was the old brewery, Jacob ventured that Irina might prefer the warmth of the cozy pub right across the street. A firm shake of the head. "*Nyet*. I want a beer from in there."

Inside, they were greeted in the foyer with interactive light displays, posters, all kinds of memorabilia. Jacob arranged for them to take a guided tour with a bunch of other tourists. Tickets and, more importantly, beer vouchers firmly in hand, he marched back to Irina, waiting patiently by a wall. As he took a seat next to her, he sensed his phone vibrating in his pocket. Then the ring tone started to play. A corny song from an old James Bond film. The melody could only mean one thing. Fletcher was calling. He knew Jacob was on vacation and wouldn't call unless it was of the utmost urgency. Irina, eyes wide, shook her head.

"Don't answer him, Yakov," she implored. "Please."

He looked at the screen of his cell and pressed the red button to reject the call. "Come on, let's go wait over there." He pointed at an unoccupied sofa twenty feet from the entry. "The tour's starting in ten minutes."

The phone rang again. The ambient noise in the foyer was growing louder, the volume of the electro-funk background music higher than it needed to be. It reminded him of the thumping music clothing stores like to play to draw in a younger crowd. More people were starting to gather near the tour starting point, their conversations ratcheting up to compete with the music. Jacob flashed Irina a look of apology. "I'm sorry, honey. If he calls twice without leaving a message, it must be important."

"More important than me?" she said with a pout of her full lips.

He furrowed his brow. "You know that's not fair."

She gave a nod of understanding. "I'm sorry. Find out what he wants. But be quick."

He stood, gesturing toward the exit. "It's too noisy in here. I'll take it outside. Wait for me and don't move. I won't be more than a couple of minutes."

# THREE

THE WIND HAD PICKED UP A FEW KNOTS, AND THE SLEET was falling almost in horizontal lines. He jabbed the green button to take the call and placed a gloved hand over his other ear to protect it from the wind. "What is it, Grant?"

A half sentence uttered in Manhattan was obliterated by the wailing of a car horn 30 yards away. Jacob kept moving in the direction of the small pub on the corner, its glowing yellow lights drawing him like a moth to a flame. "I missed that. Say again?"

Halfway across the street, he narrowly avoided a collision with a woman tearing along on a bicycle; she stopped, yelled a mouthful of Dutch abuse, and waved a fist before pedaling on her way. The establishment, one of Amsterdam's 'brown pubs,' renowned for their predominant dark tan wood-paneled interior and subdued décor, was almost deserted. The exception was a matronly, large-chested woman with gauche green eye makeup behind the bar, sitting on a high stool and flipping through a magazine. She looked up, and they exchanged nods and smiles before he dropped into the welcoming embrace of a leather armchair.

"I said you need to come home, Jacob. Now. The shit's hit the fan, and you're the only person who can sort things out."

Jacob unwound his scarf and draped it over the back of the chair. He picked up the menu absently, speed-reading the list. The dishes on offer made him wish Irina had chosen this place instead of the brewery. They served the exact same Heineken beer, after all, and hot snacks. In hushed tones, he said, "I'm giving you two minutes to convince me." He smirked to himself: The only thing that would get him to voluntarily change his plans would be if Fletcher had a hot lead on Sally-Anne Vincent's murder. Which he wouldn't because it was a personal matter and had nothing to do with Skia.

"You don't get to dictate terms with me, Jacob."

It was true. If he couldn't worm his way out of an explicit order, he'd have to abandon the vacation. Still, he'd give it his best shot. "Irina needs this distraction to get over Zerina's death. I pull the pin now, and who knows how that's gonna work out for her."

A sigh of exasperation came from the other side of the Atlantic. "Don't make me beg. Or worse, invoke Article Seven. I'm sorry, but the lives of innocent people caught up in a shitshow take precedence over Irina's emotional state."

Jacob checked his watch. The brewery tour would start in seven minutes. "I've gotta be someplace. Make your case or invoke the damned article." Article Seven was a key element of the binding contract between Jacob and Skia. The no-get-out clause.

"A group of American aid workers have been taken hostage in South Lebanon. The terrorists have made a laundry list of demands, but the president outright refuses to negotiate. We don't have the slightest idea where they're holding the hostages. You need to find out where they've been taken. That's all. No rescuing anybody, no..."

Jacob's burst of laughter made the woman drop her magazine. "You said that last time, and I ended up dodging bullets with Cuban mercenaries firing AK-47s at me!"

"Tough shit." He heard the sound of Fletcher inhaling on a cigar. "You're paid more danger money than Tom fucking Cruise. Get your ass back stateside so I can brief you before deployment.

My secretary's already got flights organized for you and Irina. This is a real tricky problem, Jacob——one of the hostages is related to Hannah McIvor."

Jacob rubbed a sheen of sweat from his forehead. The new lady president was making a lot of waves, demanding loyalty from every federal agency and employee. Failure to carry out one's duty as per contracted conditions had already seen a number of people fired, even imprisoned. The woman made Margaret Thatcher look like Mother Theresa. "Listen, what about that new guy on the Middle East desk? Oberon Pirak? You should have chosen him from the outset instead of annoying me while I'm on vacation."

"Oberon's a good agent, you're right. But he's untested in the field."

"So test him. The guy has an Egyptian mother and speaks Arabic better than me. Besides, he's physically more suitable. He could easily pass himself off as an Arab or North African. I could never do that. Even heavily disguised."

"You passed yourself off as a freakin' Argentinian, Jacob." Fletcher could barely hide the frustration in his voice. "To a Cuban government minister, no less. Don't be disingenuous."

Jacob waved away the woman as she approached with a notepad and pencil, nonchalantly chewing gum. She shook her head, tut-tutted under her breath, and returned to her position, roosting on the stool. "That was easy to pull off, Grant. Argentina has plenty of tall, blond men who look more like Swedes than South Americans. And Spanish is my second-best language after Russian, you know that." Fletcher went to say something, but Jacob cut him off. "I've gotta go."

"I'll have a chat with Oberon." Jacob heard the sound of Fletcher swallowing, no doubt the usual Hennessy XO cognac.

"You do that."

"If I feel he's not up to the task, you'll have no option but to come home."

"Gottcha," said Jacob before hanging up. He quickly walked

over to the bar and placed a 50 euro note on the counter. "I appreciate you letting me shelter from the weather for a moment. *Dank U wel.* Thank you."

Her eyes widened, crow's feet disappearing in an instant. She stammered a few incoherent syllables, but Jacob was already turning the door handle.

---

THE SOFA she'd been sitting on was now occupied by a family of three. The tour guide for the group, an attractive raven-haired woman beaming a hundred-watt smile, appeared and began her upbeat spiel. The first line was a corny "Are you ready for the best day of your life?" It was a script she would have memorized and repeated many times. Still, she came off as fresh and enthusiastic. As she beckoned the group to follow her inside, Jacob cleared his throat and held up his hand like a kid in class. "Excuse me. My girlfriend must be in the bathroom. Could I ask you to wait a couple of minutes until she comes out?"

"Sure. As long as everyone else doesn't mind?"

A moan or two of annoyance, but most heads nodded understandingly.

Two minutes went by; still no Irina.

"Could someone please have a look in the bathroom for me?" Jacob bent his neck pleadingly, fixing his eyes on a middle-aged woman in an *I Love Amsterdam* T-shirt. "Would you mind?"

"Sure, no problem," she huffed in a northern British accent. Liverpool, he guessed.

Jacob quicky described Irina, what she was wearing. He thanked the woman with hands clasped together in a prayer gesture. She stomped toward the nearby bathrooms, her stiff body language proclaiming exaggerated martyrdom.

A minute later she was back. "There's no one in there, luv," she said with a shrug. "I even got on my knees and peeked under the doors of the stalls."

"I'm sorry, but we can't delay for much longer," said the guide, infusing genuine sympathy into her words. "We've got a schedule to keep. The good news is, your tickets are valid all day, so you can always tack on to the next one."

"Thanks," said Jacob distractedly, cell in hand. "We'll do that."

He dialed Irina's number, always a faster option than going via stored contacts. Which was a moot point with his new satellite phone, which looked exactly like a late-model Samsung. There were no numbers saved to the phone or the SIM card. Every number he would need to call was locked inside his steel-trap memory. The call rang out to voicemail as the last tourist disappeared into the belly of the brewery.

Jacob gnawed a fingernail. *Don't panic yet. She's gone wandering, gotten lost; now she's patiently waiting for me to find her.* He searched every inch of the foyer: snack food stands, a small bar for folks to enjoy their free beers post-tour, even the men's bathroom. No one he spoke to could confirm having seen her, even when shown a recent digital photograph. As he ruled out each location inside the foyer, he kept dialing her number. After five unanswered calls, he finally left a message. Three short words. *Call me please.*

A consultation of his watch told him twenty minutes had now elapsed since he'd exited the brewery to answer Fletcher's call. A lot of bad shit can happen in twenty minutes. He dashed outside, blinking away snowflakes. He jogged around the building, careful not to slip on the slushy pavement, with patches of ice forming here and there. A ramp to a basement car park disappeared under the building on the north side. He searched the darkened space thoroughly, yelling out her name as he went. No luck.

His heart pounded like a trip hammer. *Where the hell is she?*

Back up on the street, he ran the wet sidewalks until his breath became ragged, ducking into cafés and tourist shops, stopping random people on the street. *Have you seen this woman?*

No one had seen her.

*Think, Hunter think. Pretend she's not your woman, that it's not personal, that you're in the field and you've lost a valuable asset. How would you proceed?*

Plan formulated, he turned on his heel and marched back to the brewery. Inside, he found an Indian man who was traveling Europe solo. He showed the man a photo of Irina, slipped him 100 euros, and asked him to stand guard at the entrance in case she turned up. "Her name's Mila Dmitrieva." She hated having to use the fake name, but when traveling anywhere with Jacob, it was a non-negotiable condition. "Hold her and call me if she shows." He gave the man a business card with his alias for this trip, Michael Barrett. "Do not move an inch until I return." The man agreed to the terms with a handshake, a broad smile, and a slight head wobble.

Next, he spoke to an employee at the ticket office, a pasty-skinned youth with bad acne. He flashed the kid a fake Interpol ID he carried around with him—just in case he needed to get past stubborn gatekeepers—and demanded to speak to the manager on a matter of the utmost urgency.

---

"ARE YOU OUT OF YOUR MIND?" The manager of the facility, an officious man in his mid-forties with pallid skin and greasy auburn hair, shook his head vigorously. "I cannot put the brewery into lockdown just because you can't find your girlfriend. Don't be ridiculous."

Jacob glared at the junior employee who had brought him here, rooted to the spot as the agitated American asserted himself. "Step out of the office, please, son. I'd like some privacy."

The kid vacillated, legs shaking, eyes darting from Jacob to his boss. "*Meneer?* Sir?"

The manager barked in Dutch: "*Blijf waar je bent, Pieter. Deze klootzak gaat binnenkort weg.*" Jacob translated the simple sentence in his head. *Stay where you are, Pieter. This asshole will be leaving soon.*

Jacob shot a laser stare at the youth, pointing at his own chest. "This asshole is going nowhere, Pieter, until your boss agrees to help me. I've changed my mind. Close the door behind you. I want a witness in case this guy later claims I did something to him."

"Watch him closely, Pieter," said the manager, in English this time. "If he tries anything weird, run for help."

The kid closed the door softly and stood there, fear twisting his face as surely as if he was about to face the firing squad.

Jacob returned his attention to the manager. The man was nodding slowly, lips pressed together firmly. He stood from behind his desk, revealing his height to be an inch or so taller than Jacob. No surprise, the Dutch were reputedly the tallest nation in Europe. He sat on the corner of the desk, draping one leg over the other imperiously. Adjusting his designer spectacles, he said, "How long is it since she...is disappeared too strong a word?" Like nearly all Dutch people, his command of English was excellent.

"It's exactly the right word." Jacob stood with his feet shoulder width apart, arms across his chest. "But I don't have time to play word games. Something has happened to her, I know it. She has to be inside the building somewhere."

"Like I said, I can't..."

Jacob smashed his fist against the top of the walnut desk, rattling a glass jar full of beer bottle caps. "You don't want to push me, Mr...."—Jacob flipped around an embossed name plate—"Wapstra."

"Call me Hendrik," he said, then snickered in a dismissive way that set off a haze of red mist before Jacob's eyes. He made a quick assessment before acting: no obvious surveillance cameras in the office. Jacob's right hand snapped out like a cobra and grabbed the manager by the throat. He squeezed hard enough to let Wapstra know he wasn't kidding around, then just as quickly let go, his gaze unflinchingly fixed on the man's face. The man spluttered as a gasp came from young Pieter. "I will seriously hurt you if you refuse my reasonable request," Jacob snarled. "I believe something terrible may have happened to my partner. I'm not leaving this office until you take action. And if poor security is to blame, you'll be looking for a new job tomorrow!"

"OK, OK, calm down, for God's sake." Wapstra staggered back, rubbing his neck. Although he was taller than Jacob, he was as thin as a rail and posed no physical threat. He blinked rapidly and said, "We have no protocols for such an incident. The only thing I can do for you is call the police. Unless you would like to do that yourself." He made a be-my-guest gesture in the direction of his desktop telephone.

"I'd like you to call the police after you've shut down the brewery and we've searched it top to bottom. This is no longer a request."

"Very well. But I warn you, there will be repercussions after the way you manhandled me."

Jacob smiled. "No there won't. I've been nothing but polite." He turned to Pieter and growled. "Haven't I?"

The young man nodded quickly. "Yes."

Jacob tapped a fingernail on the desk and said to Wapstra, "Call whoever's in charge on the floor downstairs, shut the place down. No one in or out until you and I and your senior people have combed every inch of this building. How long to search everywhere?"

"An hour, tops. You might also like to view CCTV footage? We've got a bank of cameras installed, outside and inside."

"Yes, I would." Jacob relaxed a little as Wapstra showed his cooperative side, perhaps realizing Jacob wouldn't back down. "Actually, I've got a better idea." He turned to Pieter again. "Give me your cell number." The young man gave the number readily. Jacob tapped it into his satphone and sent the photo. A ding sounded as the image transferred to Pieter's phone. "I've sent you a recent picture of Mila. She's only 5'3", I mean about 160 cm. She's wearing a dark blue puffer jacket with a distinctive red-and-white scarf, blue jeans, and black Asics sneakers with white cross-hatch logo. Can you remember that?"

"I...I think so."

"Never mind, I'll text you those details in a minute. I want you to give the information to whoever mans the security room. Get them to analyze the video while Hendrik and I look for her. It won't take long to run through the footage because we weren't here long before she vanished. Look at video from 13:30 hours, just before we arrived, to now, 14:12 hours. Can you organize that for me?"

"Yes, sir!" The young man's fear had evaporated, replaced by a wide-eyed eagerness to assist.

Wapstra picked up the phone and started punching in numbers. He fulfilled Jacob's order and stood up, smoothing his trousers.

"One more thing," said Jacob.

"Yes?"

"Organize me a refund on the two tickets I purchased."

# FOUR

JACOB GRUNTED AS HE CLAMBERED OUT OF THE GIANT copper vat. It was a delusional idea to climb into it in the first place, he knew that. Shining bright flashlights into the vats had already revealed them to be empty, but a desperate man leaves no avenue unexplored. Two burly men reached up and assisted him to the ground, muttering words of encouragement and consolation at the same time. He stood with his shoulders slumped, breathing hard like a boxer had ripped him a good one in the solar plexus. This surely couldn't be happening. This was the Netherlands, one of the safest places in Europe. And yet Irina was gone.

Wapstra, who had done a complete U-turn in his attitude and was now fussing about like a mother hen, grabbed Jacob by the cuff of his jacket. "That's the last possible place left to look for her." He frowned apologetically. "We've swept the entire museum. Your girlfriend is definitely not on the premises. You must begin looking outside."

Clutching at straws, Jacob said, "A building as old as this, there has to be secret passageways, doors...maybe?"

"If there are, I don't know about them." Wapstra hesitated in thought for a moment. "I might be able to get hold of some old building plans. I'll speak to the owners later, see what I can come up with."

"I apologize for my manner before," said Jacob, giving the man his best open-and-honest expression. "Not like me at all."

"All forgotten." Wapstra smiled. "You must be frantic with worry." He excused himself to speak to the assembled tourists. He told them they would have to wait until the police had arrived and questioned them before they could leave. The cops were expected to turn up within the next fifteen minutes. "In the meantime, did anyone get anything on their cell phones that could assist us to find Mila?"

Jacob's heart leapt with hope. Wapstra was on the ball: tourists were forever taking selfies and videos. Dumb, because you never got to appreciate the moment. Humans today had this insatiable need to document everything. If it's not on Instagram, it didn't happen. His heart just as quickly sank when no one replied in the affirmative. Just his luck to strike a sensible crowd.

One petulant man, an Australian with a tattooed neck and a strident nasally accent, objected to the holdup. "We've been hanging around long enough, mate. We didn't see the woman you're looking for. And you can't force us to stay. In fact, I'm sure you had no right to lock us inside in the first place. Only the police can do something like that, and they ain't here, so we're buggering off. Come on, Raylene." He grabbed his companion by the upper arm and began to lead her away. Wapstra was about to speak when Jacob cut in.

"Ladies and gentleman!" he roared, bringing their murmuring to an end. "Of course, you are all free to leave if you want. But I beg you not to. Even if you think you can't help, the police are very clever at asking questions when they're gathering evidence. They can get you to remember things you think you've forgotten. Like Mr. Wapstra said, they are not far away now."

A sea of sympathetic eyes blinked back at him as Raylene steered her recalcitrant man back to the group. Jacob looked directly at them. "Thank you." He reached deep to summon his unflappable persona, the one that never panics or loses heart. "Next step. Can we look at the CCTV quickly before the cops get here?"

With the slightest nod, Wapstra addressed the group once again, asking everyone to wait in the foyer. He beckoned Pieter, ordering him to stand by the door and bring the police to the security room the second they arrived. Jacob by his side, Wapstra headed down a set of metal stairs and barreled along a dim corridor until they reached a black unmarked door. The manager rapidly pressed a combination of numbers; out of habit Jacob subconsciously memorized the sequence. The door gave a metallic click, and Wapstra nudged it open.

Inside, an overweight man, whose bulk stretched the stitching of his company uniform, sat behind a row of monitors, concentrating hard. All had action unfolding on them: some screens were split into quadrants, others were full-screen. A color print-out of the photo Jacob had supplied sat beside the man's mousepad. Next to that, in large print, was the text he'd forwarded to Pieter. Wapstra cleared his throat, and the man spun around. A shake of the head and a pout didn't instill confidence in Jacob. Without bothering with introductions, the manager asked in English, "Geert! What did you find?"

Geert went to stand up, but Jacob gestured for him to remain seated. The man ran his eyes up and down Jacob, taking note of his appearance. He let out a puff of air and said, "I've isolated clear images of you, sir, and the lady arriving, you getting the tickets, then you leaving and returning a few minutes later." He pointed at the screen with quadrants. "See?"

"But you didn't see Mila leaving?" He failed to disguise his incredulity.

"No, sir."

"We've just trawled the entire building, and she's not here! If she didn't go out the front door, then what? If she went out a fire exit, would your cameras cover those areas?"

A vigorous nod of the head. "Absolutely. That would be the easiest to pick up, because those doors are very rarely used."

"Windows?"

Wapstra shook his head. "There are no windows that a member of the public could get out of except by smashing them. You need special keys."

Jacob paced back and forth. Nothing made sense.

There was a tap on the door. A serious-faced Pieter admitted three uniformed police officers. Their leader, an athletic woman in a sharply tailored navy blue uniform and jaunty peaked cap, introduced herself as Inspector Eva de Kok, and then her colleagues. She was flanked by Sergeant Mark Jansen and Constable Sophie Bakker, both standing to attention, awaiting instructions from their boss.

"We need to act fast," said Jacob, eyeballing the cops. The inspector gave off an aura of professionalism; her junior colleagues looked almost too young to be on a job like this. Smooth-skinned and wide-eyed, they could have been fresh out of the academy.

De Kok, strawberry blond hair tied back in a ponytail and her oval face sporting a patina of wrinkles earned after years on the streets, gave Jacob a steely glare. "And we will, Mr. Barrett."

"Please, call me Michael." International travel for whatever purpose mandated an alias. Once he retired from Skia, he could go back to using his own name and his real passport. That time couldn't come soon enough. "We were just talking to Geert here about his examination of the CCTV footage." He repeated in his own words what the security man had seen.

"It's like one of those locked-room mysteries," said Bakker flatly, taking out a notebook and pen. "Could you please give a detailed description of what she was wearing?"

Jacob clenched his jaw, suppressing his irritation. Conflating a possible kidnapping with a locked-room mystery trivialized the issue. He pointed at the printed notes on Geert's desk. "Take a copy of that."

"Anything else that could help us find her?"

"Like what?"

"Distinctive perfume, for example. Other traits, like a limp, a nagging cough. Anything like that."

Wracking his brain, all he could come up with was "She speaks Russian and English with a distinctive accent."

Bakker pocketed her notebook and said with a wan smile, "Thanks. That could be helpful."

Geert put his oversized headphones on his desk. He stood and said, "The officer is right, you know. It is like a TV mystery because we've got her coming in but not going out. Annoyingly, the sofa where the missing lady sat waiting for Mr. Barrett's return is in a camera blind spot." He quickly showed the police the images of Jacob and Irina he had isolated. "But I hadn't finished telling them the other things I saw on the video that might be useful."

"And what was that?" said de Kok, narrowing one eye.

In the small room, those present fanned out in an arc behind Geert as he turned to face the screen. "It's not a long time frame to analyze," he said, almost breathless with excitement. "But some things happened that looked pretty weird." He froze the video. "This happened near the bar."

Everybody leaned forward and watched intently. On the screen, a medium-set man of average appearance with a dark bushy beard and wearing a black sweater, jeans, and black boots attempted to pick up two large beer glasses. As he turned, the glasses appeared to slip from his grasp before smashing on the tiled floor. His hands shot to his head dramatically; he paced back and forth as a number of visitors and staff quickly approached.

"That could have been a choreographed distraction," said Jacob with an edge to his voice. "Why did no one mention this?"

De Kok said flatly, "Because you, quite understandably, would have focused everyone's attention on your girlfriend and her physical appearance." She adjusted her cap with the flat of her hand. "Am I correct in calling Mila Dmitrieva your girlfriend? Mr. Wapstra used the word partner over the phone."

"Yes, she's my girlfriend," said Jacob, irritation choking his voice. "Does it really matter? I just want you to find her."

She shook her head slowly. "For the record, I'm differentiating between a business partner and an intimate relationship. But no, I guess it's not vitally important. What I wanted to say was dropped glasses are hardly a novelty in a bar setting. Our witnesses might have thought nothing of it."

"She's correct," said Wapstra. "Every day we have a breakage or two. Sometimes more. Cleanups are done quickly and with minimum fuss."

Geert wasn't finished with his assessment. "Yes, that's true. We see them all the time. But it's the way this fellow exaggerates his distress that raises my suspicions."

"He could just be a nervous type of guy," ventured Jansen.

"No," said Geert. "Watch his behavior."

On the screen, a couple of staff arrived to clean up the mess, as if materializing from thin air. As they bent over to soak up the beer and pick up glass fragments, the man stepped around them, and with long, confident strides headed for the exit. "Jesus," said Jacob. "That's a 180-degree shift in demeanor."

"Now, a minute later..." Geert clicked his mouse a couple of times, and a different camera picked up the man smiling broadly under the beard and extracting a packet of cigarettes as he walked. A switch of camera again, and the man was captured outside, smoking a cigarette and chatting to someone inside a black VW Touareg. "We'll stay with this camera for another minute or so." The glass-dropper turned back toward the brewery entrance, saying something as two other men, both of large build and wearing dark green hoodies, and a small-framed person appeared in the shot. The third person, face obscured under a woman's leopard-print fedora and an expansive raincoat poncho, head down, walked with an unsteady gait, supported on either side by the two men. All clambered into the vehicle. The doors slammed shut before the VW drove off at a leisurely pace in an easterly direction toward the harbor. Another minute of jerky time-lapse images before the camera picked up Jacob, returning to the brewery from the small pub on the corner.

"That's gotta be her with those guys," said Jacob. "Can you get a closeup of the license plate?"

Geert clicked to zoom in. "No good, dammit," he said. "Nothing clear, not even a partial."

De Kok inhaled deeply. "Are you sure it's her? I mean, you can't see her face and..."

"It has to be. The height matches. They've injected her with something. Sedated her with a tranquilizer. Drugs aren't hard to come by in this freakin' narco-paradise, are they?"

"Excuse me?" said de Kok, eyes bulging. "Do you want our help or not?"

"Sorry, that's my frustration boiling over," said Jacob. He ran a hand over his face. "They've put that stupid hat on her, thrown the poncho over the top. All while people were focused on the guy who dropped the glasses." His heart beat faster. "The men in the hoodies. I guarantee they're the same men who accosted us yesterday evening in the red light district. Same build, the hoodies are identical." He paced for a moment, then had an idea. "Zoom in on the shoes, Geert." He waited a second, then he jabbed a finger at the screen. "That's the Asics logo. Blurry, but you can make it out. It's a hundred percent her, I know it."

"I agree," said Sergeant Bakker. "The only logical scenario."

"I also agree," chimed in Jansen. "Everything points to a clever kidnapping."

Just hearing the word 'kidnapping' made Jacob's heart sink. He'd dealt with kidnappings before, but it had never been personal. His motivation to find—and kill—whoever did this was higher than for any mission Fletcher had ever assigned him.

"Here's what we'll do," said de Kok, sucking air through her perfect white teeth. She turned to Wapstra, who inclined his head obsequiously. "You will deliver me the entire day's security footage, and I will get our specialists to go over it. See when the alleged abductors arrived."

"Alleged!" roared Jacob, pressure building behind his eyes.

"At this stage when nothing's proved, yes," said de Kok, unflustered. "We may be able to enhance the vision beyond what you're capable of. Perhaps pick up the license plate, but because of the angle the camera's pointed, I'm doubtful. Facial recognition software might give us a hit on the guy who dropped the glasses. We got a good look at him."

Jacob kept quiet now because he didn't want to inject pessimism into the mix, but it was possible the bearded man was disguised in a bid to beat facial recognition.

"Copy it all for her, Geert," said Wapstra.

"Actually, make it from 6 a.m.," de Kok clarified. "In case the alleged abductors were doing some prep work in the vicinity."

"That's not possible," said Jacob, his mind spinning. "We weren't even planning to come here. I'd already gotten tickets for the Rijksmuseum, but Mila wasn't interested."

"The Rijksmuseum's not far from here. Perhaps they had contingencies for a number of venues."

"But why?" said Jacob. "She's been missing well over two hours now, and I've received no demands. Something stinks." He had bought the canal boat tickets on the spot and made the booking for the Rijksmuseum online via his unhackable satellite phone. "For argument's sake, let's assume they followed us discretely or phoned ahead to let others know of our approach. If so, I have a huge question."

"What's that?"

"How the hell did they know I'd leave her side long enough to snatch her? They couldn't possibly have known that."

"Why *did* you step outside? The weather's absolutely shitful."

Bakker and Jansen stifled chuckles, perhaps not used to hearing their boss cuss so creatively in English.

"I wanted to make a phone call. A private matter I didn't want Mila to overhear." No way would he drag Fletcher into this. If the cops were as thorough as he expected they would be, they'd eventually be asking Jacob to let them have a look at his cell.

They'd find nothing—the satellite phone was operated through Skia's low earth orbit satellite network that was patched into the wider National Reconnaissance Office network. Which meant he could manipulate the call log and no one would be any the wiser.

"But why go outside on such a miserable day? You could have easily found a quiet spot here in the museum."

It was an excellent question—if he'd been telling the truth. He could not admit that his boss, the head of a secret organization, had been desperately trying to get hold of him. "I don't know. It was a delicate personal matter, and I wanted no one eavesdropping. Stupid of me in hindsight. And the loud music was a distraction." He didn't like the way her questioning was going. "Look. We're wasting time over these details. We need to get out there looking for Mila!"

The detour worked. "You're right." De Kok held out a hand as Geert dropped an orange USB drive into her palm. Her manicured fingers curled over it, and she smiled. "Sergeant Jansen. Take this back to the station. We want names attached to faces, vehicle locations. Whatever the techs can come up with. Go!"

He snapped out a semi-casual two-finger salute. "Right away."

"What's the coverage like with LPR cameras in this country?" said Jacob, mentally crossing his fingers. If the Dutch police's technology was up to par, an extensive camera network would be a massive bonus.

"Excellent." De Kok smiled. "Theoretically, we could track a car all the way along the A2 to the Belgian border. Or in any direction." Her lips compressed for a moment. "It would take a lot of work, but even without picking up the plates, if we can cross-reference time stamps, it's possible to examine traffic surveillance footage to look for all vehicles of this make, model, and color and...maybe...get a lucky hit."

The Inspector turned to Constable Bakker. "Sylvia. Let's head upstairs and interview everyone who stayed behind. Ask if anyone saw a pair of men in dark green hoodies. Maybe they were close enough to hear a conversation."

"What do you suggest I do now?" said Jacob. Nervous exhaustion was about to strike; he could feel it creeping up. The only way to avoid a crash was to keep moving. Besides, his conscience would not allow him to rest.

"Don't stop trying to call her on the phone," said de Kok, empathy warming her tone. Jacob's gut told him she was the consummate professional cop—exemplified by the overzealous insistence on using the word 'alleged'—and would explore all avenues to find Irina. "Despite all the apparent evidence, everything may not be quite as it seems."

He shook his head. "Wishful thinking, I'm afraid."

She clapped him on the shoulder. "Not necessarily. I've seen plenty of cases where someone went missing, then turned up safe and sound. Go back to your hotel, take a shower, then make your way to the station to make a formal statement. Perhaps bring some items of Mila's clothing."

He nodded. He didn't dare ask what the personal items were for because he could already guess. DNA and possibly sniffer dogs.

"We are open 24/7, so no need to rush. Of course, best to do it when things are still fresh in your mind. After you've given your statement, you will be free to go and pursue whatever other avenues you want."

"Like what?"

"Hire a private investigator, perhaps. I don't know. We have them here in the Netherlands, you know. And keep ringing her number. Meanwhile, rest assured, we'll do everything we can to find her."

"I appreciate it."

"One thing. Please do not leave the city without first informing me."

"As if I would."

"Indeed." She handed him her business card. "Get the duty officer to escort you to my office when you arrive."

The realization hit home that a whole can of worms could

open up. A statement would require personal details he didn't want to give. Exposure. Photographs of him and Irina plastered over Dutch TV claiming to be Michael Barrett and Mila Dmitrieva and being recognized by people back home who knew them as different people. How could he alert de Kok to the delicate nature of the situation without actually telling her? Intervention via Fletcher seemed the only answer. But there were no guarantees that his influence, or that of the State Department, would hold sway in this jurisdiction.

Did Jacob think it was too late to try and stop his cover being blown?

Truth be told—yes.

# FIVE

Jacob declined the inspector's offer of a ride back to the hotel in the Transporter van. Motion was key. He had to keep moving. Ideas were formulating in his head, steps he could take individually in case the cops couldn't find Irina. His best ideas came when he was walking, swimming, running, lifting weights, punching the bag. Solo activities with no distractions. A couple of possibilities were already forming in his mind. He could make use of underground contacts on Skia's list, based in Amsterdam and other Dutch cities—there was a strong chance this had something to do with the 2019 Belgian operation.

Another option: ask for assistance from Fletcher's end. Send a spare agent over to assist with the spadework. A last resort—sound out a local PI like de Kok had suggested. If those pathways proved fruitless, he'd find another way. He would not stop until Irina was back in his arms and whoever took her was punished severely.

The sleet had backed right off now as the clock edged toward mid-afternoon, the biting wind now a meek breeze. Although still bitterly cold, he felt nothing but numbness in his soul as he trudged the streets back to the hotel. People, bikes, and vehicles went past, blurs and shadows; as ever, his subconscious was on high alert. He called her number non-stop the whole way. Every time—voicemail. Desperate, he stopped random strangers, showed them a picture of Irina. *Have you seen this woman?* Each time the answer was a shake of the head and scurrying footsteps away from the unhinged stranger.

---

The ginger-haired, gold-vested concierge at the exclusive Mondrian Suites, tucked away on the pretty Leidsegracht canal, greeted him with a smile, a wave, and a friendly hello. It barely registered as Jacob hurried past the man, taking the stairs instead of the elevator, bounding up three steps at a time. In the wide corridor, the subdued, dark tones of the décor and austere abstract paintings in cold blues, grays, and blacks perfectly matched his somber mood.

Room 304 was in prime position, offering an uninterrupted panoramic view across the canal. Compact and cozy, it was a standard package in this space-deprived city but with luxury fittings and appointments and every mod-con imaginable. He'd have traded it all for a flea-infested dorm room at the YMCA to know she was safe.

He inserted the card into the slot, hearing the click as the green light glowed. Inside, the heating and all the lights were on. A glance to the bench on the left revealed that a second plastic card had been inserted into the slot for the power. First thought—Irina was back. Then he remembered. Since they were always together, he'd requested only one encoded card be issued at check-in.

*Housekeeping?* Impossible—there was no cart outside with the usual replenishments. No cleaning paraphernalia, no piles of sheets and pillowcases and towels.

Was someone lurking in here, waiting for him? Maybe more than one person. Were they the same people who'd nabbed Irina? If so, they would have heard the buzz and the click of the door opening. They'd be waiting, safeties off pistols, fingers primed to shoot.

His stomach did somersaults as he switched from tourist to operative mode.

In the narrow alcove that preceded the living area and bedroom, he pressed his back hard into the wall, slowly and silently sliding to his haunches, not letting go of the door handle. In front of him was a small closet for hanging clothes, and under that a void of a couple of cubic feet. Inside that—two pairs of his and two pairs of Irina's shoes. Holding his breath, he stretched his body as far as he could, fingers acting like tweezers to grab his size 13 sneakers. He used one to wedge open the door to facilitate a rapid exit and gently let go of the handle.

Keeping his breathing flat and shallow in his upper chest, he counted to three. He tensed his core muscles and hurled the other shoe as hard as he could at the window pane across the room, where it connected with a loud thud. He held his breath, waiting for a voice, a gunshot, some kind of reaction.

Silence.

"Police. Show yourself, hands in the air!" he barked in reasonable Dutch. "We are heavily armed." He repeated the words in English, which the cops might do in a touristy hotel with patrons from around the globe. Always a good bluff to exaggerate your identity and numbers to an unknown adversary.

The continuing silence told him the location was likely clear of danger. At least in the form of humans. There could always be booby traps, bombs, or other nasty surprises. But those things were beyond his control. As insurance in case he was wrong, he took a heavy iron from the closet, gripped the handle like it was a lifeline, and wrapped the cord around his wrist for stability. It had a heavy steel bottom plate to knock a foe into next week and a pointy end that could poke out an eye.

With slow steps, treading lightly on the parquetry floor, he advanced into the living area, brandishing the iron as if it was a firearm.

A minute later, he'd looked under the bed and everywhere someone could hide. Absence of immediate danger confirmed, he raced to the bathroom, thrust his head over the bowl, and spewed out a stream of bile. After a few moments, his stomach stopped heaving. He filled a glass of water, rinsed, and spat out the foul taste. The second glass he drank greedily, then a third. He wiped his dripping mouth with a hand towel, then moved to the bedroom, cell phone in hand.

First step—call Fletcher. Jacob needed help here. Too much ground to cover on his own. About to punch in the number, he hesitated.

A flash of white on the bedside table caught his eye. He placed the phone on the bed, stretched his arm to its maximum extent, and plucked an envelope bearing assured, cursive handwriting. The kind that spoke of a good education, that belonged to a person who didn't rely purely on keyboards for written communication. On the front of the plain standard-sized envelope were two words: *Michael Barrett*. He flipped it over. Nothing on the back. The writing desk had a supply of stationery, including envelopes, but they all carried the distinctive logo, a pencil portrait of the master Dutch painter, Piet Mondrian, after whom the hotel was named. Which meant this envelope didn't contain a notice from management.

His heart hammered as he slid a finger under the flap and tore the envelope open. Hands shaking, more with fury than anything, he pulled out a piece of lined paper, folded in half. The text confirmed his fears—it was from the kidnappers.

# SIX

Jacob's hand trembled as he unfolded the piece of paper. He paced the floor, reacquainting himself with the contents of the note. Even though every word and punctuation mark was burned into his brain, he read the paper another three times. He collapsed on the bed, the backs of his hands over his eyes. He never cried, even in private, but God dammit, this time it was close. His eyes scanned the text for the fourth time, the words cutting him like a razor-sharp machete.

*Hello, Michael. You don't know who we are, but you know who we have in our custody. Do not panic. Mila Dmitrieva is safe for now. She will not be harmed in any way, as long as you do as you are told. We will release her to you, but first you must do one little thing for us. As soon as you have finished reading this letter, call 06 5554 9381 and you will be issued with a set of instructions. Introduce yourself by giving your name. Say nothing else unless we ask you for information.*

*This is your one chance to save her. Do not fuck up, Michael.*

*If you tell anyone you have received this note or try to trace the number, which would be pointless because it will only be valid for one call, then Mila will die a slow and painful death. Do precisely what you're told and at no time deviate from your instructions. The good news is that you will have 48 hours from midnight tonight to complete your task. Complete it successfully, and we hand over Mila, no questions asked. Fail...well, you can guess the rest.*

*You have tried countless times to contact her on her cell phone, but the number comes up as unknown. We are monitoring, and we know it is you. Be prepared to share your cell phone number with us when we ask. We may need to reach you at any time.*

*Last warning: We know you have spoken to the cops, perhaps your boss, too. Do not do that again. If you are contacted, play along, but you must NOT divulge that we have established contact. If you have contacted anyone else for help, call them again and cancel the request. No funny business. Or Mila is dead.*

Jacob crumpled the paper into a ball, squashing it in his fist. He gave himself a mental head-slap, unfolded the note and smoothed it out. Evidence—if he decided to present it at some point.

His fingers trembled, his breath coming in jagged bursts. The room closed in on him, the ceiling rushing down, the walls pressing from all sides. He so wanted to give a primal scream. Instead, he buried his face in a soft pillow and let out a bestial growl. Flipping onto his back, he stared at the ceiling, no longer trying to crush him, and blinked hard. He must not get flustered, lose his cool. The threats were to be expected. And he had to take them seriously. They had snatched her with ease, and they would kill her with even less fuss. On the surface, obeying them seemed the only way to get her back. But he knew from experience: people like that have no honor. To beat them, he would not—*could not*—play by their rules, but they had to believe that's exactly what he was doing.

Logic reared its big ugly head and screamed at him. Two scenarios seemed most likely. One: the kidnappers—it had to be de Vries and his cohorts—had hacked into Skia's supposedly impregnable IT systems. Perhaps looking for David Reeve, his cover from 2019. Then they found an itinerary for Michael Barrett with a photo that matched their records of David Reeve.

Two: a traitor inside Skia had dropped them in the shit for money, providing the details of their travel plans to de Vries. Traitors were rare, but the two he recalled had caused a lot of damage, both to the organization and to the country. They had disappeared from the face of the Earth and all efforts to track them down had failed.

A thought stirred in his brain. Someone had casually strolled into his room with a key card, no forced entry. A person on the reception desk must have given it to them. Was it the ginger-haired man? Had he been threatened, paid off, or both? Jacob would press him hard for information, yet at the same time use discretion.

His stomach heaved as he contemplated the potential surveillance of him and Irina. Had bugs been planted in the room before their arrival? Miniature cameras? Were they watching him now as he squirmed, helpless? He had to assume the worst and play it accordingly.

The seconds ticked by, slow and torturous. His mind raced, scrambling for options, backup plans. Despite the warning, he *would* alert Fletcher after he'd spoken to the kidnappers. A quiet alleyway, noisy coffee shop full of dope smokers, inside a hooker's kiosk: there were plenty of options to hide and speak quietly in this city. The bonus was having a totally untraceable satellite phone. When he did speak to Fletcher, he would infuse plenty of urgency in his plea. Not that Fletcher would need much convincing. He doted on Irina like she was his own daughter. He absolutely needed another set of eyes and ears, someone to act as his proxy, then discreetly funnel information back to him. But only on Jacob's terms.

Among contacts in the Netherlands, one loomed larger than all others as an important asset: Bram Wessels, a part-time agent who lived on the outskirts of Amsterdam. A man blessed with incredible IT skills. If Jacob was going to be totally honest with himself, Wessels' talents even surpassed those of Irina. Wessels had assisted on the Belgian operation against de Vries. The man was smart as a whip and, even better, owed Jacob a favor, one he'd figured he'd never have to call in.

Finally, the cops.

That was another matter. De Kok and her crew were more or less off limits. He would not initiate contact, and if *they* did, could he work in tandem with them without the kidnappers knowing about it? Theoretically yes, but there was so much to lose.

They were watching.

Somehow, some way, they'd know. If he made the wrong move, Irina was dead. The proxy agent on the ground was key. Fletcher simply had to find the best man for the job and authorize it, no matter the cost.

# SEVEN

"What a pretty little thing you are," whispered Valentijn de Vries, arms folded regally across his chest as he regarded the captive beauty. The veteran head of a long-standing and successful Dutch crime syndicate, de Vries considered himself to be a good judge of female flesh. And this pint-sized minx, who his crew had expertly snatched only hours before, was a stunning specimen. Slavic women were a particular weakness for de Vries. They were the sweetest fruit, and this part of the world was awash with them. Many had come to Western Europe voluntarily, but many hadn't. They were promised a bright future, only to be sold down the river, driven into prostitution that barely paid them a penny. Others were forcibly removed from their homes and trafficked as slaves. A sad reality of the modern world. De Vries' business interests excluded that kind of thing, but if the drug trade were to ever go quiet, he wasn't opposed to re-examining his options. As for the attractive qualities of the women themselves, Ukrainians and Czechs were his favorites, but a sexy Russian doll, well, there was always something earthy and raw about one of those.

He walked around her, head angled like a matador circling a wounded animal. So vulnerable and helpless. She was stripped to bra and panties, secured to a wooden chair with half a roll of gray electrical tape and cable ties. A length of the tape had been plastered over her mouth. Her hazel eyes blazed with fury. "I hope you're comfortable?" he said, loosening the belt of his terry cloth dressing gown. Her eyebrows elevated, making him laugh. "Don't be scared, sweetie. I'm not going to hurt you. I just don't want you running around and hurting yourself."

He glanced up at the eggshell-colored clouds visible through the glass roof, the snowflakes splattering against it. Humid air formed droplets on the underside of the glass roof and walls of the heated indoor pool, which was attached to the sprawling 19th-century country villa. Industrial electric heaters maintained a subtropical ambience inside. Orchids and cacti in terracotta pots dotted the paving that wrapped around the pool. The oasis in a secluded part of the Chaam Forests, just on the Dutch side of the border between the Netherlands and Belgium, had served him well for several years.

De Vries shook off his dressing gown and draped it carefully over the back of a white plastic chair, revealing a well-toned and tanned body in snug black swimming trunks. Low BMI, a rippling six-pack, firm muscles, and long limbs. Aged forty-five, he attributed his rude health to a disciplined fitness regime and, most importantly, staying away from the filthy drugs he distributed all over the Netherlands, Belgium, and Luxembourg. A big part of that exercise regime included swimming lots of laps in his twenty-five-meter pool. Forty a day, minimum, often double that, depending on his schedule. Today he'd been a busy man, but he needed to get those laps in. Since some of his associates were here and had been splashing around earlier, he decided to make it interesting.

He rested a hand on Irina's shoulder. She cringed, trying to shy away, but it was pointless. Turning to his assembled men, two chatting animatedly, three scrolling mindlessly on cell phones, he made a proposition. "Listen up. If any of you dickheads can beat me over ten laps, that man can have two hours alone tonight with this Russian babe. You can do whatever you like with her. Within reason, of course." His cheeks hurt from smiling as he delighted in Irina straining in vain against her bonds. She was safe from his animals; he wouldn't let them touch her. For now. She was too valuable an asset at this point. One that would, if Michael Barret —or David Reeve or whatever the fuck his name was—did the right thing, set him up forever. De Vries would be able to purchase the firepower to crush his Mocro mafia competitors and corner the Benelux market, virtually monopolize it.

Another voice in his head told him the funds raised could be enough to cut all his ties with the drug and arms business forever. He liked the lifestyle of his current vocation, but the associated stress? Maybe he could—and should—do without it. Time would tell. De Vries nodded toward a heavy oak door set into the brick wall, leading from the pool enclosure—what he liked to call the conservatory—into the main house. "It's all set up in the jungle room for debauchery. Clean sheets, champagne, snacks, a bag of blow. Any takers?"

In a heartbeat, the conversation and doomscrolling were over, and his soldiers were standing on the pool apron, dressed only in swimming trunks. De Vries took the middle lane, to his right young Moroccan enforcers Youssef Ben-Salah and Khadir El-Fassi and to his left Serbians Veselin Petrović and Stefan Marković, plus a sadistic but loyal-to-the-core Chechen, Adlan Ibishev. He knew Ibishev would beat the rest of the boys. Not because he was the fittest but because dangling a beautiful woman in front of him was like offering a year's supply of meth to an addict. But he would not beat de Vries. Despite him being at least ten years older than them, none would get within a lap, he was sure of it.

"On the count of three. Ready?"

Eager murmurs of assent.

"No cheating. The security cameras are on, so I'll know." He grinned. "Besides, our Russian friend is keeping an eye on proceedings from her ringside seat." He rubbed his hands together. "One last thing. If you fail to complete the ten laps, you'll be docked a week's wages." He paused to let the threat sink in; it was an empty one, but they didn't know it. His finger shot up in the air as he counted. "One, two, three. Go!"

He dived in and kicked hard underwater to maintain the momentum of the dive. Breaking the surface, he saw, three lanes away, Ibishev already half a body length in front. The incentive had clearly worked on him. Breathing on both sides as he drew level with Ibishev, de Vries saw none of the other men in his peripheral field of vision. He cast two sneaky backward glances. There they were. Arms and legs thrashing, water flying, they would try their best but fail. A tumble turn at the end of lap one, a split second ahead of the Chechen, the others there purely to make up the numbers and demonstrate their tenacity. De Vries wasn't extending himself yet, and he wondered whether Ibishev's plan was to go flat-out or leave some energy in reserve.

Five laps in, and Ibishev was hanging around like an annoying mosquito. De Vries put on a turn of pace, quickly stretching his lead to several body lengths. But the Chechen dug deep, caught up and then, with a lap to go, somehow wrested the lead. This could finish in humiliation; de Vries turned on the afterburners. Shoulders, legs, and lungs screaming for respite, he churned the water around him into a roiling foam.

He touched the wall, then immediately glanced left. The motherfucker had beaten him. Ibishev was already standing up in the pool, brilliant white teeth glowing under his neatly trimmed beard. He ran his fingers through his jet black hair, gave de Vries an apologetic smile, climbed up the ladder, and collapsed onto a folding sun lounger. De Vries followed him, grabbing two bottles of water from a bar fridge and handing one to the victor.

A full minute later, the rest of the men had touched the wall. Spluttering with exhaustion, they clambered out of the pool. Each man in turn slapped Ibishev on the back, offering hearty congratulations. They only did so because de Vries was smiling, obviously preparing to be magnanimous.

"Well done, Adlan." De Vries extended his hand, which the

other man shook with a viselike grip. He had been foolish to underestimate Ibishev. He trained like an MMA fighter; his fitness was beyond question. "Are you ready to enjoy your prize?"

De Vries drew a sharp breath as Ibishev frowned and slowly shook his head.

"I am too drained to make love to the woman the way that I want to. It's a matter of principle for me not to have sex half-heartedly. May I defer until tomorrow?" Ibishev was a tough son-of-a-bitch, but he also knew which side his bread was buttered on.

"Sorry," said de Vries. "I made it clear. The offer was for tonight only." Noticing the man's head droop, he added, "Don't worry. My friend Jochem recently received a consignment of fresh Romanian beauties for his kiosks in the Hague and Antwerp. You can enjoy one or more of them once we've finished with the woman and this Michael Barrett. Fair?"

"More than fair." Ibishev leered.

---

THE MEN SAT around a long wooden table, drinking bottles of cold Amstel. Except for the strict Muslim Ibishev, who contented himself with diluted cranberry juice. The conversation naturally centered around their unwilling guest and the next stage of the operation. De Vries had already confirmed she had no grasp of Dutch, and so they freely discussed matters in her presence.

"Shall we untie her?" said de Vries once they had all confirmed they understood how the plan would unfold. "Has she been trussed up like a Christmas turkey long enough to know we aren't messing around?" As he let out a throaty chuckle, the men joined in the laughter. He doubted they were all totally genuine. De Vries had no illusions; it was impossible that they always thought his jokes were funny. Sometimes he'd toss out the lamest gags which he himself thought were stinkers. Nevertheless they always laughed along with the boss, a bunch of brown-nosers but with good cause. People fucked with de Vries, they usually didn't live long enough to regret it.

"I say let her out of the chair," said Ibishev. With his square jaw and obsidian black eyes, he was a ruggedly handsome male who attracted women easily. Even so, he had a weakness for prostitutes because they did the kinky stuff he liked. Usually with unbridled enthusiasm and eagerness, but sometimes they needed a little gentle persuasion. "I wanna hear if she's sad she didn't get the chance to experience a real man." He flexed his iron biceps for good measure.

More laughter. This time it was genuine, since no one was beholden to the Chechen. To their credit, the Moroccans and Serbs had no fear of him, although he could take them apart as easily as buttering a piece of toast.

"Yeah," agreed Ben-Salah, one of the two active kidnappers from the brewery. He had performed the magic trick of 'disappearing' Irina with the leopard-print hat and poncho. "She's not posing any threat to us, even if the propofol has fully worn off."

"She ain't no Lara Croft, that's for sure," chimed in El-Fassi, the second kidnapper and the one who had injected Irina with the fast-acting tranquilizer. "Look at the size of her. She's built like one of those tiny Olympic gymnasts, only with bigger boobs."

"Hey," said Marković, a Muay Thai champion in his youth. He was the only one of de Vries' inner sanctum whom Ibishev considered a potential physical equal. A loyal deputy to Petrović, he played a team game, always putting his own self-interest second. The brand of violence he dished out was clinical and elegant. De Vries also liked having him on board simply because it gave Petrović an outlet to converse with somebody in his native tongue. A happy Petrović meant de Vries had one less thing to worry about. "Did you see the way she was thrashing around in the chair? I wouldn't underestimate her."

Uproarious laughter echoed in the conservatory. Marković thumped his fist on the table, drawing silence. "I wasn't joking," he said sternly. "We must never underestimate anyone. Even her. Doing so can be fatal."

De Vries took a draft of his beer. "Stefan is right. I underestimated a man called David Reeve once—only I didn't know at the time he'd resurface as Michael Barrett—and one of my best friends became a paraplegic. Now he is a shell of a man, uninterested in life." He tugged at the golden hoop ring in his left ear. "With her as bait, he will not only score us a fortune, but I will also make sure he pays for what he did to Sjaak."

They all looked at Irina, still strapped to the chair but not exhibiting any signs of resistance. Like the men, she had probably worn herself out. De Vries had been mindful to monitor her from time to time, ensuring she was conscious, breathing, and not choking on her own saliva.

De Vries cast a studious gaze over his men. It had been a huge day for everyone. Their conversation was drying up, eyelids drooping, mouths hanging open in wide yawns. He sent them back to their quarters, a separate bungalow on the edge of the estate, backing onto the woodlands. They would return to their homes once Barrett had stolen the recently discovered Rembrandt, "Portrait of a Noble Stranger," from the private collector and it was in de Vries' possession. The collector had paid an undisclosed amount for it, but rumor had it the sum was close to that outlaid for da Vinci's "Salvator Mundi," which had gone for $450 million at auction in 2017.

Only his most trusted deputy, Veselin Petrović, would stay behind tonight to help convince the woman it was in her best interests to actively cooperate. Petrović was not only the most diplomatic of his employees, he was a borderline genius. It was he who had come up with the heist idea and composed the note to Barrett. With Petrović's help, de Vries would steer this audacious operation through to its stupendous conclusion.

If Barrett played by the rules, he'd be making a phone call soon.

# EIGHT

His heart hammered against his ribs. He'd made the decision to call from the hotel room's landline phone. The satellite phone was untraceable—Skia's tech experts guaranteed it—but using the phone in his hotel room somehow seemed the safest option. He dialed 9 to get an outside line, then the number he'd been given. A whooshing pulse roared inside his skull, like the sound you hear when you're holding a conch shell to your ear.

*Click.* The line opened to a greeting of silence on the other end. He casually touched the screen of his phone, resting in the top pocket of his shirt, to activate the voice recording app, then placed the landline on speakerphone.

Silence reigned on the other end.

His throat went dry. "This is Michael Barrett." He kept his tone neutral, fighting the upwelling of combative instincts. How it pained him to bend to their will. It would only be a temporary concession. There were a thousand other words he wanted to add, to scream at the asshole on the other end. He dug his upper teeth into his bottom lip as he waited for a response. The guy was in no hurry.

"You're calling nice and early. I like it," a voice rasped, deep and lightly accented. "Gives us confidence that you won't try anything stupid to put the lovely lady in jeopardy." Unmistakably Slavic, but too generic to pin down to a nationality. If he had to bet money on it, he'd opt for Croatian or Serbian, the melodic tones suggesting the latter.

"You harm one hair on her head, and I swear..." He prepared for a torrent of abuse as his plan to play along came unstuck.

Instead, the man said calmly, "Don't take us for monsters, Barrett. We have no intention of hurting her...unless you give us reason to." Some background chuckling of one other man present, then indistinct scraping. He listened hard to the sounds but couldn't identify anything. "And that will be the last time you break the rules. They are simple ones that a highly trained operative like you should be able to follow."

Jacob bit down on the temptation to speak Serbian to the man, to get a feel for this new and invisible adversary.

"Do not speak unless spoken to and do not ask any questions. It can't get any simpler than that. Before I go on, are you alone?"

Was that an amateur mistake? Jacob wondered. The man had just more or less confirmed there were no cameras in the room. Or had he? It could always be a well-disguised double bluff.

The ensuing pause vibrated with tension.

"Yes, I am alone."

"Good." Another pause, and what sounded like the shuffling of papers. Was the guy reading from a script? "Have you spoken to anyone since you got our message?"

"No." Jacob's mouth drew into a hard line. "I've only just returned from the police station and found your note."

"Excellent. We anticipate the police will be in touch with you again."

"No shit, Sherlock."

"No need for sarcasm. As for the police, of course it is only natural that you cooperate with them. Otherwise you will arouse their suspicions, perhaps see you as a suspect. That is something we simply cannot have." Murmurs of agreement from the other person present. "Have you given a formal statement to de Kok?"

"Yes." His heart skipped a beat. They even knew the name of the officer leading the investigation.

"What was in it?"

"I can't remember verbatim," he lied.

"Summarize it."

"I just told them what I remember happening. How I ducked out to talk to a friend on the phone about a personal matter, came back, and she was gone."

"You know if you hadn't done that, we would have had to wait for another opportunity."

He felt a vein in his temple throb. The bastards had been stalking them, waiting for the chance to strike. And he had provided them that chance.

"The police have no idea where we have taken her, and neither do you," continued the Serb. "Please don't worry, though. We are taking excellent care of her."

If this was baiting, he would resist it. Jacob held his tongue. If there was an uncomfortable silence, he would wait it out. The other guy could blink first.

Finally, the blink. "Perhaps you are wondering about the 'task' we want you to carry out."

Tricky. Sounded like a question, but it wasn't. Again, he remained silent.

"We need you to steal something for us. Are you prepared to do that?"

"If you release her after I've done it, of course."

"I'm glad you agreed. Otherwise you would have received a package containing a dainty female finger. You will always do as we say, when we say it. Simple enough?"

Choking off his anger at the words, spoken so calmly, wasn't easy. The pressure in his head was creating the ideal conditions for a migraine. "Yes."

"Perfect," the man continued. He dictated another phone number that Jacob was to call at 7 a.m. sharp tomorrow morning. "You will arrange to meet two men who will deliver you to me."

"Where will I meet them?" He spoke softly, breaking the don't-speak-unless-asked rule.

A short, sharp laugh. "You'll find out tomorrow."

*No rebuke.*

He pushed his luck. "Tell me more about the job."

"Again, you'll get the details tomorrow. Suffice to say, what we want you to steal is guarded. Most people would fail in such a mission. You will not fail. Your motivation will get you over the line." A pause accompanied by the sound of a cigarette lighter, a sharp inhalation of smoke. "You've been rather a good boy, Michael. Just a couple of times you spoke out of line, but I think we can forgive that under the circumstances. Perhaps we could allow you a word with your paramour."

Some mumbled words in Dutch, too hard to hear, let alone decipher. Clattering noises, like plates on saucers. A nice tea party among the kidnappers. Then scraping—the leg of a chair? More words, a female voice. Irina's voice. English, but unintelligible. They were bringing her to the phone. His breathing hitched. *Please, you better not have hurt her.*

"*Zaichik?* Darling?" The tone was fragile, shaken. In rapid-fire Russian, she said that she loved him and not to worry. An underlying defiance permeated her croaky voice. How proud he was of her.

"English only!" The grating voice belonged to a different man.

"*Oni tebya byut?* Are they beating you?" Jacob ignored the demand.

"*Nyet.*"

"English only goes for both of you!" said the original man. "And no, we are not beating her." The Serb understood Russian. Good to know.

He spoke to the other man in Dutch. Jacob understood that was the end of the conversation. All he'd gotten out of her was a couple of sentences. No more than ten lousy words. It stirred something primal and visceral inside him.

"Allow me to repeat," said the Serb. "Ring at 7 a.m. tomorrow and be ready to meet our representatives soon after that. Understood?"

Jacob couldn't help himself. "*Da, mudak!* Yes, asshole!"

The Serb laughed then disconnected the phone. Jacob smiled grimly. He'd recorded the entire conversation on his cell. Bram Wessels might be able to do something with it, match the voice to a known criminal.

Jacob showered under cold water, then switched it over to the hottest temperature his body could take. He closed his eyes tight; whatever discomfort he was experiencing was nothing compared to the distress Irina must be going through.

Drying off, a million thoughts raced through his mind. The men who had taken her, although they didn't know it yet, were on borrowed time. He would find them and take them down. Every last one of them.

# NINE

De Vries picked his teeth with a match while he contemplated his captive. Facial muscles twitched, a satisfied grin creasing his face. The phone call had gone exceptionally well, better than expected. Petrović had played his role perfectly, not allowing Barrett off the hook at any stage. De Vries was particularly pleased with how the Serb had stopped Barrett and the woman from exchanging any secret messages in Russian. It wouldn't have worked anyway—Petrović was fluent in the hideous language.

Best of all, the American had shown his hand, his willingness to act. He would do anything, take any risk, to save the life of his precious woman. That was more important to him than getting the better of de Vries. He smiled to himself. The priceless Rembrandt painting was as good as in his possession.

The woman groaned as he circled back to face her. "Did you say something, my dear?" He flicked her under the chin, as a father might do to a misbehaving daughter. "What was that, Mila? If that's even your real name. I wouldn't be surprised if you were some kind of spook, too."

Another muffled sound leaked out the sides of the electrical tape. It could have been words or a grunt of anger. De Vries smiled and stood back, arms hugging his chest tightly. He shivered. Like a boxer finding his opponent's vulnerable areas, the freezing cold was finding weak spots, seeping through cracks in the building. He'd paid a small fortune to have the place extensively renovated just after he'd purchased it, installing the best heating systems on the market. But with an old beauty like this, the maintenance was never-ending.

The woman was shaking a little, too. He'd tossed a cashmere blanket over her, but it wasn't helping much. She'd be tucked up in a warm bed soon. As he leaned in close to observe, to check her teeth weren't chattering under the restrictive tape, her wide eyes shone like glass. Ear pressed close to her mouth—no chattering detected. He flattened his palm against her brow. She recoiled, the legs of the chair clattering on the floor. Skin damp and warm, but not hot. No fever. Good. The last thing he wanted was a sick hostage. No, she was just frightened and mighty pissed off. Which set off a fire deep in her hazel eyes.

That was another thing he loved about Eastern European women: their eyes. A different quality, a different shape. Slightly turned up at the far edges. Historians and demographers would say it was a reflection of migratory patterns over the centuries, the influence of the Mongol hordes spreading their seed in the 13$^{th}$ century. Plenty of years for a genetic pattern to emerge. To de Vries, the old saying that eyes were the windows to the soul held true. His slutty, know-it-all ex-wife, Janneke, had told him the expression came from Shakespeare. As if that uneducated fool would have known! He knew for a fact it was Leonardo da Vinci who'd coined the phrase. He grinned as he recalled how Janneke's stupid cow-eyes had turned into windows to terror when he and some of the boys drove her to the edge of the Chaam Forests and made her dig her own grave. Serve her right to die in a ditch after her two-timing ways. The funniest part was de Vries had made the latest boyfriend shoot her before himself being shot at point-blank range and tumbling onto her in the hole. His lip curled up at the right side as he fondly remembered the scene.

"I'll take the tape off your mouth soon, but first I want you to understand why you are here."

The woman rocked from side to side, mumbling loudly under the tape. Her eyes bulged, every muscle in her lean body tensed and twitching. Whatever did she hope to achieve with such a ridiculous carry-on? de Vries mused. A totally pointless exercise that did nothing but waste precious energy. He slipped the blanket from her shoulders, bundled it neatly, and placed it on a portable table.

The sounds of hushed voices and footsteps came from the left as Petrović and Marković entered the cellar through a heavy oak door. "Take the tape off her," commanded de Vries, nodding at Marković. "Now," he addressed the woman, "don't try any funny business like you did last time." When they'd moved her from the conservatory to the dank cellar, she had lashed out with slaps and punches the second her hands were free. Surprisingly powerful for her small stature. And so the tape had had to be reapplied. Her spark of anger also meant she didn't get to add more layers of clothing; as before, she sat in nothing but bra and panties. De Vries worried that it might take her a while to realize cooperation was the only option. Keeping her half-naked with a bunch of men around could arouse passions best left cold. "Do you promise to behave, like a good girl?"

She nodded, eyes rounded, muscles tensed. He gave an upside-down smile as he admired her gymnast-like physique. Toned, no spare fat apart from the natural layers around the hips, ass, and breasts that made the Eastern European babes so damned attractive.

"Sorry, I didn't hear you."

Another unintelligible noise came from behind the gag; de Vries took it to be a 'yes.'

"Excellent." He gestured to his men. *Get it done.*

Marković moved toward the front of the makeshift prisoner-chair, smiling an empty smile, a tongue moistening his lips. He knelt and with searching fingers found the elusive starting point.

He scraped at the tape with a well-manicured fingernail to get it going, then began to unwind it slowly. As the gray ribbon reached the point of contact with skin, he slowed down. The way the tape tugged at her lower leg, pulling on tiny blond hairs, seemed to fascinate him.

"Get a move on, Stefan," growled de Vries. "She's spent hours wrapped up like a Christmas present. The poor creature has had enough."

From behind, Petrović had already removed the tape around the body, exposing red marks on her bare stomach and shoulders.

Finally, the last of the tape came away from the legs. She kept them perfectly still, arms dangling loosely by her side. De Vries saved himself the final honor of removing the tape from her mouth.

The hostage spluttered, then gave a light ladylike cough into her small fist. With the back of her hand, she wiped chapped lips, coated in a light sheen of spittle, then let her head slump forward.

De Vries wondered, had they gone too far?

He came closer, squatted, and craned his head to see whether her eyes had closed. With his face inches from hers, she snapped her head back. A stream of spit flew from her mouth, hitting de Vries in the chin, lips and nose.

Marković's hand darted back, ready to let the woman feel the harsh sting of his open palm.

"No!" said de Vries, now standing, rubbing the gunk from his face with a handkerchief. "Don't hit her. We do not hit women. There are other ways to teach her to behave."

"Indeed there are, Stefan." Petrović placed a small crocodile-skin valise on the floor beside the woman, still sitting in the chair. She fired death stares at the three men, now arranged in a straight line in front of her.

"There are some clothes in the bag," Petrović said with the emotion of a robot. "Nothing fashionable, but they will keep you warm and comfortable."

De Vries gazed admiringly at his lieutenant for a moment,

then back to the woman. "In the world out there"—he gestured at a window—"spitting in someone's face is considered a serious assault. You could get three years imprisonment. Lucky for you I'm a nice person and won't press charges. However, try it on again and you will receive no food or water until your boyfriend has delivered me the painting."

"What painting?"

"Never mind about that."

Her brow wrinkled. "I don't care if you starve me to death, you fucking asshole." She looked from one man to the other. "Make that assholes, plural." She sucked in a deep breath. "You fools have no idea what's going to happen to you, do you?"

Hands on hips, de Vries said, "Nothing is going to happen to us. It's you who should be worried. Your boyfriend can't get you out of this one."

"He is just one person. Of course he's not going to be the one to rescue me. The entire Dutch police force will be out looking for me."

He tilted his head to the side. "You have a high opinion of yourself, don't you?" He chuckled softly. "The cops have got much better things to do. You are one missing person, that's all. Why would they devote scarce resources to search for you when serious crime is happening in Amsterdam and other Dutch cities every day?" He sighed. "Enough of that. Time to settle you into your new accommodation." He waved a hand around at the bare brick walls, illuminated by caged bunker lights. "Not as grim as this cellar. It's a special room. A place where you can sit and contemplate life's eternal questions. It's basic, yet comfortable enough."

He gave a nod to his two associates, indicating that the time to end the chit-chat was fast approaching. "She can get dressed in her new accommodation. Take her to the guest room." He winked at the woman, drawing a grimace of disgust. "Are you going to go quietly? It's dinner time in a couple of hours. I'm sure you'll be hungry. And..."—he clapped his hands together merrily—"I'd like to offer you a nice cold beer before bed, since you missed out at the brewery. How does that grab you?"

Petrović and Marković were already grasping her by an elbow each. Her legs swayed slightly as she strove to regain her footing after being stuck in the same position for several hours. "I'll go quietly, but I just wanna say one thing."

"Oh yes?" said de Vries, cocking an ear.

"Fuck you!" She flipped him the bird, drawing belly laughs from all three men.

"That's enough," said Petrović. Before she had time to react, a hood was slipped over her eyes and tied in a knot at the back with strong fingers.

Marković draped a dressing gown over her shoulders. "Let's move."

---

THE SERBS ESCORTED Irina along a corridor. The men smelled strongly of expensive cologne and cigarette smoke. Hollow sounds of boots against concrete echoed, accompanied by the slap-slap of her own bare feet. A right turn, another corridor; the walls felt close, the ceiling not far from her head. Then outside into the bitter cold, across a field, into another building, and then down a short flight of stairs. She counted her steps. One hundred sixty-seven.

A futile exercise? Perhaps not. Yakov had told her if, in the unlikely event she ever got snatched, blindfolded and thrown in the trunk of a car, she must pay damned close attention to her surroundings. What you remembered later, even if it's just a little bit, could help track down the perpetrators. That's if things turned out well: you managed to escape, the cops busted the door down, or a ransom was paid and you were released. Pray to God things didn't turn out badly.

The memory flooded back vividly. She had been in a sports bar in downtown Manhattan. Two years ago, give or take.

Drinking with Yakov, Fletcher and, for once, Susan Stonehouse. Irina could never remember the Skia secretary being in a social setting with them before or since. They were Fletcher's guests that evening. He was cock-a-hoop; his beloved Jets had won a close one, made the playoffs, and were a game away from reaching the Super Bowl. Irina could picture the scene like it was yesterday, recreating the conversation in her mind. The irony of what was said in light of her current plight felt like molten metal rolling around in her stomach.

*Fletcher brought an armload of beers to the table.*

*Irina: No one's going to kidnap me, Yakov. Why should I know this stuff?*

*Fletcher: Everyone needs to know it. Should be taught in schools.*

*Stonehouse, giggling: Kidnapping Survival 101?*

*Yakov: Something like that.*

*Irina: So what's the secret?*

*Yakov: You have to listen to every sound, every word, take note of environmental factors: the sounds of animals, birds, machinery. Listen out for words exchanged, accents, languages. Smells, like gas, smoke, a person's own body odor, are also important. Even taste. The kidnappers will feed you something. You have to be finely attuned to everything. We're so used to relying on our sight for a lot of our day-to-day activities that our other senses get put on the back burner.*

*Irina, playfully: Maybe we could play some blindfold games later and...*

*Fletcher: Oh no. I don't wanna hear about that!*

*Stonehouse: I do!*

And that was about the end of that topic of conversation. Except Yakov took her at her word, literally. They did play a series of blindfold games. But not like the steamy sex scene in that famous movie, *9 1/2 Weeks*. Well, not that time, anyway. Instead, they acted out a couple of abduction scenarios. Of her own free will, she donned a blindfold, climbed into the trunk of his car, and let Yakov drive her around for an hour. He then grilled her on what she remembered. How did the car's engine sound? How many lefts, how many rights, how many stops? Did she hear any railway crossings or church bells? She'd scored pretty low on that first test. Missed a ton of details. They repeated the exercise twice, and she got better at it. Once, they reversed roles. She drove Yakov's car to Stamford, Connecticut, an hour from his apartment. She popped the trunk, he climbed out, and she removed the blindfold. "Give me a map," he said. His index finger landed on a point within a hundred yards of where she'd parked the car.

The man called Stefan, the slightly friendlier of the two Serbians, led her gently into the room while the taciturn Petrović remained in the corridor. The fabric of the silk hood dragged across her face, and her hair caught in it, creating static as it was slipped over her head. She blinked a couple of times to adjust to the bright light shining down from the ceiling.

"Where's my stuff?" she demanded, arms spread wide and palms open.

He dropped the valise at his feet, pointing at it. "Make do with what's in the bag. You will get your own clothes back later. Cell phone and handbag too. Maybe."

"I want my phone now. I need to call my..." She choked back a tear, her lips trembling. "My son. My parents."

A shake of his head. She glared at him, daring him to show a spark of sympathy. His face remained as inscrutable as that of a granite statue. "Not allowed."

"They at least need to know I'm alive!" Her heart burned with pain thinking about the stress they'd be going through.

"I'm sure Mr. Barrett would have called them, no? If he cares as much about you as you think he does."

"He loves me!"

A knowing smile. "I'm sure he does. Because he's gonna do what the boss wants. Only a man who truly loved you would agree to it. Or a crazy man."

She tugged the waist cord of the dressing gown tighter. "He will be angry. Angrier than me!"

He nodded. "We expect he might try something silly, but we are prepared."

"Not prepared enough!"

"Let's see." Stefan paused a beat, gathering his thoughts. "As long as me and him," he said, jerking his head toward the unseen Petrović, "...are on watch, no harm will come to you." He allowed himself a leering grin. "The Moroccans you saw at the pool? They're not as..."—he wracked his brain for the right English word—"*cultured* as us. Don't treat women so good, know what I mean? That Chechen, too. No morals. He swam like a shark to have the chance to fuck you."

"You all did." She hugged herself, taking a step back from him. "So don't think you're a gentleman."

"We did." A slow nod. "But it was just to have a bit of sport with the boss. None of us could have beaten him." He swallowed, a prominent Adam's apple rising and falling. "Count yourself lucky those other guys are gonna be kept well away from you. Otherwise your boyfriend really would have something to worry about."

"You're avoiding my original question. I want my phone."

"Please, I have to go." Stefan spun on his heel.

"Wait..."

"What?"

"At least tell me what the time is, dammit."

"Close to 6 p.m. Someone will bring you food in a little while. And a beer." He shut the door behind him with a thunk.

"*Mudak!* Asshole!" she screamed at the door. There was the sound of a key turning in the lock, brief words exchanged, retreating footsteps. Hands on hips, she examined the room. Three by three meters, give or take. Not a lot of space, but it was warm and dry, and there were no creepy men ogling her. Exposed walls, the brickwork no doubt centuries old. No windows. No pictures or decorations of any kind. No television or other electronic equipment, not even a wall clock. No reading material. Utter silence. All alone with nothing but the rushing of blood in her own head for company. One positive: the room was heated; she could feel a gentle warmth radiating under her feet.

She ran her eyes along the walls. No switch for the light. In fact, no sockets anywhere that she could see. She pushed the end of the queen-size bed six inches away from the wall. No sockets there, either. Who would construct a room like this? The assholes were remotely controlling her environment, her sensory perception. No doubt there was a tiny spy camera somewhere in the brickwork.

A bed and a blue wooden chair, a perfect match for the one she'd been strapped to for what seemed like days, were the only pieces of furniture. At the far end of the room, a door led into a basic bathroom. Shower, steel basin, pump hand soap. A toilet with no seat like you'd find in a prison. No surprise—this was a prison.

First things first. *What's in the bag?*

She unzipped the valise and tipped its contents onto the bed. Two pairs of black cotton panties, one wireless bra, a plain white T-shirt, a gray flannel tracksuit. Flip-flops and a pair of sheepskin boots.

In the bathroom ensuite, there was a soft plastic zip-up container. Inside were a tiny travel-sized tube of toothpaste, toothbrush still in its packaging, headache pills, tampons, and a bar of soap. A quick inspection of the bathroom cupboards revealed nothing except three white, fluffy towels.

Where were the clothes she was wearing when they took her? The scarf was a gift from her mother. She could care less if she never saw the other stuff again.

She took off the underwear she'd been wearing, rinsed the panties in the basin, and dressed in the 'prison' garb. The ugly tracksuit felt like a warm hug.

*Dammit, Yakov! Why did you leave me alone?*

She lay on the bed, rolled onto her stomach, and bawled her eyes out.

# TEN

The heel of a fist pounded dully on the door, sending his heartrate into overdrive. An amiable female voice that he instantly recognized called out, "Hello, Mr. Barrett? Police."

Jacob, out of sight of the officer, stuffed the crumpled letter in the top drawer of the bedside table. His head was still spinning, coming to terms with the wild conversation he'd just had with the kidnappers. One he would keep from the law.

He turned to see the youthful face of Constable Sophie Bakker. She had the kind of mouth that formed a smile easily and on almost any occasion. An internal battle was raging; Jacob could see she was fighting to suppress her natural happy demeanor. She lost the battle; however, she did manage to make the slowly forming crescent-smile one of sympathy.

"Please, come in." Jacob raked his fingers through his hair, sprang off the bed, and moved toward Bakker at the threshold.

She glanced down at the sneaker as she took a step inside but said nothing about it. He held his breath, realizing he'd been speaking to the kidnappers with the door still wedged open with that damned shoe. *Stupid.* His body, arms outstretched with palms flat against the wall, blocked her from going farther inside than a couple of feet. "The inspector insisted we come and fetch you. She wants your statement ASAP, while your memory is still fresh." Over her shoulder, he saw a hulking male officer with the gloomiest expression he'd ever seen on a cop's face.

"I'm quite capable of making my own way there." He wanted more time to think about his next move.

She sucked air through her teeth. "Perhaps, but the inspector is rather insistent. Anyway, we've just finished attending another incident nearby, so...yeah...here we are." That reflexive smile again.

The instructions in the letter said not to do anything to arouse the suspicion of the police. Refusing to accompany Bakker and her large friend would do exactly that. "Give me a moment, will you?" The officers stepped back into the corridor, exchanging words he couldn't hear, while he grabbed one of Irina's blouses, a pair of socks and—she'd hate him for it later—unwashed underwear. These items are worn closest to the skin, and she'd worn them yesterday. Sniffer dogs would latch on to them if, heaven forbid, it ever came to that.

---

JACOB SAT IMPASSIVELY in Inspector de Kok's comfortable modern office. Steel, glass, and black leather dominated the furnishings and fittings. The Dutch police were represented by the inspector and another detective, Daan Vos. He presented as an old-school investigator with abominable taste in clothing, reflected in a mauve shirt and mustard-colored tie. Vos sported a mane of thick hair as white as the snowflakes falling outside.

Jacob was pleasantly surprised they weren't conducting the interview in an interrogation room. It's what they might have done had they suspected an inside job. It wouldn't be the first time the lover was the guilty party. The Dutch cops wouldn't be doing their job properly if they weren't at least entertaining that possibility. Then again, maybe the ambience of the cozy office was their way of luring him into a false sense of security. He beat them to the punch.

"Thanks for your time, Officers." He reached for the percolator and poured himself a cup of coffee. "I appreciate that you're anxious to get my statement. But before we begin, I'd like to say something, if that's OK."

"Sure," said de Kok.

Jacob cleared his throat. "In my line of work, I have a lot to do with the American justice system. So to clear the air, let me ask right off the bat. Do you suspect me of being involved in Mila's disappearance?"

De Kok set her cup down with a clatter. "Wow. He's different, isn't he, Daan?"

"Original," Vos agreed with a nod. "We of course keep an open mind, but no, you are not officially a suspect."

Jacob took note of the qualifier 'officially.'

"We know you went to great lengths to find her," said de Kok soothingly. "We've had a thorough look over the entire day's CCTV footage, including images of you scouring the building and the surrounding streets. No one appeared to be watching you, and we don't think you were putting on an act. Your body language said you were frantic with worry."

Vos tapped a pen against his palm and said, "We are pretty confident you have nothing to do with her disappearance based on that alone."

De Kok blinked twice, as if gathering her thoughts. "We have a clear picture in our minds how events unfolded. But as a formality, we would like you to write down, in your own words, everything that happened in the lead-up to Mila going missing and us arriving. Can you do that?"

"Of course. Now?"

A shake of the head. "No. When we're done. It's OK to summarize; bullet points will be sufficient. Don't take hours over it. We know you must be worn out with worry and keen to get some sleep."

"I appreciate that." Sleep was the last thing he wanted. His instincts were screaming to get back out there on the streets, pound the icy pavements and look for her until he crashed with exhaustion.

"This interview won't take long either," said de Kok. "There are a number of finer points we'd like to clarify, to get an idea of why someone might want to kidnap Mila."

Jacob shrugged. "If only I knew."

Vos crossed his legs, revealing mismatched socks. He cleared his throat and said, "Just to definitively rule a line under you, Mr. Barrett. And please, don't take this personally. Is there any way you could benefit from Ms. Dmitrieva disappearing?"

The question was a fair one for the cops to ask and not unexpected. "Like me being a beneficiary in a will or something like that?"

Vos answered wordlessly with tightly bunched lips and a tiny nod of confirmation.

"Then no. There is no financial gain for me whatsoever." Jacob was actually glad the man had asked the question. It reminded him of the need to get his own will updated, make sure Irina was taken care of. "We are a couple, but we don't live together, so we aren't even de facto in the eyes of the law."

"Hmmm." De Kok waved a cup in the air, as if the action were an aid to her thought processes. "Have you been to the Netherlands before?"

He had, many years ago, but not as Michael Barrett. He had crossed the border in a vehicle from Germany; there was no presentation of a passport so there would be no record of the visit. "No. It's my first time here." He paused, placed his head in his hands, then fixed his gaze on one cop, then the other. "I never imagined anything like this would happen on our vacation. Never."

"Have you been contacted by anyone claiming to have Mila? Any demands?"

Jacob shook his head, looked up and bellowed, "You don't

think that's the first thing I would have told you when I walked into this room!" His hands trembled slightly under the table. Was it wise to withhold the note and the recording of the phone conversation? If someone else was in his position and asked for advice on what to do, without hesitation he would recommend putting his faith in the professionals, the police. But even assuming the Dutch police was the greatest force in the entire world, his gut told him the best way to get her back safely was by running his own rescue mission.

He'd let the cops plug away with the clues they had. Maybe they'd trace her whereabouts, send in an elite force of ninjas, eliminate the threat, and rescue Irina. It wasn't beyond the realms of possibility. But by dealing directly with the kidnappers himself, he figured the chances of success improved by an order of magnitude.

He let his shoulders slump, looked up and offered an apologetic frown. "Sorry for that outburst." A heavy sigh. "No. No one has contacted me." He flashed them a sudden hopeful look. "Have they contacted you?"

"No," said de Kok firmly. "We have heard nothing either."

His eyes stared at the ceiling for a moment, then he looked squarely at de Kok. To direct their thoughts in another direction, he said, "I don't like that. If they have no demands...does that mean they snatched her to...work as a sex slave? I've heard about that kind of thing. I mean, she's a beautiful woman."

The ticking of the clock filled a short silence before Vos said, "I doubt it. The method was too elaborate. The bastards who run the sex trade can source their human cargo much more easily than that."

Jacob blinked hard, nodded, then took a sip of coffee. It was cold already and tasted bitter.

"So," said Vos, "you don't have any enemies in this country?"

He shook his head hard, perhaps overdoing it a little. "Of course not. Why would I? I already said I've never been here before."

Vos interlaced his fingers, flexing them before drumming his nails on the table. "Perhaps you offended someone online? It happens from time to time. We live in a global world these days."

Jacob guffawed, no exaggeration necessary. "Are you for real?"

"Who knows? The abduction of Ms. Dmitrieva was sophisticated. In our considered view, it was targeted. She wasn't some random victim."

"I've got nothing." Jacob shrugged. "You two geniuses are the detectives, not me."

Without hesitation, de Kok said, "Before you told us your work brought you into contact with the American justice system. Maybe you pissed someone off unknowingly. What exactly do you do for a living, Mr. Barrett?"

"I work for the government." Seeing their eyebrows raise in unison, like a pair of seagulls taking off, he added, "Nothing exciting. I'm an employee of the Municipal State Archive in New York. As boring as a PowerPoint presentation."

De Kok said, "What does that work entail?"

He took a sip of water from a paper cup, squeezing its sides as he formulated the rehearsed lines. "In my area, we work with records from various federal agencies, including the Department of Justice."

"Impressive," said Vos.

"Not as great as it sounds. Occasionally I might work with DOJ officials to enforce federal laws and represent the government in legal matters. Like I said, boring."

"Could your work potentially include cases involving foreign nationals, Dutch citizens?"

He gave a half smile. "I know where you're going with this. I hate to disappoint you, but I'm an anonymous backroom guy surrounded by dusty manila folders. I spend all day opening and closing those big rolling storage units, reading twenty-year-old documents." A pause. "So no, I doubt that I've made enemies through my work." He felt a vein pulse slightly in his neck. He'd made more enemies than he'd care to contemplate. And he was starting to connect the dots. Valentijn de Vries *must* be behind Irina's abduction. He was the only person in Europe who might hold a personal grudge against him. The fact that he knew Michael Barrett was David Reeve meant there could have been inside help. Someone in Skia. If so, that person needed to be rooted out—but not before Irina was safe.

The inspector leaned so far back in her chair, hands behind her neck, that Jacob thought she'd topple over. She quickly righted herself and said calmly, "Let's focus on Mila. She's a Russian citizen and—"

"Incorrect," Jacob interrupted. "She's a US citizen. Has been for three years."

"My mistake. I meant to say she's a—"

Jacob held up a finger to stop her. "Before you go for a walk down Hypothetical Lane about who or what she is or isn't, let me save you the time." Jacob invented a story on the spot but with some factual details to add plausibility: he had met Ludmila, now simply and officially Mila, on a vacation in Cyprus four years ago. Plausible because the island at the time—before the invasion of Ukraine—was crawling with Russians. They'd struck up a conversation in a bar. She explained she was being harassed for speaking out against the government online. She asked him for help. Over the next week, they fell in love. Mila was frightened, desperate not to go back to Russia. Jacob called in a favor from a friend who worked in a highly classified section of the government. The guy, who must remain nameless, pulled a few strings, and Mila was granted political asylum. Her identity was altered, and she now led a peaceful life as a bank employee.

Vos was shaking his head, one eye screwed up. "Sounds like bullshit to me."

"How dare you!" Jacob stood, gripped the side of the table. De Kok's eyes widened and Vos recoiled. Jacob snarled, his gaze flicking between the two detectives before settling on Vos. "Why would I lie? The love of my life is missing, and I want you to find her." He wrote down the name and phone number of her backstop fictional boss at the Metropolitan Trading Bank. In reality she did work at a bank, only not that one. "Call Russell Warren on this number. He will confirm she's been an employee there almost since the day she arrived on American soil."

"I, ah..." Vos stammered.

"Do it now. It's about lunchtime in New York. Please don't tell him she's been abducted. Not the press either. She's got family back in Russia who would be beside themselves if they heard she'd been...kidnapped." He ran a hand over his face. "Oh my God, I can't believe I'm even using the word." A long, deep breath. "Let me be the one losing my mind with worry, OK?"

De Kok nodded, then excused herself. Through the glass wall, Jacob saw her hand the piece of paper to a uniformed woman sitting at the edge of the large, open-plan office. There were perhaps thirty people working this shift, some wearing headphones, nearly all of them looking at computer screens. The women smiled at each other before de Kok returned.

"Amanda will call Mr. Warren as you suggested."

Within a minute, a call was patched through. A man's anxious voice boomed over the phone's speaker. "What's the meaning of this? What's happened to Mila? As far as I know, she's on vacation in Europe."

De Kok introduced herself in calm tones. "Nothing to be alarmed about. It's a...visa issue that needs clarification. I just need to confirm that Mila Dmitrieva is an employee of your bank."

"She is indeed. One of our best and brightest. Is there anything I can do to—"

"No thank you," said de Kok affably. "We'll take it from here."

Jacob crossed his arms. He also had a number of backstops ready should they feel inclined to check his employment bona fides with a phone call. "Satisfied?"

Vos said, "That she works for the bank, yes. That you want to stifle publicity about the fact that she's gone missing, no. I'm not satisfied about that."

De Kok's expression turned serious, almost disapproving. "Daan is right. It's clear from all the evidence that she hasn't wandered off on her own accord. Therefore, while our regular investigative procedures unfold, we must make an appeal to the public."

This was a nasty wrinkle. Communications with the media would mean photos of Irina being released on all kinds of platforms, the CCTV images, possibly photos of Jacob, too. They might even want him to make an appeal on television. Not ideal for a spy who needs to keep a low profile. But he had to agree that this was a good idea or their suspicions would go through the roof.

He drank some water. "You misunderstood me. I meant, what can people abroad do to help find her? Nothing. Besides, her mom and dad are old and fragile. Her son is...unstable, to say the least." He scratched a forearm. "A local appeal makes sense, I guess."

Vos shook his head slowly. "It's you who misunderstands, Mr. Barrett. The appeal must be as broad as we can make it. The Netherlands is small. She may have been taken to another country in Europe. We now have to coordinate with neighboring countries, Interpol."

De Kok breathed in deeply. "We have already sent a press release to all the relevant news agencies and TV networks. And as my colleague stated, we've informed other law enforcement agencies, supplied them with the CCTV footage. If after 48 hours, there has been no progress, I will sanction a press conference. You have the choice of whether or not to participate, but I would encourage you to do so."

Jacob heartily agreed, hoping against hope he'd have her back well before the time came to front the media.

Then Vos said something to make things even worse. "We've scheduled a series of posts to go out later tonight on a number of social media sites. We'll give you the links. You might like to share them."

He felt his Adam's apple rise and fall as he gulped. "I would, of course, but I don't use social media."

"Not at all?" De Kok's mouth formed a circle of disbelief.

"No. It's a waste of time." Facebook and other social media pages were created for Jacob on an ad hoc basis for specific missions, but none existed in his guise of Michael Barrett.

"What about Ms. Dmitrieva?"

"I think she has an Instagram account, but she rarely uses it." Jacob was fully aware the cops already knew the answers to the questions they were asking about social media. Checking the online presence of all involved in the case would be one of the first jobs to cross off their list.

"Never mind. Our posts will get thousands of likes and shares." She gave a smile of reassurance. "You'd be surprised how often this method gets results."

The news would now spread like wildfire. Irina's boss, her poor parents, and Vova would not escape finding out. Jacob was now in the position of having to inform them; if they found out indirectly, they would condemn him to hell for keeping quiet. Damned if he did, damned if he didn't.

A tap came on the door. De Kok called for the young officer to enter.

"I've got an update on the facial recognition analysis. Nothing on the guys in the hoodies, but a partial on the man who dropped the glasses. It's a ninety percent match on the eyes."

"Got a name?" said Vos impatiently.

"Veselin Petrović."

The blood rushed in Jacob's ears. He recalled the name from his memory banks. An organizer in the Dutch underworld, a mover and shaker from Belgrade, Serbia, who, according to rumor, had calmly dispatched dozens of men to meet their maker.

The detectives exchanged a glance. "A well-known criminal," said de Kok. "Involved in drugs, no connection with human trafficking that we are aware of. He's kept his nose clean for a while."

"I guess that's good news?" Jacob ventured.

"Yes and no," said Vos. "There's a very high error rate in identifying people on eyes alone using facial recognition tools. Unless it's a close-up retina scan, for example." He hesitated a moment. "However, it's a place to start from."

Jacob was escorted to a quiet room to write his statement. As his pen moved across the paper, he mentally rehearsed a couple of tough phone calls ahead: to Irina's family and to Fletcher.

# ELEVEN

If there were any lookouts posted on the street between the police station and the Mondrian Suites watching out for Jacob, they were expertly concealed. From the front passenger seat of the patrol car, he failed to identify any suspicious persons outdoors. A spotter could, of course, remain hidden inside one of the many buildings along the route and Jacob would be none the wiser.

Ruben Vanderghem, the burly and taciturn officer who'd picked him up an hour earlier with Constable Bakker, scored the task of returning Jacob to the hotel. He turned out to be a lot more talkative without his female partner at his shoulder. Over the five-minute drive, he unhesitatingly passed on a lot of information.

An initial forensics sweep of the Heineken brewery, empty of staff and visitors, had come up empty. Ruben told Jacob not to give up hope on that score. More work would be done throughout the night and tomorrow; evidence might still be found. The network of traffic cameras had picked up the license plates of more than twenty black VW Touaregs heading in various directions. A couple matched the time frame; officers had contacted the owners, who were able to provide solid alibis. Follow-up would continue on the remaining vehicles.

"Don't you worry, sir," said Ruben as he parked directly outside the hotel. "The key is the Serbian, Petrović. If the facial recognition is accurate."

"Do you know where he is?"

Ruben gave a sideways glance. "Me? No."

"I meant the detectives."

A slow shake of his large head. "I'm afraid they don't either, sir. He's been off the radar for some months. There was a rumor that he had gone to Russia after falling out with his old boss. He's got mafia friends there." He bared his yellowish teeth as he turned to Jacob. "But you have to bear in mind, sir, that the underworld is a rumor factory. Lots of fake ones made up to misdirect us poor police."

Jacob swore under his breath. Ruben had a point, but often rumors were gospel truth. Maybe the intel he'd heard in 2019, that a man called Petrović would be joining forces with de Vries full-time, was wrong. If the kidnappers had spirited Irina off to Russia, she was truly screwed. He pushed the thought out of his mind.

"Be assured, half the force will be out looking for him," said Ruben. "We will get your woman back."

"Do you remember the name of the old boss?"

He scratched his head for a moment. "No. But I can find out for you. Call me in ten minutes." He handed Jacob a business card.

"Will do." Jacob tucked the card into his pocket and said, "I'm only asking all these questions because Inspector de Kok said I could hire a PI if I wanted to. At first I thought it was too much of a long shot. Now I think it might be a good idea."

"You don't need to do that, sir. We are very capable." His chest expanded, seemingly with pride.

"I don't doubt that," said Jacob with sincerity; in his opinion, the Dutch police were among the best in Europe. "But I'm leaving no stone unturned to find her. You understand me?"

"Perfectly. You want me to escort you into the hotel?"

"Not necessary."

Jacob thanked the officer profusely and turned toward the door.

---

THE LIGHT inside the lobby was the kind some people describe as ambient. Bright enough to see where you're going, but forget about trying to read in its feeble glow. The amiable ginger-headed concierge was still on duty. Jacob approached quietly and coughed into his fist to announce his presence. The man jumped on the spot, then looked up from his paperwork with an affable grin. "Good evening. Mr. Barrett, isn't it?" The concierge's initial smile faltered at the sight of Jacob's intense glare.

"Listen," Jacob said in a businesslike tone that, while friendly, brooked no nonsense. "I wanted to speak with you earlier, but I couldn't. You would've noticed me leaving with a couple of police officers."

"I...ah...noticed that..." the man, whose name badge said Marten, stammered. "Actually, it was me who gave them your room number. Is everything OK? I assume you're not in trouble since you weren't in handcuffs." His laugh was awkward. Without drawing breath, he continued, "How's your lovely lady?" He voice took a wistful turn. "She has the most beautiful eyes."

The fact the man was clearly gay protected him from Jacob's wrath for the uninvited compliment. "First of all, no. Everything is not OK." He leaned in, drawing a reciprocal bending of the back from Marten, and lowered his tone. "I'm only telling you this because I'd rather you found out from me and not second-hand from the media. My partner has been abducted, and I'm hoping you might be able to help me out."

Muscles twitched on Marten's lean face, the color draining.

"Oh my God!" His hand shot to his mouth. "Abducted? From the hotel?"

Jacob shook his head impatiently. "No, from somewhere else. Are you going to help me or not?"

"OK. Although I'm not exactly sure how I can do that." His lips turned into a quivering frown; Jacob wondered whether the guy would burst into tears.

"I'll tell you how." Jacob swallowed hard. "Someone entered our room without permission. And I'm not talking about housekeeping."

"Was it the police? I only dealt with them the time they asked for your room number. If it was before my shift, I wouldn't know..."

"I highly doubt it was them." It was a fair question, although the cops wouldn't enter without first obtaining a warrant or at least Jacob's permission. Which got him thinking: they might ask to see inside the hotel room at some point, talk to staff members like Marten here. Maybe soon, although the lead on Petrović would be their focus now. He'd better be prepared for that exact contingency, in particular by not leaving the kidnappers' note in a drawer as he'd foolishly done this time. "It was someone else, and I want to know who."

"How do you know your room was entered, sir? Was something stolen?"

"No," Jacob growled. "On the contrary. Something was left behind."

"And you want me to...? I don't quite understand."

"Listen closely. Rule number one. Don't lie to me. If you do, I will know. I've been trained to spot liars." His hands balled into fists by his sides. It would be too easy to give this kid an ass-whooping, no challenge at all. There was real fear in his eyes; the threat was sufficient to get his total cooperation. Jacob took a deep breath. "Did you give someone a keycard to enter room 304?"

"No, sir." He didn't blink, holding Jacob's gaze.

"No one forced you or threatened you?"

"Not at all." Still no averting of the eyes. Marten wasn't lying.

Maybe there was another person on the desk at the time. "When did you start your shift?"

"Maybe half an hour before you returned this afternoon…" He angled his head curiously, as if comprehending something for the first time. "Without your partner."

"Who was on reception before you?"

He consulted a book. "Beatrix Snell did the morning shift from 6 to 12. She'll be at home now. Her next shift starts at midday on Friday."

"I haven't got two days to wait. Can you give me her phone number?"

Marten sucked his lips behind his teeth. "I'm not sure I should do that."

Jacob ran a hand over his face. The kid was a good and honest person, that was clear. And he wasn't as daunted by Jacob towering over him as he had been a moment ago. "No. Quite right."

"I can call her on your behalf if you like. Ask her what you want to know."

The revolving door began to spin slowly. Jacob held his tongue as another guest arrived, huddled into her coat. She pulled back the hood of her fur-lined jacket, stamped her feet, shook an umbrella, and brushed the snow from her clothes. He stepped aside as she approached the reception desk, offering that weak smile humans use when greeting strangers. Marten gave her advice on museum opening times; she thanked him and headed for the elevator.

With the woman gone, Jacob said, "I'm gonna need to see footage from all your security cameras."

Marten exhaled, scratching his chin. "I'm sorry. I'd need to get authorization for that."

"Show me the CCTV footage, now, dammit," Jacob ordered.

The kid might be a stand-up employee, but enough was enough. "Time's ticking. I have reason to believe...Mila...is in grave danger. The cops are doing their best, but they're restricted by protocol." He paused a beat. "I'm not. You understand me?"

"Oh, dear." Marten hesitated, then nodded. He placed a *Back in 5 minutes* sign on the desk and ushered Jacob into a cramped side office. A small security monitor that looked like an old Mac SE computer displayed a couple of feeds from the lobby and one from outside the entrance. The black-and-white images were fuzzy: Jacob would have expected a boutique hotel as expensive as the Mondrian Suites to have security of a much higher quality. He frowned. "You familiar with this equipment?"

"Yes," said Marten. "I use it regularly. We keep the footage for a week, then it gets wiped."

"Rewind to 8 a.m. for all feeds."

"Got it," said Marten. A couple of mouse clicks and all the recordings were wound back. "Here we go."

Moments later, the show started. Problem was, Jacob had no idea what he was looking for. He told himself all would be made obvious when he saw it. Whatever *it* was.

"Speed it up a bit, please," he said impatiently, leaning over Marten's shoulder. He could sense the tension in the young man's body, almost smell his adrenaline. Excitement had replaced his fear.

Eyeballing the video, Jacob was glad he had chosen a small hotel. Large crowds of people milling about in lobbies would have made this task all the more difficult. Most of the footage at the Mondrian was of people wandering by on the street outside and of a smiling Beatrix welcoming, registering and checking out a handful of guests. In between those jobs, most of the time she had her face glued to the computer screen, answered phone calls and had one toilet break.

Then he saw it. Not one of the Moroccans in a green hoodie, not the glass dropper Petrović, either. Instead, a man close to six feet tall with a wiry, athletic build. He wore a baseball cap and light-colored overalls. His right hand clutched a black tool bag. On the back of his uniform was a logo of a lightning bolt. "Stop it there."

Marten clicked the mouse. "Done."

Jacob thrust his finger at the screen. "Looks like someone trying to impersonate an electrician."

Marten swung around in the swivel chair. "No. That's the company we use."

"The uniform tells you that, does it?"

"Yes. The logo."

"Recognize the man?"

"No."

"Would the visit by any chance be logged somehow?"

A quick head shake. "Not if it's a minor job. Someone would have called them to attend a problem, but it's not always written down." He scratched his head. "Maybe it should be. Anyway, the firm will invoice us later for the work carried out, and that's it."

"Terrible accountability in this place," Jacob mumbled under his breath. "Start the video up again."

On screen, Beatrix and the 'electrician' exchanged a few words, she smiling, he with his back to one camera, his face showing on another, but the images weren't clear. She tilted her head back, laughed, reached under the desk, then handed him a white key.

"Stop the video."

The images froze.

"Call Beatrix now, I don't care what time it is." Jacob told Marten what he wanted the concierge to say.

Marten found her name in his cell phone contacts and placed the call on speaker as Jacob had instructed. A sleepy voice answered in Dutch. Marten apologized for the disturbance and said he wanted to clarify that the electrician had fixed the problem in the correct room. "Apparently there are still problems in Room 311. The guest is furious."

"I can't believe he got it wrong," said Beatrix. "Although he was a new guy I hadn't seen before, so that could be why."

"What room did you encode the card for?"

"304. Mr. Barrett's room."

"Who reported the problem in the room? Mr. Barrett or Ms. Dmitrieva?"

"Um. Neither, as I recall. The electrician told me the room number himself. 304."

"How the hell would he know that?"

A brief silence, then, "I...ah...don't know."

"You didn't think to check with the guests? Make sure they were happy for a tradesman to interrupt their vacation?"

Another pause, laced with indecision and worry. "No," she said, dragging out the word. "We use this company all the time, so I...didn't think to call up to the room."

Jacob gritted his teeth, fighting down the urge to scream at the stupid girl.

"I do recall the man said he was in a hurry. I guess he kind of flustered me." Her sigh of distress down the line was as tangible as if she'd been standing there with them. "It must have been someone else the guests reported the problem to. Who was on shift before me?"

"Kasper Blom, if I remember the roster correctly."

"Maybe he called the company and gave the room number...to save time?"

"I highly doubt it, but thanks, Beatrix. I'll make sure the problem's resolved."

"Am I gonna be in trouble?"

"I'll cover for you."

"Oh wow! Thanks, Marten. You're the best."

Marten hung up and began to explain what was said in the conversation. "No need," said Jacob curtly. "I understood the thrust of it.

"You did?"

"Yeah. Now call that Kasper fellow. I know for a fact I never reported an electrical problem and neither did Mila."

Marten looked up Kasper's number and placed the call. The man was at home watching the replay of a big soccer match from South America and wasn't happy to be disturbed. No, he knew nothing of any electrical fault in a guest room.

"If the electrician is a phony," said Marten, swiveling his head around to look at Jacob, "how did he know your room number? Did you tell anyone?"

"I've got a theory on that, but I'm keeping it to myself for now." When they arrived at the hotel in a taxi, he had a feeling someone was watching them from a distance, but he put it down to paranoia at the time. "Please zoom in on that motherfucker's face."

Jacob focused on the grainy screen as the face got bigger. The man's features were so blurry as to be unrecognizable, and the more Marten zoomed, the worse it got. You could barely make out his trim beard. The dim, ambient light was a disaster for capturing good images on the cameras. Still, there was something about the guy that aroused his curiosity. "Show me footage from another camera. I wanna see him from the street when he arrives and after he exits the building. Maybe it's clearer."

Marten complied, his tongue sticking out of the side of his mouth slightly as he concentrated. Jacob had the feeling he was totally enjoying the exercise. Outside, the same man climbed out of a van, a cell phone pressed to his right ear. The other ear caught Jacob's attention. This was it. "Zoom in on his head." Thankfully, the image on the street was much clearer.

"He should have worn a beanie," Jacob mused aloud.

"Because it's cold?" ventured Marten.

"No. Because it would have covered his cauliflower ear. The man's a wrestler or a boxer. Maybe a rugby player." The image of his face overall was also better from the street-facing camera.

"It sure is an ugly look." Marten frowned hard.

"That's enough. I've seen what I needed to see. Make me a

copy of everything we've covered." He plucked a USB off the desk. "Put it on here."

"That's my music collection," Marten pouted. He opened a drawer and found another flash drive. "Let's use this one."

"I don't care which one, just hurry up, dammit." He felt a weight crushing his chest from the inside out. Someone would know this man. If he couldn't go hunting for him himself, Fletcher could send someone to do the spade work. Maybe the geek Wessels would find something.

Marten clicked around with his mouse, executed a flourish of keystrokes, pulled out the USB drive, and dropped it into Jacob's waiting palm.

"Now erase the footage. I want it all gone."

"That's not scheduled until the end of the week."

Jacob let out a sarcastic laugh. "After seeing the slapdash attitude toward people accessing guest rooms without proper authority, you think I give a fuck about that?"

"I...guess not," Marten stammered.

"I'm not leaving until it's all wiped."

"Wouldn't you like the police to see this?"

"I might give them a copy from this drive." He tossed it in the air a couple inches and caught it. "See how I feel. If anyone asks, say you deleted it all accidentally. Got it? Better still, say Beatrix did it. Your management will be more inclined to believe that idiot fucked up."

A quick nod. "Got it."

Jacob stepped back into the lobby, his mind racing.

His phone buzzed in his pocket. A glance at the screen, heart racing. Not the kidnappers, but Vanderghem. A text message. *Sorry I couldn't get back to you sooner. Had to attend another matter. The name of Petrović's old boss is Willem Koornstra, nickname Big Pim. Currently serving time for manslaughter in the Nieuw Vosseveld prison.*

Another piece of the puzzle, but one that probably didn't fit. The key was Irina's location—not criminal history lessons. *Don't get disheartened*, Jacob mused. *One thing will lead to the next.* It had to.

It was late, and his body craved sleep. But there were a couple more jobs to do—call Irina's parents and her son. Then Fletcher. But not from the hotel. If Cauliflower Ear and his associates had managed to work out what hotel room he and Irina were staying in, they must not be underestimated.

# TWELVE

"Have you changed your mind about going to Beirut?" said Fletcher, the joyous optimism in his voice like a church bell ringing on a Sunday morning. "Because if you have—"

"Irina's been kidnapped." Jacob looked both ways as he stood at one of the discreet entrances to the Begijnhof, a historic courtyard a short walk from the police headquarters. The space afforded a 360-degree view, meaning no one could observe him undetected if they entered the small amphitheater. He'd encountered a mere three people on the way here, none of them arousing suspicion, none of them the fake electrician. He was on high alert now—he was positive no one had seen him enter the cloister. Thick snow cascaded from the sky, blanketing the central lawn.

"What!" Fletcher bellowed.

Jacob held the phone away from his ear.

"You heard me."

"Please don't be playing games with me, Jacob."

"That's not my kind of humor, Grant. The news is going to reach your ears eventually. I wanted to get the jump on the media. Mainstream and all the others." He had, unfortunately, been too late conveying the information to Irina's folks. Her mom and dad had seen a brief item on the afternoon news. When the image of Irina flashed briefly on the television, even though the name given was strange to them, they knew instantly that the victim was their daughter. Vova was with them at the time, which at least saved Jacob one extra uncomfortable phone call. They were inconsolable and blamed Jacob, cursing him in the foulest of Russian cuss words. His promise to get her back fell on deaf ears.

"The media? What the hell, Jacob!"

"I would have thought your primary concern would be Irina's well-being, not bad publicity." Jacob huddled in a narrow doorway as the wind gathered strength. He was being a tad disingenuous because the press getting hold of the story was in fact a monumental problem for Skia.

"They're both my concern," he growled. "Don't be so naïve. You'll be totally exposed when this is over. This is now an existential problem for Skia."

"That's not a given. I've been on a dozen missions, been photographed and analyzed from all angles. Doesn't stop me finding new ways to do my job."

"This is different, this is...Oh Jesus."

"What?"

"Just scrolling through X as we speak, I did a search for Mila Dmitrieva. Dutch cops have already put out a couple posts. Retweets galore. All the networks, too, with links to their goddamn YouTube channels."

"Don't stress, Grant. The news cycle moves like quicksand—what's gripping today sinks into oblivion tomorrow."

Fletcher ignored the comment, getting down to brass tacks. "This is a fucking nightmare, Jacob. How the hell did it happen?"

A quick explanation ensued. Jacob expressed no certainty about who was behind it, although he mentioned the names of likely suspects: de Vries and Petrović, a possible link to Koornstra, and the mysterious man with the cauliflower ear. He lowered his pitch when mentioning that he'd taken his eyes off Irina when answering Fletcher's insistent calls. "That's when they created the diversion and struck."

"You didn't have to leave the premises. You could have spoken to me without leaving her side."

Jacob's answer was a five-second guilt-laden silence. Then a half-hearted justification. "Do you think it's reasonable to watch her like a hawk 24/7? In one of the safest cities in the world?"

"Of course not," Fletcher relented. "Tell me more about these leads."

"I have a theory Valentijn de Vries is the mastermind behind it. After what happened in 2019." A black cat scampered across the snowy courtyard, standing out like a hockey puck on a rink. Hopefully not a bad omen. "The cops have a partial facial match from the CCTV from the Heineken brewery. A guy called Veselin Petrović."

"That tells me nothing."

Understandable. Compared to Jacob, Fletcher's memory was average at best. The operation had happened five years ago; the Serb had been a minor player on the fringes. So minor nothing could be pinned on him. "What if I tell you Petrović was rumored to be part of Valentijn de Vries' *penoze* organization? A cop told me the Serb might be in Russia now. My instincts tell me that rumor was probably started by de Vries to throw investigators off the scent. This is an act of revenge. Because I turned his friend into a cripple."

Short, sharp breaths came down the line. The penny had dropped. "Dammit, Jacob. Why didn't you finish that prick de Vries off when you had the chance?"

The boss made a good point. De Vries had been five feet away, dripping in sweat and hands in the air, Jacob pointing a gun at his forehead. One squeeze of the trigger and today's tragedy would have been averted. Hundreds of thousands of euros wouldn't have gone into the pockets of lawyers defending de Vries and his buddies. The butterfly effect that never happened. There was good reason, though. "Why? Because five members of the Belgian Directorate of Special Units were standing right next to me. The aim was to arrest him, not kill him in cold blood."

"You're too soft sometimes, Jacob. I can't believe someone hasn't killed you by now."

"Soft or not, I need help here."

"What can I do? Just say the word. I'll move heaven and earth to save that girl. She's almost as valuable to me as you are."

Jacob laughed softly. The irony was brutal—she'd be the first person he'd turn to if he needed to track down a target. "Send someone over here to do the running around on my behalf. The kidnappers will have eyes on me."

"Have they got eyes on you now?"

"Don't think so. It's hard for them to sit too close to the hotel without me seeing them. There could be bugs in the room, though. Cameras. Fuck knows."

"Won't they be suspicious if you're out on the streets at this hour?"

"It's a risk I'm willing to take. They can have their suspicions, but if they don't catch me breaking their rules, I think I'm good. And there was no rule that I had to stay cooped up in the hotel room."

"Just be careful."

"Tomorrow I'm expected to call them early, then meet with someone. I think that's when the freedom to come and go from the hotel will end." He rubbed his face to relieve cold-induced numbness. "If I were in their shoes, I'd demand a move to a secure location, away from the city, where they can keep a close eye on me."

"What's the end game? You've said nothing about a ransom."

A light went on in a building across the park, curtains parted, then closed again before the light went out. He took a deep breath. "There is no ransom. They want me to steal something."

"What?"

"I don't know. They're drip-feeding me information. I probably won't know what the target is until minutes before I'm supposed to swipe it."

"Clever."

"And expected. Whatever this thing is, the guy I spoke with said it's guarded."

"Since you're in Amsterdam, I'd bet a lot of money it's a piece of art."

"I'm thinking along the same lines." He blinked, snowflakes falling from his lashes. "Jesus. It's going to be a fool's errand. Either in a museum safer than Fort Knox or some private fortress. If I'm lucky, it'll be something in transit. A van I gotta hold up."

"Want me to get an expert to look into it, Jacob? Maybe there's something new and lucrative on the market they want to get their hands on."

"Wouldn't hurt." Jacob instinctively shrugged. "All knowledge is useful." He paused. "Are you gonna send someone over to help me or not?"

He heard Fletcher pop a can of soda and take a swig. "Before I do that, maybe there's someone closer to the action."

"Who?"

"One minute while I check."

"Can you be quick about it? I wanna get back to the hotel. I'll die of hypothermia if I stay out on the streets for too much longer."

"You happy with CIA, or one of ours?"

"I don't care, Fletcher. Someone we can trust."

"I think I've found just the man. A CIA operative. Marcello Ricci."

Jacob's heart skipped a beat. "Perfect. He's the guy who foiled a plot to assassinate the Pope."

"Your memory for details never fails to astound me. Ricci's regarded as one of the best."

Jacob remembered the case from five years ago. Ricci had a super high IQ and was tough as nails. An ex-Marine with a degree in, of all things, theology. Spoke fluent Italian and French, as well as basic Arabic and Hebrew since his studies encompassed the Quran and the Torah. A pious believer, he was shot in the upper arm and stomach by the pontiff's would-be assassin, barely surviving. With blood gushing from his gut, Ricci chased down the maniac, who 'mysteriously' fell to his death from a high balcony. "Is he free right now?"

"Let me make a couple phone calls. Get yourself indoors. I'll email you when I've found out. In the meantime, I'll see if there are any other likely candidates in Europe right now."

"Let's keep the comms to emails from now on. Unless I call you. And whatever you do, don't call me."

"Agreed. What else can I do for you?"

"Nothing. Just get Ricci here, pronto. I'll handle what I can from this end. If I need anything, I'll be in touch."

"One more thing," said Fletcher. "You don't think there's a Russian connection to this, do you?"

The thought had certainly occurred to Jacob. That somehow, Irina's identity had been compromised and the word filtered back to Moscow. There were people there she had angered, people who would want to get their hands on her, prepared to pay whatever it took. "I damn well hope not." The chance that scenario was reality was too much to contemplate.

He pulled up his collar, exited the courtyard, and headed back to the hotel. He stopped in an alcove. From his memory he plucked the local cell phone number of Bram Wessels, punched in the digits and waited. A raspy voice answered. The guy smoked a pack and a half a day. "*Hallo, met Bram.* Hi, Bram speaking."

"Bram. It's a voice from the past. Remember David Reeve?"

"Holy shit, man. I saw the news. But now you're who? Michael Barrett?"

"That's right."

"I guess this isn't a social call, right?"

"Right again. Remember that favor you owe me?"

"Sure." Jacob had made sure Wessels got an extra bonus for his stellar cyber sleuthing work that helped track down de Vries in

2019. The failure to secure a conviction wasn't Wessels' fault, and he had deserved every penny he got.

"I'm calling it in."

Over the next ten minutes, Jacob spoke uninterrupted. The entire time, Wessels' jagged breathing came down the line.

"You're in a fuckin' bind, man," Wessels said when Jacob declared that all the salient facts were now on the table. "If it's that de Vries *klootzak* again, I'm on board."

"You owe me, so you're on board whether you want to be or not. Listen good in case something happens to me. I need you to get an ID on the guy in the hotel security camera footage I got my hands on. Analyze a voice recording I made of someone from the kidnapper's side. See if it's Petrović. Look into Willem Koornstra."

"That last one I know. Koornstra's in prison."

"I know that, too," said Jacob testily. "Crime bosses have been known to run shit from inside, you know."

"True."

"One other thing. See if there's any chatter about a piece of art someone like de Vries might like to get his grubby paws on."

"I can try. No promises. Want to meet somewhere discreet?"

"Can you get into the center now?" Wessels lived the quiet life in the town of Volendam, roughly 13 miles from Amsterdam.

"No chance. I'm not even in Holland right now."

*Perfect.* Jacob's jaw tightened. "Where are you?"

"Catching up with a cousin in Cologne, in Germany."

"I know where Cologne is," Jacob drawled.

"Hey, no need to be sarcastic. You Americans always have to clarify obvious shit in the movies. It's like, Paris, France, or London, England. As if any reasonable person would think it's some other Paris or London!"

"Yes, I know. Rather patronizing to the public, but I don't make those decisions, do I?"

"I guess not. Anyway, I've got no access to a car to drive home now. Besides, the weather here isn't great. I know it's freaking cold in the Netherlands, but it's even worse in *Deutschland* right now. The government's warning people to stay off the roads. But...hang on...just looking something up on the Internet. I can take a high-speed train tomorrow."

"If the roads are that bad, how are you going to get to the train station?"

"I said the government was warning, not ordering. Don't sweat it."

"When does the train pull in?"

"It arrives at Amsterdam Centraal Station at 9:32 a.m. That's the earliest possible."

Jacob sighed with frustration. "That will have to do. I'll reimburse you the price of the ticket."

"I should damn well hope so. Ninety euros ain't cheap for a guy who lives hand to mouth."

Wessels earned plenty of money as a work-from-home accountant. But he had a terrible gambling problem that kept him from getting out of the lower-middle class trap. Liquid cash was the greatest incentive you could dangle in front of the guy. "If you help me get Mila back, you will be well rewarded." Jacob gave him the name of the hotel and his room number. "Do not call me. I'll come to the lobby at 10 a.m. You follow me outside at a discreet distance. If I'm confident we haven't been followed, I'll hand you the material in a sheltered doorway at 14 Zieseniskade. Got it?"

"A hundred percent. See you in the morning."

# THIRTEEN

AT 6:45 ON A THURSDAY MORNING IN MIDWINTER, IT was still a good two hours before sunrise. Dirk, the old boat captain, had been annoyingly accurate with his grim weather forecast. Out the window lay an Arctic landscape. In the semi-gloom, illuminated partly by streetlights, as well as the glow coming from a couple of cafés preparing to open for breakfast, Jacob could see flecks of hoarfrost on blue tarpaulins covering houseboats and on the nearby bridge's metal railing. The water in the canal was turning to ice; small plate-sized chunks floated on the surface. In a day or two, if the temperatures continued to drop, the waterways would be frozen solid. Ice skaters would flock to the canals. Two positives this morning—the wind had died down and no extra snow had fallen overnight. People should be able to get around, albeit with increased risks of falls and bicycle and automobile crashes. The hotel room's thermostat was blindly oblivious to the cold outside, maintaining a toasty warmth. Despite that, a shiver ran down Jacob's spine.

In another fifteen minutes he had to make the second phone call to the kidnappers. His mind wasn't as sharp as he'd have liked. Sleep had come fitfully; whatever shut-eye he'd managed was punctuated by horrific dreams. Nightmare scenes of Irina being abused by snarling men with cauliflower ears. He'd awoken in a drenching sweat three times, guzzled water, and forced himself to try and go back to sleep. Easier said than done. Rest, even of an inadequate quality, would make it easier to cope with the demands of what lay ahead. Whatever the hell that might be. Without it, he'd be relying on muscle memory and adrenaline.

In boxer shorts and T-shirt, he cinched the blinds closed and turned away from the window. Stifling a yawn, he flicked on the coffee machine and made himself a strong double espresso. He sat on a hard dining chair created by a Scandinavian master with more focus on design than comfort. Sipping his coffee, he prayed that Ricci was on his way and IT alchemist Wessels would be able to turn the CCTV footage and voice recording into evidential gold. His own Internet searches for potential theft-worthy artwork came up with too many results to be of any use. A local like Wessels, with a feel for the place, would perhaps have better luck.

Coffee drunk, he gathered together Irina's small supply of bathroom items, clothes she'd hung on hangers or placed in drawers, and put everything back in her suitcase. Touching the objects, *her* objects, made his heart ache with worry. A worry blended with anger and a thirst for revenge. Channeling the power of those forces to rescue her was now his sole focus. It was a tightrope: the energy of those raw emotions mustn't disrupt rational thought, the ability to make the right choice while seeing through the red mist.

The alarm in his watch bleeped: 7 a.m. He dialed the numbers on the hotel desk phone, for no real reason with extra force. The call was answered in seconds.

"You ready to do our bidding, Barrett?" said the same accented voice. Jacob would bet anything it was the infamous Veselin Petrović.

"Yes," he hissed. "Let's just get this over with, shall we?"

"I understand your anger." The scraping sound of a cheap, plastic cigarette lighter, the inhalation of smoke. "I would feel exactly the same if I were in your position. It's only natural." He paused for a second. "Hell, in my culture, you touch my woman, I turn into a homicidal monster. But you're going to have to curb your instincts. Forget about being the hero. You might get lucky, break through our defenses. Maybe hurt or kill one or more of us, but that will only sign poor Mila's death sentence. You understand?"

"I understand." Jacob paced a few feet to the right, then back again. His heart raced like he'd run a mile.

"Get dressed to meet your new associates." The last word set his teeth on edge. "Warmly, I suggest." A soft laugh. "Have you seen the weather out there? Crazy, huh?"

Jacob wouldn't be sucked in by the sudden pally tone. "I've got a coat and a pair of gloves."

The Serb erupted in laughter. "You are a very funny guy." The man instantly flipped the switch on his delivery, became deadly serious. "Vondelkerk, you know it?" he snapped.

"No." The name of the place was unfamiliar. The 'kerk' part told him it must be a church; logic suggested it was in or near Vondel Park. It was the most famous park in the Netherlands, named after a 16th century writer, van den Vondel, whom many called the Dutch Shakespeare. Trivia like that would have bored Irina to tears, but it was the kind of stuff that clogged the megabyte highways in Jacob's brain.

"It's very close to your hotel." The Serb confirmed Jacob's guesswork and gave him precise directions on how to get there. "Do not speak to anyone once you exit the hotel. Got that?"

"Yes."

"Two colleagues of mine will pick you up. Wait by the front door of the church. They will approach you. Do exactly as they say."

"When is all of this supposed to happen?"

"You will check out of the hotel in the next half hour and make your way to the meeting point. Do not take a cab, Uber, or any form of public transportation. You are to walk. And walk carefully. I wouldn't want you to stumble on black ice and hurt yourself. If you do, and you are not there by 8:30 a.m., Mila will be executed."

"You can't do—" Jacob's breath hitched.

"Shut up!" A slow, steady inhalation of smoke. "Don't make this more difficult than it has to be. For the next two days, you will be staying at an undisclosed secure location. You will steal the item for us, and then you will be released together with your woman. Any more questions?"

"When I check out, what do I do with my suitcase? Mila's suitcase?"

"Leave them at the hotel."

"Come on! They'll only allow me to leave luggage there for a couple of hours at the most."

"No problem. We will send someone to fetch them on your behalf later. Leave the name Abel Smits at the desk. Tell the concierge that's who will pick up your stuff. If the staff get nosy, say you've been advised by the authorities that you have to move ASAP. Security concerns. You'll think of the perfect answer, I'm sure."

Jacob looked about the room, scanning, for the umpteenth time, for signs of a hidden camera. Failing to locate any, he nevertheless extended his middle finger and spun around on the spot. "What about my clothes? I'll need fresh underwear, shirts. Can I bring a sports bag with some basics?"

"No, you cannot. Just come as you are, in the clothes on your back. You may bring your cell phone, and that's all. Trying to smuggle anything else is pointless since we're going to strip search you. Rubber gloves and all. Hope you don't mind." He chuckled, perhaps relishing the upcoming indignity. "Don't worry about underwear and the like. We will provide clothing for you to wear until you are reunited with your belongings. And everything else you'll need to get the job done."

Jacob rubbed his forehead, hot and damp. These assholes were making things very difficult for him. Fletcher was yet to confirm that Ricci was available—indeed if anyone was available. Bram Wessels would be on the train already, mentally preparing for the drop. Jacob had to find another way of getting the material to him. *Damn it.*

A lot of work would now have to go on behind the scenes with Jacob completely in the dark. There was a good chance no one would be coming to help, and it would be all down to him. Totally under-resourced, relying on his wits alone. He'd done it before, but shit...this was gonna be a tough assignment.

"That's it, Barrett. Have a hot shower, get dressed, and get moving. The clock's ticking."

---

HE TOWELED off after a one-minute lava-hot shower, stepped into the oldest pair of underwear he had and put on his least favorite shirt. Jeans, sweater. Teeth brushed in record time, no shaving. Things were moving too fast, and time was not his friend.

Fletcher was taking too long to get back to him. Wessels wasn't briefed. Ricci not confirmed. No resources in place. Again, the nagging thought that he'd have to handle this gig unaided. The odds looked terrible.

The satellite phone would have to be packed away in the suitcase; he'd take the backup Samsung, pretend it was his regular phone. He had another idea—if Marten was on reception, he'd leave the satphone with him and come for it later. He'd built a rapport with the kid.

He fired off an encrypted text message to Fletcher. Yes, he'd said emails only, but emergencies overrule rules. *What's happening?! Is Ricci available? I have to move within minutes, then I'll be incommunicado.*

A quick mental calculation. New York was six hours behind. 01:00 hours. Fletcher would be sound asleep, dammit.

7:30 a.m. Time to leave the room. He grabbed both suitcases, wheeled them into the corridor. A woman waved good morning. "Shall I hold the lift for you?" A sweet, educated English accent with rounded vowels.

"You go," he said with a smile. He nodded at the door he'd just come through. "Just waiting for the better half. Last minute search for a pair of earrings."

She gave an understanding laugh. "Women, huh?"

"You bet."

When the elevator swallowed the woman, Jacob dragged the bags to the stairwell exit, wrangling them onto the internal landing. He gave silent thanks that both of them traveled light. Heart pounding, he made one last Hail Mary call to Fletcher before it was time to ditch the SIM card. A call from the confines of the stairwell would surely be safe from prying ears.

"Jacob? The notification alarm woke me. I just saw your text. I was about to—"

"Never mind. I'm meeting the kidnappers in an hour. They're taking me to a secure location. Any news on Ricci?"

"Yes and no. He's available, but his superior at Langley has to OK a locum job like this. There's no reason to believe he'll stymie the request."

"Right." Jacob clicked his teeth. "I'm going to assume the worst and hope for the best."

"There could be others in Europe who—"

"No time, Grant. Here's the deal." He dictated Bram Wessel's phone number, address, and email.

"Got it."

"When Ricci, or whoever you can get, is on board, hook them up with Wessels. They're going to have to coordinate on this. I can only do so much on my own. I've got a feeling the team I'm up against is big and powerful."

"Where are they taking you?"

"I wish I knew." He stopped for a second as a pair of voices rang out behind the door, then grew fainter. "The only solid lead I have is the name Veselin Petrović, the guy whose eyes were ID'd at ninety percent. I'm going out on a limb and saying it *was* him at the Heineken brewery. My gut says he's on de Vries' payroll."

"Have the Dutch cops leaned on de Vries yet?"

"I don't know." Even in the cold and drafty stairwell, a bead of sweat ran down his rib cage, tickling his skin. "But these guys are heavy on the protocol. They may have paid him a visit, but they won't act without probable cause or whatever the hell equivalent term they use here. De Vries could have her in his basement, but without proof, the police won't bust the door down. Get Ricci and Wessels to find that damned proof!"

"I'll pass all of that on." A brief pause. "Anything else?"

"I managed to get a USB drive with footage of the prick that left the letter in our hotel room. I wanted to hand it over to Wessels last night, but now I won't be able to meet him."

"What are you going to do with it?"

He looked to his left. There was a windowsill, upon which sat a number of dust-covered items that looked like they had been there for several months. Odds were, they would remain untouched for at least the next 48 hours. "Fourth floor stairwell. If Wessels can't get here for any reason, the flash drive will be inside a plastic potato chips bag tucked behind an empty can of Coke."

"Roger that."

"The guy on the video had a decent cauliflower ear. Could point to a boxer, wrestler, cage fighter, something like that." He sucked in a deep breath. "Look, I have to move. If I'm not at the rendezvous point in the next"—he glanced at his watch—"45 minutes, they've threatened to kill her." He rattled off the coordinates in case the kidnappers left evidence there that Ricci and Wessels could make use of.

"What are you waiting for, then? Move!"

Before 'moving,' he fired off a text to Wessels. *Can't make the drop.* He explained where the USB was secreted, then told him to check his email, where he would find the sound file of the conversation with the kidnappers. He added that Ricci would soon contact him. He pressed send, waited a moment, and powered down the phone.

Jacob sat on the edge of the top step, prized open the satphone's slot, and removed the SIM. He snapped the card in half, scratching the gold contacts with the zipper of his jeans. Back out onto the corridor and down the elevator. Around the corner from the elevator shaft on the ground floor was a small bathroom. He wheeled the luggage in behind him, checking that there was no one else inside. He entered the first stall and flushed the two halves of the satphone SIM down the toilet, wishing them bon voyage. He popped a replacement SIM, preloaded with random calls, texts, and contacts, in the Samsung and fired it up. The kidnappers could waste a couple hours playing with this one.

A man walked in and gave Jacob a friendly smile as they brushed shoulders. In a Midwest accent, he said, "Take care, buddy. The weather's hell out there today."

*No shit,* Jacob thought to himself. As he palmed open the door, he replied, "Nothing I can't handle."

# FOURTEEN

"Could you repeat that please, Mr. Barrett?" said the concierge. Not Marten on duty this morning. The badge said Kasper Blom. He looked up meekly from his keyboard. "I'm so sorry about the mix-up with your room." He tut-tutted. "I shouldn't speak out of turn, but that Beatrix..."

Jacob leaned in. "Abel Smits is the man's name."

"Of course, sir." No nosy questions about why he was checking out two days early, why he was leaving the luggage, nor about his absent partner. Perhaps he hadn't heard the news. Young people spent more time on TikTok than they did keeping up with current affairs. He tapped the details into the computer. Whoever was on reception when Smits fronted would be clued in on the arrangement and hand over the bags without raising a fuss.

Kasper looked up again, a lopsided grin brightening his freckled face. "Have you enjoyed your stay?"

"No complaints," said Jacob vaguely.

"Anything else today, sir?"

"Yes, as a matter of fact." He now regretted not leaving the satphone together with the USB drive on the window ledge for Wessels. "I need to leave another item, but I don't want Mr. Smits to pick it up." He unzipped a side pocket of his suitcase and handed the compact satellite phone over to Kasper. "This item is worth a lot of money."

"Really, sir?" Kasper inspected the phone from all angles. "Isn't it just a mobile phone?"

A confiding nod. "It's a prototype. Could revolutionize the market."

"Wow."

"I'm trying to get a patent for it. I'd rather return later and pick it up myself. Put it in your safe, and I'll get it in a week or so."

Kasper raised his eyebrows. "I'll need to clear it with the manager. Only he's not in until 9 a.m. If you don't mind waiting in one of those comfortable armchairs over there." He pointed to a far corner of the lobby. "I can bring you a coffee while you wait, maybe you'd like to read an English-language newspaper? *The New York Times*?"

"No need to wait for the manager, surely? I'm in rather a hurry."

Kasper shrugged.

"Listen. How about you look after it for me?"

"I thought you said it was worth a lot of money?" Kasper was starting to smell a rat.

"Never mind what I said." Jacob flashed his best affable smile. "You look like someone I can trust. Can I trust you?"

"What about that Abel Smits guy, the one who's coming for your luggage?"

"I don't know him personally. He's just an employee of a security company. What's in the suitcases isn't as valuable as this phone."

"I see."

A quick check of the watch. He really had to get moving. "You gonna help me or not?"

Kasper gave a firm nod. "After the mix-up with Beatrix, let me do you this favor."

"One more thing." Jacob knew the cops would be back after he disappeared. Maybe soon. "Want to make a bonus 200 euros?"

"I beg your pardon?"

"A hundred now, another hundred when I come back for the phone."

Jacob's request was met with wide eyes, but the extra cash proved too tempting. The morning's CCTV footage would be wiped.

Jacob set his jaw as he took back his Michael Barrett credit card, tucked it in his wallet and headed for the exit. He could have sacrificed the satphone to the kidnappers. He'd erased every text and wiped the call log of all records. This was simply a matter of principle. They'd stolen Irina, damned if those bastards would score a bonus satellite phone on the American taxpayers' dime.

---

JACOB REMEMBERED Vondel Park in summer as a mecca for walkers, joggers, and exercise enthusiasts in general. Fields of flowering bulbs. This morning, with the mercury hitting -4°F, he was the only fool taking the air on the walking tracks.

Two men awaited him at the entrance to the church. Zipped up in parkas, their black beards and olive skin contrasted with the backdrop of bright white snow. The sun shone weakly through a gap in the clouds, a pallid light in a tiny patch of china-blue sky. Jacob squinted: These were the two men from the bridge. Highly likely they were the same men in hoodies captured on the Heineken brewery's cameras. The urge to lash out was strong; Jacob overcame it by conjuring an image of Irina in his mind. Safe. With him.

"You guys looking for a light again?" Jacob laid on the sarcasm.

"Don't be a smartass," said the smaller of the two.

"Hand over your cell phone," demanded the taller one.

Jacob offered a token sign of indignation. "You must be kidding," he said with a deep frown. "How am I supposed to..."

The other man reached into a deep pocket and extracted an

old Nokia 3210. "No code, you just turn it on. You will be using this phone from now until we let you go. It will only allow you to call pre-installed numbers." He passed the device to Jacob, who scowled and tucked it away.

"So you *are* going to let me go, are you?" Jacob wriggled his toes inside his boots. The temperature seemed to be dropping as the morning wore on. "Very reassuring."

Tall stepped forward, his rubber-soled shoes squeaking on the compacted snow. He held out his hand. "Please, Mr. Barrett. Your mobile phone. Do not make this more difficult than it has to be."

Jacob reached into the pocket of his overcoat and delivered the decoy Samsung to the Moroccan. He couldn't be sure of the nationality of these punk-henchmen; however, Moroccans comprised the bulk of the Arabic demographic in the Netherlands, and that's how he would label them. It was in his savant-like nature to grade, classify, and categorize things.

"Thank you. We will, of course, examine this later." He turned to his companion and said in breathy Arabic, "Let's get this show on the road. I'm dying of hypothermia out here."

Jacob kept his face impassive. With luck, they knew nothing of his linguistic abilities. Did de Vries know? Possible—he seemed to know a shit-load of things already. Things that were supposed to remain confidential. He decided to throw them off the scent. "Hey, is that Turkish you guys are speaking?"

The small one laughed. "Wrong."

"Albanian?"

"Wrong again."

"I know," said Jacob with faux excitement. "It's Arabic, isn't it? You guys are part of that Mocro mafia I've been hearing about, right? You two Moroccans?"

Tall grabbed Jacob by the lapels of his coat, pulling him close. The garlic on his breath was like a dose of smelling salts. Jacob quashed an impulse to throw a head butt at the guy's nose. "Shut the hell up, American. You talk too much. From now on, you say nothing unless either one of us asks you a question. Understood?"

Jacob nodded briskly, giving himself a mental fist-pump at the same time. Goading the Moroccan like that, getting him to lose his cool so easily, was a positive sign. He was the type of person who would stop thinking rationally in a crisis. *Do dumb shit, leave an opening for me to strike.*

Small chuckled softly, then spat a glob of phlegm onto the sidewalk. "Walk slowly to that white van over there." No clarification needed: the VW Transporter—ironically the same model as the one Inspector de Kok and her crew rode around in—was the only van parked in the narrow street, in addition to a couple of other compact sedans and a handful of padlocked bicycles. The van's only glass was in the front windshield, driver and front passenger windows; metal panels filled the other slots. Nice and private. Every step forward felt like there was lead in his boots. Jacob despised being in this position of weakness. He clenched his jaw. Fletcher would come through with the needed support. He had to.

"Open the sliding door and get into the cargo section," said Small in a monotone.

Jacob did as instructed, both men following in behind him. The door slid shut with a thunk. Inside, benches lined both sides. Upholstered with soft leather, lap-and-shoulder seat belts installed. Marine-grade carpet. A small diamond-pressed metal box sat on the floor. Jacob's imagination conjured an array of torture and restraint tools inside it. This was a purpose-built hostage-taking machine, not the commercial van it appeared to be from the outside.

No messing about with niceties, Small commanded him to undress. As each layer peeled off quickly, the cold in the depths of his body increased. Soon Jacob was buck naked. Not caring about having his shrinking genitals on view, he instinctively folded his arms across his chest in a vain attempt to keep warm. He shivered like an aspen leaf in the fall as Tall swooped on the clothes, rifled through all the pockets, and turned them inside out. He palpated every item of clothing, woolen hat and gloves included. Checked his belt for a secret compartment. Boots were shaken, socks inverted. Jacob's eyebrows rose as the man removed the bills from his wallet, placing them in his own pocket. Tall, satisfied he had found nothing, eyeballed Jacob. "Speak the truth now. Are there any tracking devices disguised in credit cards or in the lining of the wallet?"

"No." Jacob held the man's gaze.

"Phone?"

"No."

"Wristwatch?"

"No."

"If you are lying, the woman dies instantly. Then you. Again, no tracking devices?"

"Absolutely not."

Tall nodded at his friend.

"Now," growled Small, "time for your physical." He gripped Jacob's jaw. "Open up, raise your tongue." Jacob complied, eager to get the ordeal over and done with. Forceful fingers probed inside his mouth, and his saliva dried up. Next, the man palmed Jacob's scrotum, lifted and peered behind it, muttered something incomprehensible. Looking down, Jacob pictured himself pile-driving his elbow into the top of the man's skull.

The Moroccan's breathing quickened as he donned a blue rubber glove. He spun Jacob around by the shoulders and shoved him in the middle of the back. "Bend over!" A lubricated index finger slid smoothly inside and moved around uncomfortably. Jacob grimaced throughout the humiliation, vowing to himself that this sadistic bastard would experience exceptional levels of pain come the hour of retribution.

"I found nothing in his clothing," said Tall in Arabic.

"Even his ass is clean," chimed in Small, again in Arabic. "He must have had an enema this morning. How thoughtful."

Both men laughed heartily, high-fiving each other.

"Quickly," snapped Tall. "Get dressed so we can start the engine and turn the fucking heaters on." He glared at Jacob, as if it was entirely his fault they were freezing. The man then simulated a broad, open smile, revealing a gold tooth toward the back of his mouth. "We want your journey to be as comfortable as possible."

Jacob stepped into his underwear, then sat on a bench to don socks. The rest of his clothes were back on with the speed of a one-man stage performer.

Once Jacob was fully dressed and buckled into his seatbelt, Small placed a black hood over his head. Jacob offered no complaint, no resistance. "My friend will be driving slower than usual because of the weather, so you will have time to think about what will happen if you try anything stupid." As if the rectal exam wasn't enough to seal his fate, the fool double-tapped Jacob hard in the temple.

He did not flinch. He would obediently do their bidding verbatim, watching and waiting for an opening.

"Will you be a good boy?"

"Yes," he replied in a strong and clear voice.

"Say it!"

"I will be a good boy."

"Correct answer."

The Moroccans took their seats in the front. The engine turned over, the sound a soft thrum in the library-like silence of the morning. He heard the street slush sputter as the tire spun slowly before it bit into the road. The sensory recorder in his head snapped into action. Subconsciously he began to count the seconds until he felt left and right turns; once out onto arterial roads, seconds became minutes. Every external sound that didn't fit in with normal traffic noise was noted. The entire hour and a half of the journey elapsed to the accompaniment of up-tempo Arabic music and the wafting scent of the occasional cigarette. Both Moroccans indulged in the habit, with the windows lowered the tiniest fraction to allow some of the smoke to escape. The fans blew at full blast to make up for cold air leaking in.

Jacob maintained the memorizing until they reached their final destination as a mental exercise to defeat the boredom.

He needn't have bothered.

There was no physical barrier between the front seats and the rear cargo section. He could hear every Arabic word spoken, even those uttered by another man in Dutch in a quick hands-free call five minutes into the trip. It sounded like de Vries, but he couldn't be totally sure. The Moroccans, who in a display of ignorant arrogance, revealed their names to be Youseff and Khadir, provided Jacob with other tidbits of information—enough to launch a full-scale rescue if he could share the location with the police.

He would not try and contact the police.

He would not try and contact anyone.

Not yet.

# FIFTEEN

In the dim cabin of the chartered 14-seat Bombardier Global Express XRS with only himself, the pilot, and co-pilot on board, Marcello Ricci focused on the hastily assembled instructions from Langley. The black text stood out on the glowing background of his iPad. A description of the abduction, last known whereabouts, details for his first contact—Bram Wessels, names of various Amsterdam Station operatives. Swipe left. Provide assistance to Wessels recovering intel. Utilize him every which way to achieve the goal. The task was monumental—a 48-hour deadline, which had by now eroded to about 32 hours. The chance of failure, two dead hostages, and collateral damage galore was high.

Uprooted by a late-night phone call from his winter getaway in Calabria, ordered to rescue the girlfriend of a careless NSA operative—and the operative himself—also ironically on vacation, Ricci was mightily pissed. He'd spent two amazing nights making love to Carmela, a busty brunette he'd met in a noisy Reggio bar. She was a dynamo between the sheets but also a smart woman, discerning in food and wine and capable of intelligent conversation. Now this upheaval had destroyed his hopes of extending the holiday romance. If he could perform a miracle and get the job done in a hurry, he might have one more taste of the delicious Carmela before she had to return home to her unsuspecting husband and doting kids. He smiled wistfully. The married ones were always the most enthusiastic.

Ricci absently touched the crucifix around his neck, a gift from his late mother and shiny after twenty years of regular rubbing. Casting his eyes around the luxurious interior of the airplane, he noted that money had been no object for this blitz mission. Bombardiers aren't cheap to hire, especially at midget-sized short notice. A suspicion nagged. For Uncle Sam to drop so much coin on a clandestine rescue mission, this operative must be more than a run-of-the-mill NSA employee. It wasn't Ricci's place to question budgets, of course. His only job was to find the hostages, get them out unharmed, and go back to his vacation apartment overlooking the Tyrrhenian Sea. On a clear day you could see across the sparkling water all the way to Sicily, sometimes Mount Etna. He pinched the bridge of his nose, a migraine looming, and cursed his bad luck.

He dismissed the throbbing in his temples, re-addressing his thoughts to the mission. If he couldn't secure the rescue himself —and there was a good chance he couldn't—his plan was to create a diversion, possibly with Wessels' help, and let the operative do his thing. The brief said the guy, Michael Barrett, was a polyglot elite, handy with his fists and weapons, who had completed a number of dangerous assignments over the years. Apparently a hybrid HUMINT and SIGINT wunderkind, assisting with JSOC special mission units. Sounded like a crack agent, yet he had somehow managed to fuck up big time in a damned brewery. Ricci muttered a faint tsk-tsk to himself.

The plane's engines changed to a lower tone and frequency. Landing was imminent. In confirmation, the co-pilot emerged from the cockpit and with an affable smile instructed Ricci to make sure he was buckled up. A nod of acknowledgement. The plane breached the clouds, revealing a whiteout below. Snow covered everything as far as the eye could see. He shook his head, recalling the pleasant 77°F he'd left behind in southern Italy.

The plane glided to a halt at the reserved Jet Center. He donned enough clothing to withstand a blizzard in Iceland and descended the mobile staircase. A VIP shuttle bus waited on the tarmac. He wasted no time getting inside, where the warm air made him break out in a sweat and question his decision to put on so many layers. Hat, gloves, and scarf were immediately discarded and placed on the empty seat beside him.

Through the terminal in under ten minutes, he spied a couple of waiting vehicles curbside, billows of fumes pouring out of exhausts. Winter gear back on again, the blast of cold air as the automatic glass doors parted slapped him in the face like a spurned lover. A glance at the diplomatic tags on the dark gray BMW 5 series sedan told him this was his pre-booked ride. Ricci's breath clouded in front of him, gloved fingers eagerly gripping the rear door handle and flicking it up. Brought up in the southern state of Arkansas and with a list of missions carried out in warmer climes, these conditions were going to test him as much as any adversary.

He stuck his head in the door and said to the driver, "Who are you here to pick up?"

"I recognize you from the photos, Mr. Ricci. Hop in."

Ricci placed his duffel bag on the seat, clambering in next to it. He took a deep breath.

"Tip Bradbury at your service," said the driver, a box-headed man with a wide nose. His short, blond hair was parted at the side with geometric accuracy, his pin worn on his chest like a badge of honor. The serious way he announced himself gave Ricci the impression the guy thought picking him up was a pivotal moment in international diplomacy. Bradbury turned to shake hands. "Sorry about the weather, sir. It's been building up, and the worst is yet to come. Another couple of days and the canals will freeze over. Can you imagine that?" Ricci hated this false bonhomie among a certain breed of diplomat, especially the junior attachés. He preferred to keep things businesslike. At least until the job was done, and only then would he ever loosen up with new acquaintances.

"No, I can't imagine it," Ricci replied blandly, gripping the man's offered hand firmly. "You got a phone prepped for me? I like to hit the ground running."

"One second." Lips turned down at the edges in the slightest frown, Bradbury flipped open the center console and handed over a brand-new, sleek smart phone. "There're some numbers stored on it that might come in handy. Set your own PIN. There's a second slot in there in case you need to use your own stored contacts."

"Thanks." There would be no need for that. He had memorized the numbers he'd most likely need in Amsterdam, a couple in Belgium and Luxemburg. Anything else he could look up.

"I've been instructed to take you from here immediately to the consulate for a briefing with the chief of station. You good with that?"

Ricci already had the phone pressed to his ear.

The driver showed his profile. "Did you hear me, sir? I said..."

Ricci held up his hand. "One second please."

"I've got my orders, sir."

Ricci held the cell phone to his chest. Through gnashed teeth, he said, "Damn your orders. My mission is time-sensitive, and the chief of station can wait his fucking turn. I need to make contact with this..."

Wessels picked up on the third ring, answering in a breathy voice, "Yes?"

The vehicle eased to the curb. Ricci sensed Bradbury's eyes watching him in the rearview mirror, unhappy with the maverick agent who would get him in trouble for disobeying orders.

"I've been told you're my best hope of tracking down a man called Barrett and his lady friend," said Ricci. "That right?"

"I've been waiting for your call." Wessels explained how he'd been left in the lurch by Barrett after racing to the Netherlands at short notice, the reason for being stood up coming in a phone call from a guy from the NSA, Fraser Ketill.

"Who the hell is he?" said Ricci. "Never heard of him."

"Barrett's boss, I guess."

"You guess?" The name was unfamiliar, and he knew of most of the top-level chiefs at the agency.

"Yeah..." The Dutchman described his interactions with Barrett in 2019, although he was known by another name for that mission. David Reeve. "It was a wild couple of weeks, gave me some premature gray hairs." The deal had been struck hastily, Wessels at first disinclined to help as he feared the local gangsters, but the offer was way too tempting to say no to. He'd been contacted anonymously to render assistance on a drugs bust. "I asked for payment in Bitcoin, which they were more than happy to do."

"Why you?" Ricci had already partly figured out the answer. The guy was smart—Bitcoin had appreciated a thousand percent since that time.

An intro cough said, *I'm gonna be embarrassed by what I say next.* "Because I'm the best computer hacker in the Benelux region."

"Why haven't you been hired by an agency full-time?"

"Ah..." This time the embarrassment was real. "I've got some personality disorders. I'm not a good choice for an employee, but as a contractor for one-off jobs, I'm your man."

The fact that Wessels had a gambling problem was laid out in the brief. Interesting that he *almost* admitted it, framing his weakness as a personality disorder. "I need to meet you, set things up."

"Yeah, I'm in a coffee shop downtown." He gave the address. "I was supposed to meet Barrett in a side street, but the arrangement changed when the kidnappers decided to bring him in early."

Ricci knew the deal, that Barrett had to steal something for the kidnappers or his lady was dead. An invidious position to be in. Wessels had received his information direct from Barrett and this so-called boss, Ketill, whereas Ricci had been briefed through Langley. He doubted he and Wessels were exactly on the same page. Once they had met and had a chat, he would make sure they were.

As Bradbury pressed gently on the gas, making for the rendezvous point, Ricci leaned back in the embrace of the soft leather seat, the rosary coiled loosely in his hand. He made the sign of the cross with slow precision: *In nomine Patris, et Filii, et Spiritus Sancti. Amen.* Then, fingering the crucifix, he began the Apostles' Creed. His lips barely moved, but the words came from deep within, steady and familiar. On the next bead, he whispered the Our Father, followed by three Hail Marys—faith, hope, and charity. As he reached the first decade of the Sorrowful Mysteries, he paused to reflect on the Agony in the Garden, then prayed in silence, the beads slipping one by one through his fingers.

Prayer over, Ricci's gaze fell on the snow drifts outside the window, the bare trees bending in the cold wind. He shivered in his seat just looking at it. "Turn the heating up, will ya, Tip?"

The driver obliged with a nod before returning his knuckles—white to match the streetscape outside—to the wheel. Ricci clocked the speedometer: they were maintaining a steady 85 km/h, which he mentally calculated to be 52 mph. That was fine; better to arrive in one piece than skid on ice and plow into a guardrail, as two reckless suckers had already done. Ricci would have expected more traffic than this on the major arterial roads of a European capital, but the big freeze was scaring many into staying indoors. Judging by Bradbury's anxious eyes, flicking between the rearview mirror and the frosty landscape, he was scared too. Or it could just as well be in anticipation of a dressing down back at the office.

Beyond the edge of the highway extended wide, flat polders, the odd charming windmill. The rural landscape quickly give way to denser conurbations, then modern office blocks and a couple of traffic interchanges. Finally, they entered the outskirts of the city itself, Amstel River to the left, across a number of canal bridges.

Ricci had been to Amsterdam twice before but had never seen it under this crushing winter mantle.

"Hazy Haven. That was the name of the coffee shop, right?" Bradbury inquired, his voice trembling a touch. His eyes darted around like he was waiting for an accident to befall them on the slick surface.

"That's right, pal. And please, for heaven's sake, relax. There's hardly any traffic."

A bicycle bell rang out, then another. "It's not the cars I worry about; it's these crazy cyclists."

"Just watch the road in front of you." The car stopped with a gentle skid before a crosswalk. Time to offer some encouragement or a fender bender was guaranteed. "Listen, sport, you've done a great job so far. The cyclists will take care of themselves."

"Will do." Bradbury nodded. "I do apologize. Never in my life have I driven in conditions like these."

"No biggie," Ricci replied without emotion. "Drive on."

The so-called coffee shop wasn't about flat-whites and lattes; it was one of many sanctioned venues for stoners and hippies in the city. A place where red-eyed losers could waste their miserable lives away, puffing weed behind stained glass windows and chipped ceramic tables.

Out the window, Ricci noticed handfuls of brave passersby wrapped in scarves. Many of them walked with unsteady gates, speaking to themselves as they shuffled along. In this part of town, not many were heading for high-flying, high-paying jobs. A couple, dressed in threadbare sweaters, shoes with gaping holes, embraced and twirled on the spot, then slipped over and crashed to the icy sidewalk. The urge to jump out and rush to their aid was quelled by the pair's uproarious laughter. High as kites. On a day like this, if you had nothing going for you in life, perhaps it was the best condition to be in.

A neon sign blinked above a black steel door. Hazy Haven. A slim figure slumped against the wall, head down as the man scrolled a cell phone. "Park around the corner," said Ricci. "Don't leave until I tell you to."

"Are you coming to the consulate after your meeting here?"

A shrug. "No idea. You gotta play these things by ear."

A cell phone vibrated in a holder on the dash. The screen lit up: TOM J. SAVAGE. "It's the chief," said Bradbury grimly. "Gonna rip me a new one."

"Give me the damned phone." Ricci's arm reached across the console.

"I'll pop him on hands-free."

"Tip," barked a deep, resonant voice. "Have you got lost?"

"No, he hasn't," said Ricci in a firm tone. "I'm borrowing him for the rest of the day. He and I really hit it off, didn't we, Tip?"

The scowl Ricci gave the man implied only one answer was acceptable. "Ah...yes we did," Bradbury agreed.

"Mr. Ricci. Welcome to Amsterdam." Savage's smooth tones filled the cabin, polished, authoritative, and ever-so-slightly smug. "Listen, I'm sorry to spoil your fun, but I want you in the consulate for a full situational brief in the next hour. This kidnapping of two US citizens has got us all upset. The Dutch cops are efficient, but they're way too 'by-the-book' to get the job done without risking lives. Not to mention ruffling feathers in our security services, since the woman's boyfriend is an NSA man. He's gone AWOL, too, by the way. Either he's decided to be the hero or the kidnappers have got to him. Together, we can figure it all out. We can get assets in motion fast, as long as I know what's going on. I assume you'll be working under my coordination?"

Bradbury blinked hard, eyes flicking to Ricci, who casually leaned back into the headrest, fingers absently touching the cross around his neck.

"Negative," said Ricci.

There was a pause. A long one. "Come again?"

"I'm well aware of what's going on. I've been thoroughly briefed, and I have a key asset already on the hook."

"You can't do this alone. This isn't your turf. Amsterdam's not Rome."

Ricci sighed in frustration. "I'm not under your coordination, Tom. This one's above station. I'm here on a Special Access Program, directly tasked by Langley. You'll be looped in when and if the need arises."

"Bullshit." The word hit the air like a slap. "Every mission in my Area of Operations runs through me. I don't care what stamp you walked in with—"

"Langley cares," Ricci said. "And that stamp? Signed off by someone three floors above your clearance level."

More silence. Then a clipped statement: "You go rogue in my AO and we're going to have problems, Ricci."

Ricci let a note of conciliation creep into his voice. "Tom, I'm not here to cause problems. I'm here to solve one. Fast, clean, and without leaving a mess on your desk. I'll call you if I need you. And no blowback on Tip for acting under my orders, you got me?"

He nodded at Bradbury, who ended the call with a press of the finger. The cabin fell silent.

Bradbury exhaled like he'd been holding his breath underwater. "I've never heard anyone speak to Mr. Savage like that. He didn't sound happy."

Ricci leaned back in the seat, eyes on the coffee shop's blinking neon sign. "He'll get over it. Or he won't. Either way, you're in the clear now."

A broad smile, then a relieved "Thank you."

Ricci stepped out into the cold, stood, and tapped on Bradbury's window. The glass rolled down a couple inches. "Don't park more than five minutes away. Got me?"

A quick nod. "Understood." The sparkle in the man's eyes told Ricci this might be the most exciting day Bradbury had ever had in Amsterdam.

# SIXTEEN

The man looked nothing like his file photo. It had nothing to do with the dim lights or the pungent curtain of cannabis fumes that hung in the air like smoky gossamer. The photo Ricci had been provided must not have been updated for a while. In the years since it was taken, Bram Wessels had put on at least fifteen pounds, his eyes had grown puffy, and his hair was thinner and grayer.

Wessels sat in the corner of a booth, his head bent close to a small-format newspaper, a pen hovering over the page. On the table sat his glowing cell phone, tuned in to some app or other. He jumped in his seat as Ricci touched him lightly on the shoulder. "Interesting reading material?"

Wessels scrabbled to put a hand over the publication before folding it in half and stuffing it in the pocket of a threadbare olive drab overcoat, the kind you might find in a military surplus store. "Not really." He quickly pressed the side of his phone and the screen went black.

Ricci had just enough time to see the cover image—a jockey in a two-wheeled sulky behind a handsome chestnut horse on the trot—before Wessels managed to hide his shame. "I can't believe there's horse racing in this freezing weather."

Wessels' eyebrows dipped in the middle as he formulated a terse response. "There isn't."

Ricci gestured at the man's coat pocket, the top of the magazine still visible. "I like working with honest people." A come-on request with curled fingers. "Show me."

A reluctant hand produced a colorful publication. "Here."

Ricci read aloud in a perfect French accent. "*Les immanquables de Paris Turf.*" Then, "You know French? I'm impressed."

The Dutchman side-eyed him. "No, not really. Barely enough to order a croissant."

"Or maybe enough to understand this form guide?" Ricci tapped a finger on the cover.

Wessels laughed uncomfortably, his eyes darting from the table back to Ricci. "What can I say? I like horses. It's a silly little pastime of mine."

"You looking to place a bet on the Prix d'Amérique, are you?" Ricci asked.

Wessels blinked hard. "You know that race?" he said, barely able to conceal his surprise.

"Yeah, I've heard of it. Biggest trotting event in the world." He slid into the seat opposite Wessels, locking his gaze on him. "I remember you saying something about a 'personality disorder.' That's bullshit, isn't it?"

"No, I..." he stammered.

"Pal, I've done my reading. We know you've got a gambling problem with a particular fondness for horse racing." He cocked his head. "Rather esoteric, when you've got football matches to bet on in your own country. Casinos too."

Wessels tugged the lapel of his grungy coat. "Do I look like the type of person who frequents casinos?"

"I guess not." Ricci shook his head disapprovingly. "Until we locate Dmitrieva and Barrett, I'll be looking after your little book, OK?"

Bram's cheeks flushed a shade darker than the feeble amber

glow of the overhead lamp. "It's not a problem. I've got it all under control."

"Really? What was on your phone that you were so anxious for me not to see?" He scoffed. "Hiding it like a teenage boy caught by his mom looking at porn?"

"Nothing to worry about."

"Please, don't insult my intelligence." He blew out his cheeks. "Personally, I don't care about your...addiction. I care about the truth. From now on, I will not tolerate lies from you."

"I haven't lied to you."

"Like all addicts, you probably do believe you have your problem under control, so, technically, that may not be a lie in your own mind. However, I will easily spot any deliberate lies. Got me?"

Wessels answered by pursing his lips petulantly and nodding.

"A test for you. Have you been smoking weed in this coffee shop?"

"Yes. I had a joint when I arrived. Just one."

"Any drinks?"

"A pint of Amstel and a shot of jenever."

Ricci reached across and grabbed his wrist. "Excellent. We're off to a good start."

Wessels sighed with relief.

"I've been authorized," continued Ricci, retracting his hand, "to make a substantial payment to you should we succeed in finding the targets. Even—and get this—if you only play a minor role in it. But I've got the discretion to cancel the payment entirely. I make the rules. No more gambling, no more pot, and no alcohol until the job is finished. Do you understand what I'm saying to you, Bram?"

"Perfectly."

Ricci pressed his lips thin and wide. "I'll be keeping an eye on you."

Relief uncreased the crow's feet around the Dutchman's eyes, the white sclera tinged with red from the weed. "Let's go and get that USB, shall we?"

"Lead the way." Ricci donned his woolen hat, pulling it down low over his ears. "Another five minutes of this passive smoke contagion and I'll be getting the munchies." Marching to the door, he dialed Bradbury and told him that he and his contact would make their way to the Mondrian on foot. He was to park in the general vicinity and await further instructions. He'd be on call for the rest of the day and was to hang solid and ignore any orders that came from the consulate. Bradbury agreed with alacrity.

Under leaden skies, the men walked briskly along the slick sidewalks, alert for patches of black ice. Wessels stumbled a couple of times, Ricci quick to grab hold of his coat and prevent a fall. Fifteen minutes later, they turned a corner, the black and tan stonework of the Mondrian Suites looming opposite the frozen canal.

"I'll engage the reception staff," whispered Ricci as they neared the revolving door. "You go get the material Barrett left behind. Can you do that in your mind-altered state?"

"Easy." Wessels rubbed under his nose and made his way across the lobby floor.

No other guests in sight, Ricci drifted up to the concierge, an affable young man with a light dusting of freckles. Arms spread wide on the mahogany counter, he grinned like a halfwit, playing the innocent tourist. In his peripheral vision, the shambolic figure of Wessels ambled toward the twin elevator shaft. He squinted as he took in the name tag. "Kasper, I wonder if you can help me. First time in Holland." He shook his head and laughed. "Sorry. I mean the Netherlands. You're not offended?"

"Of course not, sir. Even some of us say Holland. What can I do for you?"

"I'm thinking of changing hotels," he said. "The one my wife and I are staying at is older than Jesus, freezing cold, and she's blaming me for it! Don't suppose you've got a spare room?"

"One moment." A faint light reflected off his glasses as he read the computer monitor. "Yes, a guest checked out just this morning. Room 304 is available. A lovely room, and warm as a blanket."

"Terrific. What are the rates?"

---

THE ELEVATOR REQUIRED a keycard to operate, yet anyone could access the stairwell. So much for security. Wessels looked around, made sure no one could see him, and shouldered open the door. Inside, the concrete stairwell walls were spotlessly clean, not like the ugly graffiti that adorned the fire stairs in his own apartment block. No smell of spilled beer and stale piss either. Just the scent of nothingness.

Adrenaline-fueled pulse racing, he began the ascent. In the cold, empty shaft, his nose pinched as he breathed in hard, the effort of climbing the stairs testing his low level of physical fitness, made worse by a sedentary lifestyle, as well as smoking a pack a day and the odd joint. He stopped to rest a moment; a cough came from nowhere and rattled his ribcage. A short wait to see if another one was coming. No more coughs seemed imminent, but his teeth began to chatter a little, his body to shake. Was he coming down with something? He prayed not; last winter, the flu had laid him up in bed for weeks. Worse than that, Ricci wouldn't pay him the money for the assignment if he succumbed to illness. And with those gambling debts hanging over his head, and that other problem...

*Stop the negative thoughts. Regroup. Get a move on.*

Wessels moved as fast as his flabby legs would carry him, his footsteps thudding softly on the concrete steps as he climbed, counting the floors under his breath.

"Two. Three..."

He stopped. Looked up at the windowsill under the reinforced pane of glass. There it was. The Coke can, wedged between the sill and the damaged wall. Half-crushed chip wrapper behind it.

He stepped over, peeled the wrapper back, and felt the USB drive tucked safely inside. Cold plastic against his fingers.

He exhaled. Pocketed it. Time to vanish.

As he turned, a cleaning trolley clattered through the fire door below. He froze against the stair rail, out of sight. The cleaner's footsteps faded.

Wessels moved quickly, slipping down the stairs, shoulders hunched.

He pushed through the ground-floor stairwell door, crossed the lobby without making eye contact with anyone, and exited through the revolving door.

Thirty seconds later, Ricci strolled out behind him, having just cut short his conversation with the concierge with a promise to call back if the wife agreed to moving to the Mondrian Suites. He looked to the right and spotted Wessels, stooped over and waddling up the deserted street.

At a moderate pace, he caught up in less than a minute. A quick call to Bradbury informed him that he and his contact were waiting outside a canal-side house a block from the hotel.

# SEVENTEEN

Soulful music—jazzy trumpets and drums with intermittent soaring strings—poured from the five surround-sound speakers placed strategically around the room. Heavy timber beams adorned the white walls and ceiling, lending the place a Tudor-style feel. Jacob had no clue who the vocal artist was; it sounded like a Dutch version of Tony Bennett. He did know where they were, though, thanks to eavesdropping on the Moroccans in the van. Adding Arabic to his linguistic repertoire was paying off, but not in the way he had hoped for. Although the men spoke in Darija, a dialect significantly different from standard Arabic, it shared enough vocabulary for Jacob to understand the gist of their chatter. In particular, the destination—the middle of the Chaam Forests, close to the Belgian border. He was pretty sure he had his mind-map location down to within one mile. *If I could somehow funnel that information to the outside world...*

From his seat of honor, bang center of the twenty-foot long chestnut table in the cavernous hall, Jacob felt small and powerless. Relieved of everything but the clothes he wore, he knew that getting himself and Irina out of this was going to take every innate talent, every skill he had ever learned, combined with a liberal dose of luck.

Across the table, the surly man with the cauliflower ear stared back at him, his gaze cold, calculating. He was dressed in a blue pinstripe suit, the sharp attire starkly contrasting with the electrician's overalls Jacob had seen him wearing on the CCTV footage. He didn't recognize the man from any files or records in his memory bank. A newbie on the scene or a thug who had managed to fly under the radar? The coldness in his eyes spoke volumes. This wasn't just some hired muscle; this man was deadly and totally lacking in any sense of remorse.

Flanking the Ear, two other men sat like shadows—tall, athletic, a sculptural quality to their hard-edged features. Exquisitely tailored suits belied the dirty work they undoubtedly performed on behalf of de Vries. One of them was Petrović, whom Jacob had briefly crossed paths with in 2019. The facial recognition software had been too conservative with its ninety percent match. Clearly, the man had risen in stature since the Belgian sting. The other guy was a new face, but his features suggested he, too, could be another Slav. Birds of a feather and all that.

Jacob's eyes darted between the goons, but he didn't let his gaze linger. He'd learned a long time ago that it was best to remain circumspect when dealing with stony-faced men you didn't know. There was an uphill job of Everest proportions to be completed to secure Irina's release. He could not compromise that with empty bluster in a pointless dick-swinging contest. A contest he couldn't hope to win.

Valentijn De Vries, somehow looking even younger than he had six years ago, casual in jeans and a striped sweater, stood at a triple-door liquor cabinet. He decanted a smoky, golden liquid from a cut crystal decanter into two matching glasses. He swirled the contents of one glass and brought it over to Jacob, who accepted wordlessly. Jacob took the smallest of sips and set the glass down.

"You like it?" De Vries rested his hand on the back of Jacob's chair, looking down and sideways at him.

"It's OK." The whisky was breathtakingly good. "I've tasted better."

De Vries slapped his thigh, moved back around the table, all loose limbs, and sat to the right of his men. "I like your honesty. I have also drunk superior scotch in my time, but this was all I could get my hands on from the local suppliers." He whispered in a mock-conspiratorial tone, "In case you hadn't guessed, we're kind of hiding from the law, aren't we, fellas?"

The men guffawed in unison. They might be hiding, but they weren't afraid.

"The cops have nothing on me, Barrett. Or should I say David Reeve. That's the name of the man who tried and failed to put me in prison." He waved a hand dismissively. "Anyway, they already came calling at my officially registered address. One of my staff sent them away with...what's the expression?...a flea in their ear."

"The police didn't tell me they suspected you, and I never mentioned your name," said Jacob. "I'm surprised."

De Vries grinned and took a sip of his scotch. "They don't suspect me, at least not directly. Their visit was based on a rumor. That this fine fellow to my left"—he gestured like a product demonstrator on television—"works for me. The police thought they'd ID'd him from a camera shot. My butler sent them on their way, told them I was indisposed and that he'd never seen the man they were looking for."

Jacob nodded at the sullen Petrović. "I don't know any of these other guys, but Veselin I remember. I'm sure if he said a few words now I'd know it was him I spoke to on the phone."

"You guessed right." Petrović tugged one of his emerald cuff links. "It was me. As they say, it's nice to put a face to a name. Or, in this case, a voice."

"Enough small talk," said de Vries. "These three gentlemen will assist you with the heist, Mr. Barrett. They'll be watching from the rearguard, so to speak. You alone will be tasked with breaking in and stealing the item. My men will provide cover but also watch closely. Any silly attempts to contact the police, friends, anyone, and Mila will have her throat cut. Any questions so far?"

Jacob's grip on the glass tightened, though he didn't take another sip. His mind was already elsewhere, focused on the next steps, trying desperately to formulate a plan that would get him—and Irina—out of this alive.

But one question had to be asked. The obvious one. "Where is Mila?" He kept his voice neutral, though the ache in his chest was anything but. *Mila. Irina.* He was the reason she had been kidnapped, and he would be the reason she got out alive. The next 24 hours would be a tightrope. If anything went wrong, the slightest wobble, and her life would be over.

De Vries didn't answer immediately. He gave Jacob a sidelong glance, his lips curled into a smile that didn't reach his eyes. "Perhaps you'd like to see my buddy, Sjaak, instead?"

Jacob knew this was coming; nevertheless, the words were a blow to the gut. He stiffened in his seat, his heart pumping.

De Vries flicked his wrist, and a glossy photo landed on the table in front of Jacob. The image was graphic. A man in a full-body cast, his face bruised and swollen, tubes running from his nose and mouth. The man's eyes were closed, lids bright purple, but it was obviously Sjaak Kuiper, the close friend of de Vries whom Jacob had accidentally run over and crippled.

The photo wasn't just a history record. It was a warning. *You hurt someone close to me. I won't hesitate to hurt someone close to you.*

"Your handiwork," De Vries stated like a prosecuting district attorney. "You cannot deny it. There were witnesses, including me." He folded his arms imperiously. "And it's the reason you are here. To make amends." He paused. "You know, as valuable as it is, it's not the end of the world whether I get to own the painting or not."

*So it is a painting*, thought Jacob.

"Oh, you're not drinking?" said de Vries, looking at Jacob's barely touched glass. "Actually, that's good. Shows you're serious about this. Can't have you with a fuzzy brain tomorrow." He ran a finger down the center of his forehead, giving it a couple of light taps. "You know, Barrett, I admire your loyalty. When I told you that I wanted you to steal an item and then asked if you had any questions, the one I expected was *What's the item?* Instead, you wanted to know where your lady was. Admirable, very admirable."

"Well, where is she?"

"She's safe. Tucked away in a separate secure building." He pointed at the wall. "Miles from here, so don't even think of breaking free and searching."

"How do I know you haven't killed her already?"

"A fair and reasonable question." De Vries nodded. "You will get to speak with her soon. Via Zoom or Skype or one of those damned programs I know nothing about. Veselin has organized it."

"Thank you." The insincere words were said through a tightly clenched jaw.

"As for the item, it's a priceless Rembrandt. Discovered two years ago in some dusty attic in Antwerp, apparently. Found its way into the hands of a collector. It's now in a private home just outside Brussels."

Jacob grimaced. Belgium again.

"As I said, if you secure the painting, bring it to me, it's a win for everyone. I sell it to a corrupt Middle Eastern sheikh for a fortune, split the money with my men, you and Mila get to go free." He paused and drank more whisky. "You fail—I don't get the painting, but you and Mila die. So not a total loss for me either."

Again, the assembled goons broke into laughter.

"Look at the photo again," demanded de Vries. "Hold it in your hands."

Jacob did so. "Look, it was a genuine accident. I feel terrible for your friend, but honestly, he came out of nowhere, the rain, the panic on all sides..."

"Enough!" De Vries slapped his palm on the table, a crack echoing in the hall. "Did you forget you were also pointing a gun at my head? Did you think I was going to forgive and forget? I had nightmares for months after that."

"I never would have pulled the trigger. Even if the police weren't there with me. It's not my style to murder in cold blood." *But the first time is rapidly approaching.*

De Vries tilted his head back, lips knotted and chin jutting, then rocked forward. "Aren't you a saint!" He stood and refilled his glass. China cups on saucers sat in front of the other men. None had even touched whatever was inside them. Like dogs, they were perhaps waiting for de Vries to say *drink*.

"No. I have killed before." He set down the photo of Sjaak. "When my life was in danger, in self defense. I'm not an assassin."

"Were you defending yourself when you ran over my friend?"

Jacob suppressed a sigh of frustration. "I didn't kill him."

"Semantics." De Vries rolled his eyes. "Near enough to attempted murder; it was obvious you lined him up."

Jacob's mind ticked over. He could keep claiming it was an accident, but there was no point. De Vries had made up his mind. Sjaak had been an unfortunate casualty, nothing more. Leading the life he did, it was no surprise he got hurt badly. But it was a universal human trait—a defense mechanism—to blame others when things go wrong. De Vries was no different than everyone else in that respect.

Jacob rubbed knuckles on his trousers under the table, deciding what to say next, if anything. Petrović spared him the bother.

"Is it time to wind things up here?" The Serb glanced at his boss.

"I think so," said de Vries in a tone that suggested he was in the habit of allowing Petrović a degree of independence. "We've got a lot of things to do to prepare for the job." He redirected his gaze to Jacob. "One night's rest here, then tomorrow we move. You'll be briefed in detail on the drive to Brussels."

"What time tomorrow?" Jacob asked.

The Ear suddenly decided to contribute. "What fuck difference it make?"

Jacob quirked an eyebrow as he regarded the man. Handsome by most standards, his misshapen ear was the only obvious blemish. Compared to the others, his English was woeful. Its structure carried the traces of a substandard education, perhaps received in a far-flung Russian republic—Chechnya or Dagestan—with the former being most likely in Jacob's opinion. The man had that unmistakable North Caucasus edge—high, angular cheekbones, a slightly hooked nose, and deep-set eyes, always watching.

"No difference," said Jacob with a shrug.

De Vries smiled again. "Forgive my colleague. He comes from a place where people speak their minds no matter what. No filters, I believe the expression is." He paused a beat, then said, "We move tomorrow morning, 6 a.m. sharp."

"Who's we?"

"You, me, Veselin, and our colleague to his left."

Jacob noted that no name was given to the second Serb, or Serb Two, as Jacob had labeled him in his mind. Nor to the Chechen.

"Not the Moroccans? I'm disappointed."

De Vries laughed. "Did the boys who picked you up tell you they were Moroccans?"

"No. I guessed."

De Vries tugged a loose thread on his sweater. "They will be staying behind to keep an eye on Mila. Make sure she's comfortable for the rest of her regrettably short stay with us. And to repel any intruders, should they be clever enough to sniff her out."

Jacob ground his teeth. He didn't trust them one inch with Irina. He nodded at the Chechen. "What about Meat Ear over there?"

"Fuck you." The Chechen stood, pointed a finger, and snarled, "Do not insult me. I twist *your* fucking ears off and feed to dogs!"

"Calm down," said de Vries, looking at the man, face florid with rage. "You know better than to react to a cheap shot like that." He turned and said to Jacob, "I was planning on taking him with us, but that little outburst has changed my mind." A creepy-uncle smile, then, "He will assist the Moroccans, as you called them, in keeping Mila comfortable while we attend to business in Brussels."

The Chechen took a deep breath, his muscular chest rising and falling under his tight suit. Slowly, his face broke into a leer. "*Hartelijk dank, baas.* Thanks a lot, boss."

Jacob's eyes formed slits. "You even think about touching her..."

"I guarantee he won't," said de Vries with finality. "He might have a temper, but he does what I say. Don't you?"

The Chechen gave a slow nod. "*Natuurlijk.* Of course."

De Vries drained the rest of his scotch. "Tonight, Mr. Barrett, you will carefully study a plan of the building in which the painting is kept and a map of the surrounding area. We have made an anonymous payment to one of the collector's peers with the promise of more to come if we are successful in lifting the piece. This person visited the collector, a Mr. Arnaud van Eekhout, a couple of days ago, to offer him the opportunity to buy a modern abstract work. The offer was politely rejected. The important thing is that our guy managed to hide in the collector's library a drug that will be used to knock the collector out cold—the same one we used to sedate the lovely Mila. Except a stronger version." He shrugged. "We could make it a fatal dose, I suppose, but like you, we're not monsters."

The men laughed, but with a little less enthusiasm than before. Jacob sensed they were all getting fed up with the process but still smart enough to pretend they cared, if just a little.

"A heads-up," continued de Vries. "The property is protected with an advanced security system. No onsite guards, but if the system is tripped, people will be on their way to investigate in minutes." He leaned forward and acknowledged Serb Two with a hand gesture. "Luckily, our in-house expert here will disable the system upon arrival at the address."

"Doesn't sound too difficult," said Jacob. "The painting can't be worth that much."

"Oh, but you are wrong. It's worth, as you Americans say, a shit ton."

Jacob frowned. "Then why isn't it under heavier guard?"

"Because the fool of a collector thinks no one knows he has it. The rest of his collection is average stuff at best."

"What about surprise visitors?"

De Vries shook his head. "There will be none. Van Eekhout has cleared his diary to meet our second inside man, who contacted him on a gay dating site. They have arranged for a night of what they call"—de Vries made a face as if he'd sucked a lemon —"...kinky man fun."

His men burst out laughing; this time it was genuine.

"Our man will slip van Eekhout the drug and leave the premises at 11 p.m.," continued de Vries. "My guys will then disable the security system, you will enter at midnight, steal the painting, and leave." He did a dusting-off-the-hands gesture. "Easy."

"Any dogs on the property?" said Jacob.

"No."

"Cats," said Petrović with a grin. "As you might expect of an effeminate man like that." He tipped his head slightly. "You think a couple of pussies might cause you trouble?"

The laughter reached its loudest level of the evening. Jacob held his tongue.

"During the day tomorrow," said de Vries, "we will drive past the house a couple of times, also around the neighborhood, to give you a feel for the place and identify potential escape routes in the unlikely event that, to use another American expression, the shit hits the fan."

Serb Two cleared his throat. His thin lips barely parted as he spoke for the first time in impeccable English. "No shit will be hitting any fans. As long as you keep your cool and do exactly as instructed, there will be nothing to worry about. We are certain there will be no interruptions. You will be given a tool kit to get the job done, including a tiny amount of plastic explosive. It's new-generation material: maximum power, minimal noise. You know how to use this stuff, I imagine?"

"I've had some experience, yes."

"If you can do that, the rest will be easy for you."

"One thing I don't understand. If it's so easy, why do you need me to do it?"

"Because Mr. de Vries wishes it so," said Petrović flatly.

There was a moment of silence, then de Vries clapped his hands and said, "That's enough talking shop. The rest we can go over on the way to Belgium." He looked at Jacob and gestured toward the door. "Time for your chat with Mila. It won't be a long one, I'm afraid, since you have a lot of homework to do tonight. Let's go."

# EIGHTEEN

Serb Two took him down a long, faintly lit hallway. Jacob was grateful the loathsome Chechen wasn't given the job; the urge to take to him with his fists might have been too hard to control.

A door at the far end led into a stark, windowless room. The walls were bare red brick, chunks of ancient mortar poking through here and there, the floor a shiny polished concrete. A steel chair sat in the center of the room, a small foldout camping table beside it. On the table sat an open Lenovo laptop, the screen dark. A glass of water. The scene reminded him of an enhanced interrogation room at Guantanamo Bay, except the CIA wouldn't be as accommodating with the water.

"Sit," said the Serb. "Press enter. You have three minutes. I'll be watching and listening. English only, but if you try to be clever by speaking Russian, I will understand that too."

He took a seat, took a deep breath, and pressed the button.

The screen flickered, then came to life.

Irina's face appeared. Even in the poor light coming from behind her, it was clear that she had changed, perhaps irrevocably in a mental sense, even in such a short time. Her hair was lank, her skin sallow.

The playful sparkle in her eyes might have dimmed, but a steely determination was still evident. She was tough by nature, able to withstand adversity. Her face showed no signs of physical mistreatment—no bruises, swelling, or cuts. Everything below her neck was out of view, so he couldn't be a hundred precent sure they hadn't roughed her up.

He squinted in a vain effort to see better. The room around her was indistinct—patches of gray and cobalt blue. It could have been a fake digital background. But that didn't matter. What mattered was that she was alive, that he was able to talk to her. A silent prayer went up to his personal God. *Please, keep her safe until I've dealt with these scum. And forgive me for what I plan to do to them.*

"Michael," she said, barely a whisper. He blinked twice. It sounded so strange, her using his alias. Then she made it better. "*Zaichik*. Darling."

"Mila..." Not calling her Irina, or even Irene, was even weirder. "I'm so sorry I got you into this damned mess. But don't worry, everything's going to be OK."

"You couldn't have known this would happen." Her lips trembled slightly, but she held herself together. "I love you," she whispered, her voice soft but steady, "I—I don't know how much time we have."

"Three minutes." His heart pounded against his ribs. "I love you, too. Have they hurt you in any way?"

She shook her head, keeping her eyes fixed on him. "I'm all right. Bored. No mental stimulation." She laughed sarcastically. "I'd settle for a Dutch newspaper, even though I can't understand it. Just to look at words on a page would be nice." A slow, drawn-out sigh. "De Vries promised me it will all end soon."

"Yes, it will end," he said. "Tomorrow, they want me to—"

"No!" barked the Serb. "Keep it personal, no business."

He glanced back at the Serb and gave a small nod. Straight back to Irina. "Hang in there, my love. De Vries won't allow his men to do anything to you, I'm sure of it." He ran a hand through his hair. "I just have to do this one thing for them and he promised to let us both go. Just stay strong, okay?"

"What thing?"

"No business," repeated the Serb. "Want me to end it now?"

Jacob's hand reached toward the screen, his fingers running down the image of her face. "You have nothing to worry about." If he had to burn this world to the ground to get her out, he wouldn't hesitate. "Before you know it, we'll be sitting in our favorite bar, and this will just be a bad memory."

She nodded, her eyes searching his face, looking for reassurance in more than words. "I'm scared...Michael," she whispered, her voice barely audible.

"I know."

"Please...don't ever leave me after this. Promise."

The words cut through him like a knife.

"I'll never leave you," he said, his voice hoarse. "I promise."

Without warning, the screen flickered. The image of Irina's face began to distort, the connection wavering. Jacob's pulse surged in panic. He turned to the Serb. "No way that's three fucking minutes!"

The man shrugged, half a smile curling his thin lips. "Perhaps it's a technical problem with the Internet connection."

"Mila!" Jacob called out, his voice breaking. "Stay with me—"

The screen went black.

For a moment, Jacob sat paralyzed. Then, a surge of cold, bitter rage flooded through his gut. He was gripped by a feeling of utter powerlessness. In the face of everything he'd promised her—if he failed, they were both screwed. De Vries said the job would be easy; Jacob was under no illusions. If genuine, the painting must be worth an absolute fortune. Pieces like that aren't easy to steal, no matter how meticulous the preparation.

"Get up." A strong hand gripped his shoulder. "Homework time."

The chair scooted back on the concrete with a screech. He

stood, fingers flexing. The goon shoved him in the small of the back. “Move.”

As they marched back the way they’d come, he couldn’t shake the thought that the heist was all a sideshow, that something else was at play. Perhaps a handover of Irina to the Russians for an amount of money exceeding the value of this mystery painting. Maybe he’d be sacrificed to the Russians, too. Putin would be lusting for revenge after the embarrassment he and Irina had caused him.

There would be no sleep tonight.

# NINETEEN

LIGHT SNOWFLAKES STRUCK THE BULLETPROOF windshield and disappeared on contact, the wiper barely having to do any work. The consulate BMW hummed low through the working-class suburbs of southeast Amsterdam. Their destination was an apartment in the neighborhood of Bijlmer, famous for its brutalist residential architecture. It was even more famous for an aviation disaster in 1992, when a Boeing 747 crashed into a residential building in the suburb, killing forty-two people.

The car's air conditioning was turned up high, the vent in the back blowing hot air straight at Ricci's neck. Still he shivered under his layers of clothing. He tapped on the driver's head rest. "Can you make it any warmer?"

"On it," said Bradbury, reaching to his right to adjust the temperature.

"Are you serious?" grumbled Wessels, his face the color of cooked shrimp. "I'm dying in here."

"Tough shit." Ricci pointed at the large brown satchel lying between them. "It's another twenty minutes till we get to the safe house. Let's make good use of the time instead of thinking about the next horse race, shall we? I wanna know what's on the USB."

With clumsy fingers, Wessels undid the buckle and pulled out a laptop, battered and covered in stickers like a rockstar's favorite guitar, setting it on his knee.

"I want to see it too, you know," said Ricci.

"Don't hassle me," Wessels groaned, adjusting the position of his butt cheeks as he prepared. "I'm getting it ready." He reached back into the satchel, located the flash drive in a side pocket, and inserted it into the slot. The video files from the hotel were the only data on the drive. He worked the touchpad and keyboard deftly with one hand, as only a true computer geek can. The other hand fidgeted absently with the buckle of his satchel. No talk, just a finger circling a square, fingers tapping keys, and the low, rhythmic whoosh of tires on slushy asphalt. A double tap on the touchpad and the first of three AVI files opened. Wessels expanded the window to fill the screen. He placed the laptop between them on the seat, adjusting the angle of the screen so both could watch what unfolded. "Ready, Marcello?"

A nod. "On first name terms now, are we, Bram?"

"Looks like it." Wessels smiled wanly, pressed the play button, and eased back in his seat. For a full minute they stared at the blurry image of the female concierge behind the counter, head down, occasionally smiling and laughing.

"No audio?"

"You wish," Wessels chuckled.

"Quality's shit," complained Ricci. "Can you make it clearer?"

Wessels pouted. "Afraid not. They're using an old system at the hotel. The SISO principle applies here."

"Meaning?"

"Shit in, shit out."

"Can you speed it up a little?" said Ricci, worrying his necklace crucifix for a moment. "I'll lose my shit if we have to look at her scrolling her phone for the next twenty minutes."

Wessels obliged, and the action on the screen sped up x2 times. Seven people spoke to the concierge over the next ten minutes before a longer encounter with a man in overalls and cap.

"That could be the man with the cauliflower ear Barrett's boss told me to look out for." He paused the video and frowned. "Can't tell for sure in that crappy lighting."

"Roll it again, but slow it down to normal."

They observed for a minute or so as the two engaged in what looked like an amicable conversation, ending with the woman handing over a small white keycard, the man heading to his right, presumably toward the elevators. "Could you grab still shots of any of those people we've seen and run a scan on them?"

"I could try," said Wessels. "But you can see for yourself. The images are so—I hate to use the word—grainy that I doubt I'd come up with anything useful."

"Try anyway."

"There are two more camera feeds. I'd like to review them first."

The man had a good point, Ricci conceded to himself. "Do it."

The second AVI file contained footage from a camera set above and behind the reception desk. The images captured on video were clearer than from the angle facing reception but only marginally. The video ended and they watched it a second time, but both men were none the wiser.

"Last one," said Wessels, lining up the file with the street-side camera feed.

They watched thirty or so people walk by, a handful entering the hotel. When a VW Transporter van pulled up in a loading zone, Wessels froze the footage. License plates not visible. Still, he flashed a hopeful grin at Ricci. "This might be the money shot."

"Let's hope so."

He slowed the speed to x0.25, and both men craned their necks. Wessels zoomed. Although the man's features weren't in razor-sharp focus, there were enough specifics to get interested. A beard, square jaw. And the clincher: the mangled ear, ridged and puffy. Wessels could barely contain his excitement. "If this *klootzak* is on any database or website anywhere in the world, I'm gonna find him."

Bradbury's voice carried into the back of the car. "Sorry to interrupt. We've arrived at the address you gave me. Sure this is it?"

Outside, motionless bikes were chained to fences. Broad and towering apartment blocks. Curtainless windows showing flickering TV light. Shadowy figures loitering in darkened doorways. "Yes," said Ricci. "I'll put in a good word for you. You're free to go back to the consulate. Don't mention anything to Tom Savage about what you overheard, OK?"

"Understood." Bradbury failed to hide the disappointment in his voice. Still, he wished the men the best of luck.

---

THE THUDDING, repetitive sound of bass gripped Ricci's temples like a vise as they approached the glass doors. He scanned the monolithic building, almost 1000 feet long and eleven stories high, cursing the noise that was coming from everywhere and nowhere all at once. Inside the cramped elevator, the noise faded as they ascended. He prayed the residents weren't partying on every floor. He glanced at Wessels, clutching his satchel like it was an oxygen tank.

The ninth floor, and those immediately above and below it, must have been reserved for seniors, since there was an absolute blissful silence as they exited the elevator. He touched his cross and gave thanks for the peace. He was in no mood for arguing with rowdy neighbors. Ricci inserted the key, pushed open the door that was slightly stuck, perhaps due to warping in the prevailing high humidity, and waved Wessels across the threshold.

The décor in the apartment was sparse to the point of being non-existent. Bare white walls, tan carpet, drab beige sofa and armchairs, tiny coffee table in the living area. Sterile and clean as a hospital. There was a separate kitchen and two medium bedrooms, each furnished as plainly as the rest of the place. In one of the bedrooms sat a large, long pine desk, a couple of pivot chairs, a computer and monitor, a printer, and stocks of paper. The view from the window extended over the urban sprawl, blanketed in snow to the horizon. The vista would soon be swallowed by the fast approaching night.

"Get to it," Ricci said, pointing at the desk.

"Got a Wi-Fi log-in?"

Ricci tapped his phone then showed the screen to Wessels, who nodded and entered the code into his laptop. Ricci left him to settle in, fixed them both a cup of instant coffee with plenty of sugar, placed a couple of cookies on a plate, and brought the refreshments into the makeshift office.

"Found anything yet?" said Ricci.

"I've only just started. Gimme a break."

"What's your plan?"

Wessels outlined how he would scour a number of sites where scammers buy and sell identities, then sneak into the systems of a number of renowned global security agencies, which their directors vainly imagined were unbreachable. His best chance would be to upload the best still images he could isolate to a number of darknet forums, ex-military databases.

"Which ones?"

Wessels touched the side of his nose. "The necessary ones."

Ricci grunted under his breath, then retreated to the living room. As the Dutchman hunted, Ricci placed a call to an analyst he'd known since he started with the CIA, a man who worked deep in the heart of Langley's HUMINT labyrinth.

"Hank," he said, infusing an unspoken apology into his tone. "Sorry to disturb. I need a lead on a person of interest." He described the faux electrician.

"That's not a lot to go on."

Ricci ran a thumb over the wooden arm of the sofa. Not a speck of dust. "I've got someone looking on this end. He's good at his job, a bit cocky. Be nice if you found the lead before him."

"Leave it to me."

"Bingo!" came the cry from the bedroom.

"Too late. My guy's having an orgasm."

"Let me try anyway. If we come up with the same result, the higher the chance of a correct match."

"Do it. I'll forward you some images to run through your databases, in case my guy's got it wrong." Ricci terminated the call. Wessels was back in the living room, feet outstretched on the coffee table. A couple printouts lay by his feet. He pointed at them. "Chechen."

Ricci broke into a broad grin. "You're fucking good, Bram."

"I can get lucky sometimes."

Ricci read aloud from the page. "Adlan Ibishev, thirty-six years old." He looked up and nodded. "MMA fighter. That explains the ugly lug." Back to the printout, he ran a finger along the page. "Ex Russian army. Two years ago led troops in the attack on Mariupol, Ukraine, before joining the FSB, which he quit only six months later." He whistled. "A hell of a CV."

"Look why he quit."

"Accused of raping five women in Ukraine. Was about to face trial when he disappeared. According to rumor, he found protection under the wing of crime boss Sergei Kumarin in Moscow." He looked up. "If Barrett finds out about the guy's past...He's gonna lose his mind."

"Turn the page over. Once I had the name, it was easy to find some other links. Local ones."

Ricci continued to read aloud. "In October—gee, that's recent, only three months ago—he reportedly joined forces with... Valentijn de Vries as an enforcer." He sat at the dining table and ran a hand over the piece of paper. "This is all well and good, but how does it lead us to where they're holding Dmitrieva and Barrett?"

"It doesn't. But I'm assuming you've got a lot of people in Moscow. Maybe they can find out something about this crime boss?" Wessels combed nicotine-stained fingers through his graying hair. "If Kumarin was prepared to shield Ibishev from a rape trial, he might be willing to do other things for him. Like organizing a new life in another country."

Ricci blew out his cheeks. It made sense. "I'll make some calls." He grabbed Wessels' ankles and swung them off the table. "You're not finished. There was a voice recording emailed to you. Have you had a chance to analyze it?"

"Not yet."

"How about I make you another coffee and you can get cracking. Don't forget, payment to you is at my discretion. Don't give me a reason to decline the transaction."

"Would it be pushing the friendship to ask for an ashtray? I concentrate better with cigarettes to stimulate my brain cells."

Ricci swore under his breath. He hated smoking, but he hated the idea of failing the mission even more.

Four minutes later, Ricci had delivered the acidic brew and a glass ashtray and was making a call to Moscow station.

"Marcello? Long time no speak!"

There was a good reason for that. Ricci despised Anthony Judd with a passion, although Judd was unaware of it. The reasons for the hatred were petty to the point of juvenile and were lost in the mists of old cases. Ricci *was* one to bear a grudge, but he could mask his feelings better than most. It was totally ironic, Ricci thought, that he was the more diplomatic of the two, yet Judd had received a coveted diplomatic post. Moscow, no less. A hub of intelligence gathering and prime real estate for career advancement.

"Good to talk to you," Ricci said, stifling his disdain. "Love to have a long social chat, but I haven't got a lot of time." He gave a two-minute precis of what he wanted—intercepts on Kumarin's communications. "If he's been talking to Ibishev, I want to know. More precisely, I want to know where he's holed up."

"I'll set the wheels in motion," Judd said cheerily. "It's a hell of a long shot, especially in the tiny time frame you've given me."

He paused a moment. "This woman who got kidnapped. She must be a valuable asset to have you on the case."

"Yeah." He didn't want to get drawn into a long conversation. "She's got a protected identity back home. I don't know what her real name is, and I don't wanna know."

"Too late, Marcello. Her photo's been plastered all over social media and the Russians were damn quick to pick up on it."

"I thought social media was banned in Russia?"

"Only those deemed 'foreign agents.' The Russkies have their own socials: VK and Telegram. TikTok is allowed. And the evil Western outlets that are taboo? Well, that's just for the common folk. Agencies and the big-wigs continue to use whatever the hell platforms they like."

"Perfect," huffed Ricci.

"They quickly figured out exactly who she is. Irina Frolova, used to work for the Ministry of Finance. Dropped the minister in the shit a couple years ago, and he wound up dead. She fled the country with a mystery American man. Apparently, the rumor goes, the pair of them caused a great deal of embarrassment to the Russian government and Putin personally. Vlad's particularly pissed at her, and he ain't one to forgive and forget."

"Jesus." Ricci whistled through his teeth. None of this had been revealed to him. Had it been, he might have told his boss to take a hike and continued the fun times with Carmela in Italy.

"So now the Dutch cops are looking for her, only now she's called Mila Dmitrieva, huh?"

"That's right," said Ricci. "And we want her back. I'm at arm's length from this, but apparently she's highly valued by the State Department. I've been told to get this done without turning to the local cops for help. Which makes my job ten times harder."

"You know it's weird," drawled Judd. "But in our world, is anything really weird? Anyway, I'm reading in the online tabloids that the missing woman's known as something entirely different to her work colleagues in New York. Irene Frobisher." A sardonic chuckle. "Man, with so much identity concealment going on, no wonder she made for a gold-standard kidnapping victim. Only another weird thing—no one's mentioned any ransom or other demands. You think the kidnappers are planning on turning her back over to the Russians for a reward?"

Ricci closed his eyes and massaged the bridge of his nose. The information Judd was spewing made his gut churn. Barrett was more than likely the mystery American that had gotten her out of Russia. His cover was also now at considerable risk—perhaps it was already too late to salvage it. If Judd's guess was right and the scenario of Barrett being forced to steal something was a ruse, the Russian woman's fate would already be sealed. Maybe Ricci and Wessels were wasting their time with this wild goose chase?

"I just need to find out where she is and extract her," he said firmly. "So please, look for that link between Kumarin and Ibishev. You'd be doing me a solid."

"Don't hold your breath, Marcello."

"I won't."

Back in the noxious smoke haze, he reconsidered the idea of holding his breath. Wessels had donned a pair of headphones and was staring intently at the screen of his laptop, eyes scanning from left to right. A cigarette smoldered in the ash tray. Ricci dropped into an armchair opposite, steepling his fingers. Wessels ripped off his headphones. "Yeah?"

"You're all over this stuff more than me. Are you aware of Mila Dmitrieva having another name and or names?"

"What about the voice analysis?" Wessels couldn't look at the intense stare coming his way. "I've...ah...run the phonetic profiling. Accent, cadence, regional tells. All points to a Serbian."

"That's not what I asked." He jabbed a finger. "Dmitrieva. What do you know?"

"No more than you do." Trembling fingers reached for his cigarette, but Ricci had already pulled the ash tray out of reach.

"Remember our terms? You lie, you don't get paid. There are other more painful disincentives I can think of too. So I'm giving you one more chance before I throw you out of this apartment in your underwear. Won't take long for hypothermia to finish you off." He took a long, deep breath. "Do you know of any aliases Dmitrieva might go by?"

A rosy blush crept into the Dutchman's otherwise pallid cheeks. "I...ah...yeah...maybe."

"That's better." Ricci squinted one eye. "I've got a feeling you know a lot more than you've been letting on to me. Am I right?"

A slow nod that got faster. Ricci shoved the ashtray with his foot. Wessels plucked the Marlboro and sucked greedily.

"I did some snooping on Barrett," said Wessels, stubbing out the cigarette and lighting another with fumbling fingers. "A while back." He looked at the ceiling, tiny muscles in his cheeks throbbing, a quickened pulse in his neck. "I shouldn't have. Because I'm shit-scared this whole situation is down to that."

Ricci held his head in his hands, fingers massaging the skin near his hairline. Bad news was on the way. He looked up and saw the anxiety wrinkling the edges of Wessels' eyes. "And why the hell did you do that?"

Wessels shrugged as he fidgeted with a steaming mug of coffee. "As pathetic as it sounds, curiosity. It's my nature to want to know everything I can about people. Like how I study the form of race horses. Others might call it snooping..."

"That's exactly what I'd call it," said Ricci. "It's something I'm paid to do on a daily basis."

"He works for a clandestine organization. I'm not even sure of its name. Their mail servers are loaded with fake Hotmail accounts, very cleverly disguised. By probing their—"

"Stop!" Ricci rolled his shoulders as he ambled to the refrigerator. Fingers on the handle, he turned to Wessels and said, "I've been told he works for the NSA. If there's one thing I don't wanna hear, it's that what Langley told me is bullshit."

"Thing is," Wessels continued in *mea culpa* mode, "Imke, that's my wife, well, she's even more curious than me."

"What's your fucking wife got to do with this?" said Ricci, throttling an urge to cave Wessels' head in with the ash tray.

"She snooped around my computer. To confirm what I told her was true."

"What the hell did you tell her, Bram?"

"One night I got drunk, let some information slip about a certain person coming to spend a couple nights in Amsterdam. Someone I knew as David Reeve six years ago."

Ricci cradled his head in both hands. That last name rang a bell. "Oh, shit."

"I...I suspect she sold the information to that de Vries guy I mentioned before." He dragged his cigarette through the ash like he was plowing a tobacco field. "I—"

"And what exactly did you find out?"

"Barrett's and Dmitrieva's real names—at least the names their employers know them by. And...a whole bunch of other stuff."

"What stuff?" Ricci thundered. "Would her name be Irina Frolova, by any chance?"

He nodded. "You find that out from your contact in Moscow?"

"Yeah. It's all over social media, too." He flared his nostrils. "And I've changed my mind. Tell me everything you know, including who Barrett really is and who he works for."

For the next ten minutes, Wessels painted a picture of digging and discovery and, now, despair. How he had let his guard down while under the influence, perhaps subconsciously trying to impress Imke, who'd been riding him hard about his gambling for months.

As Wessels began to confess, in earnest and in detail, Ricci felt like he'd assumed the role of priest that his mother once thought was her son's destiny. And a wonderful career it would have been, too, if it hadn't been for that inconvenient celibacy thing.

# TWENTY

A SCROLL THROUGH THREADS ON REDDIT AND anonymous posts on X unearthed a cornucopia of theories on steroids. Dmitrieva is FSB-adjacent, in the WITSEC program, a personal enemy of Putin. Careless in Amsterdam, her cover got blown, and now the Russians have snatched her. And that was just one line of speculation.

Earlier in the day, de Kok had made a number of blunt enquiries seeking confirmation of Dmitrieva's identity and any sealed residency transfers. She sat with her chin cupped in her hands, staring at the replies on the screen. The Dutch General Intelligence and Security Service, aka AIVD: *No comment due to ongoing operations.* Europol: *Denied. Information not available at your clearance level.* US State Department: *Classified information.* Finally, a message from the commissioner's office telling her to be more proactive on the case. Easy for him to say when so-called friendly agencies were giving her the cold shoulder.

She put the computer into sleep mode, grabbed a notebook, and scooted back her chair. The news was worse than discouraging. Daan Vos might have some thoughts on the matter. Together, they often came up with good ideas by kicking around scenarios, brainstorming until it all made sense.

Vos was thumbing his way through a tall stack of files when she tapped on the side of the door frame. "Got a minute?" she said.

Stubble dotted his dimpled chin, his unruly white hair badly in need of a comb. "Do I look like I've got a minute?"

She pulled up a chair opposite him. "Make time." She waved a hand at the mountain of folders. "What's all that?"

"Cold cases. I've got a ton of them to prioritize in terms of... solvability. Is that a word?"

"Probably. I don't really care. I've just read a couple of disheartening emails." She held one forefinger against the other to start the count-down. "One. From the commissioner. He's not happy we haven't called a press conference yet on the kidnapped woman. He said with both of them now missing, it's a bad look for the city."

Vos pushed the pile to one side, giving de Kok his full attention. "He can go fuck himself," he said in an oddly supportive tone. "What's the point when, apparently, we don't even know who we're looking for? And now the boyfriend's gone AWOL from his hotel, we're chasing ghosts. Maybe the pair of them staged the whole thing!"

"No way. You saw the Heineken brewery security footage, how frantic he was searching for her. That was no act."

"That's true," he conceded. "Who else has pissed you off?"

"Two, the AIVD, and three, Europol." She finished the count on middle and ring fingers. "The AIVD was particularly dismissive. In response to my inquiries about Mila Dmitrieva, or Irina Frolova as the rumor mill has it, I basically got told to sit on my hands." She gave a head shake of incredulity. "And there was no response to my questions about Michael Barrett either."

Vos said, "They know plenty, and hiding behind the confidentiality curtain just confirms it. What about the American agencies?"

"Same brick walls, of course. It's like they don't want us to even try to find their citizens."

"If that was so, wouldn't the commissioner have been contacted by the spooks, told to back off? You just said he wants us to fire up, call the media in, that this incident was bad PR for Amsterdam."

De Kok chewed her bottom lip for a moment. "That I can't answer. Maybe the US secret services think they can clean it up while we stumble about in the dark."

Vos grunted. "Or they don't want to be seen to be exerting pressure on the police force of a sovereign nation?"

A sarcastic laugh escaped her lips. "As if!" She helped herself to a mint from a bowl on his desk. "No. I wouldn't be surprised if they've already got boots on the ground, people hunting for the missing pair."

"Then why should we bother?"

"Because the commissioner is accountable to the government. He's right to push us to get a result."

Vos sighed. "It *would* be a feather in our cap if we could solve it before the spies, wouldn't it?"

She nodded. "So what do we know for sure? Barrett's story checked out. And we spoke to Dmitrieva's boss. Apart from the waves of rumors, I can find nothing that contradicts their claimed identities."

Vos tapped a finger on the desk. "Precisely. Whenever something like this happens, the Internet always lights up with speculation like New Year's Eve."

"Yeah. There's even talk she was a whistle blower in the Russian Ministry of Finance, can you believe it?"

"Holy shit. That's a stretch." He cracked the knuckles on his left hand with loud pops. "Did someone talk to the hotel staff who checked Barrett out this morning?"

A nod accompanied by rose-knot lips. "Jansen and Bakker. Here's an odd detail about that. The guy on the desk said Barrett didn't take his and Dmitrieva's bags with him, said they'd be collected by a man called Abel Smits."

"That's bizarre."

"Very. This so-called Mr. Smits rocked up and collected the bags just before midday. Another weird thing. No cab was called to take Barrett to his next destination. He simply walked out the front door and took a left."

"In this crazy weather? Did he say where he was going?"

"No," she sighed. "And the concierge didn't ask."

"A pity. Whatever happened to curiosity?" He followed de Kok's lead and unwrapped a mint. "Did Bakker and Jansen at least get a look at the hotel's CCTV?"

She stood and hugged her chest. "Mysteriously, there was no footage for the last 24 hours. The hotel has a policy of wiping the videos once a week, but this time there was a glitch. Unreliable system or some such bullshit excuse."

"But they'd reset it for the next day, surely? There should be something of him checking out this morning."

"It seems not. The footage only started up again after this so-called Smits had been and gone. The officers did, however, see the computer log of Barrett's credit card payment."

Vos shook his head; de Kok winced as a sprinkling of dandruff flakes escaped his mane. "Dodgy. Let's get a warrant to trace any future transactions on that card."

"Already done it. And I've requested a warrant to search the room they stayed in, the entire hotel if necessary." She sat again. "I'm not letting go of this. I'm going ahead with a press conference first thing tomorrow if we haven't found them by then. And I'd like you to back me up. Someone out there knows something."

"I agree."

"In the meantime, you and I are taking a little drive down to Amsterdam Nieuw-West. Petrović's old boss runs his show from down there."

Vos dipped his eyebrows. "What? Isn't Koornstra in prison?"

"His son's taken the reins. That *was* Petrović on the video, I know it. I'm officially calling the ninety percent facial match as a hundred. It's the best we've got at this point."

Vos was already shrugging on his jacket. "Great idea. I was getting sick of those cold cases."

---

A BELL on a string jangled merrily as a stocky man in his early sixties opened the door. He had a sparse black-and-gray beard, head covered in a traditional Albanian skullcap. The man's apron was splattered pink and red, a knife gripped in his thick, hairy wrist. The fingers of both hands were streaked with blood. He smiled like he was greeting old friends. "Inspector de Kok! What can I do for you? I just closed, but I can sell you some nice lamb cutlets." He waved the carving knife casually, like it was an extension of his hand. "But get in quickly before you freeze to death."

The two officers stamped the snow off their shoes and followed the man inside, past a long glass display cabinet and into the rear section. The carcasses of slaughtered beasts hung on hooks, silently guarding a row of stainless steel benches not, de Kok mused, dissimilar to those in the morgue. The butcher rinsed off the knife and placed it on a magnetic strip alongside a number of other implements. He quickly washed and dried his hands, then turned, beckoning the detectives into a small lunch room abutting the work area.

"Please make it quick," he said, his initial bonhomie replaced with a sense of urgency. Rufat Duriqi was a Kosovan Albanian who'd migrated to the Netherlands in 2005. His Dutch was excellent. His product was so good, it wasn't only the ethnic layers of the community who shopped here. People flocked from far and wide to buy his meat. Which meant he got to practice his Dutch on a frequent and intensive basis. Most importantly, he was one of the inspector's most useful informants.

"What's the hurry?" said Vos. "You said you've just closed. And what about the lamb cutlets? My wife loves them."

"Actually, I sold out. And...ah...I need to give the shop a thorough clean. Someone from the health department's coming tomorrow to give the place the once-over." He laughed disingenuously.

"Give me a break, Rufat," said de Kok, running a finger over the small kitchen table then looking at her finger. "This is the cleanest butcher shop in the country. You could practically eat off the floor. A quick mop and you're done."

Without being asked, she moved to a sink, rinsed a chipped mug, filled an electric kettle from the faucet, and flicked on the switch.

"OK," he said, leaning against a wall. "I'll tell you the truth. I've got a meeting with someone soon. The person doesn't like the police very much. Hates them, in fact. No offense to you."

De Kok nodded. "I get it. We're not especially popular in this neighborhood."

"Who's coming?" said Vos, reaching into an overhead cupboard and pulling out a clean mug and a glass jar full of tea bags. "Like one yourself, Rufat?"

"No thanks."

Vos opened a battered old AEG fridge, pulled out a carton, and poured milk over a tea bag. "You didn't answer me. Who are you expecting?"

"A friend."

"Yeah, who hates cops. Thing is, we aren't leaving until you provide us with some information."

Duriqi shrugged. "You guys haven't been here for months. Why the sudden interest?"

De Kok pulled out her cell and showed Duriqi a still taken from the video of Petrović outside the Heineken brewery. "Not this guy coming to see you, is it?"

He took the phone, frowned and squinted, then shook his head, handing it back. "Never seen him."

She scrolled until she found better photos of Petrović, taken in good light. "What about this man?"

He didn't have to squint, and although he shook his head again, the gesture was a lot slower, without confidence. Even in the cool of the room, tiny beads of sweat formed on his forehead. "No idea."

She paused as the kettle whistled. Vos poured the water into both their cups, Duriqi looking on with twitching eyes which kept glancing at a clock on the wall. "That's a shame." She pulled up a chair, and Vos did the same. "We'll enjoy our hot drinks, then be on our way."

"Please," said the butcher, hands clasped entreatingly. "He'll be here any minute now. If he finds out I've had police drinking fucking tea in my shop, they'll smash my windows in."

De Kok knew Duriqi laundered money and allowed other dubious transactions to take place in the safety of the butchery. Drugs sometimes exchanged hands here. Low-level stuff, and she cut him some slack in return for information he heard through the grapevine.

"Don't worry," said Vos. "We came in an unmarked vehicle."

A pounding came on the front door. Loud and insistent. De Kok wondered whether Duriqi, whose face had turned the color of a ripening plum, was about to have a stroke. "Tell me who the man is in the photo and we go out the back door. Your friend won't even know we've been here."

The sweat was running thicker, dripping from the tip of his nose. "I think the man's name is Petrović."

"Where can we find him?" said de Kok. "A correct answer means we leave now."

Duriqi closed his eyes tightly, then looked up with nostrils flaring. "I don't know. He used to work for Big Pim Koornstra. What I hear, he's now on the payroll of a man called de Vries."

"Valentijn de Vries?"

He shook his head. "Don't recall a first name. But"—he inhaled deeply, his face contorting into a pleading expression—"I swear I have no idea where you can find either of them."

"Good enough." She tipped out the contents of her tea in the sink, rinsed the mug, and sat it upside down on the drying rack; Vos left his on the table. Hand on the back door, the inspector glanced back at Duriqi and winked. "We were never here."

Back at the car, Vos said, "What makes meat halal?" He took off his thick skiing-style gloves and shoved them in his coat pocket. The coat was a souvenir; a calf-length, heavy duty garment abandoned by a Russian suspect fleeing a raid on a meth lab three years ago. The guy got away because Vos had drunk too much coffee and left his observation post to take an urgent piss. The coat was a constant reminder to Vos to keep his mind on the game.

"Something to do with the rituals performed before they slaughter the animal, I think. Why do you ask?"

He shrugged. "My wife's got this thing against Muslims, but a lot of that meat looked damned fine. Next time we drop by, I think I'll—"

As Vos pressed the start button, an almighty boom echoed through the almost empty streets.

# TWENTY-ONE

"It started with the payment," Wessels said, fingers reaching for his crumpled packet of Marlboro. Ricci grabbed the lighter and pulled it toward him, flattening his palm over the top of it.

"You can have the next cigarette once you've finished the story," said Ricci, like a father telling his kid no dessert until the vegetables are eaten. "So talk."

"Crypto, back in 2019," Wessels sighed. "A simple job. Well, simple for me. Tech support for a guy named David Reeve on an international drugs bust. All kinds of agencies working together, but my brief was to help Reeve."

"Why you?" Ricci couldn't believe a guy as flaky as Wessels would be chosen for a job like that.

"I get results. I'd worked on ad hoc projects for the Israelis and the French intelligence agencies for a couple of years; they must have shared my name around. This was my first job for the Americans." He pronounced the last word like it was the proudest achievement of his life.

"If you can't redeem yourself, pal, I guarantee there won't be any more jobs offered to you." He gestured for the Dutchman to continue.

"I was tracking communications between Valentijn de Vries and his Moroccan suppliers in Antwerp." He allowed himself a flicker of a smile. "I had my sights locked on him in no time. We heard every phone call, intercepted every text. Read every email and supposedly encrypted chat. Stuff the Belgian cops were incapable of." He frowned. "Problem was, de Vries is a smart *klootzak*. A lot of the communications we intercepted were as fake as a three euro note; when the prosecutor presented our material in court, his lawyers managed to convince the judge *we* made it up." A shake of the head. "As far as brains go, you cannot beat a cunning lawyer over even the smartest scientist."

Ricci was growing impatient. "Get to the point or I toss these smokes in the trash."

"All right, all right." He drew a deep breath and let out a raspy cough. "A while ago I heard a whisper de Vries was getting involved in big drug shipments again. I don't give a flying fuck about that, but it got me thinking about the excitement of the 2019 operation. One train of thought led to another, and I got this weird urge to do a little digging on David Reeve. And the only way I could think of to do that was to try and track the crypto payment. I wasn't too confident of cracking it, but I had some ideas, plus a load of spare time." He rubbed his hands together slowly like he was washing them. "The company I do accounting tasks for cut down on my hours. Not good, because I started gambling more to make up for the loss in income." He slapped his forehead twice. "Dumbass!"

"Please," said Ricci. "Break it down for me, then we'll figure out what to do next."

"Right, yeah. So I started with the wallet that was used to pay me. Sparked my curiosity, if you know what I mean."

Ricci's stomach tightened. The heater hissed and popped, like it might give out at any second.

"I couldn't help myself; I tracked it," Wessels continued. "I started by checking the usual public sources—blockchain explorers and transaction histories. But then I dug into some of the darker, less visible stuff I still have access to: old accounts on dark web marketplaces, data from scraped forums, and open-source intel archives that track suspicious wallet activity."

"Make it make sense, for fuck's sake." The jargon was making Ricci's head spin.

"The wallet they used was part of a much bigger group. Addresses that routed through exchanges linked to private brokers. No Russian IPs either, which surprised me. But I found something else."

He reached into his coat and pulled out a notebook. Flipped pages with nicotine-yellow fingers. Stopped.

"One group—let's call it UmbroNet—kept popping up in weird corners: shut-down exchanges, old blogs, hidden forums on the dark web. I tracked a few wallet addresses. Most were dead ends. But one—just two steps from the one that paid me—was tied to a server used by scammers running fake travel sites."

Ricci raised an eyebrow. The language Wessels used was totally arcane, but he was starting to get the gist of it. "Is this what they call a phishing operation?"

"At first I thought it was just a scam, but it wasn't stealing info—it was spreading it. It sent confirmation emails to fake inboxes only someone monitoring would see. Hundreds of them. All Hotmail. Stuff like flight bookings, VPN renewals, delayed messages. But none of the links were real—they were just dummy sites."

Wessels licked his lips.

"Eventually, I got into one of the servers—someone had left an old key open by mistake. I thought it'd be full of junk, like spam bots or random files. But it was surprisingly neat. Organized mailboxes, no plain text stuff. One email stood out. Just one."

Ricci said nothing. Somewhere down the hallway, a door slammed, and raised voices bounced off walls.

"It referenced a man named Michael Barrett. Said he would be arriving in Amsterdam with his girlfriend. Provided a date. Mentioned he'd been in Belgium back in 2019 to take part in a covert operation. And that's when it clicked. Could Reeve be Barrett? My gut told me they were one and the same man."

Ricci felt a dull weight press against his chest. Fingers absently caressed his crucifix. If Wessels was right, the implications were explosive. Barrett was a huge asset whose identity was indeed compromised beyond all repair. And Dmitrieva—or Frolova or whoever she was—was in mortal danger. De Vries would now know the Russians wanted to get their revenge for her treasonous betrayal and would pay handsomely to have her turned over.

"Did you find out who sent the email?"

"No. There was no signature. No IP trail I could isolate. But there were some internal project tags. 'RZ/41-Dashlink' and 'Node Amsterdam SE-5.' Nothing else."

"And what did you do with this?"

"I stored it. Didn't tell anyone."

Ricci twisted his neck to the side. "You sure about that?"

Wessels faltered. His hands twitched. "I... I mentioned it to my wife. Stupid, I know." Another forehead slap. "I'd had way too much to drink that night, smoked a couple of fat reefers. Man, I was fucking wasted." He looked up with a thin smile. "I even won a few euros on the horses. I'd never been in a better mood. Wanted to share my joy with whoever was there. Just so happened to be Imke."

Ricci sensed the dam wall had broken. He slid the lighter across the table. In the blink of an eye, Wessels' face was obscured behind a sheet of smoke. "I got all cocky. Told her if I could crack that, there was nothing out of my reach. She kept asking about the name of the guy. I refused to tell her, but she kept nagging at me." His head dropped for a moment. "I'm weak. She's a pain in the ass, but no other woman has ever loved me until she came along. In the end, I just said the name to end the nagging. David Reeve." He began to speak louder. "Imke's got a good memory. She would have remembered the 2019 gig, how a mysterious driver had maimed one of de Vries' men." He scratched his head. "Sjaak, his name was."

"How the hell would she know that?"

"Because it was a huge court case in Brussels. A lot of shit that happens in Belgium is of major interest to us in the Netherlands, too, you know. We all watched the TV coverage. Much of the evidence was common knowledge." He sucked a cigarette so hard half the paper disappeared.

"But not the identity of the driver?"

A shake of the head. "No. That was withheld." He turned to look at snow striking a window, then fixed his gaze on Ricci. "But I knew it. And I...told my wife at the time. It was no secret this Sjaak was close to de Vries. There were even widespread rumors they were gay lovers. Imke must have contacted de Vries when I told her what I'd learned, asked for money in exchange for information on Reeve aka Barrett."

Ricci stared at him for a long moment. "I don't get it. If no one can find de Vries right now, how come your wife could?"

Wessels rubbed an eyebrow. "Who said no one can find him? He's got an official residence. Nice place somewhere near the Belgian border, I hear. I'd bet anything the cops have already gone there looking for him."

"Can you find this place?"

"Sure. But I guarantee he ain't there. Not if he's behind this. And everything points that way."

"Where could he be then? And how would your wife have gotten in touch with him? I don't suppose his number's publicly listed anywhere?"

"His address won't be widely known, that's true. The cops would know, though. And they would have visited his house as a formality, to let him know he's on their radar. Whether he was there or not..." He shrugged as he scratched the surface of the table with dirty nails. "If he'd been charged or arrested, believe me, we'd know about it by now."

"But your wife. She wouldn't have just turned up at his front door, would she?"

"No chance!" He bent his head back and laughed hollowly,

then snapped it forward again. "There are other ways." Wessels explained how half the city knew de Vries was a silent partner in a number of bars in the red light district. Imke could have dropped a message at one or all of them, said she had critical information about Sjaak. De Vries would have seized the chance to hear it, had her on the phone in a heartbeat.

"Could you do it? Find him, I mean?"

His lips drew taut. "Now that he's most likely hiding his tracks, I'd say it wouldn't be simple."

The obvious occurred to Ricci. "So where's Imke? Take me to her and I'll make her talk."

Wessels' head dropped. "She left two days after I...what's the English expression... spilled the beans." Wessels clicked his teeth. "Practically cleaned out our joint accounts. Left me with the bare minimum. She took her passport. Left a note." He laughed bitterly. "She's probably sipping cocktails in the Caribbean somewhere, one of the old Dutch colonies."

"What did the note say?"

"Good-bye, basically. Not to go looking for her. That my gambling and other habits had finally gotten to her and that she didn't love me anymore." The man appeared close to tears.

Ricci screwed up his eyes for a second.

"I know she's gone for good," Wessels said. "De Vries has bought her silence."

*Not necessarily,* thought Ricci. "Write down her full name, as it appears on her documents. I'll make some calls, see if we can track her down through passport control points."

"What for?" said Wessels. "To punish her? She won't know any more than I do."

Ricci fell silent as Wessels sent smoke rings toward the ceiling. Wessels was right. Now was not the time for retribution. It might never come for Imke: she'd seen an opportunity and grabbed it. Her soon-to-be ex-husband was the real guilty party here.

The silence between them stretched until a text message broke it. Judd from Moscow. No one had been surveilling Kumarin since he was of zero intelligence interest to the United States. He was sorry he couldn't help with the search for Ibishev.

Ricci stood and crossed the room. He opened a window slightly. The cold blew in, fierce and biting. Down in the park, a lone figure bundled up like an Eskimo was walking a dog. Mad to be out in this weather. Ricci's heart went out to the poor animal on the lead; it had no say in it. Man and beast wandered into a dark path and vanished into the thickly treed park.

He turned back to Wessels.

"You sure fucked up," he said.

"I know."

"You exposed an asset and now two people are in the firing line. You went looking in places you should have kept your damned nose out of." It was a lecture and hardly productive, but Ricci couldn't help himself.

Wessels didn't argue.

Ricci leaned on the windowsill. "But you're not useless to me. Not yet."

Wessels looked up.

"If you want to fix this," Ricci said, "you're going to pinpoint de Vries. Find everything connected to him. Properties. His registered residence first, then shell companies that might own other properties. A man like him would be careful to shield himself from the eyes of the tax department. Look for leases under false names. You find anything in the way of properties in the Netherlands, we go there, hit the streets, talk to people on the ground. Take it from there."

Wessels nodded slowly. "It'll take time."

"Then start now, dammit." He marched to the kitchen and turned on the electric kettle. "Consider this the biggest challenge of your miserable little life."

# TWENTY-TWO

The hood was ripped off her head in a rush of stale air and static. Having to wear it each time they moved her was starting to feel almost normal. The man who'd escorted her back to the room grunted something that sounded like 'good night' in English, but she couldn't be sure. She turned around; the door was already closing. Then the click as the key turned in the lock.

Back in the box.

The same room she'd woken up in. How long ago was it? She guessed at least thirty-six hours must have passed since they'd whisked her away from the brewery. The guess was a wild one, though. She could have been way off the mark.

They'd given her so little time to speak with Jacob on the video link. Just three lousy minutes, all to convey the illusion of compassion. She suspected it was nothing more than a leash-loosening exercise, designed to instill hope before reeling it back. A way to get Jacob to do as he was told and for her to stop whining.

She rubbed her arms and moved to the refuge of the bed. Although the room was warm enough, cold sweat clung to her back. She sat on the edge of the bed, elbows on knees, listening to the overwhelming silence.

Nothing to disturb it.

No hallway noise, no footsteps. Lots of internal sounds: blood pumping, auditory neurons firing, a slight ringing in her ears she knew was a form of temporary tinnitus.

Again she made a visual search for cameras and came up empty—but she *knew* they were watching. She cupped her hands to her mouth. "*Mudaki!* Assholes!"

Irina reached up to massage the base of her skull where the hood's seam had pressed hard. An enervating fatigue gripped her, a tacky mouth and dry tongue screaming for water. In the bathroom, she craned her neck under the faucet and drank greedily, splashed water on her face, then dabbed it dry with a hand towel.

A quick look in the mirror. *Those thirty-six hours have done damage that usually takes years.*

Sitting in the middle of the bed, she crossed her legs over into a kind of lotus position. She rested her wrists on the soft sheepskin boots, a touch of luxury amid the minimalism of the bare room. The yoga pose—*padmasana* in Sanskrit, she remembered—led her to reflect on Jacob's firm belief in a higher being. One she didn't share, but right now she wished she did. Any prayers she uttered would be pointless, because she was sure that if God existed, he would see straight through her insincerity.

Irina's eyes began to water, her glands producing extra tears to compensate for the lack of moisture in the air. She dabbed the little tears away with the back of her wrists, blinking against the stark light overhead. She wondered when it would be switched off to allow her to sleep. Hopefully soon. She'd never been able to sleep with a light on, no matter how exhausted she was. Having no control over the environment in this prison cell was sending her level of frustration into the red zone.

*Breathe, Irina. Don't think about these things. Don't think about anything.*

But what could she do *except* think?

Her stomach churned with hunger pangs: a meal of grilled chicken breast with steamed vegetables lay untouched on a steel tray by the door. The taller Arab, Youssef, had delivered it with a leering smile an hour—or maybe it was two—before the all-too-short conversation with Jacob. Also on the tray was a warm and flat bottle of Heineken, as promised by de Vries.

Not eating or drinking had been a matter of principle, but her mind was slowly changing. Seeing Jacob's face—the look of determination and optimism on it—was the clincher. There was uncertainty and anxiety in his eyes, but on balance, his unspoken positivity won out. For him to get her out alive, he'd need her to be as healthy as possible, physically and mentally. Starving herself out of stubbornness made no sense. Her stomach growled as saliva pooled in her mouth. Although the chicken was cold and the vegetables soggy, she tore into the food with gusto. The beer went down in seconds, followed by an almighty belch.

Dinner over, she took a leisurely shower, taking the time to pleasure herself using fingers and the handheld shower head. The hot water generated so much steam that any cameras would fail to capture what she was doing. It wasn't easy to reach a climax, but she got there, vivid thoughts of Jacob's tender lovemaking the mental aphrodisiac required to get her over the edge.

She turned off the faucet, water dripping from her body, and stood still, breathing through her mouth as her heart rate slowed.

Dressed and on the bed in the lotus position again, she decided to try a trick Jacob had taught her, a surprisingly effective way to combat insomnia. Count backwards from 300 in threes. Rarely did she get into the 100s and still be awake. But she'd always done it in the dark. With the overhead light blazing, she had little confidence the technique would work. If she could bring herself to orgasm with the threat of execution hanging over her head, maybe she would be able to drift off under the floodlight. Mind over matter.

One last look around before she closed her eyes. The bare walls closed in around her, the empty silence pressing down like a lead weight, punctuated by the sounds made inside her own body.

The room smelled faintly of the pine-scented liquid soap from the shower; she pretended she was deep inside in a forest.

She began the countdown. 300, 297, 294, 291, 288...

A new sound broke the spell.

She opened her eyes wide, heart racing.

The door opened with a slight creak. A figure stepped through. She turned her head slowly, not wanting to give him the satisfaction of seeing her flinch.

A man with an evil eye. And a disfigured ear. Her heart hit the floor.

*If only it was Jacob, someone from Skia, come to steal her back.*

She knew the man's name—Adlan Ibishev. She'd overheard the men refer to him both by first and last name. Indeed, the men casually bandied their names about. Since they were speaking Dutch, she'd had to concentrate hard to pick those names out in conversation. Ibishev had figured prominently in discussions at the swimming pool, when de Vries had staged the swimming race. From what she could gather from their body language, she had been put up as the prize. Thank God, unclaimed.

The name told her he was from the North Caucasus, likely a Chechen. He had swum his lungs out to win her, yet for some reason he declined to take advantage when de Vries gave the green light. Offered the bullshit excuse he was too tired. No, he had wanted to show the rest of the men he had discipline, no matter the temptation dangled before him. Stefan, one of the two men she guessed might be Serbs or Croats or Czechs, had offered his opinion that Ibishev had no morals. She prayed he was wrong.

Now, alone with her, he might try something.

Her stomach clenched in instinctive revulsion. There was something in the way he stood—too casual for a man on a job, too interested for someone following orders. He looked and acted like a man who had zero respect for women, who could rape without giving it a second thought.

He was broad-chested and ugly-handsome in the way boxers and brawlers sometimes were. Thick wrists, raw hands, neck resembling a coil of knotted rope. His dark eyes explored her like a scanner—not just assessing. Enjoying.

"I thought you'd be asleep," he said in Russian, the Chechen accent thick and unmistakable. "Or curled up on the bed, weeping."

Irina didn't answer. She retained her lotus pose and kept her eyes fixed on him, watching for the slightest signal he was about to make a move. She could not defeat him physically, but she would resist with every ounce of strength she possessed.

"I know you have a beautiful body under that track suit." His lips peeled back in a cat-like grin. "You looked wonderful tied to that chair in nothing but your panties and bra. Made me weak with desire."

It was all she could do to keep it together. She concentrated on not changing her blank expression, breathing steadily.

"No warm reunion with your American hero before he goes into battle tomorrow? He was very rude to me, you know. Mocked my appearance." He pointed to his ear. "I got this from destroying men much tougher than him. He's lucky Mr. de Vries held me back."

"What do you mean into battle?" *Are they forcing him to fight in their gang?*

"Just a figure of speech." He flicked invisible fluff from his sleeve. "He's got a tough task ahead of him."

"Your boss mentioned something about a painting. What did he mean?"

"Never you mind."

She ground her teeth to prevent herself spitting abuse at him, or literally spitting at him. Both options were tempting.

"You should have smiled more on that video call to your Romeo. You might've made his last look at you a little prettier."

Still she said nothing.

Ibishev chuckled in the back of his throat, ambling toward the blue wooden chair. He dragged it slightly with his foot, positioning it in the center of the room like it was his throne. Then he straddled it backward, arms draped over the backrest, watching her intently.

"Do you think this will end with a rescue? That someone's going to come for you? Break down the walls, kill the men, throw a jacket over your shoulders and say 'It's over, you're safe'?"

She turned her head slightly. "Do you always talk like a second-rate villain, or is this just for me? I'm not impressed either way."

He smiled, showing perfect white teeth. Not all of them were his.

"I like that," he said. "Mouthy. It makes this part more interesting."

"This part?" she echoed.

He held his hands apart. "The wait."

"The wait for what?"

He lowered his tone to a whisper. "The wait until we hand you over to someone else. The next stage in your adventure in the Netherlands." He frowned disingenuously. "It will be a terrible shame for me, not getting the chance to ravish you." He waved a hand dismissively. "But there are plenty of other whores in the world."

She could barely utter the words. "Hand me over? To *who*?"

Cracking a wedge of gnarled knuckles, he said, "I think you might be able to guess." He stroked his short beard. "You know, I did a short stint in the Russian army. One thing the sadistic drill sergeants taught me was that loving the Motherland is a requirement—no, the sacred duty—of every Russian citizen." He paused to dig something out from under his fingernail, flashing her a sideways glance. "Do you love the Motherland...Irina Frolova?"

"Wha...?" *This cannot be happening.*

"The stupid Dutch police thought they were doing the right thing, but they actually did you a disservice when they released photos of you. Asked the public for assistance. They thought it might lead them to us via a tipoff. Wrong. Instead, it had a most unfortunate side effect. People back in Moscow saw the pictures, people you don't want to meet...again." He clasped his hands together. "So we're just waiting for Barrett to steal the painting for Mr. de Vries before some friends of mine come to collect you. *And* your boyfriend. Because they recognized him, too. A dirty fucking spy." He rubbed his index and middle fingers against his thumb in the universal gesture for money. "The pair of you are worth more to President Putin than the priceless painting is to de Vries."

Blood rushed in her ears, bright spots danced before her eyes. *Keep bluffing.* "You're a fantasist. Your threats are empty words." Her nerves jangled as she tossed out the paper-thin bravado. She and Jacob had been rumbled—how did she ever imagine they wouldn't be after this?—and their fates were all but sealed. She refused to show him fear. While she was alive—while Jacob was alive—there was still a chance they would survive. "My name is Mila Dmitrieva."

He laughed. "Why are you even bothering to lie? It's pathetic. Oh dear, the color's drained from your beautiful face."

He let the words hang. The quiet stretched between them like a string about to snap.

Irina stood and crossed the room to the bathroom door, barely feeling her legs as they wobbled beneath her. She opened the door—not to go in, but to break his line of sight. It didn't work. He turned his body slightly, eyes following, soaking in the motion.

"I see the way you look at me," he said after a beat. "You're weighing up options. If you let me have my way with you, perhaps there's a chance I'll do you a favor, keep you out of harm's way."

"You don't see anything. You are the most repulsive man I have ever laid eyes on."

"You think I don't know what goes through men's minds when they see you?" he said, her insult bouncing off like water striking a hot frying pan. "That soft skin, that pretty anger, the gymnast's body. Even in that cheap tracksuit, you still look like something expensive and desirable."

She gripped the frame of the door. "If you think I'm scared of you—"

"You should be."

She turned and faced him fully now. "I'm not. I've been threatened by better men. And worse ones."

Ibishev's mouth twitched. "Then you understand what happens next."

She said nothing. Her face gave nothing away, like she'd taken a couple of Botox shots.

"I'm not here to hurt you," he said after a pause. "Not tonight."

"You're here to play mind games."

"No. To remind you. You're in a box. You don't get time. You don't get daylight. You get what we give you. If we give you warmth and something to eat, you feel grateful. If we give you silence, you fill the void with fear. If we give you someone to hate..."—he pointed at himself—"then maybe you last that little bit longer. Some people like having a face to hate."

Irina stepped back into the room. Her arms were trembling, fingers shaking.

"Most of all, I wanted to remind you how important it is to love the Motherland."

"You want to scare me? Then stop talking. Come closer."

That threw him off guard.

For a moment, he stared at her like he was mentally running a cost-benefit analysis of doing exactly that. He stood, the legs of the chair squeaking on the concrete floor.

She didn't move, just watched his fingers flexing by his sides. *Have I pushed him too far?*

He took one step toward her. Then another.

The tension between them stretched like piano wire.

He stopped, just outside her reach. She could see the rise and fall of his muscular chest, the gleam of sweat at his hairline, his

Adam's apple jut as he swallowed hard. He leaned slightly forward.

"You think you've won something, *suka*?" he murmured. "You think you have any power here?"

She leaned in too, very slightly. The 'bitch' slur was nothing compared to the thought of being handed back to the Russians. She'd keep it personal. "I think you're a lonely man with no moral compass."

Ibishev stared at her, and in that moment, something flickered behind his eyes. He turned and walked to the door, then paused. "This room," he said, "is your whole world now."

Then he was gone.

She stood still, her chest rising and falling in shallow, quick breaths. Her skin felt electric. Not from fear, although she was afraid—but from the sheer, exhausting effort of maintaining control.

She sat down on the bed, her hands shaking. But her eyes were dry.

He hadn't touched her.

And that, for now, was her victory.

# TWENTY-THREE

Irina didn't know how long she sat there, frozen, after the Chechen had gone.

Time was an abstract concept in this place with nothing to gauge its passage apart from her own body clock. Her circadian rhythm had been knocked out of kilter, rendering that body clock useless. The only thing to occupy her mind was the tangle of her random thoughts, the effort of willing her body to maintain normal temperature, pulse, respiratory rate and blood pressure, or as close to normal as possible.

She sat on the edge of the bed, arms wrapped tightly around her knees. Cold seemed to seep into her spine even though the floor was warmed by the coils set into the concrete.

No, it wasn't perception. It definitely seemed to be getting colder.

Her breath misted slightly in the air. Had they dropped the temperature on purpose? To unsettle her even more, signaling an invisible punishment for refusing to be afraid? Sadistic pricks.

Her thoughts kept circling back to Jacob's face on the laptop screen. His eyes. She couldn't stop staring at them for the duration of the call. There was more said by them than any of the few words he had spoken. There was guilt there, too. It wasn't his fault, and she would never see it that way. He had done more to improve her previously miserable life than she could ever have imagined. Saved her parents and her son. No, this was merely a hiccup on a long journey.

She shivered.

No mistake, it *was* getting colder, and fast. She lay on the floor, on her back, to get closer to the buried heating coils. Palms pressed to the concrete, she could tell that the temperature was definitely lower now than it had been when they'd first locked her away. Apart from her clothes and the bedding, the underfloor system appeared to be the only source of warmth.

She could warm her body through exercise, take another hot shower. She quickly checked that there was still hot water—there was.

The thick quilt made for an improvised exercise mat. She tossed it on the floor and stretched standing for a couple of minutes: shoulders, neck, hamstrings. Not sure what to do, since she always worked out with a trainer or Jacob bawling instructions and encouragement, she opted to play it by ear. This would be an improv session of her own invention. Chaos calisthenics.

She hit the deck and busted out a set of twenty burpees, focusing on maintaining form, then took a minute to get her breath back. A good start. Cross crunches next, elbows swinging around to touch opposite knees. Another short rest. She flipped over onto her stomach, grinding through thirty push-ups before her arms gave out. Her PB for push-ups was fifty in a row, but she cut herself slack due to the circumstances. Then back to the burpees, more crunches, culminating in a herculean effort to make another thirty push-ups. Hands on hips, she sucked in massive breaths. A third set and she called it quits.

What she really wanted was to run. Five or six miles. Long, slow, loping strides. To feel the cool wind in her face as it blew off the Hudson River. Then a leisurely coffee and bagel with lox and cream cheese at her favorite diner on West 42$^{nd}$ Street.

Physically drained from the burst of exercise, her brain, too, demanded a workout. Math problems, a crossword or jigsaw puzzle. A book, even pen and paper to write an escape plan on. Something!

An iPad would be the perfect medium to record her thoughts.

Eyes shut tight, she imagined herself presenting a gift.

Not a sentimental one. Not flowers or chocolates or jewelry. It wasn't even something you could touch. It was more valuable than any of that stuff. A tool.

When she got out of here, she would build something for Skia. Something custom. Something no one else in the world had.

A new programming language.

Not one of the clunky, bloated ones that everyone used. Not something built by a committee. This would be hers. Lean. Elegant. *Bespoke.* A language for people like Jacob who moved in shadows and couldn't afford to make mistakes. Something you could use wherever, whenever, with absolutely zero chance of being caught. Something so smart it could cover its own tracks, like sweeping snow back over your footprints.

She smiled faintly, fingers tracing imaginary lines of code on her thigh.

A name flashed in her mind's eye like a beacon. MIR—*Modular Intelligence Runtime.* In Russian, *mir* meant *peace.* That made her smile. Peace, born from this evil place.

She thought about the rules it would follow. Clean lines. Simple commands. The kind of system where every instruction meant something sharp. It would leave no traces on devices. Every time it ran, it would rewrite itself. Anyone who tried to open it would find only gibberish—like trying to read a book that rearranged its letters every second.

She pictured an agent, years from now, slipping MIR onto a USB stick the size of a match head. Plugging it into a hostile terminal. Watching it slip under the radar, gather what it needed, and vanish before anyone knew it had been there.

She sat up slowly and hugged her knees. Irina swore if she

survived she *would* create this language. *Built in captivity. Designed for freedom.*

She repeated the phrase in her head like a mantra.

And for the first time since she'd been taken, Irina felt like she was doing something useful again.

The plan to create the language now formed, she took a final shower, as hot as she dared, put on fresh underwear and the tracksuit, hopped under the covers, and closed her eyes.

300, 297, 294, 291...

She sat bolt upright.

His face—that sadistic leer—suddenly appeared in her subconscious, snapping her back from a semi-dreamlike state to full wakefulness.

Ibishev had unnerved her more than she cared to admit. Physically, he could intimidate most people. His mind games, though, were on another level.

Odd that he should show up just like that. Not to deliver food or drink or clean clothing, or even a message from de Vries. His only aim—fulfilled perfectly—was to intimidate her.

She compressed her lips tight. What was the point of it?

A head shake before she punched the pillow, fluffed it, and lay on her side in the fetal position. No. It had just been a bit of sport for him, an amusing diversion. He had simply come to mess with her head. To crush her spirit with the ultimate in bad news. A return to Russia was the worst possible fate—for her and for Jacob.

The clicking sound of footsteps rose above the silence.

The door opened, a soft light spilling into the room.

She sucked in a deep breath as relief washed over her. Not Ibishev this time. Stefan. Dressed casually in jeans and an old-school Rolling Stones T-shirt, the one with the iconic red mouth and tongue. Hair tousled, like he'd been roused from his sleep. His face bore no expression. He held something square and boxy in his hand.

A well-worn paperback. Dostoyevsky's *Crime and Punishment.*

"A small present to make up for the inconvenience." He spoke in Russian. Not with the fluency of the Chechen, but the accent was softer. He extended his arm; she snatched at the book, like a starving person offered a piece of bread. "Hey. Easy does it."

"This hardly makes up for what you've done to me," she snapped, although she cradled the book like it was a newborn baby. "Is it from de Vries?"

He shook his head. "No. From my countryman. He would have brought it himself, but he's busy making preparations for tomorrow. That's when Barrett has to do his job."

"Your countryman is Veselin?"

He nodded, head inclined to one side. "You know his name?"

"Yes. And yours, Stefan." She laughed. "You can't be that naïve."

"How?"

"I heard your exchanges by the swimming pool."

"We were speaking in Dutch the whole time. We were sure you don't understand it."

"Not a word. But your names don't change, do they, genius?"

He gave a knowing smile and nodded. "Of course. Veselin said he hopes reading will help you sleep."

"How did you know I wasn't sleeping?"

He touched the side of his nose.

"Was it Ibishev?" She placed the book on the bed and crossed her arms. With a defiant pout, she said, "I know his name, too. Even the Arabs. Did Ibishev say I was still awake?"

A furrow momentarily etched on Stefan's brow. "No, why would he?"

"Because he was just here, maybe fifteen minutes ago. He told me everything, that you were going to hand me over to the bloody Russians."

He laughed. "You don't have to worry about that. Mr. de Vries knows they're looking for you. In fact, it's probably common knowledge. Adlan was just doing what he likes to do best. Frighten people."

She sighed, fanning the pages of the novel. Without looking up, she said, "I don't believe him, and I don't believe you. The Russian government would pay a lot of money to have me back." She pointed at the cover of the book, landing on the word *punishment*. "To punish me. I can't believe de Vries hasn't tried to cut a deal."

He shrugged. "Believe it or not, Mr. de Vries is a rarity—a man of his word. He hates Barrett for what he did to his friend, but he made an agreement with Barrett, and he will stick to it." A barely audible chuckle, inclining his head toward the book by Irina's side. "Did you know the word for 'punishment' in Serbian is *kazn*?"

Irina swallowed hard. The word *kazn* in Russian, perversely, meant execution. "You just said de Vries wouldn't..."

He waved a hand in the air. "My idea of black humor. Don't worry; you're not going to be executed, and neither is Barrett." A pause. "Unless he fails, because that's a condition of the agreement. And like I told you, de Vries is a stickler for keeping to the terms." He paused again, longer his time, then said, "You'd better pray Barrett doesn't fail."

She picked up the book, opening it at the first page. She had a thought and looked up to ask Stefan to pass a message on, but he was gone.

She moved to the spot where he'd stood. Crouched. Listened.

Nothing.

She smiled, just faintly.

She sat again.

Waited.

Ten breaths in. Ten out.

Eventually, she propped the pillow against the wall and sat up to read. She hadn't read a physical book in bed in years, preferring e-readers. She started reading, her eyes devouring the words. Five pages in, unable to focus anymore, she dropped the book; it landed on the edge of the bed and fell to the floor.

Sleep, blessed sleep, had come. Restless, shallow, broken by phantom sounds and half-formed dreams. At some point, she thought she heard the sinister voice again—Ibishev—just beyond the wall. A low chuckle. Or maybe it was in her head.

When she finally woke, bathed in a light sweat, she had no idea how much time had passed.

The book was on the floor, splayed open with the spine facing up. When she was younger, leaving a book like that was considered a crime in her family. Dog-earing pages was also not acceptable. Only a bookmark or remembering the page number you'd finished on. Books were treasured items in a household that was broke most of the time and barely had any material possessions. In some ways, life is so much simpler when you have nothing to lose.

The air was appreciably warmer now, the heating turned back up again to a more civilized setting.

A fresh T-shirt, socks and panties had been laid across the end of the bed. A human touch.

But that wasn't the message.

The message was: *We control when you change. We decide when you're dirty, when you're clean.*

She rolled over and stood, ready to bolt into the bathroom. Nature was calling, loud and insistent. She cursed under her breath as the door opened again. Ibishev stood in the frame, arms at his sides.

"Did you bring the clothes?" she said, nodding at the small pile on the end of the bed.

"No. One of the Moroccans did. By the way, those two and I are on babysitting duty while you wait for Barrett to get the job done. We will take very good care of you." He inspected a fingernail, then through pursed lips said, "Personally, I don't fancy his chances. There's a very high risk he'll be caught, identified, arrested. Then the police will easily figure out why he suddenly fled the hotel—to commit a crime. And they'll possibly join the dots, realize that he made sure you were out of the way so he could get on with his law-breaking activities."

"Why are you here, spinning your bullshit?" she demanded. She picked up the novel and placed it close beside her, like she was a little girl and the book was a favorite teddy bear she couldn't stand to be parted from.

"This time? Just to pass on Mr. de Vries' best wishes. He'll be keeping a close eye on Barrett. I'll be notified when the job is done —successfully or otherwise—and then pass on the news to you." He leered for a second then added, "Personally, I hope he pulls it off. Much as I'd like to ravage you, show you what a real man can do, I don't like unwilling partners, and I can see you're in love with the American."

She stared at him. "Trying something new now? The good cop routine?"

He smiled. "No. I've never been good. But I am consistent. I do what my bosses tell me, which basically guarantees I get rewarded for my service and loyalty." He combed his beard with his fingers. "Sometimes I push the boundaries, can't help myself. But if I'm told to rein it in, I always do."

He stepped inside and walked toward the bed.

Irina's body tensed and her breath hitched, but she didn't move.

He stopped, one pace away.

"You're tougher than I first thought," he said. "I like that."

She squinted as she squarely fixed her gaze on him. "I hope you like disappointment too. Because this is going to end very badly for you."

He smiled again, wider this time. "I don't think so," he said. "Your man is in a locked room, very much like this one. To be honest, his is furnished a little more generously than yours."

If he was expecting her to rise to the bait, to complain about her conditions, he was mistaken. "That's nice," she said. "I'm glad for him."

"In a few hours, he'll be on his way to the target. Armed only with what he needs to get the job done, with three pairs of eyes glued to him every step of the way." He grabbed the blue chair and straddled it backwards as he had before, steepling his fingers. "And if he somehow gets away, or if he fucks it up, then your life will end. All of this guarantees his total compliance. So no, it will not end badly for me. Potentially, it can only end badly for you and Barrett." He winked, making her stomach roll. "You've got another twelve more hours in here, maybe more. I'll see you at least one more time before they return." He stood and walked out, the door shutting with a metallic clang and the click of the lock.

She must have been getting used to him, because he wasn't instilling fear in her anymore. Rather, she felt revulsion and loathing beyond anything she'd felt for a human being in her life.

Exhaustion embraced her. She started counting backwards again, only reaching the low 200s before she was fast asleep.

# TWENTY-FOUR

How many people had he rescued over the years? Spies, businessmen, diplomats, politicians, even a criminal or two. And yet none of those people mattered to him. They were names on a piece of paper, grandiose job titles, an operation to be carried out. Every last one of them could have all been executed before his eyes and Jacob Hunter would not have shed a tear, even if he had been physically capable of crying. On the flip side—a botched operation, the loss of innocent bystanders, a black check mark on his record, a reprimand from Fletcher or the president—those things would worry him much more than the death of an extraction target, someone who got mixed up in something they shouldn't have.

This was the only rescue mission that mattered to him. Irina. He had to save her. If he died in the attempt, too bad. As long as she was able to get herself free, back to her son, mom and dad, Jacob would die with a clean conscience, a rare luxury in his line of work. A clean soul? That was harder to argue. But a meaningful death—that he could get behind.

Despite an optimum level of motivation, the odds of saving her were stacked against him. It would take a lot more than just wanting it. All that *believe it to receive it, visualize it and it will happen, manifest to make your desires reality* crap, none of that would help. Jacob knew a bunch of rational, sane people who gave credence to these theories. He knew better. Valentijn de Vries held all the cards. In this situation—keeping two people isolated in separate locations—he was more powerful than the Russian SVR and FSB, the Cuban DI, even Jacob's own allies, the CIA and every other acronym agency known to mankind. In the hostage trade, power belonged to the one who had the body. De Vries had two.

And Jacob had none of the advantages he usually relied on. No outside support. No gear, no gadgets. He was the asset now. Alone.

On every other rescue mission Jacob had successfully completed—and that was all of them—he had been coming in from the outside. If not, he was a plant, embedded on the inside, trusted by enemies and enjoying freedom of movement, at least to a degree.

This time, he had nothing. No bargaining chips. No tricks to pull out of the bag. For this to go right, outside help *had* to come.

"Get your eyes back on the map," snapped Serb Two. "Learn it forwards and backwards. Your life and the life of your lady depend on it."

Jacob blinked and raised his head like he was surfacing from a daydream. "Right." He adjusted in his seat, elbows on the table, chin resting on the heel of his hand. The blueprint lay stretched beneath him—paper creased, corners curling. "Sorry." He smoothed out the plan, pretending he was studying it. In reality, every line, elevation, blind spot, and contour of the building and surroundings was already burned into his brain. It was a 3D model in his head. He could walk through it blindfolded. He could see the painting where it sat behind two feet of steel in the media room. He made an effort to appear engaged. "Hmm. Right. Yep. That wing's definitely tricky." He looked up at the man. "You know, my friend, I think I've just about memorized it all. What else is there I need to know?"

"Bullshit," Serb Two scoffed. "It's a complicated drawing. You have only spent one hour looking at it."

Jacob turned in his swivel chair, gestured at the plan. "Be my guest. Ask me anything about it."

"Bring it to me." Petrović sat behind the table, sipping tea from a delicate china cup. "Quickly now. It's getting late, and I want to get some sleep." Nostrils twitching, Serb Two carefully picked up the paper by the edges and transferred it to the kitchen table like he was carrying a delicate explosive device. Petrović placed spread-out fingers on the drawing and spun it around in order to view it right side up. He drilled a challenging look at Jacob. "OK, smartass. How many meters long is the main house?"

"Twenty-five and a half. And as a bonus, it's fourteen meters wide at its widest point. Horseshoe gravel driveway at the front, a small gate leading to a laneway out the back."

"Correct. However, that was an easy one. What..."

"Let me spare you the bother." Jacob smiled smugly. "Footprint of the ground level, or *begane grond* as it's written on the drawing, is 288 square meters. Total living space—575 square meters. There are four bedrooms upstairs, an internal staircase bang in the middle of the house. Overall plot size including gardens 4,632 square meters. A small shed and a structure for pool equipment, a greenhouse, as well as..."

"All well and good," said Petrović, his tone nevertheless implying he was impressed by Jacob's detailed grasp of the setting. "Let's get to the important stuff. Where is the painting and how do you get to it?"

"In a safe in the library-slash-media room to the rear right of the ground floor. If I'm entering the house via the front door, I first go through the front gate, which is flanked by a screening hedge. The plan doesn't tell me how high it is."

"It's high, as you will see shortly from photographs," said Serb Two. "Go on."

Jacob pretended he was reaching into his mind for the answer. "Lemme think. That's right, yes. A ten-meter pathway leads to a covered portico. A hallway takes you past a large kitchen, a WC and bathroom, then something generically labeled as a utilities room, into a large living room; in the far right corner is a door leading into a media room containing a large safe. I'm assuming that door will be locked, perhaps electronically."

"No. That one is a normal lock. Can you pick it?"

Jacob nodded. "Probably."

"You stumble at this point, it's game over." He dragged his thumb along his neck in a throat-slitting gesture.

"I won't stumble."

"Good. We will provide you with a lock-picking kit. What next?"

Jacob sipped water from a glass. "The Rembrandt is inside the safe, which I will blow open with a small amount of plastic explosive, as you mentioned before. You sure you can't open the lock remotely? That would increase the chance of success a hundredfold."

Serb Two, standing with hands on hips, was shaking his head. "No, you dumb shit. Why the hell do you think we're giving you the plastique?"

"I just wondered..."

"Don't wonder. Just do as we tell you. We have confirmed that the lock is not an electronic one." He let out a deep breath, the scent of double-mint gum reaching Jacob's nostrils. "All alarms and security will be knocked out. All you have to do is get the safe open, lift the painting, and get it out the back gate."

Petrović placed his cup on a saucer. "If van Eekhout wakes up and sees you, liquidate him. Understand?"

"Of course," said Jacob, harboring no intention of killing the man. "How do you want me to do it? A Glock would come in real handy. You giving me a gun?"

A burst of staccato laughter came from Serb Two. "Of course not, are you crazy? But I'm sure you will find something inside the house to get it done." He grinned pointedly. "And don't think about cutting any corners, showing him mercy if you have to off him. We will be watching you through the pin cam on your jacket, video and audio. We will see and hear everything you do. Got it?"

Jacob nodded. "Got it."

As promised, he was then furnished with a series of photographs of the exterior of the house, as well as interior shots taken by a realty company when the property was last on the market seven years ago. The house was gorgeous; something like that would be perfect for him, Irina, and Vova in Upstate New York. A dream to pin his hopes on. Photos memorized, he picked up the next item.

The fold-out map of the general area of Lasne, a village for rich folks on the outskirts of Brussels, instilled an initial burst of hope. The property was only about a forty-minute drive from the Belgian capital. The CIA station there was a regional coordination node, of strategic importance due to NATO being headquartered nearby and a host of other reasons. If he was able to neutralize the two Serbs and de Vries, send word back to whoever was guarding Irina that everything was peachy, no casualties, the painting had been recovered, perhaps they would let her go, and he could make his way to Brussels, then...

He gave himself an almighty mental head slap. That could not possibly succeed. For starters, whoever was watching Irina would expect to hear directly from de Vries or Petrović. A text message would not be enough for that crazy idea to work. Planning ahead like this was useless as long as Irina's exact location was unknown. His mind map told him where *he* was being kept, but so what? Irina could be miles away from there. He thought back to his college football days, how he often improvised his way to a touchdown when set plays broke down. He sucked his bottom lip. That's precisely how this was going to pan out—*play what's in front of you.*

Petrović stood slowly, rolling his shoulders. "Enough for tonight. I am satisfied you will be able to orient yourself in the strange environment."

"Just as well," said Serb Two. "Lift the painting and your lady might get to live yet."

"Can I get some sleep now?" said Jacob, making a show of rubbing his eyes.

"Do you think you can?" said Serb Two. Without waiting for a reply, he added, "If the excitement of what's coming is too much for you to relax properly, I can give you a pill."

"No thanks." He eyeballed both men in turn. "I'll sleep all right."

The men led him back to his quarters. At the door, Serb Two produced a small plastic bottle with a capsule inside. "In case you change your mind."

Jacob was alone again. The house was quiet now. He moved to the double-glazed window, pulled the curtains apart, cupped his hands on the glass, and stared out into a pitch-black night. In the daylight, you couldn't see much anyway, just some old barns, rolling meadows and a solid wall of forest.

Irina was out there. Somewhere. De Vries had said miles away, but that could be a lie. Perhaps she was close, in one of the outbuildings on the edge of the fields. He doubted it, though. Putting himself in de Vries' place, keeping them separated by a long distance made a lot of sense. His gut told him she was telling the truth when they spoke, that she wasn't being mistreated. Unfortunately, that would not save them all from the pain he would rain down upon them.

He sat at the writing desk by the window and realized his knees were shaking. No need to panic. Nervous system and muscle fatigue, anxiety. A highly trained operative, he was still a human being with human weaknesses. He poured a glass of water, drained it in two gulps, and filled it again. A hand fingered the bottle in his pants pocket. Take the pill or not? No. He'd keep it and have it analyzed later, out of sheer curiosity.

He extended his arms: no trembling. But it might start if he didn't sleep, maybe develop into a full-blown panic attack.

He stripped to his underwear and lay on his back on the

thickly carpeted floor. Even with his eyes shut, the overhead light penetrated his eyelids. He stood, flicked off the light, moved to the center of the room, and lay down again. He concentrated on the rise and fall of his chest. The old building whispered around him, pipes clicking in the walls.

He brought to mind the blueprint of van Eekhout's property, the photos. Let the patterns burn deep. Observed the flow of the house like it was a chessboard.

He pictured himself opening the door of the beautiful house in Lasne, stepping inside. Flashlight in one hand, he set off. Like in a first-person perspective video game, he made his way down the corridor with slow, deliberate steps. Searched everywhere until he found van Eekhout, sprawled naked on the floor of his bedroom, a peaceful look on his face as he snored. Back down the stairs, pick the lock, blow the safe, out the back door with the painting tucked under his arm and into the waiting van.

After that...?

God, what *would* happen after that? Could he trust de Vries at his word? Only a fool would believe a career criminal like him would act with integrity, honor the conditions of the deal. Jacob hoped against hope that he was wrong, that de Vries would surprise him.

Satisfied in his mind that he could pull off the heist, he began to meditate. Letting go of his thoughts had never been more challenging, the stakes never this high. And yet, somehow, he did.

Twenty minutes later and as relaxed as he figured he could possibly become, he recited the Lord's prayer in his head in English, Russian, and Spanish. At the final amen, he realized he was still much too agitated; no amount of meditating would put him to sleep. Damn it, he was tired. He figured out the problem—his heartrate was too high. He tried the classic 4-7-8 breathing technique: in for four seconds, hold for seven, exhale for eight. After a couple of minutes, his heart rate had fallen to a very respectable 59 bpm. Almost there. Time to apply the failsafe method.

300, 297, 294, 291, 288...

A pounding on the door jolted him into wakefulness. Heart thundering in his chest, he sat upright, hand subconsciously patting around the bed for a weapon that wasn't there. Where was he? The Mondrian Suites in Amsterdam. With Irina, on vacation.

*No...Sweet Jesus, no.*

In seconds, reality hit him in the head like a heavyweight's right hook.

He had no idea if he had slept for one minute or one hour or five hours, since he had no means at hand to measure the time; they had even taken his watch away. The door eased open, and a smiling Petrović stood in the threshold. "Time to move. As you Americans say, it's show time."

*Stay calm, don't show them any stress or anxiety.* In a steady, measured voice, Jacob said, "Close the door while I take a shower and get dressed."

Petrović took a stride inside, closing the door behind him. Finger jabbing, he snarled, "You do not dictate to us. Not a single demand, you get it?"

Back turned toward the Serb, Jacob said nothing as he strode to the adjoining ensuite.

"Did you hear me, Barrett?"

Jacob turned around. "I heard you." He grinned. "Want to come in and scrub my back for me?"

"Fuck you!" Petrović exited the room and slammed the door behind him. The smallest of victories, but a good start to what would undoubtedly be the toughest of days.

# TWENTY-FIVE

THEY WORKED IN SILENCE, SAVE FOR THE SOFT HUM OF the refrigerator and the bubbling of the coffee percolator. Two men, strangers until today, concentrating, searching for clues that didn't want to be found.

While Wessels did his arcane research, plugging away on dark web forums and various government databases that were supposed to be impenetrable, Ricci surfed the Internet, looking for leads on obscure paintings in the Netherlands. In no time at all, his mind was a confused mess. He stroked the silver cross that hung at his throat and prayed that the gambling addict would come through with the goods.

Ricci soon gave up the search. He was getting too many hits to make sense of it. He glanced at his watch: 02:37 a.m. More coffee was needed to keep sleep at bay. He also made one for Wessels, who grunted his thanks before Ricci flopped onto the couch, pressing his hands against his eyes.

The clock was against them. Compounding the time problem was the lack of weapons. A firefight loomed as an inevitable component of the rescue. Avoiding one would be ideal, but his gut told him that was wishful thinking. De Vries wouldn't be taken down by clever negotiation tactics; that was a given.

There was a limited range of armaments at the Hague embassy, but it was too far away and the pickings too slim. At almost 3 a.m., everyone that he needed to be at their post would be asleep. He didn't know if there were any decent weapons at the consulate; somehow he doubted it. He could wait until office hours, but that was more wasted time. Station Chief Tom Savage could earn his pay tonight; Ricci would call and demand he rustle up a couple of guns and whatever other goodies he could lay his hands on. Immediately.

He sat up, thumbs steady, about to enter the after-hours number he'd memorized, Savage's personal cell. He punched in three digits, then stopped, remembering something Tip Bradbury had said. There were numbers stored in the phone that might come in handy. He found the one he needed in seconds, listed under the obvious code name: *E. Jones — Tool Supplies*. The first attempt rang out with no voicemail service to leave a message. He rang again. An annoyed male voice answered, spitting something in Dutch. "*Weet je wel hoe laat het is, klootzak!*"

Ricci, assuming the guy was whining about being called in the dead of night, said in an even voice, "Sorry to disturb. I'm looking for the tool supplies guy. Is that you?"

"Who gave you this number?" the voice growled. "I was not told to expect a call. Is this a prank?"

Ricci didn't flinch. "I'm legit, don't worry. I'm calling from a suburb of Amsterdam. I need a couple of cordless drills and bits to go with them. Small ones that don't make too much noise and won't upset the neighbors. You've come highly recommended as my go-to man."

Silence. Then slow breathing. "You didn't answer my question. Who gave you the number?"

"Tom Savage."

A sigh of relief. "Correct answer. And who are you?"

"Marcello Ricci. You may have seen on the news that a couple of US citizens have gone missing. They are very important people, and I'm here to find them."

A pause, then what sounded like the rustling of papers. "What do you need exactly? I'm fresh out of cordless drills."

"A compact handgun. Suppressor to go with it. A simple, reliable model. I've got someone with me who I don't think has had a helluva lot of experience with weapons, so nothing flashy."

"Glock 19?"

"Perfect." Low recoil, easy to reload. He could teach Wessels how to load, cock, and fire it in five minutes.

"And for you?"

"Something bigger. A heavy-duty sidearm."

"Happy with a FNX Tactical 45?"

Ricci grinned. He'd spent a sunny day in the mountains of Sicily taking pot shots at beer bottles using one of those bad boys. Even with a six-pack of Peroni under his belt, the gun was so accurate he'd barely missed a target. "Also perfect. I'll take as many magazines as you can spare and I can carry. Subsonic rounds preferred. If you've got some gloves, ski masks, maybe a couple of flashlights, that would be great."

"I think I've got most of what you need. Not sure about the masks, though. Where are you right now?"

"Bijlmer."

A low whistle. "You're really trying to keep it classy. Good news, you're only twenty minutes' drive away from the pickup site."

"I'm not sure when we'll be leaving. Or where we're going. Could be fifteen minutes, could be a couple of hours."

"We?"

"Yeah, there's two of us. I can vouch for the other guy, a hundred percent."

The voice shifted, more professional now. "OK. I'll await confirmation. I'm located in Kockengen, west of the A2. OK to text the address to your number?"

"Fine."

"I'll send you the exact GPS coordinates, too."

Ricci heard a cigarette lighter sparking up on the other end.

"Please be discrete when you arrive. No party music, you got it?"

"Understood."

"Text me when you're leaving so I can get to the location and let you in." A pause. "When you arrive at the warehouse park, look for freight shed #4. Don't take any detours; it's fucking freezing. I don't want to be standing outside waiting longer than I have to."

"Fair enough. Payment?"

"Don't worry about it. I'll invoice Savage."

"See you in a little while." Ricci hung up.

Wessels was making indistinct noises as he stared at his laptop. Ricci walked to the desk and plucked the headphones from Wessels' head. The man jumped in his seat. "What the hell, man?"

"You said something just now?"

A head shake to accompany the look of displeasure. "I'm humming tunes to stay awake. You know how staring at pixels for hours on end can send a person to sleep? You don't want me to crash now, do you?"

Ricci shrugged an apology, relayed the conversation he'd just had with the 'tool supplier,' and reiterated the importance that Wessels come up with a lead.

"If you stop interrupting me, I might find it quicker, huh?" said Wessels, donning the headphones with a flourish.

Ricci grunted and glanced at the darkness outside the window, broken by the occasional light from surrounding buildings. He moved to the sill, looking down at the streets below. The vicious winter weather outside pressed hard against the sealed window—wind rattling glass, snow whipping across the streetlamps in tight spirals.

Wessels hadn't spoken in fifteen minutes. He sat hunched over his laptop, fingers dancing in a blur. Eyes darting left and right, up and down, like he'd taken too many uppers. A wadded-up Marlboro packet sat on the table beside him. The air was thick with acrid smoke and brewing coffee. Ricci poured one for himself, then refilled Wessels' mug.

Twenty minutes later, Ricci, frustrated, lifted up Wessels' left ear cushion. "You gonna find something soon, or are you just wasting everybody's time?"

Wessels didn't look up. His fingers stilled on the keyboard. Only the corner of his lip twitched. Then he said, "How many people has de Vries really loved in his life, you think?"

Ricci squinted. "What? How the hell would I know that!"

Wessels leaned back in his chair, its bolts cracking under the strain of his bulk. "A ruthless crook like him. Can't be too many. His ex-wife disappeared under mysterious circumstances, and apparently he didn't mourn for too long." He blinked, eyes bloodshot and ringed with purple. "You remember that guy, Sjaak Kuiper?"

"Yeah, you told me about him." Ricci frowned. "How Barrett ran him over in the car."

"Barrett. Reeve. Whoever you want to call him." Wessels rubbed both temples for a moment. "I think Kuiper is a more important figure in this whole mess than we might have first thought. A central figure, actually."

"And how did you come to that conclusion?" Ricci crossed his arms, wondering where the heck this was heading.

Wessels turned back to the laptop. "Listen. I was doing a bit of shell-company tracing last year for a tax job." He lit a cigarette, took a deep drag, and sipped coffee. "I kept seeing these patterns—recycled names, reused initials. But one name popped up more than once, and I never made the connection until now." He typed fast, mouth moving silently. "Just bringing it back up again."

"Something to do with this Sjaak Kuiper guy?" Ricci asked.

"Yep. Slightly altered. S. Kuiper Beheer B.V." He tapped off a collar of ash. "FYI, B.V. is roughly the Dutch equivalent of your American LLC."

"Could you fit any more acronyms in one sentence?"

"Here's another one," said Wessels, ignoring the aside. "Sjaak K. Logistiek. And one with an English-sounding name, S. Kuiper Property Management. Always a minor variation, like someone trying to be clever but not clever enough to be invisible."

Ricci stood behind him now, bending low and looking over his shoulder. Wessels tapped into a property registry tunneling through a VPN that geolocated him to Slovenia. Ricci watched as the list populated. "Four properties in total," said Wessels. "Three with buildings on them, one a vacant block of several hectares. All these addresses are in or near the Chaam Forests area, not far from the Belgian border. But most interesting, they're owned by the shell companies I just showed you."

"OK..."

Wessels wiped his nose with the back of his hand, leaving a tiny smudge of cigarette ash on his cheek. "And guess what else?"

Ricci shrugged. "Surprise me."

"One of the properties got a new leaseholder three months ago—a firm with no website, no phone number. Registered in Lithuania. You know how many Lithuanian companies de Vries used between 2019 and now?" He held up three fingers. "Same naming pattern. I double-checked. And the owner's address? A shell in Antwerp."

"This could be mere coincidence."

Wessels nodded hard, his gray curls bouncing. "Yes, it could. Except for one thing. Valentijn de Vries legitimately owns one property in his own name. Guess where?"

"Chaam Forests?"

"You got it." Wessels clapped his hands.

Ricci felt his heart starting to pump faster than it had since his last frantic romp with Carmela. "Holy shit. How far away is it?"

"About 130 km." Wessels looked up. "Tell me I'm not crazy."

Ricci's jaw flexed. "You're not." He grabbed his coat from the back of a chair. "We go."

"Hold on. You want to go now?"

"You want to sit here and wait for someone else to do the next bit? I've got news for you. There is no one else."

Wessels looked toward the window, ice blooming across the corners of the glass. "It's a 90-minute drive in good conditions. Snow's thick. Roads are crap right now."

"I didn't ask for a weather report." He cursed his stupidity under his breath. He should have seconded Bradbury. The BMW would have handled the conditions nicely.

"Know anyone around here whose car we could borrow?"

"Are you being serious now?" Wessels shook his head. "Of course not. This isn't my turf."

Ricci paced. "We need wheels, even if we have to carjack someone on the street."

"Wait," Wessels said, rising slowly. He grabbed his scarf, threw on his heavy coat, and buttoned it up tight. "No need for that. There's a side parking lot by Holendrecht hospital. Employees leave their cars there overnight. It's dark, barely watched. I'm guessing there'll be a wide range of vehicles to choose from."

"How far?"

"Only 15 minutes' walk from here. It's not going to be fun trudging through the snow, but there's no other way at this hour."

"You know your way around the hospital?"

Wessels nodded. "Imke had some 'women's issues' a while back. Got treated there. We traveled down from Volendam a couple of times."

"OK. We gotta go now." Ricci gave him a hard look. "Don't forget, I'm gonna show you how to use a Glock on the way to de Vries' country pad. Pray you don't need to use it. I need you focused in case you do."

"I'm focused," Wessels said, packing up his laptop and tucking it into a case, which in turn went into a shoulder bag. He forced a smile, uneven teeth ruined by years of nicotine. "This is me focused."

Ricci dug around in the cupboards, pulled out a steel thermos, and filled it with coffee from the pot. He placed the thermos and an assortment of highly processed snacks in his duffel bag. He turned to Wessels. "You got enough cigarettes? I don't want you going nuts having withdrawal."

"I wouldn't mind stopping at a gas station for more."

They stepped out onto the dark landing, Ricci locking the door behind them.

# TWENTY-SIX

WESSELS ZIPPED UP HIS PARKA AND CHECKED HIS phone. "Three-fifteen. If we push hard, we can be inside the hospital parking lot by three forty-five." He donned thick gloves and patted them together, making a show of how cold he was. As if anyone needed reminding.

Ricci pulled a black beanie low over his ears. "Just don't slip and break your leg."

"If I do, I'll make sure it happens on the grounds of the hospital." He gave a gritty smoker's cough. "Then you won't have so far to carry me to the doctor."

Ricci couldn't help grinning. The guy was a hopeless case, yet he liked him instinctively. Not that he intended to show it. He feigned a sarcastic laugh. "You like race horses, so you should know what happens to them when they go lame." He chambered a new round into an imaginary pump-action shotgun, pointed the barrel, and pulled the trigger. "Bang."

"Very funny."

They descended the nine floors to ground level via the fire stairs. Not out of a desire to improve fitness—the elevator was out of order. At the bottom, Wessels bent double and puffed like he'd just finished a triathlon. Ricci gritted his teeth and made a hand gesture. "No time for rest. Lead the way."

Head bent low against the biting wind, Ricci stayed a pace behind Wessels. The Dutchman struggled, lifting his legs like he had weights around his ankles. Pushing him was pointless: they'd get there when they got there.

Ricci looked over his shoulder, hoping to see a passing vehicle they could flag down. Take by force if necessary. Nothing but darkness and empty road. The grim Bijlmer apartment block behind them loomed like a brutalist tomb. Ice glittered on the sidewalk under streetlights. Snow barely fell now, but the air temperature chilled to the bone. Both men's breath came out in billowing clouds, their boots crunching over salt and grit.

Ten minutes in, Wessels pulled up. Hands on hips, he gasped, "We're lucky they treated the sidewalks near the hospital. Otherwise..."

Ricci's hand gripped Wessels' shoulder. "Enough stalling already." He gave the man a slight shove in the small of the back, eliciting a moan of protest. "Move!"

Another block down, Ricci said, "Listen to me, Bram. When this is over, you get out."

Wessels stopped, glancing at him sideways. "Out of what?"

"Whatever's left of this life you think you're living. You've got skills many would envy. But there's no control. No discipline."

"I've got nothing left to control." His eyes grew moist. "Imke's gone..."

"Fuck Imke," Ricci spat. "You're better off without her, man." *And she's better off without you*, he mused. "Get help with your addictions, for God's sake, before they destroy you."

Wessels didn't respond to the rebuke. He didn't need to. They both understood where that conversation ended. "Let's get a car," he said instead. "And then we go find that bastard's forest hideaway."

"Which one?"

"All of them."

The cold wind howled down the street behind them, but the two men didn't look back. By the time they made it to the rabbit warren of a hospital at Holendrecht, Wessels was limping from a cramp in his left calf. "There," he said, pointing. "That white Opel. What do you think? I can break into it easily if you can hot wire it."

"Too small. Not enough grunt for the conditions. Which my gut tells me could get even worse."

"Really? I think it's quite a good..."

Before he could finish, Ricci was already on the move. A chunky silver Toyota Hilux beside a concrete column had caught his eye. He looked back and beckoned. Wessels hobbled over. Ricci winked. "You're not the only one who knows how to break into cars. I need to do it more often than I'd like."

As expected, the hospital parking lot was totally deserted at this hour, snow packed hard between the rows of cars. Ricci moved with a purpose, no wasted motion, breath tight in his chest as he stepped between glinting bumpers and frost-veiled windshields. The Hilux sat beneath a lamp that still had hours to burn before sunrise. The vehicle was a diesel model, short cab.

He gave it one slow circle, checking for alarms. Nothing obvious. Seemed to be a standard factory build. Doors locked, of course.

He placed the duffel bag on the ground and unzipped it, pulling out a slim steel wedge and a stainless steel bypass knife. He slid the wedge into the upper corner of the driver's window, gave it a shallow wiggle until it bit the seal. Then the knife slipped in behind the weather strip, aimed at the control rod.

Tension.

Twist.

A soft click that sounded like a gunshot in the snow-muffled silence.

He opened the door slowly, willing the dome light not to activate. It blinked anyway. Not to worry; there was still no one around, apart from Wessels, standing sentry. Inside the cabin, it was all cold plastic and vinyl with the gift of sheepskin seat covers to warm their frozen asses. The faint aroma of cigarettes combatted the stronger pine scent from a little green cardboard tree dangling from the rearview mirror. He reached under the dash.

"Pass me the bag, Bram. Hurry up."

Wessels did as instructed before resuming his post, extra fidgety under a temporary smoking ban.

From deep in the bag, Ricci fished out a flathead screwdriver and a short length of stripped wire. With one hand he popped the ignition shroud, exposing the harness. Lots of wires. He ran his fingers down the column and found what he needed: power, starter, ignition.

Strip. Twist. Connect two wires. The dashboard flickered to life.

Touch two more—the starter buzzed.

He gave it two seconds, then separated the wires. The engine caught and settled into a smooth idle. Diesel fumes fogged the frigid air.

He shut the door, tossing the shroud into the passenger footwell. Windshield wipers sensed moisture, thudded once, and stopped. Ricci sat still for a second, holding his breath, fingers twitching on the wheel. No alarms went off. No cameras in this section of the lot. No one had seen them.

He shifted the gear selector to drive, took off the handbrake, and gently pressed on the gas pedal. The Hilux slid past a line of snow-covered cars and eased out onto the icy access road, its tires crunching softly on the gritted surface.

"Seatbelt," said Wessels with a head gesture. "Traffic cameras are everywhere in this city." He laughed. "Wouldn't want to get a fine, would you?"

"Shit," said Ricci. "You just reminded me." He leapt out of

the truck and attached a patch of black tape to the license plate, turning a C into an O. It was a crude effort and unlikely to pass close inspection, but he was planning on ditching the vehicle for another as soon as the chance arose. He jumped back into the truck, said a silent prayer, and eased out of the lot.

# TWENTY-SEVEN

The Hilux rolled out of suburban Holendrecht, its headlights cutting through the thick pre-dawn darkness. The streets were totally deserted, lined with silent buildings and skeletal trees. Small snowflakes drifted lazily across the windshield, melting on contact, the moisture activating the wipers. Ricci fussed with the control on the stalk, killing the automatic function. The heater was pumping air at maximum output, creating a toasty warmth.

Nearing Kockengen, the roads became tighter and less maintained. Ricci slowed down as snow piled along the shoulders and wind whipped across broad open fields. The village finally appeared, quiet and dusted white, nestled in the flat Dutch countryside.

"How far from here?" said Ricci. "I'm going to feel a lot more confident with a pistol under my jacket."

Wessels consulted the integrated GPS, fingers hovering over the screen. "Not far. Two rights, a sharp left, then straight for a hundred meters."

Minutes later, the Kockengen industrial park loomed, dark and quiet. "Look out for freight shed number four."

Wessels counted them off aloud as they slid past a line of

closed roller doors, a caged light above each one. "I think that's our man." He pointed at a thin figure in a knitted cap, thick scarf wound around his mouth.

"It's him," agreed Ricci. "No one else would be mad enough to be out at this hour."

The man hugged his body and stamped his feet like he was putting out an invisible camp fire. He went to light a cigarette but put it back in the packet as he spied the newcomers.

Ricci pulled the hood of his coat tighter and muttered a prayer under his breath as he rolled to a stop. The diesel engine clicked, cooling quickly in the freezing conditions. He ordered Wessels to remain in the vehicle, the Dutchman delighted to oblige.

Out of the car, the cold cut Ricci to the bone. All he could think of was getting this job done and wending his way back to Italy, into Carmela's lusty embrace. He approached the man, holding his gaze with each step. "You the tool man?"

A nod. "Follow me." The man worked a key into a padlock and hoisted up the roller door. Ricci frowned. Pretty lax security for a warehouse storing armaments. His worries evaporated when he saw a second door behind the first. To access it, tool man entered a complex sequence of numbers, at least ten. Ricci had no hope of logging the numbers in his mind since the man shielded the keypad with his body.

The inner door clicked and rolled to the left on smooth rails. Inside, fluorescent lights hummed to life, revealing a compact but meticulously organized storeroom. Black cases, hard plastic crates, a wall of pegboards holding tools and weapons like surgical instruments. Ricci stepped in on the heels of the tool man, grateful to be out of the weather, even if the space was far from warm.

Tool man gestured at a long metal workbench. "You wanted discreet and functional." He reached beneath and produced a matte-black Glock 19 Gen 5. "Compact. Reliable. Standard sights." He handed it over. Ricci checked the slide and racked it once.

Next came the FNX Tactical .45, a full-sized beast with threaded barrel and optics mount. "This one will get you out of most predicaments." The man grinned, then reached into a crate. Out came two suppressors, one for each pistol. "Not the quietest on the market, but they'll stop the neighbors from waking up and calling the cops."

He opened a smaller crate: boxes of 9mm and .45 ACP. "Hollow points. FMJ too, if you're expecting armor."

"I've got no idea what I'm expecting." Ricci nodded and holstered the Glock under his coat as the tool man slipped the FNX into a padded case. "Gloves?"

"Here." The man pulled out a pair of insulated tactical gloves. "Good for touchscreens. Kevlar weave. Won't save you from a sharp knife but better than protecting yourself with bare hands."

Tool man dragged a hard case off a low shelf and popped open the clasps. "For when it gets too dark to see." Inside, two pairs of night-vision binoculars nestled in packing foam.

Tool man zipped everything into a black duffel. "The bag's a bonus. There's also an assortment of other goodies in there. Unbreakable stainless steel cable ties, some basic first aid supplies. Best of luck with whatever it is you're doing."

Ricci nodded. "Thanks. I'm gonna need it." A firm handshake before the tool man escorted him to the exit.

Back outside, he tossed the duffel into the back seat and gestured for Wessels to roll down his window. "I'd like you to drive the rest of the way."

"Sure." Wessels climbed out, crushing a cigarette under his boot. "Get what you wanted?"

"More than I wanted."

"Can I see?"

"Later."

Wessels took the wheel, his mouth a thin line of concentration. Ricci had to know the guy could handle a vehicle in case he himself was incapacitated at any stage. The roads westward were still slick and empty of traffic. To Ricci's relief, the Dutchman drove with care and skill in the icy conditions. Kept to the speed limit, eyes never leaving the road apart from regular glances in the rearview mirror. Ricci rubbed his crucifix between thumb and forefinger, asking the Lord to give Wessels the strength and courage not to crumble under pressure.

---

THEY TRAVELED WEST, threading through empty industrial roads in the last dark hours of the night before swinging onto the A2 and heading due south. Twenty-seven minutes later, they stopped for a bite at a 24/7 BP station in Utrecht. Inside, Ricci found a booth with a clear view of the bowser apron and parking spots while Wessels bought two coffees, a couple of ham and cheese sandwiches, and three packs of cigarettes.

Ricci nodded thanks as the breakfast landed on the table. They ate and drank in silence until they'd consumed everything. Ricci scrunched up the wrapper from his sandwich, stuffing it inside the empty coffee cup. "We're switching to that Subaru Forester over there."

"What?" Wessels' eyebrows formed a steep V. "There's a man getting out of it. How...?"

"I'm going to lift it," said Ricci in a whisper. He gestured with his head at the approaching man. Late fifties, slight of build, he took slow and careful steps over the icy concrete. He hadn't bought any fuel. "He's coming in to buy something, maybe just to use the bathroom. Wait here. I'm going to bump into him and pick his pocket." He drew a deep breath. "Once I'm in the driver's seat, make your way out there as fast as you can without looking guilty or suspicious." He gave him a stern look. "And don't fall over."

"Wait. My gear's in the Hilux. Your bag. The weapons, too. We need to get that stuff out first." He squeezed Ricci's wrist. "Actually, are you sure this is a good idea? Perhaps we should keep the Toyota for now."

"Why?"

"The Hilux owner might not notice it's gone from the hospital lot and report it for hours. We steal this one, the owner's calling the police in minutes." He glanced up at the ceiling. "We're being watched, too."

A deep breath. Wessels had passed the test. "Yeah, you're right. We'll swap later." Ricci gave himself a mental fist pump. Wessels not only possessed a massive IQ, but it was matched by an ability to think clearly in stressful situations. Ricci glanced at his watch. Still plenty of time until the sun showed itself above the horizon. "Let's go." He was up on his feet, moving to the automatic glass doors, beanie pulled low over his eyes.

Wessels pulled over sharply only minutes from the service station and killed the engine.

"What's wrong?" said Ricci.

"Can I step outside for a smoke?" His eyes widened in hope. "It's been over an hour, man."

"No, you cannot. But since you stopped..." He ordered Wessels to reach over into the back seat and hand over the black duffel. "I'm going to show you how the pistol works. Better do it now than leave it too late."

Wessels gulped. "What if I fuck up in a crisis? Are you sure you trust me with a gun?"

"I'm gonna have to," Ricci said with a sigh. "But don't worry. After I've shown you, there's no chance you'll make a mistake."

Ricci reached into the duffel bag and withdrew the Glock 19, holding it flat across his palms.

Wessels stared at it, not blinking. "You sure I need to... I mean, I thought I'd be more of a behind-the-scenes man."

Ricci gave him a stern look. "There's no behind-the-scenes where we're going. If you're with me, you're part of the action."

He passed the gun over solemnly. Wessels held it delicately with his fingertips, as if it might explode in his face at any moment.

"The first and most important thing," Ricci said, calm but

firm, "is to treat it like it's always loaded. Always. That rule never changes."

Wessels grimaced as he nodded, holding it away from him like a stinking dead fish.

Ricci leaned over, grabbed his hands, and adjusted the grip. "No, this way." He stared into his eyes. "You right-handed?"

"Yes."

"OK. Right hand high, ensure a strong wrap-around. Your left hand acts as a support; keep your thumbs forward, don't cross 'em. Do that and you could lose a thumbnail or worse."

"Jesus Christ," Wessels muttered pitifully. "I'll never remember all of this."

"Damn straight you'll remember," Ricci rebuffed. "Feel the heft of it. You know what this bad boy is telling you?"

A head shake. "No idea."

"This is not just a weapon, Bram. It's your last word in an unwinnable argument."

Wessels glanced down, shifting his butt cheeks in his seat. "I don't like this one bit."

"You don't have to like it. You have to be competent with it. There's a difference."

Ricci reached over again and gently tapped the slide. "You pull, or *rack*, it back like this. Be firm, don't molly-coddle the damn thing. That action loads a round into the chamber. For now, it's empty. Just get a feel for it."

Wessels hesitated, then gave it a try. He was slow, his fingers shaky, but he got the slide all the way back and let it snap forward.

"Not the worst I've ever seen," Ricci said. "The safety's internal. You've got to keep your finger off the trigger until you're ready to shoot."

Wessels looked down at his finger resting against the frame. "Okay. Got it. I think."

Ricci reached for a spare magazine, pulled out a round, and held it up. "Nine millimeter shell. Small enough for a novice like you to control, powerful enough to stop someone in their tracks—if your aim is true."

He loaded the magazine halfway and showed him how it clicked into the grip. "Eject with the button when there's no rounds left. Reload with a fresh magazine fast. You'll have maybe ten seconds of clear thought in a situation. Less than that if you're scared."

"I'm already fucking scared!" Wessels said, his voice a little higher.

Ricci smiled thinly. "Excellent. A little bit of fear keeps you sharp. But scared with no training under your belt is totally useless. We'll stop for a spell before we get to the first of de Vries' properties. Somewhere nice and private in the woods. I'll take you through some basic drills. You'll practice loading and firing until you can do it with your eyes closed."

"What about the noise?"

"The suppressors will make sure no one hears us."

"Great," he said with zero enthusiasm.

"You'll be a crack shot in no time."

Wessels exhaled. "All right. I'll give it a try."

Ricci tousled Wessels' hair. "That's a good man." He took the Glock and gave it a final tap. "In a tight spot, this weapon could be the difference between you living and dying."

"How about avoiding tight spots altogether? How about that?"

Ricci laughed. "Drive on, Bram."

# TWENTY-EIGHT

The streets were still dark at 07:32 a.m., sunrise not due for another hour. The outside temperature was close to 14°F, icing-sugar snow dusting the roofs of houses and cars lining the street. Wessels drove slowly past the target address in Meierijstraat and parked around a corner at the end of the street. Killing the engine, he glanced at Ricci. "This can't possibly be it."

"Why not?" He agreed with Wessels but wanted to hear his reasoning.

"Too many neighbors. If one or both of the Americans are being held captive in this street, someone would have noticed."

"In theory, yes. But have you ever heard of Ariel Castro?"

"Cuban revolutionary?"

"No. Psychotic sex maniac. He held three women captive for more than a decade and abused them with impunity. One of them eventually escaped and alerted the authorities. The neighbors claimed ignorance." He gestured out the window. "In a quiet suburban street like this. There have been many such cases all around the world."

Wessels rubbed his chin. "Holy shit. Maybe they *are* in there?"

Ricci shook his head. "I doubt it. But let's check anyway. I wanna cross this one off the list before we move to the more likely candidates."

"How do you propose we do that?"

"We break in and see for ourselves."

"What if someone sees us? A jogger or something?"

"Act normal. Like we're out for a walk or something." Ricci gave the bridge of his nose a tired, lingering pinch. "FYI, I spotted a dome camera mounted at the front door of the target house, but don't panic when we get there. I reckon it's a dummy."

"You sure?"

"No. So make sure to keep that scarf over your face. I wouldn't want you fingered for a B&E."

"What's that in normal English?"

"I don't want the cops arresting you for burglary."

"Me either."

"Right." A quick caress of the cross. "You good to go, Bram?"

A slow nod and a frown that morphed into a nervous smile. "I guess."

"Follow me. If you do exactly as I say, everything will be all right."

Ricci walked quickly and confidently, bag of goodies slung over his shoulder. Wessels followed on his heels, loaded Glock tucked in his waistband and a tire lever in his left hand, most of it hidden up his sleeve. They had practiced with the pistol for twenty minutes in a forest clearing ten clicks from where they were now. Not a lot of time as far as training goes—and Ricci would be the first to admit he was a shitty instructor with little patience—but it was all they could manage given the circumstances. As it turned out, Wessels surprised Ricci, and himself, with his aptitude for all aspects of weapons handling. Loaded and shot the darned thing like a veteran. Wessels credited his good performance to the hundreds of hours he'd spent playing shoot-em-up games on his computer. However, it was one thing doing drills, entirely another when faced with real danger. Ricci prayed the danger would all come his way.

Ricci stilled his breathing as a woman approached with a German shepherd pup on a leash. The dog walked with small, mincing steps, obviously anxious to get the ordeal over with. The woman smiled and said a handful of rapid Dutch words that Ricci had no hope of understanding. He smiled back genially and waved while Wessels took up the slack, saying something that drew a nod of understanding from the woman before she continued on her way. *Well done, Bram.*

They reached the concrete wall at the front of the target house with no more interruptions. "We'll go around via the right side and try and get in through the back door." On the drive, Ricci had found the address and checked it out on Google Maps and Google Earth using satellite view. Basic layout for a small suburban home. Nothing obvious that could trip them up.

Ricci moved low and fast, close to the perimeter wall separating the house from the neighboring property. He scanned window lines and corners, flashlight beam narrowed down to a needle. Wessels followed slower, heavier, the tire lever bumping quietly against one thigh. Gravel crunched with every step; there was no avoiding it even under a layer of snow.

Inside, the house was dark: no night lights or digital displays glowing. Curtains drawn. No sounds coming from the interior.

Ricci gestured—*let's go right to the back.*

The rear of the house opened to a small courtyard with scattered pot plants. A security light came on, illuminating the solid back door, fitted with a small pet door. Wessels pointed to a security camera. "Another fake," whispered Ricci, nevertheless pulling his scarf up higher over his nose. "Probably to scare off undesirables."

"Like us?"

Ricci said nothing as he placed his duffel bag on the ground and fished around inside it with the flashlight in his mouth. He extracted a lock pick set. Lips compressed, he worked for thirty seconds, jigging and wriggling the tool until he heard the clean snap of the lock cylinder. He sent Wessels back around to the front, telling him to stand guard and hold any escapees there until he came back. Waving the Glock around should be enough to do the trick. If outnumbered and outgunned, he told him, don't be a hero and take evasive action. Wessels nodded, not exactly oozing confidence. Ricci pushed open the door and stepped in with his pistol up, slicing the small laundry room in sections with the flashlight beam.

A door sprang open to the left, there was a click, and light flooded the space. A piercing scream shattered the silence. Ricci spun to the source of the sound, weapon pointing.

An elderly woman in a floral dressing gown pressed a hand to her mouth, eyes agog. Seconds later, a bent-over, silver-haired man appeared on the scene, shouldering his way in front of the woman to shield her from the intruder. Bare-chested with ribs like a washboard, he brandished a glinting, long-bladed kitchen knife. The man hollered a warning in hissing Dutch that sounded like a broken air hose. Ricci had to hand it to the old boy; he stood his ground magnificently, protecting his wife and his home like a champion.

"Jesus," Ricci growled as he flicked off the flashlight and returned the FNX to his shoulder holster, keeping his coat slightly open. "Keep the noise down, will ya."

"Get out of my house!" the man yelled in English, eyes darting from the weapon to Ricci. "I won't hesitate to stab you."

Ricci made a hands-down calming gesture. "No need for that."

"Who the hell are you?" he demanded, snaking an arm around the trembling woman. "What do you want?" He added in a raspy voice, "We don't have any cash in the house. You're wasting your time."

"I'm not here for your money. I need an address to go with a name. Valentijn de Vries. Do you know it?"

The man's legs wobbled for a moment. "No. Why would we?"

"He owns this house." Ricci pulled his coat aside wider, offering a good look at the weapon. "I'm not leaving until you tell me where he is."

The man shook his head hard. "I can't help you. We rent the house from a real estate company." He swallowed and said through dry lips, "We've lived here for five years now. Never heard of the name you mentioned." He jutted out his chin. "I suggest you try the property manager. Want the number?"

The real estate office wouldn't open for hours yet. Still, knowledge is power, and if all else failed, Ricci might be able to menace loose some information. It was a long shot, since it was highly unlikely the property manager would be able to connect the shell company owner to de Vries. "Sure."

The man whispered to his wife, who waddled off and returned in under a minute with a business card. She held it out in a shaky hand, and Ricci pocketed it. "Thanks." He wasn't quite done. He lowered his voice a fraction, injecting a note of calm. "You haven't seen anyone unusual around here lately? Strange people coming and going? No weird shit going on at the neighbors'?"

"No," the man said quickly. "This is a boring street in a quiet village where nothing ever happens."

*Until Bram and I showed up*, Ricci thought. He leaned forward slightly, narrowing an eye. "Tell no one about this, OK? No police. No phone calls. If I hear you blabbed, I'll be back." He patted the gun under his coat. "Your knife is useless against this. It will blow a hole in your head so big no one will be able to identify you. Got it?"

A nod of understanding.

Ricci stared unblinking into the man's eyes, then gave his lady the same treatment. He turned, closing the door quietly.

Wessels was waiting by the front gate, pacing back and forth to keep warm, hands buried deep in his coat pockets. "About time you got back. Find anything out?" he asked as Ricci approached wearing a blank expression.

"The residents know nothing. Let's go. I'm driving this time." Ricci tossed his gear in the back seat, climbed in the front, and slammed the door behind him.

"What happened in there?" Wessels asked, placing the tire lever in the footwell.

"A harmless old couple," Ricci said. "I scared the hell out of them. If they knew anything about de Vries, they would have said."

Wessels laughed, coughed, and laughed again. "You scaring pensioners for kicks?"

Ricci didn't respond. His jaw was set, his eyes already on the road.

Wessels kept chuckling. "Did you wave the gun at them?"

Ricci buckled up and started the engine. "I told them not to make a fuss. That's all."

"God help us. You probably made the old guy shit himself."

Ricci's hands tightened on the wheel. He turned to Wessels and said, "To be honest, he was a darned sight braver than you."

Wessels twisted to look at Ricci square on. "While you were in there, a lot of stuff went through my mind. I've fucked up big time. In many ways, this is all my fault. I'm going to do whatever I can to make things right."

Ricci dropped his chin, turning his head to side-eye Wessels. "Something tells me I can believe it."

"I promise I won't let you down," he said solemnly. "Whatever it takes."

Ricci clasped his hands together and closed his eyes. Said the words silently in his head. *"Forgive me, Father. I frightened good, innocent people. I wish it were otherwise, but it cannot be undone. But I did what was needed. Let them have no fear now. Let them be safe. And let Bram be the man he needs to be while you watch over him and keep him safe, too. Amen."*

Ricci cracked the passenger side window and nodded at Wessels. "Have a cigarette if you like."

"Actually, no."

"What? It's been over an hour. You must be dying for one."

He shrugged. "I'll wait. And I know it's not enjoyable for you."

Ricci smiled to himself. The man was serious about stepping up.

# TWENTY-NINE

National Police Commissioner Felix Vermeulen regarded Inspector de Kok with a measured gaze. His blue tie hung loosely at his throat, the starched collar of his white shirt undone. A vein throbbed gently at his temple. Two years away from retirement, he'd managed to retain a youthful appearance.

De Kok sat with one leg crossed over the other. The commissioner's office was a place she visited often. Her boss was renowned for his approachability. Usually, the atmosphere was more relaxed than it was this morning.

The blinds were half closed, the window panes unable to completely shut out the noise from the street below: the faint wail of sirens in the distance, car doors slamming, people chatting. She had barely touched her coffee, which now grew cold on the table. Daan Vos sat beside her, curious eyes following the conversation.

"You prepared for this?" said Vermeulen. He stood, hands clasped behind his back, and ambled to the window. A hand parted the blinds for a moment before he resumed his seat. "The vultures are arriving en masse. Plenty are already here, waiting in the media room."

"Don't sound surprised." De Kok scrolled through a tablet. "You pushed for this press conference, sir."

"Indeed, I did. They're still vultures."

Vos chuckled. "A necessary evil."

"So," said Vermeulen, switching his gaze from Vos back to de Kok. "You ready to face them?"

"Yes. We've done everything we can with the evidence we've collected." Her face remained impassive. "I'm not going to hide our findings from the media."

The commissioner nodded. "They'll be pushing hard about the online speculation. That Mila Dmitrieva is an imposter. That her boyfriend, now also missing, is a fraud." He paused. "How are you going to respond to that?"

She took a deep breath. "How do you suggest I respond? The Internet is awash with dubious information. A lot of it very convincing. People believe all sorts of rubbish."

Vos said, "Easy to deal with. We live in an age of so-called misinformation and disinformation. Created by humans and bots alike. AI too. It's impossible to keep up with things. Blame that."

"Daan has an excellent point, sir. And since the various security agencies aren't being forthcoming with help, I can easily frame all the chatter as misdirection."

Vermeulen tapped the arms of his glasses on his desk. "Good. It's not our job to decipher this stuff. It's our job to do everything we can to find these missing people. To maintain the reputation of Amsterdam as one of the world's safest cities." He opened and closed a silver cigarette case, then tucked it into his pants pocket. "I'm pleased your press statement omitted the rumors. We need to stick to facts. Not stir speculation that Dmitrieva is a whistleblower against the Russian government. That Barrett's some kind of spy. We don't need to be getting ourselves involved in diplomatic scandals."

"Sir," ventured Vos. "Won't you get raked over the coals by the government for organizing the press conference? I mean, weren't you warned to drop it?"

He set his mouth grimly. "I have to follow the law. Not the

demands of politicians who come and go with each election. Or faceless bureaucrats."

"We also have to follow the law," said de Kok with a smile directed at Vos. She had always admired Vermeulen for his unbending integrity, seeing him as an example to the entire force. "As far as our investigation goes, Mila Dmitrieva and Michael Barrett are who they say they are. Who their documents say they are. Anything else is mere noise until we get undisputed facts."

"The CIA and Europol don't send 'stand down' memos over noise," said Vos.

"No, they don't," said de Kok. "But as the commissioner just pointed out, their memos mean squat to us."

Vermeulen coughed into his fist. "Time to move, Eva. I want you to give them deflection when they ask the inevitable questions."

"Yes, sir. I can do deflection without raising a sweat."

"But make sure you get the message to the public that we need their help. I believe someone out there knows where they are."

"Any updates on the credit card trace?" said Vos.

"No," admitted de Kok. "But I wasn't expecting a hit on that." She looked at the commissioner. "Daan and I are tracking the Petrović lead. That explosion in Nieuw-West tells me we might be getting close."

"I thought that was a gas explosion?" said the Commissioner.

"No, sir. A device exploded in the trunk of a car. Forensics are looking into it. I believe it could be linked to Petrović, and by association, de Vries. My instincts tell me those men are the key."

"Any progress with questioning de Vries?" said the commissioner.

She shrugged. "He's a slippery bastard. So far he's managed to avoid us. But if Petrović is working for him and we can find out where he's holed up..."

Vos voiced the question no one so far had dared ask. "And if she's really Frolova and Barrett's not who he claims to be? What then?"

The commissioner stood and donned his dress jacket. "Then they're both in a lot more danger than we thought. And we're probably already too late. Come on. Let's face the vultures." He paused for a moment. "Eva, should we have another crack at flushing out de Vries? I can get a warrant to raid his estate based on the Petrović angle. Sending in the DSI might shake something loose."

De Kok and Vos stood. She said, "I'm in favor."

"Me too," said Vos. "What else have we got?"

---

THE MEDIA ROOM at police headquarters buzzed with murmurs and the flicker of camera flashes. TV camera operators lined the back wall, the red lights of their equipment blinking like sentinels. Microphones bearing the logos of a variety of media outlets—local and international—clustered at the podium in a tangle.

De Kok stepped up beside Vos. They wore expressions of quiet control, but their rigid posture betrayed the weight they were carrying.

"Good evening," de Kok began, her voice steady. She spoke in English due to the large number of foreign journalists present. "As you know, we are investigating the disappearance of two individuals: Mila Dmitrieva and Michael Barrett. Ms. Dmitrieva was last seen near the Heineken brewery two days ago before being abducted by a group of men in a black VW Touareg. There has been no contact made by the kidnappers, no ransom demanded. Mr. Barrett, who was helping us with our investigation, checked out of the Mondrian Suites on Friday morning and has not been seen or heard from since. We are extremely worried for their safety. Please, take a moment to watch this." She turned and pressed a clicker to start a montage of video material on a large screen behind her.

When the clip ended, a female reporter blurted out, "Is it true

Mila Dmitrieva is actually Irina Frolova, a Russian whistleblower?"

De Kok raised a hand. "Please. No questions until I've finished speaking." She described all efforts undertaken thus far to track down the victims, emphasizing that the police were hopeful for a breakthrough soon. She then altered course. "You'll be aware that there has been a lot of speculation online. We cannot rule out that much of this is misinformation created to put us off the scent of the real kidnappers. At this stage of the investigation, we have no evidence that contradicts the identities of Mila Dmitrieva and Michael Barrett as stated in their travel documents."

Another journalist shouted, "So you're not denying she's wanted by the Russian government for treason?"

"Did you even hear what I just said?" De Kok glared at the reporter. "We're treating this as a missing persons case until facts tell us otherwise."

A third journalist chimed in. "The American State Department and Europol have both refused to respond to my questions about your investigation. Have the National Police been ordered to back off?"

Vermeulen leaned forward into the microphone. "We're continuing our investigation with full legal authority. The police act independently and do not bend to the demands of third parties. Not on my watch."

De Kok smiled, her heart filling with pride. She could only hope Vermeulen's successor showed even half of his backbone.

The same journalist pressed on. "You said no one had claimed responsibility or made a ransom demand. This is most unusual, is it not?"

"Highly unusual," agreed de Kok. "Which is why were are so keen on appealing for the public's help. If you saw anything unusual near the Heineken brewery, the Mondrian Suites hotel, or in Amsterdam Nieuw-West in the past 72 hours, please come forward. Someone out there knows something. We guarantee complete confidentiality and your anonymity." She read out phone numbers and email addresses.

"What about a man named Petrović?" a new voice asked. "Isn't he one of the men in the video you just showed us?"

De Kok didn't flinch. "Again, we're exploring all leads." She suddenly decided to go off script. "However, facial recognition software indicates that the man you mentioned could indeed be Veselin Petrović."

The room erupted, voices overlapping and drowning each other out. De Kok raised a hand to silence the throng. "That's all for now," she said firmly. "Updates will follow as appropriate."

The commissioner and the two detectives made their way to a side exit. The thick door muffled the noise of the frustrated media left behind to make sense of what they'd heard. Vermeulen headed for another appointment, de Kok and Vos making their way back to the situation room upstairs.

"You handled that superbly, Eva," said Vos.

"Not so hard. They went exactly in the direction we expected."

"They're vultures, just like the commissioner said." He stopped on the stairwell. "But they're right to circle. If this really is about Frolova..."

"Then we're chasing ghosts we're never going to catch."

He sighed. "We gotta go through the motions, though, don't we?"

"Yes." She paused, twisting her lips. "That explosion in Nieuw-West gives me a flicker of hope. Too much of a coincidence that happening so close to Duriqi's shop just when we happened to be there. Something tells me that butcher knows more than he's willing to admit."

"Should we stake him out?"

"We've got nothing else."

They walked the rest of the way in silence.

# THIRTY

IRINA PULLED THE QUILT OVER HER HEAD, TUCKING HER elbows and knees tightly against her body. Damn, it was cold—even under the blanket, even in a tracksuit and boots. She touched the tip of her nose. It felt like a block of ice. Why were they torturing her like this? A touch of defiance didn't warrant turning off the heating. This was too much. Probably the Chechen's doing. He'd be coming with an ultimatum: give herself to him or suffer the cold. She would rather die of hypothermia than cave in.

A knock came at the door. She pulled the covers down, exposing just her face from the chin up. What was that? They'd never bothered knocking before.

Had she imagined it?

Thump, thump, thump.

No, it was real.

"Who is it?"

No reply. But the door opened.

The shorter Arab—Khadir—stood on the threshold, arms folded, observing.

"What the hell do you want?"

He edged closer. "We've had some trouble with the heating. The cold weather has led to a breakdown." The guttural edge of his accent only deepened his menace. "A temporary inconvenience, I'm glad to say." His thin lips curled into a sadistic smile that belied his words. "An airlock in the circuit."

"Airlock?" She sat up in bed, pulling the quilt around her like a tent. "You're lying. There's no radiator in here. The floor is—"

"It's a hydronic system. Relies on water flow. I won't bore you with the details, but we've called a specialist. It should be fixed within the next two hours."

"Two hours? I'll freeze to death before then."

"Possible. It's minus twelve outside, probably zero in here now." He took another step forward. "Let me get under the covers with you. Our bodies will keep each other warm until the system is running again."

Her eyebrows shot halfway up her forehead. "No chance, *mudak*. You must be insane."

Khadir rocked his head back and let out a laugh that turned Irina's stomach. "I like your spirit. But..." He glanced over both shoulders in a mock display of caution. "Did you know I've already been... what's the word... intimate with your boyfriend?"

A knot formed in her stomach. Her breathing quickened, steam forming in the air before her eyes. Instinctively, she ducked back under the quilt and curled into the fetal position. She wouldn't respond to his provocation.

She felt the bed sag as he sat beside her. She stayed still, focusing on her breathing. A hand began rubbing her hip.

"Want to know what happened?"

She said nothing. Would say nothing.

"I stuck my finger up his ass to make sure he wasn't smuggling anything." He paused. She could feel him shifting on the bed, his hand now rubbing halfway down her outer thigh. "You know, I could tell he quite liked it. I know I did."

The urge to scream, to lash out, overwhelmed her. She knew he was trying to provoke her. She would not react.

"And since I like to be thorough, I feel it's my duty to perform the same security measure on you. Can't be too careful with Russian spies."

She swallowed hard, her heart hammering against her chest like it wanted out.

"But first, I'm going to take off my clothes and get under the covers with you. If you want to avoid the finger, you're going to do something for me, okay?"

The mattress lifted an inch as he stood. She heard the sound of a zipper, then imagined he was unbuckling his belt. The bastard wasn't bluffing. But what could she do? Tears ran down her cheeks as she waited for the next horror.

She twisted her neck as Khadir whisked the quilt off, exposing her to the cold—and to him. Naked. Thankfully not fully aroused, but massively endowed. The potential damage that thing could do in its erect state was terrifying. She grabbed a pillow and buried her face in it but not before catching sight of the blue rubber glove.

Jesus. This maniac—ten times worse than Ibishev—wasn't bluffing.

Eyes squeezed shut, she felt the clammy rubber touch her face. She screamed into the pillow, turned, and spat at him.

The door opened.

Ibishev.

*No. Please—not the two of them.*

The Chechen barked something in Dutch. She didn't understand the words but got the sentiment. Ibishev was furious. He switched to English, perhaps for her benefit.

"Put your clothes back on. For God's sake, what do you think you're doing?"

Irina didn't trust Ibishev, but his timely appearance had spared her something horrific. Though it was likely temporary—especially if he was serious about handing her back to the Russians.

She dared to look up now, blinking through a film of tears.

The fierce expression on Ibishev's face was matched by one of fear on Khadir's. The Moroccan scrabbled to get dressed, the rubber glove looking ridiculous as he fumbled with his clothes. He mumbled something in Dutch, but Ibishev wasn't having it.

"Are you stupid? I know she didn't agree to this. I was watching the feed, you moron."

More Dutch from Khadir.

"I don't care what you thought. This is a professional operation. I'll be reporting this to de Vries, and you'll be looking for another job. That's if he doesn't decide to kill you."

Ibishev held the door open as a chastened Khadir slunk out, head bowed. The Chechen followed, slamming the door behind them.

Within ten minutes, the room was so warm she had to peel off the tracksuit and sheepskin boots. Irina kicked away the quilt, covered herself with just a sheet, and closed her eyes.

Within a minute, she had fallen into a deep sleep.

# THIRTY-ONE

SNOW HAD STOPPED FALLING COMPLETELY NOW, BUT the dash showed it was still bitterly cold outside. Black trees stood out like shadows against a gray background. The wind was building, bare branches swaying eerily. It would be light enough to see without aids in another thirty minutes or so. They'd been traveling in silence, punctuated only by Wessels' occasional wheezes and coughs. The rattling sounds coming from his passenger were unsettling, making Ricci think the man's lungs were beyond repair. If he made it to fifty, it would be a miracle.

"The property is coming up soon," said Ricci, glancing at the GPS screen. They had already passed dozens of quaint houses on Kloosterstraat, which was essentially a long, narrow lane. Some homes were perched on acres of land, others had small frontages. Nearly all residential buildings they encountered sat behind neatly trimmed hedging. Wide open fields, rows of hothouses and horse studs added variety to the landscape. Ricci found little to like about the bucolic beauty, swearing under his breath. "There's no decent cover around here, dammit. The buildings are set too far from the road, the terrain is too flat, the forest is miles away. Even the hedges are way too low."

"Sorry I couldn't organize a line of shielding evergreen trees by the side of the road," said Wessels. "Maybe next time."

*Sarcastic prick*, thought Ricci.

"Wait." Wessels touched the navigator screen. "See there? If you drive past de Vries' place, we can park around that corner, reassess our options."

Ricci nodded. Wessels was smarter than he looked.

The target house itself loomed on the right. Even in the bleary pre-dawn, you could tell the property was worth many millions of euros. Two stories, red brick and tile, dormer windows galore, a separate four-door garage. And that's only what was visible from the road. Ricci knew there was much more behind the house, perfect places to hide a person or two.

Wessels whistled as they cruised by. "Seeing it up close and personal is a lot different than looking at it on Google Earth. Man, that place is fit for a rock star."

Ricci took a left 200 yards beyond the limits of the estate, made a U-turn, and stopped, tucking the truck behind a massive barn. No one from the house could possibly see them here. "Way too exposed from the front. We'll have to enter from the side or the rear, access it from another property." He sighed. "And we'll have to move soon; it's getting too light. Country folk like to get up early in the morning."

"Whatever you say," said Wessels. He cracked the window a fraction and lit a cigarette.

"Toss it." Ricci wound the window all the way down. "I've indulged you enough with that filthy habit. You can have one when *I* say so."

Wessels nodded and flicked the barely smoked cancer stick onto the frozen ground. "You know, one thing's been bothering me. Quite a lot, actually."

Ricci growled as the passenger window closed again. "Just one thing?"

"Yes," said Wessels, the sarcasm completely lost on him. "Why is it just the two of us embarking on this crazy mission?" He laughed awkwardly. "And when I say two, it's really only you, isn't it? Going up against God knows how many men. I mean, isn't this the kind of thing where the cops send in men dressed in riot gear, full face helmets, battering rams? What have we got? Two pistols and a tire lever."

Ricci turned, nostrils flaring. He kept his voice even but with a hard edge. "You want me to call for backup? Not happening, sport. First, we'd have to wait twelve hours for someone with clout at Langley to wake up. Then at least another twenty-four for them to put together a team, brief them, fly them in under diplomatic cover, rent vans, coordinate actions with the Dutch. Maybe—maybe—we move in forty-eight hours. You think our hostages have got forty-eight hours? I doubt it."

"I...ah..." Wessels stuttered. "I meant that—"

"Second problem," Ricci plowed on. "Supposing we could get personnel on the ground by tonight, what then? From what I understand, de Vries is a smart guy with the instincts of a fox. He'd sniff us out for sure. Hell, he could be on to us already. Time, Bram. We don't have enough of it."

"But surely the Dutch authorities—"

"They won't cooperate with us. Why? Because I'm sure they've been told to look the other way. This is a case involving a person the Russians want dead and an American operative who officially doesn't exist. The Dutch cops will be doing what they can to appear to be proactive, but with no help from the outside." He picked at his thumbnail. "Last but not least, I won't reach out to them because my boss specifically told me not to."

Ricci leaned back, voice gritty now. "The kidnapped Americans aren't sanctioned operatives anymore. Yes, the US wants Dmitrieva and Barrett back but not at any cost. Officially, they've been left to fend for themselves. No one's coming for them, Bram. Except me and you."

Wessels swallowed, nodding. "But why me?"

"Because you're in it up to your fat neck." He offered a

lopsided smile. Time to butter him up a little. "You're actually more valuable to me than you give yourself credit for."

"I am?"

"Yep."

"What's next then?"

"I've formulated a basic plan. It's not going to work unless you can do this one vital thing for me. Now listen up. Here's what we're going to do."

---

In the confines of the Hilux, Wessels hunched over his laptop, face contorted in concentration.

"Anything?" said Ricci impatiently. "You've been at it a while."

"Not yet. It's not simply a matter of...wait...got something."

"What is it?" Ricci felt his heart accelerating.

"The security camera system's wireless. Poorly encrypted too—second-rate Asian firmware, probably hasn't had an update in years."

"You sure?" The pitch of Ricci's voice rose a notch. "Maybe you're wrong. Someone like de Vries would have spent a lot of money on his security system."

Wessels chuckled. "My guess: he paid a cowboy who told him he was getting the best but instead installed cheap shit and pocketed the difference. Happens more often than you'd imagine in the IT world." He continued to tap on the keyboard, eyes flicking between code and signal data. "They've got three cameras installed outside. One's facing the driveway, two covering the backyard. Found the IP range. Just need the admin password. Not so easy..."

Ricci glanced at the house. "Can you guess it?"

"Trying to brute-force it now." His fingers danced, the screen flashing row upon row of failed attempts. "Wait..." His fingers stilled as he leaned back and whistled softly. "No way. You're going to love this."

"What?"

"I used a program to generate a shit ton of passwords based on general information about Sjaak Kuiper. It was a hunch, and I didn't think it would work, but it did. *Kuiper1980*. Kuiper's birth year."

"De Vries really is a sentimental fool, with the emphasis on fool."

Wessels scratched his head. "No. He's smart. But no one gets everything right."

"So you're in then?"

"Of course! I've got full admin access."

"Are there cameras running inside the house? Maybe you can..."

"On it." He leaned forward, tongue poking out a fraction of an inch as he focused. "Yep. Lots of them." He glanced up at Ricci. "Doesn't trust his own people."

"Can you see what we're up against?"

"Shouldn't take too long." Two minutes later, Wessels had located three men. Two were asleep in their beds in a separate building, named 'Bungalow' in the system; a third was churning laps in the pool to the rear.

"Easy prey if we move now," said Ricci. "I can force them to tell us if there are others on sight, take me to the woman."

"Holy shit!" said Wessels. "I've just found her, too. Curled up in a bed in what looks like a prison cell." He pointed at the image of the sleeping woman. "The camera feed's labelled 'Bungalow basement.'"

"We have to go, Bram. Switch off all their cameras."

He shook his head. "No. Shutting the cameras might cause an alarm to go off. There's a way around it, though. I've looped the feeds. Ten-minute playback from twenty minutes ago. That will mask any real-time activity from the system." He looked Ricci square in the eyes. "The loop's running for ten minutes. After that, everything goes back to live."

Ricci's eyebrows rose. "Not much time. Especially if there's someone in there we missed who's monitoring the system."

Wessels clicked a final command, closed the lid of his laptop. "The feeds are looping. Let's hope the goons keep sleeping and swimming until we get there."

Ricci slid a round into the FNX Tactical. "You've done everything you needed to do?"

"I think so."

"Good." He donned a pair of insulated tactical gloves, handing another to Wessels. "These let you operate effectively in the cold."

"Thanks. I think."

"Grab your Glock and suppressor, two spare mags, and follow me."

"Not sure I can shoot at a human being," said Wessels, voice shaking.

"If your life's in danger, you'll find a way."

"You gonna say a prayer for me, holy man?"

"For both of us. Let's move."

# THIRTY-TWO

THE HOOD HAD COME OFF AN HOUR OR SO AFTER THEY left base. It was still dark outside the van, stars twinkling here and there. First light wasn't far away. Maybe another forty-five minutes. *Every new day presents new opportunities*, Jacob told himself. The chance to do good things, to achieve, to make your mark. Today, putting a positive spin on the old mantra wasn't cutting it.

His limbs felt heavy, like he'd waded waist-deep into wet concrete, but his thoughts spun fast and disjointed, refusing to slow. There were too many unknowns. Conflicting scenarios of failure and success, images of joy and tragedy, filled his mind. He was too tired to fight them off—anxiety clawed at him, a quiet, relentless vibration under his ribs. His heart thudded with the stubborn rhythm of a nightmare refusing to end. These cascading emotions boiled down to one thing—save Irina. To quell the anxiety, he focused on the one element he could control: his breathing. And, somehow, within a minute, the pressure had eased.

Jacob figured they'd be deep in Belgium by now, not far from van Eekhout's home. He wondered for a moment why the men persisted with the hood-wearing charade, then it struck him. *They* didn't realize it was pointless because they had no idea that Jacob had memorized the route. That he could lead the police straight back to the house in Chaam, even with the hood on again.

Up front, Petrović whistled tunelessly, driving extra sedately now that they had left the highway. The snow was much thinner on the ground here; the temperature on the dash showed it was two degrees Celsius.

Over the last hour, fragments of conversations between Petrović and his Serbian pal had revealed scraps of information to Jacob. Ninety percent of it was useless macho banter between alpha males: football, women, politics. The men talked in their native tongue, sprinkling it with obscure slang. Serbian wasn't a language Jacob spoke fluently, but he understood it well enough to follow along. One bawdy joke told by Serb Two—who, it turned out, was called Stefan, or Stefa for short—was so funny that Jacob, despite his anxiety or maybe because of it, struggled not to burst out laughing.

The signpost for the village of Lasne appeared ahead. Not long now. Jacob's heart thundered under his jacket. *Get it wrong, Irina dies.*

He stared out the window, pretending to be studying landmarks in the semi-gloom: a church, post office, school, park. Instead, he focused every ounce of energy on listening to the Serbs. The closer it got to the main event, the more talkative they became.

Stefan scrolled his phone, looked sideways at Petrović. "The Internet's buzzing with rumors about the woman."

"That she's not who she says she is?"

"No. Well, yes. We already knew that. But people are saying she's going to be handed over to the Russians. That they want to punish her for past actions." He looked up and blinked. "We're not doing that, are we, Vesko?"

Petrović pushed out his lip pensively then said, "I don't think that's Mr. de Vries' intention."

"Have they made an offer? The Russians, I mean?"

Petrović braked at a crosswalk, allowing a woman to cross the street. "I thought you were smarter than that."

"What do you mean? It's a legitimate question."

He eased on the gas again. "How would they even know we have her, Stefa? I haven't said anything to anyone." He paused. "Have you?"

"Of course not." Stefan shook his head. "But I don't trust that Chechen prick. It was a Russian mafioso who got him the job with de Vries, remember? Ibishev's got no respect for the poor woman, I know that much."

"You think those two Moroccans are any better? Adlan's loyal to the boss, don't worry about him. He's a big picture guy."

"But if the rumors are true, the Russians must be willing to pay whatever it takes to get her back, right?"

Petrović slammed his palms against the steering wheel. "He's loyal, I said. Listen, I've spent more time with Adlan than you have."

"I wouldn't want to spend time with him. He's a pig."

"Granted, his manners can be rather...abrupt. But if there was anything untoward going on, I'd know. Besides, the boss made an agreement with the asshole in the back seat." He jerked a thumb toward Jacob. "De Vries might be many things, but he always keeps his word."

"It's not the boss I'm worried about. I mean, what do we really know about Ibishev?"

Grinding his teeth, Petrović growled, "Enough nonsense, Stefa. Let's get this job done, then get back to Chaam with the Rembrandt. I'll bet anything you like that we'll be dropping the hostages off somewhere this evening, and that will be the end of the matter."

The Transporter rolled to a silent halt outside the collector's home. "We're here," said Petrović in a whisper. Stone façade, slate roof, high hedges. Private and discreet. You could almost smell the wealth from the roadside.

Jacob nodded. "I recognize it from the photos. Looks smaller in the flesh."

"Yes," agreed Petrović. "The front of the house is narrow, but it extends a long way toward the back."

"I remember, don't worry." Every detail was scorched into his memory.

They drove to the end of the street, turned around, and killed the engine. The sudden silence was almost overpowering. Petrović held up a finger of acknowledgement as a black BMW sedan glided past from behind, stopped a hundred yards away, and did a U-turn. De Vries, keeping an eye on things. They had encountered no other vehicles or people on any streets since the woman on the crosswalk. They sat quietly for a couple minutes before Petrović started the van and took them around the block and down the back alley. Without stopping, he pointed at a red wooden gate nestled among a thicket of ivy vines. "That's where you pop out with the prize."

"Fine," said Jacob. "What next?"

"We relax at a rented property in a nearby village. You can catch up on some sleep, eat some good food. Get you in the right frame of mind. Then we come back for the heist at midnight."

"Right frame of mind?" said Jacob. "You must be joking."

Petrović nodded. "I get your frustration. But believe me, going into this with a positive attitude is in your best interests and those of your woman."

Jacob muttered under his breath. He hated to admit it, but Petrović was right.

# THIRTY-THREE

THE EARLY MORNING MIST CLUNG TO THE FIELDS. Somewhere, a rooster crowed. Ricci glanced at his Rolex: 8:27 a.m. Extra thick cloud cover that muted the pre-sunrise light in dark tones was a distinct asset this morning. He grazed his crucifix with a light touch of the fingers. Almost time to go. They crouched behind the wide trunk of an oak tree in a neighboring property; the place was totally deserted. Perhaps a weekend summer getaway for its owners or a vacant rental. Five yards in front of them, evenly spaced posts indicated a dividing fence, its wires invisible to the naked eye.

"If you see a dog at any stage," whispered Ricci, "shoot it without hesitation."

"Oh my God," mumbled Wessels.

"Consider it practice in case you have to plug a human."

No response from the Dutchman except a noise that sounded like whimpering.

"Follow right behind me. Stay low and watch your step. Could be holes, sticks, rocks, anything."

"OK."

He heard Wessels' fast, hard breathing as they traversed the field, eyes on the ground. Thankfully, it was flat and free of obstacles. They moved silently, the snow muffling their steps. At the fence line, Ricci held apart two wires, allowing Wessels to flop through the gap, landing with a grunt. Ricci ducked under the wire and remained in a crouch. He fished a pair of binoculars out of the duffel bag and trained them on the wall of glass ahead, scanning the surrounding area. Apart from the bright light shining through the glass, he detected no other signs of life. "The pool's on the other side of that wall. Let's hope he's still doing laps and we can give him an early morning surprise."

In another thirty yards, they were bent at the waist, climbing a short, wide set of slate stairs. Each step taken was carefully and deliberately, a thin coat of ice glinting off the tiles. Scattered pot plants and garden furniture, a massive steel Weber and open-mouthed stone lions populated an expansive courtyard. "Wait behind that," Ricci whispered, pointing at the barbecue. "Come when I call you."

He flattened himself on the freezing tiles, crawling like a lizard toward the conservatory. He swiveled into a sitting position, hidden from view by the six rows of bricks underneath the glass section of the wall. Inside, a fit-looking man, back and arm muscles dripping with water and gleaming under the lights, ascended the pool ladder. Even from this distance, the cauliflower ear was evident. Ibishev. The man heaved himself out with one last effort, grabbed a towel off a lounger, placed it over his head, and began to dry his hair.

This was the moment.

Ricci sprang to his feet, squeezing the trigger twice. Two giant holes appeared in the glass, shattered fragments falling inward. The man spun around, eyes wide in fright, to see Ricci advancing upon him, gun leveled at his chest. The American bellowed one of the few Russian phrases he knew. "*Ruki vverkh!* Hands up!" Then in English, "Do not move or I will blow your head clean off your shoulders."

Ibishev glanced left and right, chest heaving and body twitching.

"Forget about it. No one's coming to your rescue." Ricci called out over his shoulder for Wessels to come inside. A moment later, he sensed his partner at his right shoulder.

"Only an idiot would bring a pair of Speedos to a gun fight," said Wessels into Ricci's ear. Ricci burst out laughing.

The Chechen yelled, "You are dead men!"

Ricci fired a shot six inches wide of Ibishev's hip, a muffled thud sounding as the bullet found a home in a cushion beside him. "I thought I told you to put your fucking hands up. Do it, or the next one goes in your stomach. I know just where to aim to guarantee a lingering, painful death."

"Fuck you," challenged Ibishev, hands remaining by his sides. "Hurt me and the Russian woman dies."

Ricci hesitated for a second, then realized the man was playing mind games. He fired another round, the bullet striking the Chechen in a fleshy part of his thigh. Ibishev dropped like a stone, clutching his leg firmly with both hands. Blood puddled beneath him, dark on the cold concrete. By now, Ricci and Wessels were upon him. Ricci glared down. "You are one stubborn son of a bitch." He hauled back and laid a boot into Ibishev's hands as they covered the wound. "Hands behind your back or my friend will finish you here and now." As Ibishev complied with a scowl, swearing something unintelligible, Ricci winked at Wessels, whose eyes were bugging out like he had a thyroid problem. "He's not as humane as I am, are you?"

"Uh...no way!" Wessels gripped the Glock in two hands, aiming the barrel at the center of Ibishev's snarling face. "I'd happily kill this asshole." He shook the gun. "Do as you're told."

Ibishev's head dropped, cockiness gone. Ricci smiled to himself: put in his place by the meek and mild Wessels. He deftly placed a steel cable tie around Ibishev's wrists and tugged it tight. As his handyman grandfather would have said—that ain't going nowhere.

"Help me get him on his feet." Ricci gripped Ibishev by the armpit, Wessels copied, and together they leveraged him to a standing position. Blood continued to drip onto the ground. Unbidden, Wessels grabbed a towel and wrapped it tightly around Ibishev's leg. Ricci nodded appreciatively.

"That's not enough," muttered Ibishev. "Too much blood flow. I need a doctor."

"Not yet." Ricci stuck the barrel of his pistol in the small of Ibishev's back and gave it a nudge, forcing the man to take a couple of unsteady steps. "Take us to where the other two men are first, then the woman. If you help us, we'll call a doctor."

"What other two?"

Ricci jabbed his thumb hard into a point on Ibishev's neck—the mandibular angle behind the jawbone and under the ugly cauliflower ear.

"Aarrgghh!" The man crumpled to his knees, toppling over onto his side.

"Don't mess with us." Ricci hauled him back up. "We know there are at least two others here. In the bungalow. Are there more?"

No reply.

Ricci gripped his pistol tightly by the slide and frame and brought the butt of the grip down in a short, brutal arc. It caught Ibishev just above the temple, the sharp polymer base crunching against bone. Ibishev grunted and sagged, knees buckling. Ricci followed through with another strike, this one to the nose, blood spraying on the ground. The Chechen dropped to the floor in a twisted sprawl, one hand twitching. "No...more. Just me...and two others."

Wessels again helped Ricci drag Ibishev to his feet. "Enough time wasting," growled the Dutchman. "Take us there now."

"Back out the way we came," Ricci said with a tight grin. Wessels was rising to the occasion better than he could have hoped for. He glanced to his left. The sun was peeking above the horizon, struggling to penetrate the thick clouds. *Please, God, let them still be asleep.*

A biting wind clawed at his face, colder than ever, despite the breaking of the dawn. Ricci watched the almost-naked Ibishev shiver as he staggered barefoot across the frost-bitten paving stones, blood seeping through the towel around his leg. Panting like a tired dog, the Chechen led them around the swimming pool toward the spot where Ricci had forced their entry. Ibishev slowed and gestured downward with his head. "Broken glass there," he complained. "My feet."

"Tell someone who cares," said Ricci. "Move."

They walked slowly back down the slate steps, Ibishev leading them around the south side of the main house. Through the dissipating mist lay a pair of quaint brick-and-tile outbuildings, each set behind wraparound gravel pathways and framed by box hedges in need of a prune. "Which one are they in?" said Ricci.

"On the right."

"There's a light shining in that small window," Ricci murmured. "Could mean nothing. Could mean one of them's up and about. Are they normally still in bed at this time?"

Ibishev didn't answer. He was shivering so violently Ricci could hear his teeth clacking. Ricci poked him in the ribs with the pistol barrel. "I said, are they—"

They were ten yards from the front door when it flew open.

A muzzle flashed in Ricci's peripherals. The shot echoed like a firecracker in the morning stillness. Starlings scattered into the gray sky.

Wessels made a gurgling sound, blood bubbling from his mouth. Ricci glanced left and saw the man's eyes roll back as his limbs folded under him like paper. He'd taken one that shredded his heart, the entry hole visible in his winter coat. There'd be a large, ragged exit wound in his back. Ricci made the sign of the cross. He would make sure Wessels did not die for nothing.

Ricci dropped to his knees, grabbed Wessels' Glock, and tucked it into his waistband. He grabbed Ibishev by the back of the neck and shoved him forward, swinging around him in one motion, applying a headlock. He'd use the Chechen's body as a living shield.

Another shot came. No love for their colleague. Ricci felt the force of the bullet striking Ibishev—thudding into and exiting the meat of his biceps. The man expelled a wet breath but didn't scream. Too cold, too numb, or too tough, Ricci didn't care. Main thing, he was useful—still standing and blocking rounds.

He narrowed his eye, asked the Lord to guide the shot, and fired twice around Ibishev's shoulder at the gap in the doorway.

The man on the other side yelped and fell back inside, his assault rifle falling onto the stone stoop. It took a clattering bounce, landing under a garden faucet. Ricci let go of Ibishev and side-kicked him hard in the kidney, drawing a scream of pain. Was that enough, though? The man still presented a serious danger, even badly injured and restrained by unbreakable cable ties. Ricci simply could not leave him alone and unguarded outside. He took careful aim, prayed for forgiveness, and shot Ibishev twice in the temple. He looked up, saw the door still open, and stormed in, firing as he went, keeping low and sprinting as fast as his legs would take him.

Inside, the man, an Arab by appearances, was sprawled on black and white tiles, fingers clawing desperately, crimson streaks marking the floor. One shot had struck him in the neck, now open and raw, blood gushing. Ricci stepped in close, closed his eyes and whispered a rapid prayer, then calmly put a bullet through the base of his skull. Quick, clean, humane.

From the end of a darkened hallway, another voice called out —male, loud, hysterical.

Ricci double-checked his weapon. Plenty of rounds. He took cover behind a refrigerator and waited. He hoped curiosity would override caution and the other man would present himself, come to check on the welfare of his buddy. A minute later, a flashlight beam illuminated the floor, creeping ever closer to the dead man. The barrel of the assault rifle was the first thing Ricci saw. He recognized the make and model. Serbian Zastava M70, significantly more powerful than the FNX .45 that he gripped tightly in his right hand. Surprise, however, always outranked power. And he wanted this last one alive.

As soon as the man's right foot was visible, Ricci tensed. The whole body was now in view—another Arab, for sure—the Zastava thrust out and waving. Ricci counted to three in his head and launched, ramming into the guy like a linebacker, shoulder driving into a hip, arms wrapping around his waist. They crashed to the floor. The Arab let out an *oof* under Ricci's 225 pounds, the rifle falling to the floor with a clang. Ricci quickly adopted optimal position astride the man, using his forearm to force the guy's cheek into the tiles. The man wailed out the side of his mouth as he threw wild back elbows, none connecting. Ricci leaned over, picked up the dropped rifle with his free hand, then pressed the barrel lengthways hard onto the back of the man's neck. There was some desperate cursing, gasps and wheezing, then the resistance stopped. Ricci pulled away the rifle and grabbed a handful of hair, bouncing the man's skull off the tiles once, twice, until his body went completely limp.

He rolled the man over, listening for breathing. Yes. Still alive. He wriggled the duffel bag off his back, extracted a cable tie, and pulled the man's wrists together behind his back. The Arab groaned, trying to buck Ricci off. The guy was a tough trooper, no doubt. But Ricci was having none of it. He slammed his head into the floor again and finished binding him. For good measure, he looped a cable tie around his ankles.

Ricci badly wanted to ask a bunch of questions. *Have you called de Vries? Is anyone on their way?* But that would take time, especially if the fellow was uncooperative.

He had to find the woman first, get the hell out of there, then ask his questions.

It was almost fully light outside now. Still, he flicked switches on as he went from room to room, searching for an entrance to the cellar. He checked every room of the bungalow. Flipped up rugs looking for trap doors. Nothing. Must be in the neighboring building.

He raced back to the immobilized Arab and rolled him over. Two purple lumps sprouted from his forehead, blood trickling from his nose. His eyes were closed. *Damn, I went too far.* Then he blinked, narrowing his hate-filled eyes when he registered it was Ricci.

"Where is the woman?" Ricci said, enunciating each word slowly and clearly. "I need to find her."

He shook his head. "Don't know nothing."

Ricci unholstered the pistol and pressed the muzzle hard in the middle of the man's forehead. "I will have no hesitation in dispatching you to Jannah to be with your dead friends."

Alarm widened his eyes. He wasn't ready for the afterlife just yet.

"Yes, they're both dead. My partner, too, which I'm *really* pissed about. I'd prefer not to kill you, but if I have to… "

"Pocket," the man moaned.

"What?"

"My…trouser…pocket."

Ricci shoved a hand in one pocket, coming up empty. A keyring with three keys was in the other, together with a slim cell phone. "The second bungalow?"

A nod.

"Where're the stairs to the basement?"

"At…back of cottage. One key opens…front door, another… door opposite bathroom…takes you down to…basement. The last key…room where woman is."

"Wait here," said Ricci, relishing the irony.

---

FNX .45 firmly in one hand, he flew down a set of narrow stairs, their sleek modern design and construction contrasting with the old-fashioned bungalow above. At the bottom was a corridor with motion-activated lights. Ten yards along, the white door. He inserted the key, turned the handle, and pushed.

A bright light glowed from the ceiling. At the end of the room, a queen-size bed, a lump in the middle, dark hair on a pillow. The air in here was notably warmer than in either of the bungalows.

"Mila Dmitrieva," he shouted. "Is that you?"

A pair of small hands appeared, pulling the quilt down a fraction.

"Mila?"

"What?" She eased herself up on her elbows, squinting. "Who are you?"

He was upon her, trying hard to keep his face neutral, not to panic her. He ran a hand across his face; he must look a fright with his dark stubble. "My name's Marcello Ricci. I work for the CIA, and I've come to get you out of here. Are you OK? Do you need medical attention?"

"No, I'm not hurt." Her eyes locked on him. "Have you got... Michael?"

A shake of the head. "I'm afraid there's still some work to do in that regard."

"Do you at least know where he is?"

"No." He paused for a second. "Get dressed quickly and come with me. I'm not sure if de Vries has been alerted about the breach." As tears welled in her eyes, he added, "Don't worry. We'll find him. Now move!"

She was on her feet and had visited the bathroom and thrown on the track suit and Ugg boots in less than two minutes. Ricci bounded up the stairs, leading Irina to the second bungalow. She caught her breath when she saw the lifeless bodies of Wessels and Ibishev sprawled on the blood-stained ground, and again as they stepped over the dead Arab in the first bungalow kitchen. The sight of the second Arab, trussed-up, battered, and bruised with a tooth lying by the side of his head, made her grimace.

Ricci stopped, turned, and handed her the Glock. "Watch him. I'll be back with a vehicle."

"Understood." She took the gun, stepped forward, and

pointed it at the back of the man's head. To her surprise, her hands didn't shake.

Ricci hared across the open field, up the country lane to the Hilux. He gunned it back to the estate, churning over lawns and flower beds as he took the shortest route to the bungalow. He slipped the satchel containing the laptop from Wessel's shoulder, grabbed his cell phone and wallet, and tossed it all in the passenger footwell. It was a pity to leave him here, undignified. But driving around the countryside with a dead body on board made no sense. He silently bade the fallen man goodbye and turned his attention to the woman.

"We have to get out of here now. The shot that killed my friend was a loud one. A gun going off back home early in the morning would barely raise an eyebrow. Here—I don't know."

"You think I'm keen on hanging around?" she said. "Let's go."

The Russian woman surprised him with her strength. She strained, her face turning red, as she gripped the surviving Arab's knees and heaved while Ricci grabbed the shoulders. They dumped him in the back seat, drawing moans of protest. Ricci pushed him onto his side, covered his body with a picnic blanket, and told him to stay down. Engine idling, Ricci took three deep breaths. With Wessels dead, he had no idea where the third shell-company property was. The information was tucked away in the laptop, but the device would a hundred percent be password protected. Even if he could get access, he'd have no idea where to start looking for it. Quicker to simply ask. "Where the fuck is Michael Barrett?"

# THIRTY-FOUR

"Where is he, Khadir?" said Ricci once again. The man had so far revealed his name but nothing else. That was about to change.

Ricci had driven the Hilux to a park a half mile from the Chaam estate, stopping behind the small terraced stadium of a local soccer team. He sent Irina to sit on a nearby bench, in full view of the vehicle, while he interrogated the hostage. He'd told her it might get ugly, and she was happy to be out of the way. "I'm only going to ask once more before I start to get serious."

The man remained silent, squeezing his eyes in an attempt to look defiant. Problem was, trussed up tight, he held no cards.

"Where is he?"

"De Vries will kill me if I say..." The man lisped slightly on account of the missing front tooth.

Ricci shoved an oil-soaked rag in the man's mouth, then demonstratively held up a sheet of coarse-grit sandpaper he'd found in a toolbox in the truck's bed. There was another gift in there that paired with the sandpaper like a fine wine with food: a bottle of denatured alcohol. Khadir blinked rapidly. Ricci pulled up the man's shirt and rubbed the paper hard against the soft skin. Then he poured a generous amount of the liquid onto the raw, pink wound. The Moroccan writhed in pain; muffled animalistic screams came from under the gag.

"Next time it's your balls, buddy." He screwed the lid back on the bottle, giving it a shake to add to the theater. The gag removed, Ricci continued. "I might even get the lovely lady to help me. Imagine not only the pain, Khadir, but the shame of that. Now give me the fucking address."

The Arab closed his eyes tight. "Village called Alphen."

"Good start."

"Sint Janstraat. Don't remember the exact number, but I can show—"

Ricci started the engine, plugged the street name into the GPS, and waved for the woman to come back.

The drive to Alphen took no more than fifteen minutes. No traffic, just pleasant scenery of evergreen forests and snow-covered fields, some cows and sheep. Along the way, Ricci warned Khadir that his survival depended on full cooperation. To the woman, he explained what had happened in the outside world while she'd been held captive, the speculation about who she was, why she was taken. "You're under no obligation to answer this," he said, "and I'll treat it as confidential, but...ah...what should I call you?"

"Irina," she whispered, offering him a smile that said she trusted him to keep his word.

He decided to push his luck. "And the man we're looking for? Is he Michael Barrett or David Reeve?"

She laughed. "Take your pick."

"I'll go with Barrett."

"Good choice."

De Vries' third shell-company property was a traditional Dutch farmhouse-style building. Rich, reddish-brown brickwork, a steeply pitched tiled roof. White-framed windows, ivy creeping gently along sections of the hedge and façade. To the right of the main house, a long single-story wing—likely a converted barn or extension—could serve as a guest annex, a place to keep Barrett on a short leash. A gravel driveway extended past the annex, providing ample parking space although there were no vehicles in sight.

Ricci drove past the house for another hundred yards, turned around, and stopped. "Khadir!"

"What?"

"What part of the property is the American in?"

"Locked room in the...don't know the word in English."

"Annex?"

"Yes, I think so."

"Cameras?"

He chuckled. "Of course."

Irina said, "I might be able to knock them out if I can access the laptop you brought with us."

"Really?" Ricci said, incredulous. "It'll be password protected."

"I can at least try." She reached into the footwell and placed the device on her lap. "We're in luck."

"What do you mean?"

"He must have been in a hurry. Closed the lid without shutting down. It's in sleep mode with no password prompt." She gritted her teeth. "Let's see now." Her breath was shallow as she navigated her way around the cluttered desktop. "Second piece of luck: he labeled his files and folders in English." She glanced at Ricci. "But his system is so disorganized, I doubt I'll find anything useful."

"There's something on there," Ricci insisted. "He disabled the cameras at the place they were holding you."

"Awesome. Means it's probably the same lazy setup here."

"What—"

She gave him a sideways look. "Could you please not interrupt me? I need to focus."

He frowned, tendons popping in his neck. "Sorry."

Three minutes later, she closed the lid. "Done."

"Are you kidding me? I mean, how...?"

"It was easy. Your friend saved the password from last time.

*Kuiper1980*. I never would have guessed that in a million years. I've set the loop in motion. Fifteen minutes and it goes back live. That's your window."

Ricci turned to Khadir.

"You're going in with me. But you'll have a gun in the small of your back."

Hobbling like the loser of a kickboxing match, Khadir made his way to the front door. He entered a code into a numeric keypad, opened the glass-panel door, and almost fell in. Quiet and still. In less than five minutes it was obvious. The place was empty. Outbuildings too.

"What next?" said Khadir, panting and struggling to stay upright. "I don't know what else I can do."

"Barrett was supposed to do a job for de Vries. We believe it's an art theft."

A shrug, but the telltale smirk gave him away.

"You know where it is," growled Ricci. "But in case you've forgotten, Mr. Sandpaper will be happy to help you remember."

Khadir's face went white. "Belgium."

"More specifically?"

The Moroccan coughed up the address in Lasne with no hesitation.

"It's a private home?"

"I think so."

Ricci patted him on the back, harder than necessary. "Good boy."

Back at the Hilux, Ricci said, "When are they hitting the target?"

"Today. That's why the house is empty."

"What time today?" he demanded.

The whites showed bright in Khadir's wide eyes. "I swear, that I do not know."

A vigorous application of sandpaper and alcohol revealed Khadir was telling the truth. It also elicited bonus information on what was being stolen. Ricci googled the name of the painting and gave a low whistle.

Irina clunked the door closed, glaring at Ricci. "I think you enjoy that process a little too much."

"I wish it were the case. Job satisfaction is important to me, but some aspects..." He clicked his teeth. "They suck."

"What now?"

He rubbed the back of his neck. Logic told him the gang would strike at night, but when exactly? He could head there now, stake out the address, and wait. Perhaps be rumbled, put Barrett in the crosshairs. Having Irina and Khadir in tow didn't make things easier. He could call The Hague station, ask for a team to be sent down to Lasne.

Another idea occurred to him.

He jumped out of the Hilux, pacing back and forth as he waited for the pick-up on the other end. Done talking to an excited Tip Bradbury, he then called his boss in Langley.

# THIRTY-FIVE

After driving around for thirty minutes, Ricci found a small snack bar two blocks away, bought a selection of croquets in bread rolls with mustard, fries in curry sauce, and takeout coffees.

Back at the boutique stadium, he parked in the corner of the lot to ensure a clear view of anyone coming their way. He and Irina demolished the food in silence. Khadir made noises while he ate—that missing tooth again. Ricci had cut loose the cable tie from his wrists so the man could eat and drink before his impending transfer to Amsterdam. Irina was going too, only she didn't know it yet.

"Shouldn't we get moving?" she said, gulping the last of the coffee and placing the empty cup back in the holder. "Didn't you say it was nearly two hours to get to where Michael is?"

"I'm waiting on something first."

"A call?"

"No."

Just then a sleek, black Volkswagen Multivan turned into the lot, followed by a dark blue Mercedes-Benz GLA. Two tall men, both dressed in jeans and puffer jackets, got out of the drivers' sides, exchanged a few words, and started walking toward them with confident, long strides.

"Who are they?" Irina said.

"They've come to take Khadir to Amsterdam. He'll be held until the brass decide if and when to hand him over to the police. Maybe they've got other plans for him."

"Whatever he gets, he'll deserve it."

"You're going too."

She shook her head, rocking her body from side to side. "No! I have to go with you, make sure he's OK. I can help you..."

He grabbed her wrist. In a soothing voice, he said, "Your talents are unmistakable. But my brief was to get you out of the hole and make sure you're safe. Right now, you are not safe. But you soon will be." He nodded at the approaching men. "From Amsterdam, you'll be flown back to New York under guard."

"I don't suppose there is any point arguing the matter?"

"None," he said with a firm shake of the head.

"And what about you?"

"The smaller vehicle is for me. I'm driving to the address our Arab friend gave me. A couple of agents are coming from Brussels to assist." He patted her on the top of the hand. "We will get him back. Alive." He smiled warmly. "Just like I got you."

**4:00 p.m.**

Ricci could smell his own body odor. Halfway to Lasne, he stopped at a Total gas station, bought a roll-on deodorant, a small tube of mint toothpaste, and a toothbrush and took a much-needed shower. He lingered longer under the hot water than he should have; people were waiting for him. A shave would have been nice, but that would have to wait.

In a small French restaurant in the village of Lasne, he met the two agents from Brussels. A man, Stan Krieger, and a woman,

Dominique Robert, the 't' silent. Both were fit and tanned, in their late thirties, spoke fluent French and Dutch, and came with a quiverful of skills to match Ricci's.

"We scouted ahead, spoke to the residents of a house two doors up from the address given by your Moroccan pal," said Krieger in a deep baritone. "Turns out the street is one where people like to keep to themselves, not much sense of community. The residents we spoke to said van Eekhout is a snob and has no friends in the street, is known for loud parties and weird people coming and going at all hours. They readily agreed, for an obscenely large fee, to allow strangers—us—to set up an observation post on the second-floor bedroom of their home."

"Is the post set up yet?" said Ricci.

"Oui," replied Robert with a nod. "I had a phone call five minutes ago. We've got two pairs of eyes directly on the front of the house."

"Quite a team you've assembled at short notice." Ricci pursed his lips in appreciation. "What about the rear?"

"Two small cars are parked fifty yards either side of the property in the back alley," said Krieger. "No one's in them, but they've got two night vision cameras pointing directly at van Eekhout's gate and two pointing back the other way."

"We can confirm the heist hasn't happened yet," chimed in Robert. "Our residents saw van Eekhout leave and return with a small bag of shopping as recently as thirty minutes ago. Said he looked in a chipper mood."

They discussed the plan: would officers storm the house once Barrett was inside, extract him? Or wait for de Vries' people to come and pick him up, then move and make some arrests?

"My brief was to extract Mila Dmitrieva and Michael Barrett," said Ricci. "There was no mention of bringing the kidnappers to justice, nothing of that nature."

"Hmmm," said Robert. "There's a problem with that."

"What?" Ricci hated problems. Especially at the eleventh hour.

"Belgian jurisdiction. We've got their special forces on standby in a garage a couple of blocks away. The police want bodies."

"Here's what I propose," said Krieger. "Once we see Barrett enter the house, from the front or the back, Marcello enters from the opposite side." Ricci nodded agreement. "He escorts Barrett back out again, drives him to Brussels." Krieger took a mouthful of herbal tea. "No doubt he's made an arrangement to contact the criminals once he's retrieved the artwork. He makes contact, they come to get him, we pounce."

Ricci had to acknowledge that the plan sounded perfect. Almost. "Are we going to brief other neighbors, tell them to keep their heads down?"

"Already done," said Robert. "We reverse-searched the addresses of every house in the street, got cell numbers by cross-referencing car registrations. All but two answered our calls. The ones who are home will stay indoors; the others will stay away until we contact them again and give them the all-clear. We door-knocked the addresses of those who didn't answer, nobody home."

"What if the bad guys show up early, spoil the plan?"

Krieger shrugged. "How badly do you want this man?"

"Desperately."

"Then we must pray they do not arrive until Barrett has summoned the pick-up," said Robert.

Ricci nodded as he felt the cross around his neck. Praying was something he was very good at.

**8:45 p.m.**

FROM THE VANTAGE point across the street, Ricci peered through the telescope. A man parked a small red sedan outside van Eekhout's place and walked up the front path. He knocked and was admitted by the owner. A huge slug of a man. The visitor remained inside until 11 p.m., when all the lights went out in the house and he exited, walking briskly and smiling like he'd won the lottery.

### 11:57 p.m.

RICCI, awake mainly thanks to a steady supply of strong coffee, observed a figure dressed in black clothing and a ski mask walk up the path, turn the door handle and walk inside.

"Go," said Krieger. "And hurry up, it's starting to snow again."

"What if he's locked the door behind him?"

"It was unlocked, so I think he'll leave it that way if he has to get out fast." He shrugged. "If not..."

"I'll find another way in, don't worry." Ricci tapped the black-market FNX pistol in his shoulder holster. "Wish me luck."

"Wait," said Robert, looking through a pair of binoculars. "I don't believe it. A delivery van's just pulled up twenty meters from van Eekhout's place. Could be de Vries' people inside." She looked at Krieger. "Weird to be arriving at this hour." She placed the binoculars to her eyes again. "Bald, fat man. He's eating something, casual as you like. Scrolling his phone at the same time. Oh dear. Porn." She exchanged a glance with Ricci. "What do you think?"

"Give him ten minutes," said Ricci. "Barrett will need more time than that to get the job done. If the van driver hasn't gone by then, I'll go down and move him on." He ran a hand through his hair, then turned to address another agent hunched over a computer screen. "Keep your eyes glued on the camera feed from the back. If Barrett manages to lift the painting quickly and get out, we might have to move faster than we thought." He sighed and poured himself another coffee.

# THIRTY-SIX

"LET'S GET YOU RIGGED UP," SAID PETROVIĆ, TWISTING his head around to face Jacob in the back section of the van, parked fifty meters from the target address on the opposite side of the street. He patted Stefan on the shoulder. "You can do the honors."

Five minutes later, the pin cam was wired up and running, the thin-profile satchel with his safe-breaking gear slung across his shoulder. He was dressed head to toe in black, a ski mask rounding off the ensemble.

"You're definitely meeting me in the alley around the back, correct?" said Jacob, eyeballing Petrović. "Not leaving me high and dry with the cops waiting to arrest me?" The nagging thought returned that this whole operation was a giant setup. The minute he entered the back alley with the Rembrandt, he'd be met by a phalanx of Belgian forces, de Vries standing in the background, pissing himself laughing.

"What a wild imagination you have," he replied with a grin and a slight shake of the head. "As soon as you have the painting, send a text to the contact listed as P. One word. *Yes.*" He stole a glance out the window. "We'll be there to pick you up in less than a minute."

"Got it." A thought occurred to him. "What if it's not there?"

"What do you mean, if it's not there?"

"Exactly that. Maybe—"

"Shut up! It's been verified."

"Fine," Jacob said quietly, leaning back against the side wall of the van. "Whatever you say."

Stefan reached under the bench, pulled out a bulky laptop, a modified Toughbook, and moved to the front passenger side. Jacob figured he'd be remotely disabling any security systems to give him a free run at the prize. For five minutes, he tapped away at his keyboard, humming tunelessly. Jacob glanced between the two front seats, trying to catch a glimpse of the screen, but Stefan's body blocked it completely.

"OK," said Stefan finally. "The cameras are still on, but I've switched off the motion-detection function that actually makes them engage. Van Eekhout had a special sensitivity adjustment on, presumably so his precious pussies don't trip the system every time they lick their asses."

Petrović chuckled, but Jacob failed to see the humor.

"Stored footage from today has also been completely wiped to protect the inside man and make sure nothing can point back to us."

"So it's safe to go in?" said Jacob. "No surprises awaiting me?"

"Yes," said Stefan, almost defensively, like he didn't appreciate his professionalism being brought into question. "I've also killed the digital override on the vault. All ready for you to blast open."

*Brilliant.*

"It's now three minutes to midnight," said Petrović, angling his watch. "Get out and get moving." He grabbed the headrest as he spun in his seat, staring a burning gaze into Jacob's eyes. "Do. Not. Fail."

Jacob slid open the side door. "One last thing," said Petrović. "Don't bother trying to use the landline phone in the house. Our man cut the wires."

"Got it," said Jacob. The idea had occurred to him, but with Irina's life on the line, he wouldn't have tried in any case.

"Go!"

No coats or jackets were allowed for the heist, which meant no dawdling in the bitter cold. Jacob shivered under the body-hugging black track suit. The chill seeped through his thin black sneakers and even thinner socks. The entire outfit made him feel like a motion-capture actor making a CGI scene for a movie. Two more houses to go...*here it is*.

A glance up and down the street. Deserted, as expected.

A look up: no lights on inside the house. Red dots blinked where a couple of cameras were mounted above the door, but Marković had promised they wouldn't pick him up.

The wrought-iron front gate opened with barely a touch of the hand, although the accompanying squeak in the still of the night gave his heart rate a nudge. He crouched and hastened to the front door, making sure to place his feet flat as he traversed the slick paved surface. A twist of the door handle, a gentle push, and he was in. The inside man had done his job.

His heart stopped for a moment as he waited for the ear-splitting wail of the alarm.

Silence.

Inside, he tugged off the annoying ski mask as a priority. Next, he flicked on a powerful pen flashlight, illuminating the hallway. Clear of obstacles all the way to the media room at the end. He stopped, shrugged off the carry bag, unzipped it, and shined the light inside. The micro-plastique charge and the burner phone with no SIM, just SMS capability. One saved number. Plus a basic tool kit for contingencies. Not much in the way of equipment, but he'd worked with less before.

Something caught his ear. A tremor from upstairs. The plan of the building flashed in his brain, telling him exactly where to go. He padded up the carpeted stairs, making his way to the main bedroom. The penlight picked up a fat, naked man, sprawled across a king-size bed. Bound to corner bedposts with silk ties. Eyes closed, snoring up a storm.

Flashlight between his teeth, Jacob checked the restraints, then retied them with constrictor knots. Only a pair of scissors would free him.

Back down the stairs, he easily picked the lock and entered the media room. With no windows, he decided to close the door behind him and switch on the overhead lights. They flickered to life, revealing book-lined shelves from floor to ceiling on two sides and a lowered cinema screen on the far wall. No vault. Must be behind the screen.

Jacob turned around; on the side of the door opposite the light switch were two remote controls in wall-mounted holders. One for the air conditioning, another with a single button in the middle. He pressed it, and the movie screen slowly raised, revealing the vault.

On the right-hand side of the vault were two panels. One displayed numbers and symbols to enter the code to open the safe. The other was something altogether different.

Jacob sat on his haunches, staring at the glowing green ring around the biometric scanner. A fingerprint reader. His pulse spiked. He hadn't anticipated this. Neither had de Vries' men. But what a bonus. No keypad. No code to guess. Best of all, no explosives. Just a little glass square waiting for a fingerprint—van Eekhout's. There was nothing appropriate in his kitbag he could use to lift a print: no glue, no silicone, no modeling clay. A big house like this one, though, would definitely have something he could make use of.

Jacob moved back through the dining room and entered the spacious kitchen, almost commercial sized. He scanned for anything he could use. Nothing obvious on the benches.

He yanked open drawer after drawer. Then his eyes landed on it—clingwrap.

He pulled out the roll and tore off a decent length. There were scissors in the drawer; he took them too. He grabbed a wine glass from a rack above the counter, wiped it clean on a dish towel, then hurried back to van Eekhout.

Jacob stood back, studying the man's arms. Both of them were flabby, the right one slightly bigger in the forearm. Right-handed; the right index finger was the likely candidate.

He cut off a square of clingwrap and pressed it carefully onto the pad of the collector's index finger, smoothing it down with his own gloved fingertip. He held it there a moment, then peeled it away gently, revealing a faint impression. Not enough to fool the scanner.

He stretched a second square of clingwrap tightly over the rim of the wine glass. Then, with extreme care, he pressed the collector's fat finger onto the taut film surface, rolling it slightly to get an entire print. He lifted the glass and held it up to the flashlight—there it was. A full, clean print.

Back in the media room, he wrapped the bit of clingwrap around his finger, aligning the ridges as best he could. One shot. Sweat beaded on his forehead as he pressed it to the scanner. The reader blinked red, then green.

Yes!

Then the green circle changed into a square, with a message.

Enter PIN.

He thumped his hand against the door of the vault. He should have suspected the redundancy. Valuable time wasted.

He took a step back and had a good look at the safe. Old-school: mechanical lock with digital override. But the override was dead. And it wouldn't have worked anyway without knowing the scanner PIN. The explosive was the only way in now.

Sighing, he unwrapped the block of plastique and shaped a piece of it into the lock seam. Not much—just enough to compromise the bolts without vaporizing the paintings behind the door. The Rembrandt must not be damaged. He inserted the remote fuse, stepped back into the hallway, and dialed the number that would detonate the explosive on the second ring.

No loud bang, no billowing smoke. Just a low, suppressed thump.

He marched back into the room and yanked the door open.

The vault was high and broad. Climate controlled. Rows of paintings, some boxed, some draped. The Rembrandt was obvious—central, encased behind a thick UV-protective frame. "Portrait of a Noble Stranger." He had seen a photo of the work, but to make it obvious, there was also a label in Dutch on the top of the frame. *Portret van een nobele vreemdeling.* Jacob was no art expert, but even he could appreciate the genius of the master's work. Soft light playing off the hollow of the subject's cheek, the glint of intelligence in the half-turned gaze. Jacob stared for five seconds, admiring. It didn't matter that the piece was worth gazillions; Irina was worth more.

He carefully wiggled the painting out from among the others. The weight was a lot more than he expected—thick glass, reinforced backing.

He stepped back into the hallway, carrying the painting flat, chest-high, like a furniture mover. Walking sideways, it was impossible to use the flashlight in his mouth to see his way. He eased the painting to the floor, turned on the hallway light, and picked up the Rembrandt again. He'd turn the light off once he got the painting outside.

Breathing hard as he edged his way along the corridor, he realized he'd wasted way too much time with the fingerprint reader. The Serbs would be getting restless. Time to send the text.

Five feet from the back door, he sensed something moving behind him.

A rustling sound.

*Jesus.*

His heart froze as he felt the prize slipping through his hands. He eased it to the floor and spun around.

A blur of fur and claws tore past him. He let out a breath he didn't realize he'd been holding. He'd totally forgotten about the cats.

The furry creature scampered away, back toward the living room, tail high.

He forced his breath to slow. Another cat padded past him like it owned the place, mewling a greeting.

Outside, he leaned the painting against the brick wall, went back in and flicked off the light, shut the door, and texted *Yes*.

Forty-five seconds passed before the van arrived. Not the one he'd arrived in; this one was brand new, bigger, German tags. Covering their tracks.

Marković stepped out and helped Jacob lift the painting into the cargo section. Straps had been pre-installed to hold the prize snuggly in place.

Jacob climbed in, sweat gathering under his clothes in every place it could gather. He sat down, and Marković handed him a bottle of water. Jacob drained the contents like a student chugging a beer at spring break.

The hood went back over his head. The sliding door opened and closed again.

A stinging slap on the back. "Nice work." Jacob's heart skipped a beat. It was de Vries. The hood came off again. The crime boss grinned at him. "There's no need for this anymore."

Jacob didn't respond.

"Nine minutes flat," said Petrović from the driver's seat. The van started moving. "You just saved two lives."

The van pulled away, slow and deliberate. "Where are we going?" said Jacob, glaring at de Vries. "Where is Mila?"

"We're taking you to her now," said de Vries. "Then we're gonna drop your sorry asses on the side of the road somewhere. You know, I was half hoping you would fuck this up so I could have the pleasure of killing you." He laughed from the pit of his stomach. "Congratulations."

# THIRTY-SEVEN

RICCI PULLED UP THE COLLAR OF HIS JACKET AS HE crossed the road. He tapped on the window. The overweight man jiggled in his seat.

"*Qu'est-ce que tu fous là!* What the hell are you doing!" Ricci barked, making a wind-down-your-window gesture.

The man dropped his phone in his lap and lowered the window. "I...had an argument with my wife. I needed to get out of the house, calm down, you know how it is..."

"My daughter could see you from her bedroom window looking at filth on your phone."

"I'm sorry."

"Are you jerking off in there?"

"What? No..."

"Get the fuck out of here!"

The man nodded, jowls flapping. "*Mais oui.* Sure thing." The engine turned over, and the van took off with a shudder.

Walking briskly up the path, Robert's shrill voice came over his ear piece: "We've got action at the rear of the house!"

"What?"

"A van's pulled up at the gate. Barrett has the painting. Someone's helping him load it in the van."

"I'm on it!" *Why did I wait before dealing with the fat man? You stupid idiot!* He ignored the front door and tore down the side path, wet branches brushing his face. He sprinted to the end of the path, leapt over an overturned wheelbarrow, and shoved open the gate.

Gone.

He glanced left and saw taillights disappearing at the end of the lane. "We've missed them, dammit."

"Don't panic," said Robert. "I'm sending a unit to cut them off."

Ricci collapsed to his knees, chest heaving.

"Return to base," said Robert. "We're going for a drive."

# THIRTY-EIGHT

He turned his head sideways, watching the headlights cutting through the snow-flecked black night. Adrenaline from the heist still coursed through his veins, breath coming in white wisps. It was hard to believe it, but de Vries was actually going to keep his word. Maybe he'd give all the proceeds from the sale of the Rembrandt to Sjaak, to help make the crippled man's life easier to bear.

Jacob sighed. Revenge would not be his after all. He would not kill anyone. Not even the Moroccan who had defiled him.

Perhaps just as well.

He hated killing. Now with the passage of time, his blood had cooled enough to let go of it. As long as Irina was safe... If she wasn't, his blood would turn hot again in an instant, and he *would* kill.

Up front, Petrović drove sedately, exchanging jokes with Stefan in Serbian, laughing like old war buddies. Jacob's curiosity had fizzled out: no eavesdropping, no memorizing the route, no listening for sounds.

De Vries had his head buried in an e-reader, one leg crossed over the other, glasses perched on the edge of his nose like some kind of academic. His face was bunched in concentration; every now and then he'd give a chuckle.

Jacob looked down at his hands. Trembling, not out of anxiety, but from the build-up of nervous energy that hadn't settled and wouldn't for a couple of days. De Vries must have sensed something; he placed his device on the seat and pulled a blanket from under the bench. Jacob gave a nod, wrapping it around his shoulders.

The job was done, all conditions of the contract met—but something still felt wrong. They'd pulled it off too easily. Then again, some days things just go right.

As the van turned left out of the long, narrow alley, Jacob caught sight of bright headlights sweeping across a line of hedges up ahead. He sat forward, peering through the gap between the cargo bay and the driver's compartment.

Two gleaming, dark sedans were parked across the road, angled in a V shape. Exhaust fumes billowed in the cold night air. No lights on, shadows visible behind the windshields.

"*Shta dodjavola?* What the hell?" Petrović muttered, easing off the gas. He turned to glare at Jacob. "Your doing?"

"Are you serious? When could I have—"

Suddenly both of the blocking cars revved to life and surged forward, one stopping inches from the front of the van; the other darted past on the left, swerving to box them in from behind.

"Hold on tight, everyone!" Petrović barked. He jammed the gear lever into reverse. Tires spun, then screeched on the slick asphalt. The van fishtailed as it backed up fast—but the second sedan got there first, skidding sideways to pin them.

The first shot boomed.

A high-caliber round punched through the van's rear panel, tore past Jacob's head, and embedded in the padding behind him. A second shot cracked, penetrating from the same direction. De Vries cried out, his eyelids fluttered, and he crashed to the floor, e-reader skittering. No blood—he'd fainted from fright. Jacob hit the deck, rummaging around under de Vries' clothes. A coward, but a gun-carrying coward. The Heckler & Koch USP Compact felt like a long-lost treasure in Jacob's hand.

Another shot broke through a side panel. Then something unexpected. A shot fired inside the van with a deafening crack, the sickening sound of a bullet driving through flesh and bone. Before Jacob could process what was happening, the sliding door flung open. Petrović stood in the gap, spots of blood on his face, firmly gripping a pistol in both hands.

"Wait—what the fuck are you doing?" Jacob shouted as he rolled onto his stomach, concealing the H&K. "Did you just kill Stefan? Tell me you didn't!"

"I'm doing what I came here to do," Petrović snapped. "Pick up the painting. Now!"

"Gimme a minute." He rolled onto his side, tucking the gun under his waistband. Why hadn't Petrović just shot him too? He grabbed the frame, twisted his body into a kneeling position, and turned around with its base resting on the floor of the van.

"Stand up now. Nice and easy," said Petrović. "No sudden movements."

"You're double-crossing de Vries, aren't you?" Jacob's voice was hoarse with disbelief. "You had everyone fooled."

"I work for people with influence and class," he scoffed. "The people who pay me make de Vries look like a wannabe loser." Petrović gave him a wink, aimed the gun at the back of de Vries' head, and calmly executed him, the head rising and falling with a thud. Jacob's heart stampeded. "And you're coming with me. My Russian friends in Moscow will be delighted to receive you and your *suka* as a gift. Even better than the painting. Now get out."

As Jacob took a step forward, trying to figure out his next move, how to deal with Petrović and an unknown quantity of his buddies, all hell broke loose.

A fusillade of flashbangs. Maybe a dozen of them. White-hot light illuminated the landscape. Through a megaphone came a loud cry: "*POLICE! AU SOL! METTEZ-VOUS À TERRE!* GET ON THE GROUND!"

Jacob took cover in the back of the van, pressing himself flat to the floor. Let them fight it out among themselves.

Sensations washed over him, heightened by a fresh surge of adrenaline. The sound of boots hammering on pavement and gravel. The staccato rhythm of automatic gunfire.

The passenger section lit up with muzzle flashes, lighting up the crazed glass in the windshield. Return fire from Petrović and his friends erupted, impossible to tell from where. Jacob dared to peek through a big bullet hole in the wall above the wheel well. Petrović, painting held above his head, and another man. Running in zig-zags toward the forest.

Bullhorns bellowed more French. Even if Petrović and his Russian buddies didn't understand the words, the meaning was crystal clear.

A sniper's rifle barked once. Petrović, a floodlight trained upon him, careened face-first into a brick retaining wall. He clutched his thigh and rolled around, wailing. The Rembrandt had fallen with him, landing glass-side down on the snowy ground. His accomplice turned, aiming wildly and firing from the hip—another shot caught him in the neck, spinning him around in a half-circle. His body spasmed before folding and collapsing.

Ten seconds passed. A beautiful silence. No more shooting.

A tinny sound rang in Jacob's ears.

Then came loud, disjointed voices, more boot stomping, the crackle of radio chatter.

Figures appeared in the open door. Two giant DSU officers in gray camouflage gear and helmets poked their rifles inside.

Jacob stood, dropped de Vries' pistol on the floor, and raised his hands. "*Ne tirez pas! Je suis l'otage!* Don't shoot! I'm the hostage!"

In a heartbeat, the officers had pulled Jacob from the van, frisked, and handcuffed him. The men were rough, almost brutal, but he couldn't stop smiling. They stood back, looking at him like he was off his meds.

One of the men spat some police jargon into his radio.

Another two officers sprinted past them, toward the downed men. Jacob remembered the painting. "Hey!" he shouted, nodding toward the officer bending over the frame. "That Rembrandt. It's worth millions—be careful!"

There was the sound of footsteps approaching from behind. Not DSU—civilian shoes. People speaking English. Jacob twisted his head around. The voice that followed was American.

"You must be Michael Barrett."

"Marcello Ricci?"

"At your service." Ricci, sporting a cobalt-blue two-day growth, bowed and extended his hand. He quickly realized that Jacob couldn't reciprocate and ordered one of the officers to remove the cuffs and leave them alone. "I'm so glad you're safe. Means I get to keep my job." He offered a wry grin.

Jacob stared at him. "Mila?"

"You mean Irina," Ricci whispered and touched the side of his nose. "Yes, she's safe. She was liberated from a property in Chaam, not far from the one you were held in. She was taken to Amsterdam several hours ago. On her way back home by now, I should imagine." He explained how Ibishev, one of the Moroccans, and Bram Wessels had been killed in the act of freeing Irina.

"Was it the shorter Moroccan who died?"

"I believe it was, yes."

Jacob sighed heavily. "Good." Karma can be a deadly bitch. He felt sorry for Wessels, though. A flawed human with a heart of gold if ever there was one.

A man and a woman dressed in smart suits approached. Ricci introduced Krieger and Robert, who informed Jacob they would be taking him straight to Brussels. He'd be given the once-over by a medico, then sent back to New York on a flight from Melsbroek Air Base.

Jacob nodded and went to speak but stumbled. Ricci caught him.

"Let's get you out of here," said Krieger, taking him by one elbow while Ricci had the other. "You need some serious rest."

The four of them walked through the cordon together. Flashing lights cut through thick snowflakes. Agents swarmed over the carnage. Three bodies were zipped into bags. Petrović and two other men—presumably his surviving Russian colleagues—were cuffed and dragged away to a waiting van that resembled an army tank. The Rembrandt was gently lifted and placed into a padded box under the supervision of three separate officials. What would van Eekhout make of it all, Jacob wondered.

As they reached Ricci's SUV, the CIA man opened the passenger-side door and turned to Jacob. "I've heard the rumors, and I don't know what's true and what's speculation. And frankly, I don't care. What I do know is this. Some powerful people stateside will be very happy to see you."

# THIRTY-NINE

Ricci smiled as he glanced sideways at his snoozing passenger. They had only been on the road for five minutes and Barrett had crashed out. Dressed in fresh clothes provided by the Belgian police, his head lolled against the window, cheek mashed into the glass, skin slightly fogging the surface with each exhalation. A thin line of drool had formed at the side of his mouth. He'd been to hell and back in the space of a few days. No wonder he was out to the world.

The cell phone in the dash mount blinked. A message from his boss at Langley. He knew what it would be about. A written report. He'd be expected to produce one as soon as possible. Sorry. Not responding.

But the flashing phone gave him an idea. He dialed the main number for the Netherlands police. A woman answered cheerily in Dutch.

"Sorry," he said. "It'll have to be English."

"Not a problem, sir. How can I help you?"

"I'd like to report some unusual activity at an estate in the Chaam Forests. You heard of it?"

"Of course, sir. What kind of activity? Terrorists?" She

sounded hopeful. Looking for a little excitement on a boring shift at 2:27 a.m.

"In a way. I believe I heard shooting, people screaming."

"May I have the address?"

Ricci gave it.

"And your name, sir?"

He pressed the red button. He put the crucifix to his lips. *Please, let them give Wessels dignity in death.*

After a couple of minutes, he pulled over, fired off a quick text to Carmela, and drove off again.

A minute later, the phone pinged. He could see the reply in preview mode. *I'm waiting for you, baby.*

He smiled, nudged the speedometer to the maximum allowable 120 km/h, and turned the heater up. Man, he was sick of the cold.

# FORTY

JACOB RAN HIS FINGER ALONG THE TOP OF THE GIANT aquarium in Fletcher's converted Tribeca warehouse apartment. "Is that one a new acquisition? I don't remember it from before."

Fletcher ambled over, bent at the knee, and pointed at a lively fish circling a plastic wrecked ship. "Well spotted. I was lucky to get that peppermint angelfish. Another guy had ordered it, but I heard about it and offered more."

Jacob regarded the creature for a moment. Bright red with stripes, it reminded him of a candy cane. "Very nice."

"And rare. The $30,000 price tag is steep, but they're hard to catch. Divers have to go down 400 feet to get 'em. Can you imagine?"

"I guess we saved on not having to pay Wessels his fee," said Jacob, a trace of sadness in his voice.

"What are you talking about?" Fletcher puffed on his contraband Cuban cigar. "It comes out of my pocket, not the Skia budget."

Jacob sat on a leather sofa, hands in his lap. "Sorry."

"Besides, plenty was outlaid on Ricci, chartering aircraft for all of you." He shook his head and chuckled as he took up residence in a plush armchair. "The thing that gets me the most is having to itemize the lost satellite phone."

"It's retrievable," said Jacob. "Send someone from the consulate to the Mondrian Suites. Kasper will hand it over."

"Really?"

"Sure."

A pregnant pause lingered before Jacob said, "All jokes aside, where do we go from here? My cover's been blown to smithereens." He sipped cognac from a cut crystal glass. "I had no idea the extent of the social media coverage of this." Another, longer sip. "And Irina? She's gonna be—"

Fletcher held up a hand. "She'll be fine, and so will you." He tapped ash into a huge green glass ashtray. "Wheels are in motion already. You don't think the best minds haven't been cranking over these past few days, trying to devise a way to discredit the information that came out?"

"I...did think something like that would be going on. But seriously, how effective can those efforts be? Everything about Irina came out into the open."

"All deniable."

"How?"

"The key agencies involved will be issuing a joint press statement to the effect that you and Irina were victims of an elaborate scheme cooked up by the Kremlin."

Jacob rolled his eyes. "Come on!" he scoffed.

"For real. A report is going to be 'leaked' to *The Washington Post* detailing how the digital footprints supposedly linking Barrett and Dmitrieva to espionage were fabricated, that these identities were invented."

"What about the fact that we used passports in those names? Checked into a hotel, used credit cards in those names? The trail is there and easily connectable. How do we refute that?"

"Watch this and I'm sure you'll start to feel a little better." Fletcher pressed the button on a remote. A large screen television came on. Fletcher connected to an encrypted cloud server. A video began to play. President Hannah McIvor sat behind the Resolute desk in the Oval office. She wore a tailored navy suit jacket over a white blouse with a subtle silk sheen, a small flag pin fixed at her lapel. Her green eyes were clear and steady.

Jacob's breath caught as she looked intently down the barrel of the camera and began to speak in her strong, confident voice.

"Hello. Firstly, Mr. Hunter, let me say how thrilled I am that you and Ms. Frobisher are back home, safe and unharmed. Please be assured that the integrity of your identity and those of Irene Frobisher and her family members will be restored. From tonight, there will be a coordinated worldwide media blitz. News outlets across the globe will broadcast breaking news that you and Irene are the victims of Russian disinformation. Interviews with cybersecurity experts and intelligence analysts will flood the airwaves, explaining how deepfake technology and fake news were weaponized to create an elaborate hoax involving fake tourists Michael Barrett and Mila Dmitrieva.

"Campaigns will be run on social media platforms over the next week aimed at educating users on identifying false information, such as that spread by a hostile actor in this particular case."

She took a sip of water.

"You are far too valuable to this country for us to do nothing. You will not be hung out to dry. Public opinion will shift rapidly. The governments and security agencies of the Netherlands and Belgium are a hundred percent on board with our efforts to control the situation. Any stories emerging from private citizens in the Netherlands or Belgium with whom you were in contact that push a different narrative will be quashed immediately."

A pause and a reassuring smile.

"America looks forward to your continuing service."

The screen went blank.

"Your reaction to that?" said Fletcher.

Jacob helped himself to a cigar from the wooden box. "I liked the previous president a lot better." He lit the stogie, inhaled and blew out three perfect rings. "But you know what? I'm really starting to warm to this one."

**Don't miss THE SAINT PETERSBURG FILE. The riveting sequel in the Jacob Hunter Thriller series.**

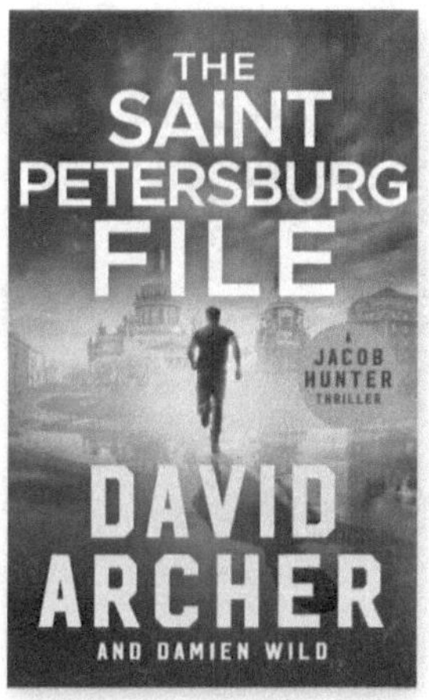


**A coup is coming. Hunter's the only one fast enough to stop it.**

Jacob Hunter believed he would never set foot in Russia again.

He was wrong.

With a new face and sharper skills than ever, Hunter slips into Saint Petersburg's shadowed streets to dismantle "Severnaya Volna" — a covert plot to topple Estonia's government and install Kremlin loyalists. But the deeper he digs, the more tangled the web becomes.

Shadowed by Russian counterintelligence, betrayed by someone he trusted, and surrounded by allies with deadly agendas of their own, Hunter has one chance to stop a European war. If he fails, his own survival won't matter.

Scan the QR code below to purchase THE SAINT PETERSBURG FILE.

Or go to: righthouse.com/the-saint-petersburg-file

*NOTE: flip to the very end to read an exclusive sneak peek...*

# DON'T MISS ANYTHING!

If you want to stay up to date on all new releases in this series, with this author, or with any of our new deals, you can do so by joining our newsletters below.

In addition, you will immediately gain access to our entire *Right House VIP Library,* which includes many riveting Mystery and Thriller novels for your enjoyment. Including a prequel novella to this series!

righthouse.com/email

*(Easy to unsubscribe. No spam. Ever.)*

# ALSO BY DAVID ARCHER

Up to date books can be found at:
www.righthouse.com/david-archer

**ROGUE THRILLERS**

Gates of Hell (Book 1)
Hell's Fury (Book 2)
Ice Burn (Book 3)
Judgement by Fire (Book 4)

**JACOB HUNTER THRILLERS**

The Kyiv File (Book 1)
The Bogota File (Book 2)
The Havana File (Book 3)
The Amsterdam File (Book 4)
The Saint Petersburg File (Book 5)

**PETER BLACK THRILLERS**

Burden of the Assassin (Book 1)
The Man Without A Face (Book 2)
Unpunished Deeds (Book 3)
Hunter Killer (Book 4)
Silent Shadows (Book 5)
The Last Run (Book 6)
Dark Corners (Book 7)
Ghost Operative (Book 8)
A Fire Burning (Book 9)
Dawnlight (Book 10)
Dead Ice (Book 11)
No Loose Ends (Book 12)

**ALEX MASON THRILLERS**

Odin (Book 1)
Ice Cold Spy (Book 2)
Mason's Law (Book 3)
Assets and Liabilities (Book 4)
Russian Roulette (Book 5)
Executive Order (Book 6)
Dead Man Talking (Book 7)
All The King's Men (Book 8)
Flashpoint (Book 9)
Brotherhood of the Goat (Book 10)
Dead Hot (Book 11)
Blood on Megiddo (Book 12)
Son of Hell (Book 13)
Merchant of Death (Book 14)
Extinction C-14 (Book 15)
A Vengeful God (Book 16)

**NOAH WOLF THRILLERS**

Code Name Camelot (Book 1)
Lone Wolf (Book 2)
In Sheep's Clothing (Book 3)
Hit for Hire (Book 4)
The Wolf's Bite (Book 5)
Black Sheep (Book 6)
Balance of Power (Book 7)
Time to Hunt (Book 8)
Red Square (Book 9)
Highest Order (Book 10)
Edge of Anarchy (Book 11)
Unknown Evil (Book 12)
Black Harvest (Book 13)
World Order (Book 14)
Caged Animal (Book 15)
Deep Allegiance (Book 16)

Pack Leader (Book 17)
High Treason (Book 18)
A Wolf Among Men (Book 19)
Rogue Intelligence (Book 20)
Alpha (Book 21)
Rogue Wolf (Book 22)
Shadows of Allegiance (Book 23)
In the Grip of Darkness (Book 24)
Wolves in the Dark (Book 25)
Olympus Must Fall (Book 26)
Children of the Empire (Book 27)
Wolf at the Gates (Book 28)

**SAM PRICHARD MYSTERIES**

The Grave Man (Book 1)
Death Sung Softly (Book 2)
Love and War (Book 3)
Framed (Book 4)
The Kill List (Book 5)
Drifter: Part One (Book 6)
Drifter: Part Two (Book 7)
Drifter: Part Three (Book 8)
The Last Song (Book 9)
Ghost (Book 10)
Hidden Agenda (Book 11)

**SAM AND INDIE MYSTERIES**

Aces and Eights (Book 1)
Fact or Fiction (Book 2)
Close to Home (Book 3)
Brave New World (Book 4)
Innocent Conspiracy (Book 5)
Unfinished Business (Book 6)
Live Bait (Book 7)
Alter Ego (Book 8)

More Than It Seems (Book 9)
Moving On (Book 10)
Worst Nightmare (Book 11)
Chasing Ghosts (Book 12)
Serial Superstition (Book 13)

**CHANCE REDDICK THRILLERS**

Innocent Injustice (Book 1)
Angel of Justice (Book 2)
High Stakes Hunting (Book 3)
Personal Asset (Book 4)

**CASSIE MCGRAW MYSTERIES**

What Lies Beneath (Book 1)
Can't Fight Fate (Book 2)
One Last Game (Book 3)
Never Really Gone (Book 4)

# ABOUT US

Right House is an independent publisher created by authors for readers. We specialize in Action, Thriller, Mystery, and Crime novels.

If you enjoyed this novel, then there is a good chance you will like what else we have to offer! Please stay up to date by using any of the links below.

Join our mailing lists to stay up to date -->
righthouse.com/email
Visit our website --> righthouse.com
Contact us --> contact@righthouse.com

facebook.com/righthousebooks
x.com/righthousebooks
instagram.com/righthousebooks

# EXCLUSIVE SNEAK PEEK OF...

## THE SAINT PETERSBURG FILE

# CHAPTER 1

"ANOTHER APEROL SPRITZ, MY DARLING?" SAID JACOB Hunter, pushing back his opaque sunglasses to rub a speck of grit from his eye. As always with her, he spoke Russian, one of the many languages he was fluent in. He squinted in the afternoon sun for a moment before pulling the shades down again. The view from the restaurant at the top of Lisbon's famous landmark, the Santa Justa Elevador, was spectacular. Lights were beginning to twinkle among the sea of terracotta-tiled roofs.

"*Davai!* Sure!" Irina Frolova—Jacob's partner in life and sometimes in work—reached out and stroked his hand gently. He relished the glow of warmth radiating from her body.

Three minutes later, he returned clutching fresh drinks.

"Thanks for bringing me to Lisbon, *zaichik*," Irina said, reaching for her glass. "I love it. Peaceful and... somehow I feel totally safe. Like nothing can touch us."

"I feel the same."

"It's weird," said Irina thoughtfully, "but even the people peddling on the streets seem less aggressive than anywhere else. Why would that be?"

Jacob ventured a guess—the local laid-back vibe was so ingrained that no outsiders could change it.

"It's just a façade, though, isn't it, Yakov? All that happiness on display?" she said, the Russian version of his name sounding like poetry in her mouth.

"Maybe," Jacob admitted, flipping a beer coaster back and forth in his fingers.

Irina took a long sip. "You think someone can track us down here?"

He pulled his lips into a tight, pensive frown. "I doubt it. We're far enough off the radar."

Even if someone were actively looking, he and Irina were experts at keeping a low profile. They had made small physical changes, too. Behavioral shifts. Irina wore her hair in a different style each month; Jacob placed a wedge of foam in one shoe to alter his gait.

Three years had passed since Jacob's last mission, two since the Amsterdam fiasco. His identity—and Irina's—had been blown apart when Irina was kidnapped. With the Dutch cops running the case, Jacob had been powerless to stop the publicity, meaning future operations abroad became problematic. To the point of being impossible. He was still officially employed by the clandestine agency, but its boss had deemed the heat was still on, and Jacob sat on the sidelines. Despite the efforts of the newly elected US president to smooth things over, his life was still in peril, although the degree had decreased over time. By Fletcher's reckoning, next year Jacob would be back in the game.

Two years cooped up in the acreage property had seemed like an eternity. A beautiful estate on the shores of Keuka Lake in upstate New York with plenty of land to ride trail bikes and horses, the home was still a virtual prison. After the first year with new fake identities, they had gotten braver, disguising themselves and embarking on short outings of varying distance. After twelve months, they took a road trip to Vegas, partying like honeymooners. And they had absolutely loved it.

This was their first trip overseas since Amsterdam, where Jacob had been forced to steal a piece of art in exchange for

Irina's release. Their freedom was ultimately won thanks to a brilliant CIA agent, without whom both of them would surely be dead. A traumatic experience, but they were both made of stern stuff.

But after two years, they'd decided enough was enough. Time to spread their wings once again and face the world head-on. It took a lot of mental preparation, with Jacob and Irina realizing they could be "made," that word could get back to a number of ruthless enemies they had made over the years. On balance, however, they concluded that the risk was worth the benefit to their mental health.

"I wasn't entirely sure about Portugal," said Jacob, picking up the laminated menu. Irina broke out in a radiant smile, and the dimples in her cheeks deepened. "That it would meet with your approval." He held his beer to the light, observing the little bubbles rising to the top. "It's not one of Europe's most glamorous destinations."

She laughed off the comment. "Shabby chic I think is the English expression, *da?*"

"You nailed it." He nodded, taking a swig of a local beer.

"Where to after this?" said Irina, studying the ramparts of Saint George's castle in the distance, then looking across to the broad Tagus River.

"The Algarve. The water's turning chilly, maybe too cold for swimming."

She shook her head, loose brunette curls waving. "Nonsense, Yakov. I've swum in icy Russian rivers. A little cold water isn't going to stop me having fun."

"That's the spirit. One more day here in Lisbon, then a week by the seaside."

A server approached, nodding deferentially as he cleared a space on the table and put down a silver platter of assorted seafood. Grilled sardines formed a small mountain in the middle, with lobster, crab, scallops, and chunks of fried cod placed around the perimeter.

Harpooning a lightly charred piece of fish, Jacob said, "This food makes up for everything else Lisbon lacks."

Irina pressed her lips together, unable to decide where to begin. Finally, she picked up a shrimp and sucked the meat with slurps of satisfaction. Wiping juice from her mouth, she voiced her agreement. "*Ochen' vkusno!* Delicious!"

The waiter returned carrying a chilled bottle of chardonnay. He uncorked the bottle and poured a small measure for Jacob to sample. In fluent Portuguese, Jacob said, "Full glasses for both of us. I don't like this tasting charade."

The waiter burst out laughing. "If I don't do it, I get my ass kicked by the boss."

"It beats me how you can speak so many languages," said Irina through compressed lips as the waiter retreated. "I spent a month learning basic Portuguese for this trip, but I didn't catch any of the exchange between you and that man!"

"You know it's all down to the knock in the head I got playing football. Before that, I barely passed high school Spanish." It was a white lie. He'd passed easily, but his capacity for learning other languages was indeed down to a skull-crushing concussion. He'd been knocked out cold trying to score the touchdown that would have given his school its first-ever championship. Jacob's freakishly acquired savant-like talent was a blessing and a curse.

"I'm still jealous," she said. "Russian and English is all I'll ever be good at."

He caressed her hand, lingering as he lightly brushed the tops of her fingers. "There are other things you're very good at," he said with a sly grin.

"You referring to my IT skills?"

He winked. "That too."

Later, they took a leisurely evening stroll through the Praça do Comércio, a vast public square hugging the banks of the Tagus River. Next, they checked out a packed bar, shared another bottle, this time a robust red, and listened to the plaintive crooning of singers performing in the melancholic fado style. Jacob and Irina held hands under the table like new lovers as the beautiful voices rang out in the smoke-filled tavern.

At a quarter to midnight, as Jacob stood at the window of their apartment in the Alfama district, he marveled at how Irina had stayed with him after all the shit she'd been through. His heart ached with love for her.

She called out his name—as always, Yakov in the Russian way—mischief in her tone. He turned to see her naked, glistening from a shower, sliding between the sheets. Closing the shutters, he approached the bed, heart hammering with desire, a feeling that hadn't faded since they'd first made love.

A glowing light on his bedside table stopped him in his tracks.

The text came from a cell phone number he hadn't seen for years. No name came up, but he knew who it was. His boss, Grant Fletcher.

And it could only mean trouble.

Big. Fucking. Trouble.

# CHAPTER 2

Clanking sounds, like metal striking metal, registered in the deep recesses of his awakening consciousness. The bleeping and blipping of medical tech, echoing voices, and footsteps. Fragments of memory began to spark through the prefrontal cortex of his brain, chasing away the fading haze of anesthesia. He remembered a phone call, urgency in Fletcher's voice. Desperation verging on hysteria—unusual for the normally circumspect man. Mention of a plea for help coming directly from President McIvor.

There was panic in the White House. Grown men and women shitting their pants in the Pentagon. Urgent action was required, but all orthodox approaches were doomed to fail. Hence, McIvor had reached out to Fletcher. There was even a vague promise to alter Jacob's contract by removing Article 7, the "no get-out clause," should he succeed in his task. Other agencies and operatives had been considered, but none were deemed capable of stopping the Russians. Only Jacob Hunter was rated as having any chance of thwarting the implacable enemy.

Then came a hastily arranged charter flight from an airfield outside Lisbon to Zurich, Switzerland. An even more hastily arranged safe house for Irina, somewhere in central Portugal. She had refused to return to the United States; her offer to assist Jacob remotely from a European base was accepted by Fletcher with gratitude. The two-hour time difference between Portugal and Saint Petersburg meant she could communicate with Jacob in near real time.

He recalled the bumpy flight through stormy skies. Greeted in Switzerland by Fletcher in an armored limousine, speeding along the snow-lined motorway to a secret medical facility.

The haze cleared faster now as he drifted back into consciousness.

Jacob blinked his heavy, sticky eyelids—once, twice, three times. The light in the room forced him to squint as he adjusted to the clinical brightness. The urge to cough struck, an insane tickling that started in the chest and moved quickly into his throat—but he couldn't do it. Nor could he close his mouth. His dry lips formed a circle but could compress no more than the circumference of the hard object wedged in his mouth. *Must be a tube running down my neck.* He sensed sweat beading on his brow. Unable to swallow, his sense of helplessness soared off the scale. His head felt like it was in a vise; the only place to look was up.

A BLUE SURGICAL mask hovered into his line of sight. Above the mask were big brown eyes beneath bushy brows. A doctor—thank God. The man spoke in a reassuring, soothing voice, the Swiss accent rising and falling. "I'm going to remove the breathing tube in a moment. The swelling has gone down enough for you to breathe on your own."

He'd had surgery multiple times before but always woke up afterward without an object stuffed down his neck—the normal way it's done. In a normal freaking hospital.

As if reading his mind, the surgeon continued, using arcane medical terms Jacob only partially understood. The gist was clear: Operations to the face and neck can, rarely, cause enough swelling to warrant the intrusive air hose. The medical team had monitored him for twelve hours, constantly observing, until the tube could be removed. "Whoever your boss is wasn't happy about the delay in you waking up."

Five minutes later, Jacob was groggy but able to pull himself halfway to a sitting position and chug half a liter of tepid water before collapsing onto his back again. The urge to cough manifested, the barking sound alarming to his own ear. The doctor assured him it would pass. A female nurse secured a cuff around his upper arm, inflated it by pressing a button, then placed a plastic clip on his index finger. A minute passed in silence before she removed it. "In the normal range," she said robotically, then left him in the bare room.

The Swiss doctor stayed, peeling off his mask and sitting on the edge of the bed. He folded his hands in his lap, calm and professional.

"I understand you were briefed on the procedure pre-op. Correct?"

Jacob nodded. "Yes," he croaked. "I know you've changed my appearance."

"*Ja, genau*. Yes, precisely," said the doctor with a curt nod. "You've undergone an RIA procedure. Rapid Identity Alteration. You may have heard something about this breakthrough protocol."

He nodded. Some months back, he'd read an article about preliminary experimentation in this area. Cutting-edge technology, far superior to traditional plastic surgery.

"Today," continued the doctor, "you have the honor of being the first person to have had the full treatment." He gave a thin-lipped smile and tapped a clipboard with a ballpoint pen. "And survive to tell the tale. Congratulations."

"Forgive me for not sharing your enthusiasm," Jacob rasped. "Care to explain exactly what you did to me?"

The doctor smiled broadly, then cleared his throat. "We placed micro-ceramic scaffolds on your orbital ridge and jawline. These have shifted your bone contours enough to reduce the chance of cameras recognizing you as... yourself. Also, your facial dermis has been layered with a bioengineered graft, subtly changing pore density and texture." The smile widened. "Best of all, we've accelerated recovery time with a hormone-laden skin regeneration gel, which is why you are not horribly bruised right now. Normally, the amount of bone and skin treatment you had would require a minimum six-week recovery. But not for you. A NATO lab in Iceland has developed what we call a recombinant peptide, KAP8—a piece of magic that will have you up and about in forty-eight hours. Is that not miraculous?"

"If you say so. I still feel like I've been tackled by a 300-pound tight end."

The doctor shook his head. "I have no idea what that means, but I shall beg your indulgence and continue." He leaned closer, lowering his voice. "Moderate discomfort is expected after the operation but will soon pass." He toyed with his spectacles. "And here's another fascinating aspect. We trimmed your hair very short, then reset the follicles. Your hair growth pattern and pigmentation will begin to alter within thirty-six hours."

"I beg your pardon?" Jacob's mind spun.

"Your hairline will recede at the sides, a bald patch will form on your crown. The remaining hair will have a salt-and-pepper appearance. Very dashing."

The urge to punch this condescending asshole in the face was almost overwhelming. "You what!"

The doctor held up one hand. "Please. This part of the procedure—all of it—is reversible with drugs and more surgery. We can make you look exactly as before. Do not panic."

"Easy for you to say." Jacob felt a hard lump bulge in his throat as he gulped. "Anything else?"

"*Ja.* We've made an adjustment to your eyes." The doctor paused to pop a mint in his mouth. "Semi-permanent overlays that bond directly to the cornea—greenish-hazel instead of your natural blue. Very becoming."

Jacob grunted.

"They will last six months before melting away."

Jacob blinked slowly. "Is that it? Didn't cut my dick in half, did you?"

"Of course not," the doctor said, blushing bright pink.

"How different am I going to look from the real me?"

"You already look very different."

"Define very."

The doctor coughed into a fist. "Perhaps a fifteen to twenty percent deviation from your original baseline. That's the margin we can create in this time frame. But similarity and difference are subjective."

Jacob pressed his palms into the mattress, wondering if he could push himself all the way up. Not yet. "What if someone who's dealt with me in the past looks me in the eye?"

"I guarantee they will not recognize you." The doctor smiled tightly. "Our medical advances guarantee your anonymity."

A tingling ran through Jacob's fingers; he instinctively held them up to look.

"I was told the place they're sending you may have records of your biometric data," the doctor continued. "Therefore, a minor procedure was performed. Effect lasts about a month, maybe six weeks."

Jacob stared at his hands.

"We micro-abraded the top layer of skin and bonded biopolymer fingerprint overlays with artificial ridges. Mild tenderness for a day or two, then exactly like your own skin."

"What about voice matching?"

"Good question. Larynx surgery was considered, but it's too risky. May I suggest—"

"No, you may not." Jacob gestured toward the door. In perfect Swiss German: he added, "Fuck off, Doc. I'd like some alone time."

---

He dozed for a while, then awoke with burgeoning strength in his limbs. The healing hormone must have been doing its job. He swung himself off the bed and walked gingerly across the cold tiles to the small bathroom, drip-bag stand in tow.

Inside, he emptied a seemingly never-ending stream of urine into the toilet, washed his tingling hands, then turned to the mirror.

The first thing that struck him was the lack of bandages and dressings. In his teens, he'd had a small, suspicious lump removed from his left ear, after which his head had been wrapped like a Christmas present. The lump proved benign, and the wound had taken two weeks to heal. This time, the surgery had been much more serious—his face had been cut, sliced, stitched back together. Objects inserted, drugs and hormones injected. No walk in the park. Yet the only evidence of the operation was an assortment of light pink marks covered with transparent strips of biofilm. Around the temples, along the jawline, under the eyes. That was it.

But the transformation in appearance was already obvious. And the changes would accelerate over the next thirty-six to forty-eight hours. The hazel-green eyes stared back at him like a stranger. He couldn't help the faintest of smiles tugging at the wound sites. The damn doctor had been right—the new color did suit him. He wondered how Irina would react if she saw him now.

Jacob grazed his cheek softly. It was the same skin in texture and underlying color, yet somehow different. He took a deep breath, feeling a sharp twinge in his right shoulder. One second of worry, then he remembered shoulder pain was a common side-effect of general anesthesia.

Returning to the bed, a wave of fatigue washed over him. The second he got himself reasonably comfortable, he heard footsteps outside the door.

The handle turned abruptly, and a man in a glossy gray suit entered. Without a word, he placed Jacob's cell phone on the overbed table. Then he reached into the carry bag slung around his shoulder, extracted a silver laptop, and put it next to the phone.

"Not even going to introduce..." Jacob placed a fist over his mouth to cover a cough. "...yourself?" His voice sounded as thick as molasses.

"Sorry. I thought you were asleep." The man was a forty-something cookie-cutter agent with a face like an alleyway rat and the body of a gorilla. With zero emotion, he said, "William Duff. CIA station, Zurich."

"Where's..." Jacob almost said his boss's name, checked himself at the last second, and attributed the near-slip to the anesthesia. "Where's the man who brought me here?"

A shrug. "No idea. I'm just a link in a complicated chain, doing one job." He fussed with the computer, fingers clicking the mouse a couple of times. A sideways glance at Jacob. "You recovered enough to use this?"

"Don't make me laugh." Jacob shook his head. "It's a computer, not heavy machinery."

The man cast an apologetic frown. "You've just had surgery, so I thought—"

"An A-plus for your observational skills," said Jacob, loaded with sarcasm. "You'll go far in your career. Cut to the chase and tell me what the hell you're doing here."

The man explained which folder Jacob needed to open, then recited a long password of random symbols, numbers, and letters.

"Want me to write it down for you?"

"No need. I got it."

The man exited as quietly as he had arrived, leaving Jacob to figure out what the hell would happen next.

# CHAPTER 3

Fletcher usually delivered the news from the luxurious confines of his converted warehouse apartment in New York City's upscale Tribeca district. Whether it came in a manila folder or on a flash drive, in a sealed envelope or as spoken instructions he had to commit to memory, Jacob received his orders in a face-to-face meeting with Fletcher.

Not today.

Today, the Skia director's benign face, bushy brown mustache front and center, occupied the entire screen of the laptop.

*Why isn't he calling me on my cell?* Jacob wondered. *What's with the dumb-ass recording?*

Fletcher wiped the lenses of his glasses, cleared his throat for the third time, blinked, redonned the eyewear, and launched into his spiel.

"I'm recording this because I don't want you interrupting me and throwing me off balance. After you've digested what I have to say, if you've got any questions, call me. But not until you reach the end of the video."

Jacob paused the recording and pressed the nurse-call button. A tall woman in crisp blue scrubs arrived within a minute, head cocked, eyes bright.

"What can I do for you?" she said in a rich, modulated Indian accent. "Are you in pain? Need more morphine?"

He shook his head. "No, but I'm starving. Could you get me a cheeseburger? A side of fries and a cold beer would be good."

"Sorry, sir, but our menu is rather spartan—just boring, healthy items on offer." She left and returned with a menu showcasing the blandest foods imaginable. Jacob sighed, choosing a ham sandwich on whole wheat bread washed down with orange juice.

On with the video.

Fletcher's face assumed an expression of utmost seriousness: crow's feet accentuated, nostrils wide, lips tight. "Hopefully, the operation didn't affect your greatest asset—your photographic memory. So I assume you recall the content of our conversation en route to the medical center."

That "conversation" had been more a rant by Fletcher. Jacob had never seen his boss so stressed out: a fake smile plastered across his face, constantly tipping little white pills into his mouth, chased down by huge gulps of water.

"Pay close attention," Fletcher continued. "Everything I'm about to tell you is important."

The upshot was as follows. A soldier had been murdered in a border observation center in Tallinn. An unidentified Russian intruder was another casualty, killed by responding Estonian forces.

The dead soldier, Corporal Indrek Laanoja, had alerted his commander, Major Robin Saar, of suspicious movements on the lake border between Russia and Estonia. The soldier was sure he was witnessing preparation for an invasion in real time. Three minutes after the call to Saar, the panic button in Laanoja's bunker was pressed, and five nearby soldiers were immediately dispatched to see what was happening. They were confronted by two agitated men in Estonian military uniforms, weapons raised. A firefight ensued: one of the hostiles was killed instantly, the other, Estonian Corporal Mihkel Vares, injured and subdued.

Laanoja was found dead beside his chair, tied and gagged, with two bullet holes in his stomach. The computer systems had been tampered with, but how and to what end was still not entirely clear.

Jacob took a sip of water as Fletcher rubbed one eye before resuming.

The traitor, Vares, was subjected to interrogation—not using the enhanced techniques favored by the CIA but good enough to get some answers. Unfortunately, not about the computer systems manipulation—his ignorance on the matter was deemed genuine. Vares admitted to being paid to arrange the safe entry of the Russian hacker via the river crossing between Narva and Ivangorod, transport him to Tallinn, and admit him to the facility's hub.

A search of the latter's body found two return tickets from Ivangorod to Saint Petersburg dated November 12. A photocopy of both tickets was in a separate folder on the laptop Jacob was currently looking at. Vares had intended to flee Estonia with the Russian because remaining in the country was not an option. Now Vares faced a decade to life in prison for treason.

It turned out that what Corporal Laanoja thought was the start of an invasion was, to use a sporting term, a dummy pass. All troops and equipment had withdrawn to original positions, which made Laanoja's murder all the more strange.

Initial suspicions that a mole had signaled Vares it was time to move naturally fell on the superior officer, Major Saar. He was questioned by personnel from the Military Intelligence Center of the Estonian Defence Forces. Saar was cleared—for the moment. The major revealed that, after talking to the corporal and looking at the live-stream, he'd also believed the Russians were on the march. He made a series of official phone calls up the chain, leading to large numbers of Estonian troops being told to prepare for mobilization. Thirty minutes later, satellite images showed the Russians moving back to their previous positions. Even so, the patterns of their assembly and the movement of so many units toward the border were considered an act of provocation.

Problem was, the Estonians were too shit-scared to call the Russians out for their act. Prime Minister Karilaid had advisers in both ears. Mild diplomatic representations had been made, encountering denials of evil intent regarding the border actions, as well as a denial of any knowledge of the intruder. The Russians had even imprisoned one of their top generals, a scapegoat, to try to smooth things over.

In Estonia, a blanket media blackout had been applied. The so-called accord that had been struck to guarantee peace, at least for the foreseeable future, had been instantly disrespected by an act of brazen arrogance. At least that was the assessment of US top brass. Fletcher was inclined to agree.

The accord was on life support, and tensions were back on the boil.

Analysts in the Pentagon, apprised of what had gone down in Tallinn, as well as operatives embedded in Estonia and Russia, believed that the dummy start of an invasion was a veiled threat to the Baltic nation: Abide by the accord—to the letter—or we will crush you. One thing the security agencies who had examined the incident agreed on was this: There was a mole in the Estonian forces and/or government much higher up than Vares. Possibly more.

*Of course there are more!* thought Jacob. *There are always more.*

The second conclusion they'd reached was extra alarming. The ease with which the anonymous Russian hacker—or whatever he was—had breached Estonian security pointed to something a lot more sinister.

The consensus was that hardline fanatics—a small group of outliers or perhaps even conspirators at the heart of the Kremlin—were plotting a coup in Estonia. Regime change. President Karilaid would be arrested and imprisoned and a Kremlin puppet installed in his place. After that, NATO would have to tread carefully if its members wanted to avoid a hot war with Putin.

Long story short, President McIvor, a staunch supporter of the NATO alliance, wanted Jacob back in the ring, whatever it took.

Jacob rubbed his eyes gently with the heels of his palms as Fletcher stopped his monologue to light a cigar and pour himself a glass of Hennessy XO cognac. The next thing he said had Jacob wishing he also had a bottle at hand containing something stronger than tepid water.

"You're going to Saint Petersburg in three days. I wanted two days, but it's been agreed an extra day of rest for you will make a big difference. I only pray you'll be there in time to defuse the time-bomb. The doctor tells me you'll be fit enough to travel in seventy-two hours and, more importantly, to work. Now let's talk about your legend," he said pointedly, scraping the wheel of his Zippo and relighting the stub of his smoldering stogie. "You are a Russia-sympathizing Estonian businessman. Thanks to the accord, which officially still exists, there are direct flights between Tallinn and Saint Petersburg. You'll fly from Zurich to Tallinn and from there to Pulkovo Airport. Your itinerary and full bio will be sent to you in an email, along with the names of contacts in Saint Petersburg."

Jacob sipped water, dreading this impending "business trip."

"You'll need to study a bunch of profiles. These are people we've identified as being those most likely to be orchestrating the destabilization campaign, which we believe is codenamed *Severnaya Volna*—in English, Northern Wave. I'm forwarding more detailed dossiers on these people and a bunch of background information."

Jacob paused the video, summoned the nurse, and demanded a notepad and pen. He wanted to test his memory. He was confident it would work as per normal, but after experimental surgery, such confidence could be misplaced. If by tomorrow he could recall what was on the paper, he'd destroy any notes he made.

"Finally," said Fletcher, "in addition to wishing you good luck and godspeed, I suggest you spend the next three days brushing up on your Estonian." A deep inhale. "That's it for now. Please delete this video file."

Jacob shook his head. Of all the Baltic languages, he had to get lumbered with the hardest. A smattering of Finnish—Estonian's closest relative—picked up on a mission in Helsinki four years ago would be his launch pad. He'd only required a handful of phrases in Finland; this was going to be next-level intensive study. Even with his own savant-like language skills, passing himself off as an Estonian would be close to impossible.

He deleted the MP4 file, confident Irina could track it down for him on Skia's cloud maze if needed. His email inbox contained the promised attachments from Fletcher. He opened and read them all over the next couple of minutes. He scooped up his cell and punched in Fletcher's number.

"Work?" Jacob's voice rose a semi-octave. "You have the audacity to call throwing me back into the fucking lion's den of Russia work?"

An uncomfortable laugh came down the line. "I make no apologies for that. You are my operative. You work for me." Another laugh, this one lightly tinged with sarcasm. "You've had a very long vacation on the American taxpayer's dime, Hunter. Now it's time to earn your keep. You get paid more than Taylor Swift, for Chrissake."

A massive exaggeration, even though he had no cause to complain about his hefty pay packet. "I needed that vacation, as you put it, because my identity was basically obliterated. Irina's, too. We needed to reconnect with the world."

"Give me a break, Hunter. That was pure indulgence. Your upstate mansion is like a freakin' resort. No need to travel anywhere."

"You might find it hard to believe, but you can still get cabin fever in a mansion with acres around you. Especially when you're someone like me, used to traveling, blowing off the cobwebs."

"I feel for you, I really do." A short pause while he sipped something then smacked his lips. "Your task is going to be difficult, but the goal is straightforward. If you succeed in stopping the predicted coup, you could be—at the president's discretion—a free man forever."

"I'm gonna need that in writing."

"I'll see if McIvor will sign off on it."

Jacob knew there would be nothing in writing from the White House. That's not how these things worked. Still, he now had a mountain of motivation. He took a deep breath, then aired his concerns about being able to pass as a real Estonian.

"I won't be able to pull that off, Fletch. Not even if I spent the next three days doing nothing but taking Estonian lessons."

"We took that into account. Your name for this mission is Robert Tamm. Born in Narva, on the Estonian border, where the Russian demographic makes up more than ninety-five percent of the population. This makes your being stronger in Russian than Estonian credible."

"You don't have to tell me where Narva is," Jacob hissed under his breath. "It's a well-known fact."

"I didn't know until recently!" protested Fletcher.

"Geography's never been your strong suit, has it?"

Fletcher plowed on without replying to the slight. "Your mother is an ethnic Russian, a Soviet nostalgist who yearns for the good old days of the USSR. I won't bore you with the rest of the legend right now. I've sent you all the material you need in an encrypted email."

"I've read it all."

"Already? No, don't answer that. I forgot that you're a fucking cyborg." He paused for a moment. Jacob heard Fletcher softly scolding someone—he guessed it was his personal assistant and rumored paramour, Susan Stonehouse. Fletcher coughed twice, then returned his attention to Jacob. "Anyway, we figured that if you were at least half-Russian, the locals would be more inclined to open up to you. Especially if you share your mother's ideals."

"You figured right. One more thing?"

"What?"

"Who are the conspirators?"

"In the list you got."

"Yeah, but it's a long list. What do our analysts think? Who are they leaning toward?"

"There are conflicting theories on our side, mainly because a lot of the information on the suspects isn't objective. Your Saint Petersburg contacts will probably have their own theories, better than ours."

"Anyone at home been able to do anything with the train tickets?" The details of the tickets flashed in Jacob's mind as he visualized the photocopy Fletcher had emailed. Purchased for cash on 9 November from Window 12, Finland Station, at 10:16 a.m. Train: 412 IVANGOROD → PETERSBURG. Departure: IVANGOROD 07:18, 11 November. Arrival: SAINT PETERSBURG 10:43. Carriage: 03. Seat: — (standing/no assigned seat). Ticket No.: PL-GT-74-9921 / PL-GT-74-9922.

A pity the tickets weren't bought with a card, he mused. Online would have been even better. A digital footprint offered a pathway to track down the purchaser, whereas with cash that task was almost impossible. A tricky one to pull off, but he wouldn't rule out trying to track down and grill the cashier who'd manned window 12 on November 9.

"No. I've sent a copy to Irina, plus a photo of the dead guy, but she's yet to get back to me about it." A pause, then Fletcher said, as if he'd discovered the theory of relativity, "If our analysts had all the answers, there'd be no need to send you into the field, now would there?"

"I guess not."

"Damn straight. In truth, the list is a guide. Like I said, your contacts in Saint Petersburg will have quality local knowledge. You can't beat that."

"I guess so," said Jacob with a sigh.

"Could it be Putin himself behind it?" said Fletcher. "I wouldn't put it past him to set up scapegoats."

Jacob chewed a plastic straw he'd been drinking orange juice through. "My gut says no. He's losing ground in ongoing skirmishes—why start another?"

"We've got what we've got," said Fletcher phlegmatically. "Which ain't much, apart from a list of names and chatter about Severnaya Volna."

"What went down in Tallinn proves it's not just chatter. Something's brewing."

"I'll leave you in peace now, Hunter." The words were sweet relief to Jacob's ears. There was nothing more the boss had to say that would make his task any easier. Besides, there was someone else he was desperate to reconnect with.

Jacob rolled over in his bed, grabbed his laptop, and logged onto Skia's encrypted communications network.

Irina answered breathlessly in less than ten seconds. "*Zaichik! Vsye v poryadke?* Is everything OK?"

"Brilliant," he said flatly, pressing the phone hard to his ear, as if that would bring her closer to him. "The surgeries went well. Just a couple of nagging aches. How are you holding up in Castelo Branco?"

"Fine. Except I'm nowhere near the town. It's like a hacienda out in the sticks. Pool, jacuzzi, gym, massive wine cellar—the works."

"Fazenda."

"What?"

"In Portuguese, a property like that is called a fazenda."

"Not everyone's a damned polyglot like you, Yakov," she laughed.

"Either way, it sounds like a pleasant extension of our vacation."

"It's not like that at all! None of these luxuries mean anything to me. I've been worried sick. Not hearing from you for more than a day when we haven't been out of each other's sight for two years. I can't bear it."

"I'm sorry, Irochka."

"I'm sorry, too. I know it's not your fault."

A silence ensued for a few moments, but silences between them were never awkward.

"Fletcher tells me he sent you a task," Jacob prompted.

"Not one I can complete. How can I trace a cash sale? And I've searched every database known to man, but that dead Russian isn't showing up anywhere. A regular John Doe."

"Worth a try, though."

"Always." She paused a short beat, then said, "I've got a bunch of burly security guards looking out for me, maids—you name it. Maybe they're Portuguese secret agents, I don't know." She inhaled so deeply, he felt like she'd sucked half the air out of the hospital room. "Yakov. I need to see you. Turn your camera on, please."

He groaned. Not in pain, but in embarrassment. "I don't think you wanna—"

"Show me your face!"

He relented, clicked the mouse, and saw his own, new face appear in the top left corner of the screen.

"*Bozhe moi!* Oh, my God!" she cried. "What have they done to you?"

"The doctor says it's all reversible."

"I hope so, *zaichik*. Because right now, you are one ugly *sukin syn*."

Jacob shook his head, dismissing the insult with a fatalistic laugh. Even when she called him a son of a bitch, he couldn't help but love her with all his being.

# CHAPTER 4

Jacob looked down and slightly to the left, to where his heart was pounding a military tattoo under his designer business shirt. Respiration was still normal, but getting that rapid heart rate under control was a priority.

A deep breath to refocus.

*Stay in your role. You have every right to be here and be treated properly. Nothing bad is going to happen to you. Don't panic. Don't act weird. Don't say anything stupid to give yourself away.*

Amid the faint sounds of announcements being made in Russian and English over the loudspeakers, a crack in a floor tile caught his attention. As he stared at the crack, the floor vibrated with the low rumble of a jet taking off outside.

The reality of lining up to be processed by the border guard at Pulkovo Airport in a country where scores of people—including the president himself—wanted Jacob dead almost canceled out the calm state he'd attained on the airplane. A state induced by deep meditation, breathing techniques, and a couple of stiff vodka sodas.

He took another deep breath and shuffled forward two steps, his feet feeling like his Oxford brogues were lined with lead. He dragged his virtually empty carry-on case behind him, which also felt heavy, as if it were full of bricks instead of a laptop and papers.

Up ahead, a male-female couple at one of the passport control booths exchanged glances of confusion. The bespectacled official frowned deeply, shook his head, held up a hand, and made a phone call. Straining his ear, Jacob caught the words *visa irregularities*, *detention*, and *deportation*, spoken loudly enough for everyone in the line to hear. Moments later, two men sporting bristly number-one haircuts and decked out in cobalt suits arrived, placed handcuffs on each of the inbound passengers, and led them away. The captives' heads were bowed, shoulders slumped, not a word of protest uttered.

Jacob's heart thundered, which pissed him off because he'd only just reined in his heart rate again, back to a respectable seventy-five BPM according to his Breitling smartwatch. This was the Russia he feared. Authoritarian and bureaucratic, quick to jump on any indiscretion and punish harshly for non-compliance.

The line inched forward again. Three more individual travelers were processed, this time with a minimum of fuss. Border guards stared intently at the arrivals, flicked their eyes to passports, computer monitors, then back to the faces before them. The clunk of a stamp, the snapping closed of passports, a green light, and they scurried away toward the baggage carousels.

At 23:47 hours, November 16, it was Jacob's turn to cross swords with the regime and, God willing, sneak under the fence in one piece. His mouth felt as if wadded-up cotton balls were stuffed in his cheeks, sucking out every molecule of moisture.

He'd expected to be faced by a grim, granite-faced soldier with the IQ and charm of a roof tile. Instead, he struck a rather attractive woman who couldn't have been twenty-five, thick mascara coating long lashes, strawberry-blond hair tied back in a ponytail. She made the uniform of dark green jacket, matching cravat, and crisp white blouse look like high fashion.

Instead of the anticipated border guard's snarl, she greeted him with an affable smile. He fought the instinct to be a gentleman and meet her smile with one of his own, keeping his lips in a straight line. Normal expression, normal words, normal behavior that didn't draw attention. *Just get in the door; your experience and skills will carry the day.*

"Is this your first trip to Russia, Mr. Tamm?" she asked in perfect English. Not too many years ago, when Estonia was a republic of the USSR, a citizen of that country would have been able to communicate easily in Russian. Nowadays, English was everybody's second language in the Baltic countries; young people barely knew any Russian at all.

"Yes," replied Jacob, unblinking. He decided to switch to Russian. "It's my first visit to Russia. I've wanted to come for many years, and now with this new accord, I get to live out my wish."

"You speak Russian very well." She studied his passport again. "Born in 1990 in Estonia, I see. Not many of your generation are so well versed in our tongue."

He allowed himself the faintest of grins. "It's my first language, as it happens." His words came out deliberately in a soporific monotone. "I've got a Russian mother. I grew up in Narva, right on the border, but never got to cross it. Ironic that I had to backtrack to Tallinn to fly here when the bridge between Narva and Ivangorod is only 160 meters long. Have you ever been to Estonia?"

The tactic was working. The woman's eyes were half-shut as she stifled a yawn. Jacob knew what she was thinking: at close to midnight, the sooner she processed this boring jerk, the better.

"State the purpose of your visit."

Commands now instead of questions. Much better.

The details of his legend rolled across his mind's eye like teletext on the morning news. "Business."

"State the nature of your business, Mr. Tamm. And don't be so long-winded about it." She nodded over his shoulder toward the line behind him. Her voice was now as firm as a school principal's, eyelids compressed and forehead wrinkled. The embodiment of soulless Russian bureaucracy. "We've still got half of your flight left to process, and some of us want to go home."

He suppressed the urge to bust out a smart-ass comment. Play it straight, according to the script. "I'm here to liaise with the Russian Ministry of Industry and Trade, looking to forge lasting partnerships with public and private companies. My sponsor is the Estonian Chamber of Commerce and Industry." He added that he ran a logistics consultancy with strong ties to Finland, but with the advent of the new accord, Russian partners wanted to reopen some of the old sea routes to the Baltic states and beyond, with Estonia as the bridge.

The rambling reply caused the woman's eyes to glaze over.

"I can show you the official documents if you like?" Jacob leaned down toward his case.

She shook her head firmly, ponytail swishing. "*Nye nado. Prokhodite.* No need. Please proceed." She stamped an entry in his fake passport with a flurry. The green light came on, Jacob's heart flooding with relief, as if an oncologist had just told him the stage-four cancer prognosis was all a big mistake.

As a parting gesture, she said, "Do not overstay your visa, Mr. Tamm. Penalties apply."

*As if I would*, Jacob said to himself. *The sooner I'm out of here, the better*. He replied, deadpan: "*Khoroshego Vam dnya*. Have a nice day."

Scan the QR code below to purchase THE SAINT PETERSBURG FILE.

Or go to: righthouse.com/the-saint-petersburg-file

www.ingramcontent.com/pod-product-compliance
Lightning Source LLC
LaVergne TN
LVHW041112080826
845145LV00007B/1779

*9781636964706*